THE LIVING AND THE DEAD IN WINSFORD

HÅKAN NESSER

THE LIVING AND THE DEAD IN WINSFORD

Translated from the Swedish by
Laurie Thompson

MANTLE

First published 2015 by Mantle
an imprint of Pan Macmillan
20 New Wharf Road, London N1 9RR
Associated companies throughout the world
www.panmacmillan.com

ISBN 978-1-4472-7192-5

Typeset by Ellipsis Digital Limited, Glasgow
Printed and bound by CPI Group (UK) Ltd, Croydon, CR0 4YY

'Characteristic of the moor is that to all
intents and purposes, it has no beginning and no end.
I would like to mention three other things that are not
to be found in this sublime landscape: cul-de-sacs,
evasive excuses, and last but not least – words.'

Royston Jenkins (1866–1953), innkeeper in Culbone

'. . . the dispassionate fluids of an eye that
tried so hard to forget one particular thing that it
ended up forgetting everything else.'

Roberto Bolaño, *Amulet*

ONE

1

The day before yesterday I decided that I would outlive my dog. I owe him that. Two days later, in other words today, I decided to drink a glass of red wine in Wheddon Cross.

That is how I intend to pass the time from now on. Make decisions, and stick to them. It's not all that difficult, but harder than it sounds, and, of course, everything depends on the circumstances.

The rain had followed me all the way across the moor, ever since I turned off the A358 at Bishops Lydeard, and as dusk set in quickly it made tears well up in my eyes like cold lava. A falling movement, then a rising one; but those tears that were forming were perhaps a good sign. I have wept too seldom in my life – I'll come back to that.

I had set off from London at about one, and after I had wriggled my way out through Notting Hill and Hammersmith the journey had exceeded my expectations. Driving westwards along the M4, through Hampshire, Gloucestershire and Wiltshire – at least, that's what I think the counties are called – and a few hours later southwards along the M5 after Bristol. It feels reassuring that all these roads have a number – and all the places a name – but the fact that it feels like that is less reassuring.

Exceeded my expectations may well also be the wrong expression to use in the context, but my apprehensions about getting lost, taking the wrong turning and ending up in endless traffic jams on the motorway heading in the wrong direction, and not arriving on time, had kept me awake for a large part of the night. The rest of the night it was the old story about Martin's sister's lover that kept me going. I don't know why he and she turned up in my thoughts, but they did. One is so defenceless in the early hours of the morning.

I'm not used to driving, thanks to the way things turned out. I remember that when I was young I used to think that it gave me a sense of freedom, sitting behind the wheel and being master – or rather mistress – of my fate and the routes I chose. But it has been Martin who has done all the driving for the last fifteen or twenty years: it's a long time since we even raised the question of who was going to sit in the driving seat when we went on our joint car trips. And he has always turned his nose up at anything to do with GPS.

There are such things as maps, aren't there? What's wrong with good old maps all of a sudden?

And then of course there was the problem of driving on the left in this stubborn old country, so the risk of something going haywire at any moment was quite considerable. But I managed it. I had overcome both the minefield of London's obsolete traffic systems and the torture presented by the motorways. I had succeeded in filling up with petrol and paying cash without any problems, and it was only when I got as far as the narrow roller-coaster of roads over Exmoor that the feeling of melancholy caught up with me. But I never stopped in a lay-by in order to raise my depressed spirits, even though I maybe ought to have done. Besides, I'm not at all sure that I saw a lay-by.

But as the fact is that in this country nearly every place named on a map also has a pub, at shortly after half past four I parked next to a white van with the text 'Peter's Plumbing' on the door in a strikingly deserted car park next to a strikingly abandoned cricket field. I hurried indoors without giving myself time for remorse or second thoughts.

So, Wheddon Cross it was. I had never set foot here before, and had never heard of it.

Well, I did wonder for just a moment whether I ought to take Castor for a little walk first, before drinking that glass of wine – I must admit that I did. But he doesn't like rain, and he had been out when we stopped for petrol an hour and a half ago. I don't think he even raised his head when I opened and closed the car door. He enjoys having a rest, Castor does – he sometimes sleeps fifteen or sixteen hours a day if he gets the chance.

The place turned out to be called The Rest and Be Thankful Inn. Apart from the big-busted bleach-blonded woman behind the bar (about my own age, possibly slightly younger in fact), there were only two other living beings in sight that late November afternoon: a frail-looking old lady with a crossword puzzle, drinking tea, and an overweight man in his thirties wearing working-clothes and a dirty baseball cap with a fancy-looking PP just above the peak, with a mug of beer firmly grasped in his powerful hand. I assumed he must be the peripatetic plumber, but neither he nor the crossword-woman looked up when I entered the room.

But Bar-Blondie did so. Mind you, she did so only after first carefully drying the wine glass she had in her hand and placing it on a shelf in front of her, but still.

I ordered a glass of red, she asked if Merlot would be okay, and I said that would be absolutely splendid.

'Large or small?'

'Large, please.'

It's possible that PP and the crossword puzzle solver raised various eyebrows, but if so it was something I registered in the same way that one notices a butterfly behind one's back.

'It's raining,' said Blondie as she poured out the wine.

'Yes,' I replied. 'It certainly is.'

'Rain, rain, rain.'

She said that in a singing tone of voice, and I assumed it must be the refrain in some hit or other. I don't know why I chose the word 'hit' – I'm only fifty-five after all. But there are certain words and phrases that my father used to use, and I've noticed that lately I've started using them as well. Top hole. Cuppa char. Brolly.

I took my glass and sat down at a table where there was a little brochure featuring local walks. I pretended to begin studying it, in order to have something to do with my eyes. What I would really have liked to do was to drink my wine in three deep swigs and then carry on driving; but it was not my intention to make a lasting impression on those present. I might eventually return – even though my reason for stopping at just this place was that I hoped never to return there. A solitary, unknown woman of mature years who pops in and drinks a large glass of wine in the afternoon would no doubt attract attention in a small village. That's the way it is, nothing to get het up about unless you are a poet or an artist. I'm not a poet or an artist.

And Wheddon Cross was not my village. My village is called Winsford, and according to the brochure on the table in front of me it is half a dozen miles to the south. The pub there is where I really must be careful not to put a foot wrong. That is where I am likely to become a regular customer, and exchange a few words and thoughts with my neighbour. That was in any case the way I had approached the situation, and after the first sip of wine I was pleased to note that the lava-like tears had subsided. There is a sumptuous, velvety quality about red wine that could turn me into an alcoholic, but that is not the path I intend to follow.

In fact I have very vague ideas about the paths I ought to be following. That's the way I have developed, and what things are going to look like in six months' time is a matter of almost laughable unpredictability. As the Bible says, sufficient unto the day is the evil thereof.

Very true.

During the twenty minutes I had spent at The Rest and Be Thankful Inn, twilight had thickened into darkness, and it had stopped raining for now. I gave Castor a special treat – dried liver: that's his secret passion – and consulted the map. I drove out of the car park and set off along the A396 in the direction of Dulverton. After a few tortuous, winding miles I came to a road turning off to the right, with a sign saying: Winsford 1. This new road led down into a narrow valley, presumably following the course of the River Exe – which as I understood it gave its name to the whole moor – but the stream was no more than a vague suspicion of trickling movement through the car window. Or perhaps a premonition, a hint of a living being: it was not difficult to succumb to mysterious illusions in this unfamiliar, almost invisible landscape as the mist began to swallow it up; and when the first buildings on the edge of the village were caught in the beam of my headlights I felt a sort of atavistic relief. I drove past the village shop, and the local post office, then turned left and – in accordance with the instructions I had been given – parked in front of a war memorial commemorating the fallen in the First and Second World Wars. Together with Castor I crossed a simple wooden bridge over a fast-flowing stream, noted a church steeple outlined against the patchy blue sky that had suddenly been washed clean of mist, and started walking along a village street called Ash Lane. Not a soul in sight. Just past the church I knocked on a blue door in a low pommer stone house, and ten seconds later that door was opened by Mr Tawking.

'Miss Anderson?'

That was the name I had given him. I don't know why I had hit upon my mother's maiden name – perhaps for the simple reason that I was hardly likely to forget it. Anderson with only one 's', which is how they spell it in this country. By means of a simple hand gesture Mr Tawking indicated that I was welcome to step inside, and we each sat down in an armchair by a low, dark wooden table in front of an artificial gas fire. A teapot, two cups, a plate of biscuits, that was all. Apart from two keys on a ring lying on top of a sheet of paper, which I gathered was the rental contract. He served tea, stroked Castor and invited him to lie down in front of the warm fire. Castor did as he was bid, and it was obvious that Mr Tawking was used to dealing with dogs. But I could see no sign of one at the moment: Mr Tawking was old and hunched, certainly well over eighty – perhaps he had had a four-legged friend that died recently, and perhaps he had felt it was too late to acquire a new one. Dogs should not outlive their owners, that was a conclusion I had recently come round to.

'Six months from yesterday,' said Mr Tawking. 'From the first of November until the end of April. So there we are – don't blame me!'

He attempted to smile, but his muscles were not quite able to follow his intentions. Maybe it was a long time since he had anything to feel pleased about: there was an ingrained sense of melancholy enveloping both him and the room in which we were sitting. Maybe it was not just a dog that had left him, I thought, but a wife as well. Wives ought usually to outlive their husbands, but that is quite a different matter and not something I had any desire to think about in the present circumstances, certainly not. Instead I noted that the fitted carpet was dirty and worn in places; there were patches of damp on the gaudily patterned wallpaper, and for some strange reason a piece of red tape was stuck to the top right-hand corner of the television screen. I felt an urge to get out of here as quickly as possible. My own feelings of impending twilight needed no further encouragement, and after less than a quarter of an hour I had signed the contract, paid the agreed price for six months' rent – £3,000 in cash (plus the £600 I had paid into his account two days ago) – and been given the keys. We had talked about nothing apart from the weather and the practical details.

'You'll find an instruction book on the draining board. It's intended for summer visitors, of course, but if there's anything else you want to know about just call in or give me a ring. My number is in that book. Be careful when you make a fire.'

'Will my mobile phone work up there?'

'That depends on which network you are with. You can always try from the mound on the other side of the road. You can usually get a signal there. The place where that woman is buried, and round about there. Elizabeth.'

We shook hands, he stroked Castor again, and we left him.

The mistress and her dog returned along Ash Lane to the monument and the car. It was becoming windy, gusts lashed and buffeted the larch trees and telephone wires, but the rain held back. The mist meant that visibility was thirty metres at most. There was still no sign of any living creature apart from us. Castor jumped onto his seat in the car, and I gave him another liver treat. We exchanged a few reassuring thoughts, and I did my best to erase the questions in his worried eyes. Then we set off and proceeded carefully along the other road through the village. Halse Lane.

After only fifty metres we passed the village pub. It's called The Royal Oak Inn, has an impressively thick thatched roof, and faint beams of light shone out of its windows onto the road. Just past it, but on the other side of the road, with gloomy-looking rectangular windows, was Karslake House, a hotel boarded up for the winter.

Then both buildings and street lighting came to an end. The road became even narrower and was barely wide enough to accommodate a single vehicle: but during the seven or eight minutes it took us to reach Darne Lodge, through a series of convoluted and awkward bends, we didn't meet a single car. Visibility was restricted by high, grassy and stony banks that had evidently been flanking the road for centuries – apart from the final section when the moor suddenly stretched out on all sides, temporarily illuminated by a full moon that succeeded in piercing the clouds and mists for a few seconds. All at once the landscape looked ethereal, like an old painting – Gainsborough or Constable perhaps? Or why not Caspar David Friedrich? Friedrich has always been Martin's favourite artist: a reproduction of *Monk by the Sea* was hanging on the wall of his office when we first met.

I was struck by an ambivalent feeling of fear and relief when I got out of the car to open the gate. Or perhaps I had been flirting with this same unholy alliance as Friedrich, darkness and light, ever since what happened on that beach just outside Międzyzdroje.

Międzyzdroje – I still can't pronounce it properly, but the spelling is correct (apart from the strange accent under the first 'e' that I don't know how to produce): I've checked it.

Eleven days ago now. A very difficult period of time if ever there was one, but despite everything, the nerve-racking, choking feelings have become slightly less acute for every morning that has passed, and every decision made – at least, I like to think that has been the case.

I have made up my mind to continue thinking that.

And if only I could switch on the electricity, get a fire started and sink a glass or two of port, I would be faced with a sea of tranquillity. Six months of winter and spring on the moor. With no company apart from Castor, my own ageing body and my misguided soul. Each day like every other, every hour impossible to distinguish from the preceding or the subsequent one . . . Ah well, in so far as it was possible to begin to envisage the coming six months, that is more or less how things looked. A hermit's life of redemption and reflection and God only knows what – but both Castor and I were well aware that we should spare no thought for the morrow, and an hour later, when he was on his sheepskin and I was in a rocking chair in front of the somewhat hesitantly crackling fire, we simply fell asleep, one after the other.

It was the second of November, it is perhaps worth noting: we had travelled further than I could ever have dreamt of and as far as I could judge we had swept away all traces of our movements. Feeling confident and secure that this was the case, shortly before midnight we moved over to the bedroom with its sagging double bed. I lay awake for a while, drawing up a few preliminary and practical plans for the following day. Listening to the wind blowing over the moor, and to the refrigerator humming away in the combined kitchen and living room, and eventually deciding that the events of the last few months had now finally come to an end. Or of the last few years, to be more precise.

And to be even more precise: of my life as it had turned out so far.

2

'I can understand that you both need to get away from it all,' Eugen Bergman had said, peering over the rim of his remarkably outdated spectacles. 'What with that mad woman and all the rest of it. And the literary timing is just about right as well. However it turns out, we shall be able to sell it.'

This is not going to be an account of what has happened in the past, these unstructured notes – no more than what is necessary in order to understand the present. In so far as I have any ambitions at all, that is just about as far as they go. You write – and read – in order to understand things, that's something I've often tried to convince myself about. There is a lot that I shall never understand: recent happenings have proved that more conclusively than I might have wished, but surely one should try to throw a bit of light on things? I've started to do that far too late – but you ought to do something while you're waiting for death to carry you off, as one of my colleagues used to say on particularly bleak Monday mornings at the Monkeyhouse. Although I'm beginning to get confused already, words and times are becoming unclear. Back to Sveavägen in Stockholm, exactly one month ago. Eugen Bergman.

'However it turns out?' said Martin, as if he had failed completely to understand the indulgent irony in what the publisher had said. 'Can I remind you that I've been sitting on this material for thirty years. If your bean-counters can't grasp the value of that, there are bean-counters in other publishing houses who will.'

'I've already said that we shall publish it,' said Bergman with one of his wry smiles. 'And you'll get your advance. What's the matter with you, old chap? I can assure you it will be translated into seven or eight languages without further ado. They might even put it up for auction in England. Get on your bike, for God's sake – you have my blessing. And the deadline will be the end of April next year. Mind you, I'd quite like to read bits of it before then, as you know.'

'Fat chance,' said Martin, then nodded at me: 'No bastard gets to read a single word until it's finished.'

It was time to leave, that was obvious. We'd been no more than ten minutes in the room, but needless to say everything had been prepared meticulously in advance. Bergman has been Martin's publisher for twenty years, and is one of those old-fashioned, solid-as-a-rock types. That's what Martin always used to say, in any case. Every new contract – there haven't been all that many, only six or seven if I remember rightly – has been confirmed in Bergman's office. Sign on the dotted line, shake hands, then sink a drop or two of amaro from one of the slightly worse-for-wear little glasses he keeps hidden away in one of his desk cupboards: that has always been the routine, and it was the routine that Friday afternoon at the beginning of October as well.

The sixth, to be precise. An Indian summer day if ever there was one, at least in the Stockholm area. I'm not quite sure why Martin had insisted on my being there, but presumably because it was a rather special occasion.

If so, it wasn't difficult to understand why.

To celebrate the fact that we were still together. That the turbulence of the last few months had not been able to undermine the solid base of our marriage. That I stood behind my husband, or wherever it was that an independent but good wife was expected to stand. By his side, perhaps?

And I admit that 'insisted' is not the right word. Martin had asked me to be present, that was all. Eugen Bergman has been a good friend of both of us for many years, even if we haven't actually been socializing together very much since the death of his wife, Lydia, in 2007. So it was not the first time I had visited that messy office of his in Sveavägen. By no means, and on most of my visits we had drunk a few drops of amaro.

When we left the publisher's Martin announced that he had several other meetings booked in, and suggested that we should meet at Sturehof about six o'clock. Although if I preferred to go straight home I could have the car, as taking the commuter train was no problem as far as he was concerned. I said that I had already arranged to meet this Violetta di Parma who was going to stay in our house while we were away – something he ought to have known as I had mentioned it in the car on the way to town that morning – and that Sturehof at six o'clock would be fine for me.

He nodded somewhat absent-mindedly, gave me a quick hug then continued walking along Sveavägen in the direction of Sergels Torg. For some reason I remained standing there on the pavement, watching him weaving his way through the crowds of unknown people, and I remember thinking that if I hadn't happened to get pregnant when we spent Christmas with his awful parents thirty-three years ago, my life would have turned out differently from the way it did. So would his.

But that was a thought about as banal as an itchy finger, and it lacked significance or comfort.

I enrolled in the Department of Literary History in the autumn term of 1976. I was nineteen, and my boyfriend and first love Rolf enrolled at the same time. I studied literature for two terms, and I might have continued longer if Rolf hadn't been killed in an accident the following summer, although I can't be certain of that. I kept feeling at regular intervals that studying literary texts through a magnifying glass was not my true calling, and although I passed the exams without much difficulty – albeit without achieving top marks – I convinced myself that there were alternative arenas in which my life could take place. Or however you might like to express it.

Rolf's death was naturally a crucial factor. He was the one of us who had been a bookworm enthralled by literature. He was the one who would recite Rilke and Larkin at night after six glasses of wine, he was the one who took me to seminars organized by the Arbetarnas Bildningsförbund – the Workers' Educational Association, or the ABF as it was called – and the Asynja book club, and he was the one who would spend the last few kronor he possessed on half a dozen second-hand copies of Ahlin, Dagerman and Sandemose at Rönnell's anti-quarian bookshop rather than ensuring that we had enough to eat over the weekend. We never got as far as pooling our financial resources – and if we had done it would certainly not have been without its problems.

But in the middle of August 1977, Rolf fell to his death fifty metres down a cliff in Switzerland, and so we never got round to considering such a venture. I abandoned my literary studies and after a few months of mourning, during which I spent part of the time living with my parents and the rest working as a night receptionist at a hotel in Kungsholmen, I signed up for a sort of media studies course at Gärdet in January, and that was the direction my career took. I was given a job by Swedish Television eighteen months later, and that was my workplace until three months ago – apart from two sessions of maternity leave and an occasional project at some other insti-tution.

It feels odd, being able to sum up one's life so simply; but if you miss out your childhood and all the things you thought were so important at the time, it's straightforward.

Barely a year after Rolf's death I went to a garden party in the Old Town. It was the middle of July 1978. I somewhat reluc-tantly accompanied one of my fellow students on the media studies course, and that was the evening when I met Martin. I was the one who was reluctant, not my fellow student, and that had been the way of things throughout the year. I was not in mourning for just one death, but for two. An old one and a new one – I shall come back to that later – and dealing with one's sorrow is by no means a simple matter.

It turned out that I had actually met Martin before.

'Don't you recognize me?' asked a young man who came up to me, carrying a large plastic mug of red-coloured punch. He had long, dark hair and Che Guevara on his chest. And was smoking a pipe.

I didn't. Didn't recognize him, that is.

'Try erasing the long hair and Ernesto,' he said. 'Lit studies a year ago. Where did you go to?'

Then it dawned on me that it was Martin Holinek. An assistant lecturer in the department – or at least, he had been while I was studying there. We hadn't exchanged many words, and he hadn't taught any of the courses I had attended, but I certainly did recognize him once the penny had dropped. He was reputed to be a young genius, and I think Rolf had talked to him quite a lot.

'That business of your boyfriend,' he said now. 'That was absolutely awful.'

'Yes, it was,' I said. 'It was too much for me. I just couldn't carry on studying as planned.'

'I'm very sorry,' he said. 'Have you managed to get back on your feet again by now, more or less?'

That was not a matter I wanted to start going into, even if it seemed to me his sympathetic tone of voice was genuine, and so I asked instead about his links with the garden party crowd. He explained that he actually lived in the same block and knew most of those present, and so we started talking about the Old Town, and about the advantages and disadvantages of various districts in Stockholm. The suburbs versus the town centre, that kind of thing. We somehow managed to skirt round the fact that it was a matter of class and nothing else – or at least, that's how I remember it. Then when we sat down to eat at the long table, we ended up next to each other, and I noticed to my surprise that I was enjoying it. Not just Martin, but the whole party. Everybody was happy and unassuming, there were lots of young children and dogs around, and the early summer weather was at its absolute best. I had been rather antisocial ever since the accident, kept myself to myself and wallowed in my gloomy thoughts – and I think this was the first time since the previous August that I laughed spontaneously at something. It was probably something Martin said, but I don't remember.

But I do recall what he said about Greece, of course. As soon as the following week he was going to board a flight to Athens, and then continue by boat from Piraeus to Samos. Western Samos, on the southern side. He would spend at least a month there in a sort of writers' collective: he had done the same thing last summer, and when he spoke about it I realized that it had been a stunning experience. Needless to say they were all high for much of the time, and all kinds of weed were smoked, he admitted that readily – quite a few of those present had their roots in California – but nevertheless everything was devoted to literary creation. A writers' factory, if you like. He wasn't able to explain exactly what happened in detail that first evening, but everything was concentrated in or around a large house owned by the English poet Tom Herold and his young American wife Bessie Hyatt. I knew who they were: Herold had published several collections of poetry despite the fact that he couldn't be more than thirty, and Bessie Hyatt's debut novel, *Before I Collapse*, had been one of the previous year's most talked-about books. Not just in the USA, but all over the world. The fact that it was considered to contain various keys to the complicated relationship between her and Herold did its reputation no harm.

Of course I was impressed, and of course I could see that Martin Holinek was proud of being a part of such an illustrious gathering. For a specialist in literary history it would mean that, for once, he could hear things straight from the horse's mouth – instead of having to plough his way through endless masses of discourses, analyses and essays that attach themselves to every writer's output, like mould in a badly ventilated cellar. I didn't know what Martin's academic research was concentrated on, but if he was working on a doctorate it was more likely that he would be devoting his studies to something Swedish, or at least Nordic.

But I never asked him about that, and a few years later when we were married and living in our first shared flat in Folkungagaten, that collective in Samos was the only thing I could remember clearly from our first conversation.

Looking back, I doubt if we actually discussed much else.

I was employed by Swedish Television because I was good-looking and could speak clearly.

One of my male bosses – in worn-out jeans, a black jacket and with the makings of a dapper little beard – summarized the appointment procedure in those words a few months later. Several of us had gone to one of Stockholm's pubs after work – I don't remember which – and since he had been involved in that procedure he suggested that I might like to accompany him afterwards to his five-roomed flat in upmarket Östermalm, and listen to some of his unique Coltrane recordings. I declined the offer on the grounds that I was not only happily married but also pregnant, and if I'm not much mistaken my place was taken by a jolly, red-haired colleague who had presumably been awarded her contract on the same well-established grounds as me.

Be that as it may, the Monkeyhouse became my workplace. That was what Martin and I used to call the television centre all the years I worked there – just as our name for the university he worked at was Intensive Care, or sometimes the Sandpit. I read the news for several years, was hostess for various unmissable discussion programmes, and then shortly after the turn of the century started working as a producer. I could still speak clearly, but my looks had undergone the subtle change that maturity brings and were no longer considered to be ideal for the screen. As another male boss with a dapper beard explained to me on one occasion.

However, for the whole of my adult life I have grown used to being greeted by people completely unknown to me. In the supermarket, in the street, on the underground. The harsh truth is that half of Sweden recognizes me; and even if it was Martin who dominated those headlines in May and June – I have no wish to take that distinction away from him – no doubt my name and my face played a significant role when it came to assessing the news value.

But I didn't resign from the Monkeyhouse. I merely applied for a year's leave of absence – a request that was granted in two minutes without specific comment by Alexander Skarman, who was temporarily in charge of such matters during the summer holidays. It was the middle of July, and hotter than it ought to have been in a house occupied by renowned primates. He stinks of Riesling after his lunch, and comes from an established and loyal media family, although he is by no means a mogul or even especially gifted. He was wearing a linen tunic-shirt and shorts. How times have changed . . . Sandals and filthy feet.

I had not given any motive for my application, nor was that necessary given the circumstances.

'From the first of September?' was all he said.

'I'm on holiday in August,' I reminded him.

'You are a very well-known name, you know that.'

I didn't respond. He suppressed a belch, and signed the form.

Our children, Gunvald and Synn, rang a few times during the summer – not *several times*, just *a few* – but it was not until well into August that either of them came to visit us. It was Synn, who flew in for a three-night stay from New York. 'Are you going to leave Dad now?' was the first thing she asked me, and in among the mass of repressed emotions in her voice it was the expectation that I heard most clearly. She and Martin had never really got on well together, and I assume that what had happened seemed to her a positive step forward in the hopes she had been harbouring ever since puberty.

But I informed her that I would not be leaving him. I tried not to sound too definite, said something to the effect that time would have to take its course, and then we would see what happened. I think she accepted that. I don't know if a private conversation took place between father and daughter during the twenty-four hours she spent in our house. Martin said nothing about that in any case, and I'm sure he thought it was a good thing that she didn't stay any longer.

I haven't seen Gunvald since last Christmas. The intention was that we would stop over in Copenhagen on our way south and call in on him, but after the Poland business happened that was out of the question. Or perhaps it was not really the intention that we would do that: perhaps there was some sort of agreement between Martin and Gunvald, I sometimes think that is the case. A gentleman's agreement not to meet face to face, and no doubt that wouldn't be a bad idea. I have the feeling that in the circumstances it would be in the best interests of our children for us to leave them in peace.

I write *us*, but I suppose I ought to reduce that to *me*.

Perhaps leave them in peace for good, come to that – I must admit that is a thought that has become more pressing during the autumn. But quite a lot of thoughts have behaved like that. The difference between a day, a year and a life has shrunk very noticeably.

3

The first morning was grey and chilly.

Or at least, it was chilly inside the house. The smell of ingrained mould was very noticeable in the bedroom, but I told myself I was going to learn how to live with it. The house has only two rooms, but they are quite large and the windows in both of them face in the same direction: southwards. That is where the moor begins, and on the other side is a rough and moss-covered stone wall that encloses the plot on three sides. Out on the moor the ground slopes gently down towards a valley that I assume continues all the way to the village – but the dense mist that has settled over the countryside this morning makes it difficult to work out the topography.

Especially when viewed from my pillow. Dawn had barely broken, and neither Castor nor I were particularly keen to fold back the duvet and leave behind the comparative warmth that had built up inside the bed during the night.

Sooner or later, of course, one needs to relieve oneself, and this morning was no exception. Castor normally seems able to last for an eternity without emptying his bladder, but I let him out even so while I crouched shivering on the icy-cold toilet seat. When I had finished and went to let him in, he was standing outside the door looking reproachful, as he does for much of most days. I dried his paws and provided him with food and water in the two pastel-coloured plastic bowls I had found the previous evening under the sink. His usual bowls were still in the car – I hadn't bothered to unpack in the dark.

Then I put on the kettle with tea in mind, and managed to get a fire burning. The uneasiness that had been bubbling away inside my head gradually dispersed, thanks to the heat and the underlying feeling of well-being that was trying to establish itself, no matter what. A truth much deeper than conventional civilization and modern fads presented itself: if you can keep a fire going, you can keep your life going.

In other respects the house is as devoid of charm as its owner. It provides the rudimentary basics, nothing more. Refrigerator and stove. A sofa, an armchair, a table with three chairs and an old-fashioned desk in front of the window. A rocking chair. Nothing matches. Quite a large picture of ponies out on the moor hangs just to the side of the sofa. A smaller embroidered tapestry with six lop-sided trees looks as if it has been made by a child.

Plus an effective fireplace. Thank God for that. Castor was stretched out on the sheepskin in front of the fire as if it was the most natural place for him to be in the world. I assume he is still wondering what has happened to Martin, but he shows no sign of doing so. None at all.

In the built-in wardrobe in the bedroom I found the two electric fires – which I have to pay Mr Tawking extra for if I use them – and plugged in one in each room. I turned them both up to maximum heat output, in the hope of creating a reasonable temperature inside the house without having to keep a fire going. And perhaps also get rid of some of the mould.

I drank my tea without sugar or milk, and ate half a dozen rusks and an apple – all that was left of my emergency rations. Then I made a superficial survey of the cooking utensils in all the cupboards and drawers, and started writing a list of what I needed to buy. A grater, for instance, a frying pan and a pasta saucepan, a decent bread knife; and by the time the clock said half past nine – we had woken up shortly after seven – I had also carried in everything from the car. And crammed stuff into wardrobes and drawers.

It's going to work, I made so bold as to tell myself. I do one thing at a time, and it works. Castor was still stretched out in front of the fire, completely at ease as far as I could tell, and I thought how interesting it would be to get inside his head for a short while. So interesting to be a dog instead of a person, even if only for a few moments.

When I had finished unpacking and the other chores, I stood out in the yard for a while and tried to sum up the situation. The mist had not dispersed much, despite a fresh wind blowing in from the higher parts of the moor to the north. Visibility was still not much more than a hundred metres in any direction, and instead of going out for a walk, which is what I had intended at first, we got in the car and drove down to the village to do some shopping.

★

Only a small part of what I reckoned I needed was available in the local shop – Winsford Stores. However, the owner, a chubby lady about sixty-five years of age, was very helpful and explained that if I drove to Dulverton I would definitely be able to acquire most things. She was probably longing to ask me who I was and what I hoped to do in her little Winsford; I had an equally unspoken response at the ready, but we didn't get that far this first morning. Instead she gave me detailed instructions about how to get to Dulverton. There were two possibilities: either take the A396 alongside the River Exe, through Bridgetown and Chilly Bridge; or the B3223 up into the moor, then down into Dulverton alongside the River Barle, the other main waterway over Exmoor. We consulted a map, which I bought from her, and agreed that it would be a good idea to take the former route there, and the latter back. Especially if I was living here on the moor – something I didn't really admit to doing, for whatever reason. I paid for the various goods I had chosen, including a dozen speckled eggs supplied that very morning by Fowley Farm, which was only a stone's throw away from the shop: according to all sensible judges they were the most delicious and nutritious in the whole of the kingdom. I thanked her for her help and wished her a very good day. She wished me the same, and I bore with me her warmth and helpfulness most of the way to Dulverton.

Half an hour later I parked outside The Bridge Inn next to an old stone bridge over the Barle. Without doubt Dulverton is a market town that can supply everything a modern person can possibly need – or an unmodern one, come to that. After strolling around the town for ten minutes – under a greyish white sky with no trace left of the mist, and even a suggestion that the sun was about to break through the clouds – Castor and I were able to establish that the place had not only restaurants, but also a police station, a fire station, a pharmacy, a library, and a variety of shops, pubs and teashops. There was even an old antiquarian bookshop, which we couldn't resist paying a visit to, as a notice pinned to the rickety door announced that four-footed friends were especially welcome.

We did the shopping at a leisurely pace, then went for a little stroll by the cheerfully babbling brook that was the Barle – oh, I am so pleased to be able to write 'cheerfully babbling brook', I think it enables me to redress matters somewhat – and I found it difficult to understand where all the water was coming from. To round things off we ate some venison pie with a large helping of peas at The Bridge Inn – well, Castor had to be satisfied with a handful of doggy treats produced willingly from a store under the counter.

I noted that there is a considerable difference between being a single middle-aged woman and a single middle-aged woman with a dog. Castor's company, as he lies there under my table in the pub, gives me some sort of natural dignity and legitimacy that I find difficult to explain. A sort of undeserved blessing that one can make the most of. I would not be able to cope with the situation I find myself in were it not for his reassuring presence and support – certainly not. Nevertheless I am of course very unsure if everything will end up happily, whatever that cliché might mean, even with this formidable companion by my side. But at least it helps me to get by in the short term. Minutes, hours, perhaps even days. Presumably that is also how a dog thinks and makes its way through life. One step at a time. They obviously have an advantage on that score.

In fact he was Martin's dog to start with. Martin was the one who insisted that we needed a pet when the children had flown the nest – and by a pet, he meant of course a dog, nothing else. He grew up with lots of pooches around the house; in my well-organized childhood there was no room for such extravagances, I don't really know why. I had to make do with unreliable cats and a handful of aquarium fish that soon died off, that was all. Oh, and a brother as well. Not to mention a younger sister – I would prefer to write my way around her, giving her as wide a berth as possible, but I can see that it wouldn't work.

He's seven years old, getting on for eight, Castor. A Rhodesian ridgeback. I had never heard of them when Martin first brought him home. I think he had a vague dream of the dog lying at his feet in his study at the university, and perhaps also accompanying him when he delivered his lectures. But of course, that never happened. I was the one who took Castor on courses, and to the vet's. I was the one who looked after all the practical details involved in owning a dog, and I was the one who took him for long walks every day.

Because I was the one who had time.

Or to be frank, who made the time: but there was never any argument about it. I enjoyed doing it, it was as simple as that.

To go wandering through woods and fields for a few hours every day with a silent and loyal companion, with no other aim than doing just that – walking through the countryside in silence – well, after only a few weeks that was an occupation I came to regard as the most important and meaningful aspect of my life.

Perhaps that says something about my life.

When I drove back to Darne Lodge – following the elevated route over the moor – the mist had dispersed altogether and the views extended for miles. I wound down the side window and thought I could just about make out the sea in the distance, or the Bristol Channel at least, and I was overcome by a feeling of being very solitary, totally insignificant and passed over. In many ways it is easier to live somewhere without horizons, in the mist and in a confined space. At least I am well aware that I need to stick to simple and practical activities, to make decisions and stick to them, as I said before – otherwise everything can go to pot. When everything, every step and every action and every undertaking has no broader significance, when you might just as well be doing something else rather than what you are actually doing at the moment, and when you can't help but think about that – and when the only thing that might possibly have some point seems to be linked with the mistakes and misdeeds one was guilty of in the past – well, then madness is lying in wait just round the corner.

Living on the moor involves an attractive but dangerous freedom, I'm beginning to understand that already. I stopped in a lay-by and let Castor move from the poky back seat to the front passenger seat. He loves being there, puts his nose over the air intake and thus creates for himself an ethereal range of scents.

Or he pokes his whole head out through the side window, like dogs do in the countryside. There is nobody in the whole world who knows that we are here.

I'll say that again: there is nobody in the whole world who knows that we are here.

4

Early in the morning of the tenth of April my husband raped a young woman in a hotel in Gothenburg. Her name was Magdalena Svensson, twenty-three years old, and she had been working at the hotel as a waitress since the beginning of the year. She reported the incident to the police after about three weeks mulling it over, on the second of May.

Or perhaps he didn't actually rape her. I don't know for sure, because I wasn't there.

Martin was interrogated, spent a night and a day in police custody and was then released on bail.

Just over two weeks later, on the eighteenth of May, a tabloid newspaper became aware of the situation – the fact that the well-known polemicist, author and professor of literature, Martin Holinek, had been charged with rape – and by the following week the whole of Sweden knew about it. Magdalena Svensson talked about what had happened that night to a large number of media outlets, and for five days running it made the headlines in the evening tabloids *Expressen* and *Aftonbladet*. My husband refused to comment and was given sick leave by the university; but it was widely discussed on the radio and television and in the press. But above all it was a hot topic on social media: in one blog, for instance, another woman claimed she had also been raped by 'that sleazy professor' – in a hotel in Umeå almost a year ago. He was alleged to have been 'as randy as a bloody chimpanzee' – an expression she had obviously borrowed from an earlier case involving a French banker and politician – but she had not got round to reporting the incident because she was afraid. Two other women wrote in their blogs that they had also been raped by different professors, and comments were as numerous as grasshoppers in Egypt.

To crown it all one of the commercial television channels offered me and Martin 50,000 kronor if all three of us would agree to take part in one of their evening discussion pro-grammes. By 'all three' they meant the rape victim, the rapist and the rapist's wife. They considered it to be a matter of considerable public interest. We declined the offer. We never discovered whether or not Magdalena Svensson accepted. Or at least, I didn't.

On the tenth of June Miss Svensson withdrew her rape accusation, and for a few days the incident had new wind in its sails in the media. There was speculation about her having been threatened, about the rapist having bought himself free in accordance with time-honoured practice, and various other theories similar in nature. A demonstration against men who hate women attracted two thousand people to Sergels Torg in Stockholm. Somebody posted a condom full of shit through our letter box.

To be fair, a handful of voices made themselves heard in Martin's defence – the usual ones. But he held fast to his decision to make no comment. So did his lawyer, despite the fact that he is one of the leading members of his fraternity in Sweden and normally can't keep his mouth shut.

The preliminary investigation was abandoned, and the whole matter shelved.

I didn't have much to say about the matter either, but when the uproar was at its height I counted more than twenty photographers and journalists camped outside our house in Nynäshamn. Late one evening Martin fired two shots of his elk-hunting rifle through the window, straight up into the heavens over the forest. The press mob had something to report now, and promptly disappeared in the direction of Stockholm to leave us in peace for a while. Being a star reporter and having to hang around outside a house in Nynäshamn is no sinecure.

I recall Martin trying to look pleased with himself as he put his gun away. 'So there!' he said. 'Shall we have a glass of wine?'

But he sounded anything but upbeat, and I declined the offer. For some reason he was never prosecuted for shooting a gun inside a built-up area.

We spoke about what had happened – or perhaps hadn't happened – only once, and never again. That was my choice, on both counts.

'Did you have sex with that woman?' I asked.

'Yes, I had sex with her,' said Martin.

'Did you rape her?'

'Most certainly not,' said Martin.

That was the day it was first written about in the news-paper: I hadn't been able to bring myself to ask before then, even though I knew about it. Neither of our children was in touch that evening. None of our friends either. I thought the telephones were remarkably quiet.

Apart from calls from unknown numbers, of course; but we didn't answer those.

'That woman up in Umeå,' I did get round to asking a few days later when it was being widely discussed. 'Did you?'

'Surely you don't believe what she says?' said Martin.

One of the things that felt remarkable throughout the summer – much more remarkable than difficult, I ought to stress – was that I couldn't make up my mind what the truth was. I sup-pose it was somehow outside my range of comprehension, I couldn't really grasp it, and what you don't understand is not something you can pin down. At least, that's what I tell myself was the situation. I used to wake up in the morning and after the first few seconds of blankness the situation I found myself in would hit me. I would realize why I was feeling so tired and melancholy – and then as I tottered to the bathroom on unsteady feet I would feel like an actress who had ended up in the wrong film. The wrong film altogether, and twenty-five years too late.

Both Martin and I had been unfaithful once before, and on each occasion we had managed to hold our marriage together. He was first, and then it was me as a sort of revenge. It was while the children were still at home, and it's possible that we might have reached different decisions if they had flown the nest. But I don't know, and it's difficult to speculate about it. In any case neither of us would have continued the relationship with the new partner if such a possibility had presented itself. That is something we have convinced both ourselves and each other about during the years that have passed since it happened. Sixteen years and fourteen, to be precise. Good Lord, I blush in embarrassment when I recall that I was forty-one years old when I went to bed with that young recording technician. He could have been a mate of Gunvald's, if Gunvald had knocked around with types like him.

After the worst was over, from about the middle of June or thereabouts, I noticed that I really did want to know what had happened. I needed to know exactly what my husband had been doing with that waitress in the hotel.

That night.

The problem was that it was too late to ask Martin. An invisible borderline had been passed, a sort of ceasefire had been proclaimed, and I felt I had no right to tear it up. I am not all that interested in sex any longer: somewhat lazily I had assumed it would be sufficient for Martin to masturbate in the shower and imagine he was penetrating some willing accomplice's pussy. But in fact it wasn't quite as easy as that.

Ask for a divorce? I would be fully entitled to do that, of course. But it didn't appeal to me. There was something basically banal about such a reaction: after all, we had been married for thirty years, we had been living parallel lives with a sort of shared mutual understanding, and we had booked a shared grave at Skogskyrkogården cemetery.

But in the end I phoned her. Magdalena Svensson. I found her details on the Eniro website. She was at home in Guldheden, Gothenburg, and answered on her mobile.

We met three days later, on the twentieth of August, in a cafe in the Haga district. It was an exceptionally warm day, and I had taken a morning train from Stockholm. As I arrived a bit early, I decided to walk all the way from the central station, and felt unpleasantly sweaty when I reached the cafe. Moreover a vague feeling of disgust had grown up inside me; I doubted whether what I was about to do was sensible, and very nearly turned back as I approached Haga. I had my mobile in my hand, was ready to ring her number and explain that I had changed my mind. That I didn't in fact want to speak to her, and that it was best if we both forgot all about the whole business.

But I didn't. I pulled myself together.

She was sitting at an outside table under a parasol, waiting for me. She was wearing a light green dress and a thin, white linen scarf, and even though I recognized her from the pictures in the newspapers, it was as if I were meeting a quite different person. She was young and pretty, but not especially sexy. She looked shy and uneasy – but considering the circumstances that was perhaps not so odd.

She stood up when she saw me. She obviously belonged to the fifty per cent of the Swedish population who recognized me. I nodded to her to indicate that I had identified her, but it was only when we shook hands and introduced ourselves that I was struck by the paradoxical hopelessness of the situation. Either this cautious little creature had been raped by the man I had been living with for the whole of my adult life, in which case one had to feel sorry for her. Or she had voluntarily agreed to have sex with my husband, in which case there was no need to feel sorry for her in the slightest.

'I'm so sorry,' she said.

Apart from saying her name, those were the first words she spoke: I thought she was going to continue, but she said nothing more. It seemed to me that if she had been sitting there waiting for me – the older woman who had been betrayed – she ought to have had time to think of something more pregnant to say than that she was sorry. That television programme that never happened would have been a bit of a disaster.

'So am I,' I said. 'But I haven't come here to tell you how I feel.'

She smiled unsteadily without looking me straight in the eye.

'Nor have I come to hear about how you feel. I just want you to tell me what happened.'

We sat down.

'If you have nothing against that,' I added.

She sucked in her lower lip and I could see that she was close to tears. It was not difficult to work out how all those quotations from her in the newspapers had come about. Journalists had telephoned her, and she hadn't had the sense to replace the receiver.

'I'm so sorry,' she said again. 'It must be awful for you. I didn't think about that.'

When, I wondered. When didn't you think about it?

'How old are you?' I asked, although I already knew the answer.

'Twenty-three. I shall be twenty-four next week. Why do you ask?'

'I have a daughter who is five years older than you.'

'Really?'

She didn't seem to understand my point – nor did I, come to that. A waitress came to our table. I ordered an espresso, Magdalena Svensson asked for another cup of tea.

'I understand that this is difficult for you,' I said. 'It's hard for both of us. But it would make things easier for me if I got to know exactly what happened between you and my husband.'

She sat in silence for a while, scratching her lower arms and trying not to cry. Her lower lip was sucked into her mouth again, and it was almost impossible not to feel sorry for her. So that's it, I thought. He did rape her.

'It was my sister,' she said.

'Your sister?'

'Yes. She was the one who persuaded me to go to the police. I regret doing so. Nothing has got any better. I've felt so awful all summer, I just don't know what to do.'

I nodded. 'Same here,' I said.

'She was also raped, my sister,' said Magdalena, blowing her nose into a paper tissue. 'That was five years ago. We have that in common. But she never reported the man who did it. That's why she encouraged me.'

She suddenly sounded like a schoolgirl. A secondary school pupil who had been caught pilfering or playing truant. Just for a second the image of her and Martin's naked bodies in a hotel bed flashed through my mind's eye: it looked so absurd that I had difficulty in taking it seriously.

Was it possible to take something like this seriously? What does *seriously* mean?

'She said you should always report the perpetrator, otherwise women will never be liberated. Will never be rehabilitated . . . Or something like that. And so I did report him. She came with me to the police station. Her name's Maria, by the way – just like you.'

I nodded again. 'So you and your sister have that in common, do you?'

'Yes.'

'Maria and Magdalena.'

'Yes – what's special about that?'

I brushed the thought to one side. 'But then you retracted your accusation later?'

'Yes. I did.'

'Why?'

'It became too much.'

'Too much?'

'Yes, with the newspapers and all that.'

Our coffee and tea were served, and we sat without speaking for a while.

'Forgive me,' I said eventually, and now I really did feel like a stern headmaster questioning a pupil at his secondary school for girls about some petty offence or other. 'Forgive me, but I don't really understand. Are you saying that you really were raped by my husband?'

She thought for a moment. Then she said: 'I was drugged.'

'Drugged?'

'Yes. That must have been what happened. I was away with the fairies. And afterwards I could hardly remember anything about it.'

'Couldn't remember? But didn't you say that—'

'I woke up in his bed. And I had his sperm on my stomach.'

I drank my espresso in one gulp. Concentrated my gaze on the back wheel of a bicycle leaning somewhat untidily against a green wall, and felt that I really ought to throw up.

'It must have been in a drink . . . That drug.'

I gesticulated, inviting her to continue.

'I finished work at nine o'clock that night, but a few of us stayed behind in the restaurant. One of my workmates, another girl, had a birthday, and we'd planned it as a surprise for her . . .'

She fell silent and produced another tissue. I thought that this detail must have been reported in the media, but I'd evidently missed it.

'Are you suggesting that my husband put some drug or other into your drink, then enticed you into his room and then . . . Well? Is that it?'

'Somebody must have done it,' said Magdalena. 'They were sitting at the table next to ours. And we started talking to them, sort of . . .'

'You started talking to them?'

'Yes.'

'So there was a group of them, was there?'

'A few men and women. About your age.'

I wondered who the others could have been. Most probably colleagues of Martin's, some academics he'd met at the conference. But it didn't matter, hardly anything mattered.

'It wasn't simply that you got drunk, then?' I asked.

Magdalena Svensson started crying. We sat there in the cafe for another ten minutes, but I couldn't get any sense out of her.

In the train back to Stockholm there was just one thing she had said that I couldn't get out of my mind.

I had his sperm on my stomach.

It was when I got back home to Nynäshamn late in the evening after that conversation with Magdalena Svensson that Martin informed me about his plans for the winter. I felt a little bit like a being from outer space, and didn't have anything much to say. Nor did I mention what I had been doing earlier in the day.

5

It was about three o'clock in the afternoon, before daylight had deteriorated too much, that we set out on our first longish walk over the moor.

By 'longish' I mean in this connection just under two hours. I had bought various maps and descriptions of walks at the antiquarian bookshop in Dulverton, but on this occasion I didn't bother to plan a particular route. I just felt the need to start becoming acquainted with the moor before darkness fell – and Castor was evidently of the same opinion as he immediately took the lead, always a sign that he thinks a walk is going to be interesting and worth doing.

We set off from Darne Lodge, I climbed and he jumped over the stone wall, and then we followed one of the several well-worn paths heading westwards. It was extremely muddy in places, but I was wearing my splendid new walking shoes bought in Queensway, Bayswater, three days ago, and Castor is never put out if the ground is a bit on the sticky side. What he can't cope with is when the going is hard and littered with sharp stones – just like me, in a figurative sense.

We had only walked a few hundred metres when we came to something marked on the maps as a sight worth seeing –

the so-called Caratacus monument: a small shelter protecting a memorial stone from Roman times. The inscription is illegible to the uninitiated, but the stone is thought to have been raised to honour a local chieftain who led valiant resistance against the superior occupying forces.

We continued southwards, parallel with the Dulverton road even though we only had occasional glimpses of it. I thought somewhat casually about the concept of 'resistance', then and now. Superiority and inferiority, male and female: but I soon lost the thread – it seemed out of place in this landscape. I still don't know what is appropriate and what is inappropriate here, but what I can say is that there is a marked sense of desolation and a peculiar kind of silence on the moor. Apart from when you disturb a pheasant, or a flock of them – there are hundreds of pheasants on Exmoor – and the colourful males at least seem incapable of flying without screeching loudly. After a while we also happened upon a little group of the famous wild Exmoor ponies. They looked both dishevelled and strong – and clearly needed treating with respect. I have read that they wander about up here all year round, and live their lives from birth to death in these spartan surroundings. They more or less ignored us. Castor restricted himself to observing them from a safe distance, and then we continued our leisurely stroll. To an untrained eye like mine, the moor is a sort of self-sufficient entity – that is the overwhelming impression it makes. It is barren and monotonous, perhaps somewhat secretive, and motionless as a petrified ocean. Nothing but low, bushy vegetation succeeds in forcing its way up from the infertile soil: heather, ferns and gorse, some of it constantly in bloom. Here and there the landscape is intersected by valleys carved out over the centuries by brooks and streams wending their way to the Exe or the Barle. But in these hollows the vegetation is abundant and dripping with moisture: we soon found ourselves in one of them, filled with beech and oak, alder and hazel – I'm not sure of the various species, and resolved to buy a comprehensive reference book as soon as possible. I recognize holly, moss and ivy, clinging stubbornly and methodically to trunks and branches. Water trickles under dense rhododendron thickets, and the smell of decay is everywhere.

I made all those observations during the first thirty or forty minutes of our walk, as we were making our way down a slope on a very muddy path, apparently used recently by both sheep and ponies: it seemed to be the very same slope we had contemplated from our bedroom window that morning. And sure enough, one of the very rare signposts indicated that the path went all the way to Winsford. However, when we came to somewhere apparently called Halse Farm, which must presumably have given its name to the road up to Darne Lodge, we decided to turn and go back home. It was four o'clock, and dusk was already beginning to fall: no doubt it would be best to walk all the way to the village the next morning or afternoon. Neither I nor Castor would want to be stranded in the dark in this magnificent, bewitching landscape. The word *bewitching* really does seem to be an accurate description.

When we got back to Darne Lodge we spent a few hours dealing with household chores. Yet again I feel linguistic uncertainty when I use the pronoun *we*. Obviously I was the one who lit the candles and the fire, and who chopped up greens and onions and slices of lamb for the stew I eventually ate myself. I was the one who did the washing up, wiped clean various drawers and cupboards, and packed away my clothes in the wardrobe and the chest of drawers in the bedroom. Castor's only contribution was to eat his evening meal – Royal Canin Maxi for dogs over twenty-six kilos – and lap up rather noisily the water in his usual metal bowl. He spent the rest of the late afternoon and evening on the sheepskin rug in front of the fire.

Needless to say my urge to cling on to the plural form is not all that difficult to understand. I have lived under the same roof as my husband for over thirty years, and that has left traces deep down in the grammar of my language. Perhaps it is just that I'm scared. A *we* has so much more weight than a mere *I*, even if it is only a dog that justifies its use. And it is the elder twin sister of Independence – Loneliness, the one who carries herself awkwardly, has skin scarred by scurf and very bad breath, who I have to kill and bury. Over and over again; that's life. She is the monstrous enemy, for both Castor and myself – I don't know why I started going on about this. Bugger it all! To hell with all this nonsensical analysis! I believe in individual human beings. I *must* believe in individual human beings.

As an antidote I drank two glasses of the excellent port I had bought in Dulverton, and took out my computer. Martin's can stay inside his black briefcase for now, the one with that irritating sticker from Barcelona. I suppose I'll get round to opening both of them eventually, the briefcase and the computer: but this evening didn't seem to be the right time. I established that there was indeed no internet connection here, as I had already been told. If at some future point I feel the need to link up with the outside world – for reasons that I can't really imagine at the moment – I can either drive to Minehead on the coast, where there are several internet cafes, or to the library in Dulverton. Or at least, I assume that's what I would need to do: perhaps there are possibilities closer at hand. Attempts to use both my mobile and Martin's in various parts of the house were also in vain: I decided that tomorrow I would try the location Mr Tawking had mentioned – that grave on the other side of the road. In no circumstances am I going to try to phone anybody – or to send an e-mail or a text message: but it could be interesting to know if anybody has been trying to contact us.

There again, perhaps it would be risky to activate my mobile. I don't really know how they work. But if somebody should try to contact us – I mean *really* try – somebody like Interpol or a detective or somebody like that, then they will find us sooner or later, of course. But the point is that it should never occur to anybody that they should start searching. Because there is no reason to do so.

After the second glass of port wine and when the fire began to die down, I let Castor out to do his business. He disappeared into the pitch darkness, and as it was getting on for five minutes before he reappeared, I had time to imagine all kinds of things that might have happened to him, and worry unnecessarily. The whole plot is certainly no more than a thousand square metres, but it would have been easy for him to clamber over the old stone wall, if he had wanted to.

Then we went to bed. It was no later than a quarter past ten, but the darkness and the house itself – and the rain which soon began pattering on the slate roof and on the evergreen bushes outside the window, rhododendrons there as well if I'm not much mistaken – somehow reduced the concept of time to a . . . to a totally insignificant theoretical construction. Before falling asleep I also began thinking about the house for the first time – about its history: how old it was, what function it used to have, who had lived there over the years and indeed the centuries, and why it was located just here in splendid isolation on the moor. There is a real farmhouse not all that far away, in the direction of Winsford, just above Halse Farm, and it's possible that Darne Lodge was originally a part of that smallholding. Outside the lodge is a boarded-up stable block that I haven't yet bothered to explore, and I suppose I can find out more details from Mr Tawking if I feel that I really want to know. Or down at The Royal Oak, which I have not yet visited.

In any case, the house is old, probably several hundred years old. The stone walls are thick, the roof low and the windows on the small side. Even if the rooms are large, the house is constructed in accordance with austere practical considerations, and when I had settled down in bed I realized that if a fire had been burning steadily all day one could benefit from the residual heat in the walls, even in the bedroom. After a while I got up and disconnected both the electric radiators. It's better to rely on the fire, I thought: the simple firewood bunker built onto the gable wall of the stable block is well filled – but perhaps my landlord will expect me to leave it in the same state as it was in when I arrived. If so, I have no idea where I would get the necessary firewood from: but that is not something I need to worry about in the near future, and when I snuggled back down under the duvet I recalled once again the bitter-sweet fact that nobody in the whole world knows where we are. Castor and his master.

Or his missus, for that matter.

And those who know that there is somebody living in Darne Lodge just outside the village of Winsford in the county of Somerset near the border with Devon – possibly nobody at the moment apart from Mr Tawking – have no idea about their identity.

A woman and her dog, that's all.

An autumn night like any other.

About an hour later I suddenly woke up. I found it impossible to decide if I had been woken by something external or something internal, but I was possessed by a highly unpleasant throbbing feeling and sat up, leaning against the bedhead. The rain had stopped, the darkness was dense. A faint musty smell. The only sound to be heard was Castor's regular breathing from underneath the bottom of the duvet, but nevertheless I sensed a new sort of presence in the room. As if somebody were standing pressed up against the wall next to the wardrobe, watching us. Or perhaps the front door had just closed with a bang, and that was the sound that had woken me up –

but that was of course a sheer impossibility. Castor would have reacted to the noise. His sense of hearing is many times more sensitive than mine, and even if he is not all that efficient as a guard dog, he always notices if some unknown creature turns up in our immediate vicinity.

But my heart was racing, and it was some time before I managed to calm down. It occurred to me that perhaps I ought to buy a little CD-player. A reassuring voice or a saxophone that could soften up the darkness and the silence would no doubt be welcome. Dexter Gordon, perhaps? Or Chet Baker? Would it be possible to find something by Chet Baker in a music shop in Minehead or Dulverton? Or would I need to go to Exeter? That is the only town of any size in this neck of the woods, and if I have read the map correctly it should be possible to drive there in an hour and a half or two hours at the most.

I eventually fell asleep again, and began immediately to dream about the grey-white beach at Międzyzdroje. Walking eastwards into the wind, and then that strange walk back again.

That strange walk back again.

6

Martin spent three summers in all at Samos. 1977, 1978 and 1979. The literary jamboree continued for another five years or so, but Tom Herold and Bessie Hyatt left both their house and the Mediterranean island in September 1979. Bessie's second novel – *Men's Blood Circulation* – was published a month later that same autumn, by which time the pair had settled down just outside Taza in Morocco, and they stayed there until Bessie's suicide in April 1981.

For a few weeks in July–August 1980 Martin was a guest at their new home in Morocco: I stayed behind in Stockholm, awaiting the birth of Gunvald. We had moved into our first shared accommodation, a three-roomed flat in Folkungagatan, in May. I don't know exactly what happened during those weeks in Taza, but something significant did. When Martin came back to Sweden he had changed in a way that I didn't really understand until several years later. Although we were about to become parents, we hadn't known each other all that long; my pregnancy was rather complicated, and I was con-centrating on what was happening to my own body – the internal changes, not the external ones.

In any case, we didn't talk much about Taza. Not before

Bessie Hyatt's suicide, and not after it. Quite a lot was written about Herold and Hyatt during those years, and an English company even began making a film about their lives – with two relatively prominent actors taking the leading roles – but the project eventually came to a halt for some unknown reason. Possibly a shortage of money, or possibly a threat of legal action from Tom Herold's lawyers.

But Martin never published anything about it, not a single word, and when I asked him about that long afterwards – more by chance than out of real interest – he simply answered that he was bound by certain promises. No, he didn't *answer*, he *implied* – looking back now, I'm quite sure that is the fact of the matter.

Tom Herold kept both his life and his reputation. He continued living in Morocco – but not in Taza – until the beginning of the twenty-first century, when he moved back home to England. He published over twenty collections of poetry, three novels and a sort of posthumous autobiography, which appeared six months after his death in 2009. He also directed and produced two self-indulgent long films during the nineties; but his fame reached its peak for a broader and non-literary public in May 2003, when he decapitated a young burglar in his Dorset home with the aid of a thousand-year-old Arab scimitar. As the burglar was armed with both a knife and a gun, Herold was cleared of any criminal offence by the subsequent trial.

He also managed to fit in another short marriage – between 1990 and 1995 or thereabouts. The woman in question was a young Moroccan by the name of Fatima: but there were no children from this relationship either.

For the whole of his life Tom Herold was constantly being written about, despite the fact that he deliberately avoided publicity. He never gave interviews, not even when he was being hounded by writers and journalists of all conceivable persuasions. Especially after the suicide of Bessie Hyatt he was subjected to what can only be called a witch-hunt. He was accused in several contexts of being guilty of his young wife's death, and there was much speculation about the use of drugs and various occult rituals. But Herold never commented at all about the relationship between himself and his wife. Needless to say, when his posthumous memoirs were published almost thirty years after Bessie's death, expectations were very high. It was unclear if he had given permission for the book to be published before he died, or if it was his publisher who had taken the matter into his own hands. Herold had no heirs at all, and had not made a will. He was killed by a malignant colon cancer, and according to his few friends his final years had been characterized by pain and melancholy.

In any case, *The Sum of My Days* was a failure, from both a literary and a commercial point of view. The reviews were consistently lukewarm, and those who had been hoping for sensational revelations, especially in connection with his years together with Bessie Hyatt, were disappointed. The so-called memoirs turned out to be mainly a series of neutral observations of nature without much in the way of subtlety or finesse. The only chapters with a more personal touch were about some summers in his childhood, spent on a farm in Wales in the company of a female cousin. Bessie Hyatt was mentioned by name twice in the whole book, and their marriage that inspired so much speculation and gossip was allocated about three-and-a-half pages. Moreover, most readers thought the book was badly edited, and although Herold was such a familiar name in large parts of the world, there was never any question of its becoming an international success.

Thirty years after Bessie Hyatt's death, her two novels – *Before I Fall* and *Men's Blood Circulation* – had achieved worldwide sales of over twenty-five million copies. Roughly speaking that is about ten times as many as Herold could manage.

'I understand,' Eugen Bergman had said that October afternoon in Sveavägen. 'And how extensive is your material, approximately?'

'A thousand pages,' said Martin with a shrug. 'Give or take a hundred. And I need six months to get it into shape. Maybe more, but let's say six months to start with.'

'Hm,' said Bergman.

'Morocco,' said Martin, giving me a look that was intended to mean we were in agreement. That we had discussed the matter, and were in the same boat. The same unsinkable flat-bottomed rowing boat of marriage in heavy seas. There was no end to the images implied, and I suddenly felt sick.

'I still have quite a few contacts down there, and it's always an advantage to be in the right place.'

'Hm,' said Bergman again, heaving himself up from his

desk chair and walking over to the window, where he gazed out for a while at Adolf Fredrik Church. Swayed back and forth in a way that one has to call characteristic. Hands clasped behind his back. Hair all over the place. It was a lovely autumn day out there. Martin signalled to me that I should say nothing, and I looked around for somewhere suitable if I found I really did need to throw up. I decided on the waste-paper basket at the side of the desk.

'And what about Bessie Hyatt? Those years?' He muttered that in a low voice, almost as an afterthought, without turning round.

'Of course,' said Martin in his typically quiet, non-committal tone of voice. 'That's what it's all about after all, isn't it?'

He could just as well have been commenting on how to cope with heartburn, or what kind of roof would be most appropriate for his outside loo. I started to feel less like throwing up. Bergman went back to his desk and put on his glasses. Pushed them down to the tip of his nose and looked at us as if we were a picture puzzle he was on the point of solving. Or something like that.

'Okay, I understand that you need to get away from here. What with that mad woman, and all the rest of it.'

Thus spake Eugen Bergman, publisher, pataphysicist and good friend for half a lifetime.

And so on as described before.

It was a simple plan: when we met Bergman it was over a month since Martin had proposed it, and I had agreed without much thought. Perhaps that was a mistake on my part – yes, of course it was: not the fact that I didn't think much about it, but that I said yes. Afterthoughts of one kind or another wouldn't have done much good; it was a situation that called for instinctive reactions and intuition, not for logical or emotional calculations.

And perhaps I made the wrong decision. Completely and utterly wrong.

But that meeting with Magdalena Svensson was fresh in my mind, I can blame that.

'Let's disappear from the face of the earth for half a year,' said Martin. 'Let's grant ourselves that luxury.'

'What do you mean exactly?'

He pretended to think it over while eyeing me with that innocent look of his which had been a trump card for so many years, but no longer was. 'I mean . . . I just mean that we should go away for six months without telling a soul where we've gone to.'

'Really?'

'Apart from the fact that we're going to Morocco, perhaps. Telling a few people that, at least. They can send post to Marrakesh or Agadir. Poste restante. That still works, and we can pick it up when it suits us. If we need to be in contact with the outside world we can always find an internet cafe. No mobiles, I'm so damned fed up with mobile phones. Just you and me . . . Time to think things over and heal wounds, and whatever else you want.'

'Have you any special place in mind?' I wondered. 'A particular house, or anything like that?'

He had been back to Morocco not all that long ago. The end of the nineties, if I remember rightly – an assignment commissioned by the university, some Sufi poets or something of the sort, and he had tagged on a week's holiday as well. Maybe he had met Herold, maybe not. We'd never spoken about precisely what he had got up to, I don't really know why. Perhaps there was some kind of crisis at the Monkeyhouse at the same time. Or in the Sandpit. Both institutions generally imploded a few times every year.

'There are several possibilities,' he said. 'I have a few contacts down there.'

'And those thousand pages?' I asked, because he had told me that as well.

'Of course.'

'And you're going to write about them? About Herold and Hyatt?'

'Why not?' said Martin, adopting his non-committal expression once again.

I thought about that promise of silence he had made, thirty years ago by this time, and assumed that death had rendered it no longer relevant. Herold's death. I didn't follow it up.

'What have you thought about doing with the house?' I asked instead. 'And Castor?'

'We can let out the house,' said Martin. 'Or just leave it, whichever you prefer. And we can take Castor with us. He has a doggy passport, getting him into Morocco would be no problem, and I don't think getting him out of Sweden would present any difficulty either. If it did, we could do a spot of smuggling – we've done that before, after all.'

He had already worked out answers to any possible questions.

'Are you sure you didn't rape her?' I asked. 'Sure that she had sex with you willingly?'

He had an answer to that as well. I didn't mention that I had been to Gothenburg and spoken to his victim.

'Okay,' I said. 'Perhaps it's not a bad idea.'

'When a hurricane's blowing you have to take shelter,' said Martin.

And so we had made our decision. I recall that the only feeling I could manage to muster was that it didn't matter.

7

We got up late. Or at least, I did. Castor is not the type who gets out of bed simply because he's opened his eyes.

I had a quickish shower. The cramped bathroom is cold and damp. And there is an odd smell that suddenly reminded me of a pair of old Wellington boots in my childhood (they were always standing in the area between the veranda and the kitchen in the home of my classmate Vera: for a year or two I used to spend about four days a week in their house. They must have belonged to her father, those boots – he was a large, big-nosed and generally unhealthy person). The water for the shower is heated up by a gas flame as it runs through the pipe: a primitive arrangement that doesn't work very well, but I suppose it's better than nothing. Maybe I don't need to have a shower every morning, as I have done for the whole of my life so far. In any case, it seems more sensible to get a fire going first and warm up the rest of the house. I'm learning a lesson: cold and damp give rise to distress and feelings of hopelessness.

We had breakfast, and made plans for the rest of the day. I let Castor out for a three-minute peeing excursion. Stood in the doorway, watching him. He wandered indifferently round the yard a few times: apparently there wasn't much here worth sniffing at – not even the dustbin over by the stable block was worth investigating this morning, it seemed. He eventually peed on both sides of the only tree, a big, lop-sided larch. That was evidently the right place: he's used it every time since we came here. I sometimes wonder what goes on inside his head.

Northerly wind. Grey-blue sky. I decided I should buy a thermometer, if for no other reason than to enable me to make more or less accurate weather forecasts every morning. Fire – shower – breakfast – weather: they seemed to be suitable hooks on which to hang up our existence.

I guessed it was about eight degrees today, and noted that figure down. The fourth of November. I also wrote that I was fifty-five years old, three months and four days.

Then a walk, of course. Dogs are made for taking exercise – or at least, African lion-hunting dogs are. I decided on Tarr Steps, a place that's mentioned in all the guidebooks I've thumbed through so far and it's only a ten-minute drive from here. In the direction of Withypool. It's an old stepping-stone set-up over the River Barle, as I understand it; from the Middle Ages or thereabouts. There are footpaths to explore on both sides of the river, and a cafe that might be open.

Then some shopping, followed by dinner at the village pub, in the early evening. A good plan. A day in the life . . .

Or perhaps the other way round – that would involve a different kind of truth. *A life in a day*. The way you live one day can be repeated every other single day. Until the end of time. Is that why I'm here? The simple plan? I must stop asking questions like that.

★

Tarr Steps turned out to be protected from the wind, but on the other hand it started raining – as unwelcome as news of a death while you're busy solving the daily crossword puzzle. Mind you, it held off until we had walked a fair distance along the river bank, and met two elderly women each with a retriever. The dogs greeted one another politely, as did the women and I, and I had begun wondering whether to continue along the path as far as Withypool. That is less than two hours' walking time from Tarr Steps, and there is a pub there.

But the rain forced us to beat a retreat. We crossed over a ford and began retracing our steps along the other side of the river: after two-and-a-half hours in all we were back at our starting point. The cafe was open, but I felt too wet and muddy to go in. We sat in the car, I took out my mobile and checked the situation: no signal. I switched off. Maybe I ought to find a place where there was a signal and then sit there for a while every other day.

At most. Perhaps once a week would be enough – presumably you would need to switch on, then ring somebody or receive a call in order for it to be traceable? But I don't know.

Martin's mobile as well. I ought to force myself to do that, the sooner the better, no doubt. And I mustn't forget our computers. For that's the way it is, despite everything: I must make contact with people, face up to facts, send the occasional e-mail, show signs of life. Our children, Eugen Bergman. My brother. Christa . . . Yes, of course, I really must see to that. Pretend that we are still going strong in the good old sense of that term, and that there's no need to worry about us.

Perhaps contact Christa first of all, that would seem logical.

But I decided to put it off until tomorrow. There is no great hurry yet. It takes time to get to Morocco. I started the car and began driving back to Darne Lodge.

I ran through the plan for the day again and adjusted it as necessary: an afternoon in front of the fire. Tea and a sandwich. A thick book – I had bought an old copy of Dickens's *Bleak House* at that antiquarian bookshop. Nine hundred pages, that seemed about right.

Then, as evening approached, down to The Royal Oak Inn. Decisions and action. To the end of time.

But they are not easy, those times spent in the car without having decided where to go to. Dulverton, Exford or Withypool. Or to the sea.

Or to any bloody place, come to that. They would all be equally sensible or senseless. And it wouldn't matter one way or another, it wouldn't matter at all. Perhaps it would be easier if we were in jail, I wondered this inhospitable morning. If we had narrower horizons, and there was somebody taking care of us. We need a plan, I thought, both me and my dog. We need a path to be following during the whole of the winter.

Or a jigsaw puzzle with five thousand pieces. Why not?

I had anticipated these bleak moments, of course I had: during the whole of that hazy journey through Europe I had been aware that this would happen – but what good did foreseeing it do? We know we are going to die one of these days, but how are we helped by knowing that as a fact?

And I must stop judging Castor in accordance with the same criteria I use for myself. No doubt there is a difference in our ways of thinking about which I haven't the slightest idea.

Or perhaps this is exactly what dogs spend all their time thinking about?

Muddy Paws Welcome

Castor stood up on his hind legs and sniffed at the notice. It was a quarter past seven. Voices could be heard from inside the pub, a man and a woman – a bit casual, slow, tired, like an elderly couple who have been talking to each other for very many years. We went inside and looked around. The woman's voice was that of the barmaid: a copy or perhaps a sister of the woman I had met in the village shop the previous day, rosy-faced and as tough-looking as a kettle-holder. The man, also in his sixties, was sitting in front of a steaming plate of dinner and a glass of beer at one of the window tables.

Checked flannel shirt. Thinning hair and somewhat skinny, an Adam's apple like a bird's beak. The most noticeable thing about his face was his spectacles.

'Aha, a stranger!' he said.

'Welcome,' said the barmaid. 'Both of you. It's a bit rough out there.'

I felt a quick rush of gratitude. For the fact that they started talking to me. But that's what people do in this country, and my existence was thereby confirmed. Castor's as well. He wagged his tail a few times, walked over and rubbed up against the man with his nose, who stroked his head gently. The way one should – no hard pats: it was clear that he'd dealt with dogs before. I felt grateful for that as well.

'My dog Winston died last spring,' he said. 'I haven't got round to acquiring a new one.'

'You have to finish mourning their loss first,' said the woman. 'They are worth that kind of respect.'

'Absolutely right,' said the man.

'Absolutely right,' I said. The image of Martin on the beach flashed before my mind's eye, but I shoved him to one side.

'You're passing through, I take it,' said the woman.

'Not really,' I said. 'I'm renting a house just outside the village for the winter. Darne Lodge, maybe you know it?'

The man shook his head but the woman nodded. 'Up there?' she said. 'Above Halse Farm, isn't it?'

'Yes, that's the place.'

'For the winter?'

'Yes.'

'Isn't it old Mr Tawking who looks after it?'

'Mr Tawking, yes, that's right.'

'And you're going to live there all this winter?'

'Yes, that's the plan. I have a piece of writing I need to work on.'

She laughed. 'Well, if it's being left alone you need, you've come to the right place. But forgive me. What would you like to drink? I sometimes forget that I'm working in a pub.'

'You'll get used to it eventually,' said the man. 'You've only been working here for thirty years.'

'Thirty-two,' said the woman. 'We do a very good shepherd's pie, if you fancy something to eat. That's right, isn't it, Robert?'

'Not bad at all, it has to be said,' replied Robert, eyeing his portion intently. He had only just begun eating it. 'I've tasted worse. I can't quite remember when and where, but I think it might have been in—'

He was interrupted by somebody else coming in through the door.

'Good evening, Henry,' said the woman. 'Pretty rough weather out there.'

Robert shrugged and started eating. The newly arrived customer – a short, slim man aged about thirty-five – nodded a greeting to all three of us, and smiled when he noticed Castor, who had already stretched himself out on the floor in front of the radiator. 'A nice dog. Yes, winter's on the way.'

'Can you wait a minute, Henry,' said the woman. 'I must just see to our new guest first. Would you like to try the pie? There's steak and kidney as well, of course. And a few other things.'

'Shepherd's pie sounds good,' I said. 'And a glass of red wine, I think.'

'Excellent,' said the woman. 'My name's Rosie, by the way. It's always nice to have a new face around.'

'What's wrong with our faces?' asked Robert, his mouth half-full. Henry, who actually looked as if he might be Robert's younger brother, or even his son, took off his jacket and hung it on a hook on the wall. I received my glass of wine and sat down at one of the four empty tables in the bar. Castor raised his head and wondered if he ought to move a little closer to me, but decided it was more comfortable by the radiator.

'Anyway,' said the man called Henry. He seemed a little more shy, somewhat more introvert than the other two,

Robert and Rosie. 'Mrs Simmons managed to get away to the hospital after all.'

'Thank God for that,' said Rosie.

'And not a day too soon, if you ask me,' said Robert.

'Nobody's asking you,' said Rosie. 'How's George?' she added.

'I don't really know,' said Henry. 'But at least he said he was going to take the opportunity of throwing out that sofa.'

'About time,' said Robert. 'The cat's been pissing on it for the last ten years.'

'George is the nicest man I've ever met,' said Rosie as she poured out a glass of beer for Henry.

'Except when he's watching football,' said Robert. 'Then he's like a male gorilla with toothache.'

Henry sat down on one of the barstools. They continued talking about Mrs Simmons and George, the sofa and the cat, for a while. All the time they avoided using Mrs Simmons's first name, whatever it was, and I wondered why. But I didn't ask. I sipped my wine and started leafing through my Exmoor guidebook. I thought that if I really was going to stay here for the winter I would eventually discover all kinds of connections and contexts that I didn't have a clue about just now. Perhaps Robert and Rosie and Henry had spent the whole of their lives in this village. Mrs Simmons and George as well. And the cat and the sofa. For several minutes none of the others seemed to pay any attention to the fact that I was sitting there, and I wondered if it was up to me to make some kind of move. To ask about something or other – but before I hit upon something a young girl appeared with my food. She was dark-haired and pretty, twenty-five at most, and somehow or other it was obvious that she didn't really belong here.

'You can take out those bottles when you've finished with the rest of it,' said Rosie. The girl curtseyed, and returned to the inner regions.

'It's hard to get good staff,' said Rosie to nobody in particular.

Robert cleared his throat and looked as if he was about to say something, but nothing came of it. Rosie switched on the television, which was attached to the wall high up under the ceiling. All four of us gaped at a sports quiz for half a minute – not Castor, he was asleep – then Rosie switched off.

'Does it taste all right?'

I had eaten only two mouthfuls so far, but assured her that it was absolutely delicious.

'She's good in the kitchen in any case,' said Robert.

'Not only there, unfortunately,' said Rosie, and I gathered that she had other sides in addition to the rose-tinted one.

I stayed at The Royal Oak for nearly two hours, and drank a second glass of red wine. While I was sitting there three other customers arrived. A young couple only stayed long enough to drink whatever it was they had ordered, but soon after they left a man of indeterminate age came in. He was tall and lanky with dark, slightly tousled hair, and sat down at the table next to mine with a pint of ale and a portion of cod and chips.

After a while we engaged in a conversation.

8

I once had a childhood.

A mum and a dad who were a dental nurse and a dentist. An elder brother who was called Göran and still is, and a younger sister called Gun. We lived in a little town in central Sweden full of small businesses, Free Churches, and spoilt youngsters who were cosseted and pampered but couldn't wait to escape into the real world. Our house had a garden with currant bushes, a mossy lawn, an old apple tree and a swing that nobody swung on any more after Gunsan, as we called her, was run over and died.

We also had a sandpit that became overgrown with weeds, and a cat that kept coming and going. Not just one cat – there were several, but only one at a time. They were all called Napoleon, even if they were female and had kittens that we either sold or gave away.

Gunsan was only eight when she died: both Göran and I were at secondary school – he was in his third year and I in my first. Some families cope with a catastrophe, but others don't. Ours didn't.

The bus driver who ran over Gunsan didn't get over it either. He had a mental breakdown after backing over a little girl and killing her in the car park outside the swimming baths; his wife left him the next year and shortly afterwards he hanged himself in a forest in quite a different part of Sweden. His name was Bengt-Olov, and much earlier in his life, before he started a family and became a bus driver, he had been the best centre forward we had ever had in our local football team. Big and strong, but nevertheless fast and unpredictable. He even played twice for Sweden juniors. At the end of the forties, I think that was.

Göran took his school-leaving exam and flew the nest, and I followed suit two years later. Mum and Dad were left on their own with their dental practice, their lovely old house, and each other. By then Mum had stopped working as a dental nurse – she didn't have the strength any more.

But before Gunsan died – and before she was born – that's when I had a childhood. That's the period I've been trying to forget about for many years. It is also astoundingly good at disappearing again the moment it crops up. It was somehow so straightforward, so full of hope and light that I am blinded. Indeed, I have often been blinded and made to feel rather ill by that mirage that manifests itself for a fleeting moment and then fades away.

And nowadays, much later in life, when I unexpectedly bump into my old schoolmate Klasse, or Britt-Inger – or even Anton come to that, the first boy I ever kissed and the one who once massaged my pudendum in a people's park that no longer exists – on such occasions I suddenly get a lump in my throat, and feel an urge to turn round and run away. Whatever happened to you? I think. I can't bear seeing you. Surely you can't be Anton Antonsson with that lovely laugh and those warm, gentle hands: whatever happened to him? Where does this miserable-looking middle-aged creature with a pot belly and a strained expression on his face come from? And then Gunsan comes into my head, as I am lying in her bed under the sloping ceiling and reading Astrid Lindgren stories to her and I think – have always thought – that I don't want that bloody childhood any more, that damned romantic glow; I don't want to recall her half-closed eyes and her arms around my neck when I lift her out of the water and onto the jetty down by the lake and she half sings, half whispers the old Swedish folk song 'Who can sail when there is no wind' into my ear.

Or my mother's and father's funerals, I can do without them as well – there was barely a year between them and I am well aware that you can create cancer inside your body at any time if you try hard enough. That's what my mum did as she sat at home in that melancholy house: she created cancer in her own body by thinking hard about it – it took seven years but she managed it in the end. And since my dad was buried – cause of death: a broken heart – I have hardly ever set foot again in that central Swedish town. On the very rare occasions when I have done so, I have always found it difficult to breathe, and thought that it's like eating breakfast in the evening even though you don't want to.

We set off shortly after midnight. It was Martin's idea that we should start with a night drive, get to a favourite hotel in

Kristianstad, have breakfast there and then take the ferry from Ystad. And that's what we did, from a geographical perspective at least. But for some reason or other we began talking about Gunvald.

'There's something I've never told you,' said Martin.

We had just filled up with petrol at that garage near Järna that never closes. Ahead of us was four hundred kilometres of the deserted E4, then diagonally down through Småland and northern Skåne along various numbered roads. It was the night between a Thursday and a Friday in October, dawn was light years away, and we could equally well have been in a space capsule on the way to a dead star. Aniara.

'What? What have you never told me?'

'I didn't think he was mine. In the beginning I simply couldn't believe it.'

I didn't understand.

'Gunvald,' Martin elaborated. 'I was convinced that somebody else must be his father.'

'What the hell do you mean?' I asked.

He laughed in that good-natured way he had been practising ever since he was forty.

'Well, like in that play of Strindberg's, *The Father* . . . It's the kind of thought that crops up in every man's mind. Just think! What if the father is somebody else? How could you be certain? And you can't very well ask, can you?'

He tried to chuckle. I had no comment to make. I thought it was best to let him go on. I started to toy with a very special thought, but it was too early to mention it yet. We had the whole night in front of us after all, maybe six months in fact: there was no hurry. No hurry with anything at all.

But as things turned out I never took up that thought.

'Anyway, please don't misunderstand me,' he said after a few seconds of silence, drumming lightly with his fingers on the steering wheel. 'It was nothing more than one of those obsessive thoughts, but it's remarkable how they can take possession of you. And the fact is, he wasn't anything like me at all – surely you have to agree about that? People commented on it, don't you remember? Your brother, for instance.'

'If there was ever a person who was like his father, that person is Gunvald,' I said. 'Not in his appearance, perhaps: but if you look inside him, you must realize that you . . . that you are looking into a mirror.'

Martin thought that over as we covered a kilometre of deserted motorway. I knew that I had offended him. That he thought it wasn't worth the effort of trying to conduct a sensible conversation with me. That he had overlooked that fact, as usual. He was a level-headed and discerning man, an optimistic person who actually believed that language could be a tool rather than a weapon; but I was a woman who swam and sometimes drowned in an irrelevant sea of emotions. Yes, *irrelevant* is the right word for it.

Or perhaps I am being unfair to him. That's not impossible, and I reserve the right to be so.

But I couldn't understand what he was fishing for. Did he want me to agree with him? To confirm that it was perfectly reasonable for him to have suspicions about how our first child came into being? That this was a new and interesting insight into what it was like to be a man? That it perhaps was some-how connected with his need to rape – or at least to have sex with and spray sperm onto – an unknown waitress in a hotel in Gothenburg many years later.

'I'm pretty sure he's yours,' I said.

'What?' said Martin.

The car swerved slightly.

'I said that he's yours,' I said.

'You didn't say that at all,' said Martin. 'You said something quite different.'

'I don't understand what you're getting at,' I said. 'How was it with Synn, did you have similar thoughts then?'

Martin shook his head. 'Not at all. It was only in connection with Gunvald. I've actually spoken to a few friends about this phenomenon. Or I did so several years ago. They admitted that they'd had similar thoughts.'

'When they had their sons?'

'Yes.'

'But not when they had their daughters?'

'Come off it!' said Martin. 'None of them have any daugh-ters, incidentally. But if you don't want to talk about this, we can drop it. I just thought it might be worth mentioning.'

'Were they academics?'

'Were who academics?'

'Those others who had problems with being a father. Were they university people?'

'Why do you ask that?'

'Because it needs a special sort of mind to come up with

something so bloody stupid. Anyway, he is yours. I didn't have any other men at that time.'

I hadn't really intended to make a response as cutting as that, but it kept Martin quiet for several minutes. For several more dark kilometres along the E4. Further out towards that dead star – for some reason I found it difficult to shake off that image.

'How do you think he is now?' he asked in a somewhat more normal tone of voice as we passed the first turn-off to Nyköping. It was a couple of minutes past one.

I thought that was a justified question, at least. Gunvald had never been in good shape, not since puberty at any rate. He had difficulty in making friends, and started having sessions with psychologists and therapists while he was still at school. We suspect he tried to commit suicide a couple of times, but that has never really become clear. He was legally of age on both occasions, and hence everyone involved was bound by secrecy. If the patient gives permission then of course the veil of secrecy can be lifted: but Gunvald refused to do so. He lay there in his hospital bed, glaring apologetically at us, and pretended he had fallen by accident from a balcony on the fifth floor. What could we say?

On the second occasion he also spent time in hospital, but by then he had already moved to Copenhagen – it was when Kirsten had left him. It was labelled food poisoning, and he refused to receive visitors.

Kirsten had taken the children with her – my grandchildren – and moved back to her parents' home in Horsens. And announced that if Gunvald made any claims on them, she would report him to the police. She wrote that in an e-mail to me.

I don't know what she would have reported him for, she didn't explain when I spoke to her a few days later. Neither did Gunvald, of course.

As we sat there in the car, driving through the night, it was exactly two years since that had happened, and Gunvald had moved into a flat of his own in the Nørrebro district of Copenhagen – he had evidently got it through a colleague at the university. Martin had visited him twice in Copenhagen, and I had met him once in Stockholm when he gave a lecture at Södertörn. That was all. It occurred to me that if Martin doubted whether he was Gunvald's father, I had as much justification for doubting that I was his mother.

I had met my grandchildren, the twin girls, once after their father's food poisoning. I went to their home in Horsens on Jutland, and stayed for three days. I spoke a lot more to Kirsten's parents than to Kirsten herself: they were pleasant and I had the impression we were on the same wavelength. But then, I don't have anything negative to say about Kirsten either.

Which makes the equation somewhat problematic.

'Maybe he's sorting his life out now, despite everything,' said Martin. 'It's not up to us to pass judgement.'

I knew they were in occasional contact by e-mail and on the telephone, but Martin never said anything about what they had discussed. Work, presumably. The academic duckpond, both here and there. Stockholm and Copenhagen. Probably not as you would expect between father and son, but more likely between two colleagues – one young and ambitious, the other old and experienced. An arts assistant lecturer and an arts professor. Linguistics versus literature history. Yes, I'm pretty sure they restricted themselves to that neutral playing field.

On my part I endured so many sleepless nights for Gunvald's sake, from puberty and for about ten years thereafter, that it very nearly drove me mad. That was probably when I lost my good looks – that quality that first fitted the bill for television screens, but then no longer did. And over time I had also developed a thick skin, hard and effective, and I had no intention of peeling it off. Certainly not. The day Gunvald comes of his own accord and asks me to, I might consider it: but not off my own bat. The impotent, misdirected primeval powers of a mother: I'm not going through that again.

But I still wondered what Martin was after, and couldn't resist pressing him a little harder.

'Have you ever mentioned it to him?' I asked.

'Mentioned what?'

'That you didn't think you were his father.'

'Bloody hell!' barked Martin, smashing his hand hard on the instrument panel. 'Are you out of your mind? I only raised it for a bit of fun. Let's forget it.'

'A bit of fun?'

He didn't respond. What the hell could he have said?

And I had nothing to add. I reclined the seat, inflated my travel pillow and announced that I was going to try and get some sleep. He slid a Thelonious Monk disc into the CD-player, then neither of us spoke again for several hours.

★

But I didn't sleep. Just closed my eyes and thought how odd it was that we were sitting in this same car, on our way southwards. After all these years. After all those occasions when we didn't measure up to each other, all those manoeuvres to ensure we ended up in the same place. How odd it was that we were still together. And that my life had come to the point where I no longer wanted anything apart from being left in peace and quiet – I thought about that as well. Perhaps that was the price of being the person I have been. That we have been the people we have been. The premier league, as my brother Göran once said. *The premier league?* I remember wondering. What on earth do you mean by that? It's as plain as day, Göran insisted. A literary colossus and a television presenter – you are playing in the premier league. You only have yourselves to blame.

He plays in division three. He explained that as well. He's a secondary school teacher in a small town in central Sweden, which means that he's slap bang in the middle of real life. Not the town he grew up in, of course not; and the business about divisions was something he'd got from a colleague, apparently. Martin disapproved of that: he had been on the list of Social Democrat election candidates a couple of times – never likely to be selected, but still – and such people mustn't belong to an elite.

That was long before the incident in the hotel in Gothenburg. Martin ceased to be a social democrat round about the turn of the century, it wasn't clear exactly when.

But the fact is that to a large extent both our lives have been lived in what is known as the glare of publicity – my brother was right about that. We have been standing on a stage – usually separate stages, but occasionally a shared one – and when you are on a stage you try to put on an act. To be good-looking and talk clearly, as I said before. Until somebody says it's time to make an exit. And on that occasion when Gunvald came home drunk, the only time he had done so, and spelled out the truth for me, his analysis was more or less identical with that, it really was.

'You're a bloody nobody, do you realize that? A made-up cut-out doll, that's what I had for a mother – thank you very much. But you don't need to feel ashamed – I've been doing that for you all these years.'

He was seventeen then. A year later he reached the so-called age of maturity, and fell off that balcony.

I adjusted the pillow against the side window and started thinking about Synn.

9

'Mark,' he said. 'My name's Mark Britton. I can see that you have a shadow over you.'

Those were the first words he spoke, and I wasn't sure I had heard them correctly.

'I beg your pardon,' I said. 'What did you say?'

He had eaten the rest of his food. Now he slid the plate to one side and turned towards me. We were sitting at neighbouring tables, with about a metre between us. Rosie had switched the television on again, but turned the sound down to almost zero. Two men in white shirts and black waistcoats were playing snooker.

'A shadow,' he repeated. 'You must forgive me, but I notice things like that.'

He smiled and reached out his hand. I hesitated for a second before shaking it and telling him my name.

'Maria.'

'You're not from round here, I take it?'

'No.'

'Travelling through?'

'No, I'm renting a house for the winter just outside the village.'

'For the winter?'

'Yes. I'm a writer. I need some peace and quiet.'

He nodded. 'I'm familiar with peace and quiet. And I read quite a bit.'

'What did you mean by "a shadow"?'

He smiled again. He seemed reserved and friendly, and gave the impression of being a reliable person. I'm not sure what I mean by that epithet, or how I justify it, but he reminded me vaguely of a religious studies teacher I had at secondary school. It's a reflection I'm making now with hindsight, as I am writing – not something I hit upon as we were sitting there in The Royal Oak. I don't remember what he was called, that teacher, but I recall that he had a daughter who was confined to a wheelchair.

I also wonder what made me start talking to this Mark Britton so casually. It wasn't just my loneliness crying out for somebody to make contact with, anybody at all: there was a simple straightforwardness about him, not a trace of that typically male scheming that is so prevalent and about as hard to perceive as an elephant under a handkerchief. Despite everything I am aware that I can still be regarded as an attractive woman. Even if Mr Britton must surely be several years younger than me.

'May I join you?'

'Please do.'

He took with him his half-empty glass and sat down facing me. I had the impression that both Rosie and Robert were watching us, but trying to give the impression of not doing so. Henry was also still there in his corner, but absorbed by his newspaper and something which looked like a horseracing programme. I observed my new table-mate furtively. He had long, slightly unruly hair, but I thought nevertheless that he looked civilized. By civilized I suppose I mean that he looked as if he was at home in an urban environment rather than on a moor out in the sticks. Perhaps he had just been to visit his ancient mother and was on his way back to London, I thought. Or a sister, or a brother-in-law, who knows? Anyway, a dark red shirt, open at the neck, and over it a blue pullover. Quite tall, on the slim side, clean shaven. Deep-set eyes that were perhaps a fraction too close together. His voice was deep and pleasant – he could well be an actor or even a radio announcer. Or possibly even a television presenter, if he paid a visit to a barber. I smiled at the latter thought, and he asked what I found amusing.

'Nothing.' I shrugged. 'It was just a passing twitch.'

Castor noticed that I had acquired a companion and came over to our table. Sniffed casually at Mr Britton, yawned and found a new place on the floor.

'Your dog?'

'Yes.'

'What's he called?'

'Castor.'

He nodded, and we sat without speaking for a few seconds.

'Anyway, my assertion about a shadow,' he said eventually. 'It wasn't just something I said in an attempt to appear interesting – I hope you understand that. I could have said "aura", but people are usually scared of that word.'

I thought for a moment, then maintained I wasn't especially

afraid of auras, but didn't believe in them. I asked if people were less scared of shadows.

'They are in fact, yes,' he said. 'Anyway, I see an absent husband and a house in the south – but we don't need to go into that. You've just arrived here, I take it? I've never seen you around before, in any case.'

I noticed that my pulse started racing and that I needed to gain time. *Absent husband? A house in the south?* But I couldn't see how I could make use of any time I gained.

'I arrived a few days ago,' I said. 'What about you? Do you live here?'

'Not far outside the village.'

'It's beautiful here.'

'Yes. Beautiful and lonely. At this time of year, at least.'

'Some people prefer loneliness.'

He smiled slightly. 'Yes, we do. Have you been in these parts before?'

'Never.'

And so he began talking about the moor. Slowly and almost hesitantly, without my prompting him. About places, walks, the mists. And how he actually preferred this time of year, autumn and winter, when there were not so many tourists about. He sometimes spent whole days out on the moor, he told me, from dawn to dusk, preferably without a map or a compass, preferably without really knowing where he was.

'Trout Hill,' he said, 'above Doone Valley, or Challacombe – you can learn a lot up there. You can get lost on the moor, of course you can: but if you don't get lost you can't find yourself.'

He laughed slightly ironically, and stroked back his hair, which occasionally fell down and covered half his face. I wasn't sure if he was trying to impress me with what he was saying, but it didn't seem so. Nor did he offer me any services, didn't ask if I needed a guide or somebody who could pass on tips about places or paths. He just warned me to be careful, and explained that when the mists fell even the wild ponies could get lost. If you were caught out by the mist, it could often be better simply to stay where you were and hope that it would soon lift. Assuming you had suitable clothes, of course: if you felt cold it was always better to keep moving.

I asked if he was born on Exmoor, and he said he was. Not quite here in Winsford, but in Simonsbath, a bit higher up and more or less in the middle of the moor. He had moved away when he started at university, but came back ten years ago. As he worked with computers it didn't matter where he lived: twenty years of city life and stress was quite enough for him, he maintained.

He said nothing about his family. Didn't say if he had any children or had anything that could be described as 'personal relationships'. I suspected he might be gay: he had precisely the frankness that heterosexual men usually lack. Even if he showed noticeably little interest in my circumstances.

I didn't ask him about details, of course not, and while he was talking I gained the time I needed. I was able to decide how much of my own personal circumstances I was prepared to reveal.

Not very much, I concluded. And I stuck to that line.

Maria Anderson, a writer from Sweden. I think I even managed to convince him that I wrote under a pseudonym. I told him I was living just outside Winsford, but I didn't go into precisely where.

What sort of books do you write? he wanted to know.

Novels.

No, I was not a well-known name, especially not outside Sweden. But I managed to keep going. I had been awarded some kind of scholarship for a year, and that was why I was here on Exmoor.

'And you intend to write about the moor, do you?'

'I think so.'

Then I asked him what he had meant by that reference to a shadow, an absent husband and a house in the south.

'I can't help it. I can see into people's minds, that's the basic truth of the matter. It's always been the case.'

We'd had our glasses refilled. He had another dark beer, and I had a drop more red wine.

'Interesting,' I said, non-committally.

'I've been able to do that ever since I was a child,' he explained. 'I knew my father had another woman long before my mother found out about it. I was eight then. I knew that my schoolmistress's mother had died the moment I saw her walking across the schoolyard that winter morning. Five minutes before she came into the classroom and told us about it. And I knew . . . No, I'd better stop. It's pointless to keep providing proof. It doesn't matter if you believe me or not.'

I nodded. 'I've no reason to doubt you.'

'And now you're sitting there wondering what I have to say

about the husband and the house, aren't you?' said Mr Britton, taking a swig of beer.

'Once you've started you might as well go on,' I said.

He laughed. Somewhat nervously, I thought – in any case it was the first time he'd done so during our conversation.

'I don't really have anything to go on about,' he said. 'I just get a fleeting image in my brain, and all I can do is describe what the image looked like. What it might mean is another matter altogether.'

'And what exactly did you see in my case?'

He thought for a moment, no more. 'I didn't see a lot,' he said. 'At first a man, then a white house . . . Bathed in strong sunlight – it looked as if it were somewhere in the south. The Mediterranean or North Africa, perhaps. Then came the shadow: it came from up above, and I had the impression that it was *your* shadow. Or that it had something to do with you at least. And it swept away the man. But the house remained standing. Anyway, that's all – but it was pretty clear. I suppose "mist" is a better word than "fog" to describe it, by the way.'

I swallowed. 'What did this man look like, did you notice any details?'

'No. I saw him standing quite a long distance away. But he was rather elderly, not really old – about sixty or so.'

'And you saw all this inside my mind?'

He adopted an apologetic expression. 'Perhaps not quite – but it's when I observe a face that images like these crop up, and that's what I did.'

'You observed my face?'

'Every man between the ages of fifteen and ninety would

want to observe your face. If he could. Do you think I'm being importunate?'

I wondered if I thought so. I concluded that I might have done in different circumstances, but now here we were in the local pub in Winsford in the county of Somerset, and with the exception of Mr Tawking this Mark Britton was the first person I'd spoken to for more than half a minute in over a week. No, it didn't feel importunate, and I explained why.

'Thank you. It's lonely, being a writer, is it?'

'It goes with the territory. If you can't cope with loneliness you can't devote yourself to writing.'

He shrugged, and suddenly looked a little sad.

'I could be a great writer. If that's the necessary criterion.'

That was of course an opportunity for me to ask questions about his private circumstances, but I desisted. Instead I extracted some practical information from him. Where I could find a launderette, for instance. Where I could buy firewood. Which was the best place to shop for food.

Mr Britton filled me in on these points and several more besides, and when we left the pub we thanked each other for an interesting conversation. He said he usually visited The Royal Oak Inn several times a week, and was looking forward to meeting me there again.

Then we shook hands and said goodbye. He went off up Halse Lane, Castor and I crossed over the road and walked down to the war memorial, where the car was parked. I realized that I had drunk two glasses of wine rather than the planned one, but I certainly had no intention of walking up to Darne Lodge in the dark. I could see no sign of Mark Britton on the road, and assumed he must have turned off into one of the narrow alleys you pass before coming up onto the moor itself.

I had left the bathroom light on, but that wasn't visible from the road and I overshot the house by some fifty metres before realizing it. It was not exactly straightforward, backing along the narrow asphalt track, but I managed it. I made a mental note to buy some kind of outdoor lantern to hang on the gatepost, so that I would be able to find my way home in future.

Before I fell asleep – but quite a while after Castor had done so at the foot end of the bed – I made two decisions. I would wait for at least a week before setting foot again in The Royal Oak Inn, and the following day I would be sure to check the computers, both mine and Martin's. Sixteen days had passed since we left Stockholm, so it was high time.

I would go to an internet cafe in Minehead – Mark Britton had said there were several there – and take a look at the e-mail inboxes. And if necessary answer any pressing messages. It would certainly not be a good thing if correspondents started checking up on where we were.

Certainly not.

10

After Synn's birth I was stricken with something that was eventually diagnosed as post-natal depression.

I don't know if that was the correct name for it, but if the two things coincide in time – the birth and the depression – I assume it must be. In any case, it meant that the relationship between myself and my daughter was disturbed from the very start. That important contact between mother and child that everybody talks about didn't happen until several months later, and by then it was too late.

It wasn't that I didn't like my child. The fact was that I had no desire to go on living any longer. I could see no light at the end of the tunnel, and nothing seemed to have any point. Every day, during the weeks I was in hospital, I asked the nurses to bring my daughter to me: but as soon as I had been with her for a few minutes I started crying my eyes out. It was uncontrollable, and after I had fed her briefly they took her away again. I know that I cried more for Synn's sake than for my own.

I received help of various kinds, and was eventually allocated a therapist. It was the first time in my life I had met one; her name was Gudrun Ewerts, and after only two or three sessions she expressed the opinion that I ought to have been given help much sooner. When I told her the story of my life up to that point – it was 1983, and I had just celebrated my twenty-sixth birthday – Gudrun put her head in her hands and sighed.

'My dear,' she said. 'Have you paused to think about what you've been through these last ten years?'

I thought about that, then asked her what she meant.

She glanced at her notebook. 'If I understand things correctly, what's happened is as follows: your younger sister has died. Your boyfriend has died. Your mother and father have died, and you have given birth to two children. Is that right?'

I thought once again. 'Yes,' I said. 'That's right. I suppose it's a bit much.'

Gudrun smiled. 'You can say that again. And I don't blame you for reacting as you have done.'

She went on to explain that what I had done was simply to bottle everything up, and that was what was now punishing me. She accepted that bottling things up could be an effective way of dealing with such happenings: but before you do that you need to have a clear idea about what it is that is being hidden away.

She liked to express herself in images, and what we spoke about in all our conversations – for there were many, definitely over a hundred – had much more to do with the fatal accident to my younger sister and the tragic fall that killed my boyfriend than with little Synn.

But it was mainly to do with me, of course.

My life had been badly mismanaged, I was informed. I hadn't

dealt with it as one ought to deal with one's life, I hadn't taken it seriously enough. But I was pretty well suited to be a television performer, she was the first to acknowledge that, and I recall that we laughed about it. On the whole it would be an advantage if the television authorities could use cartoon versions of newsreaders, Gudrun thought: it is not good for anybody to sit staring at a camera, knowing that a million anonymous viewers are sitting on their sofas and gaping at your face. Evening after evening. I actually passed on her suggestion to one of my bosses, but as expected it fell on stony ground.

We continued to meet regularly even after my depression had died down and dispersed. The meetings covered getting on for two-and-a-half years, reducing eventually to just once or twice a month towards the end; and I know that nobody has contributed more to my understanding of myself than this Gudrun Ewerts.

'You have been living all your life on other people's terms,' she said. 'Since your little sister's death, at least. You have been living a mirror image of yourself – do you understand what I'm saying? If you bury your own free will in a desert, you can't expect it to survive.'

I know that she came into my mind as I was walking along the windy beach at Międzyzdroje, that dear old therapist of mine; when I was walking in a sort of dream after having closed that heavy door. Maybe it's not all that surprising, and I have the impression that I smiled at her. Or at least, at her memory: she has been dead for more than ten years, and it must have been a strange sort of smile.

★

But the relationship between me and my daughter never improved. She became an introverted child, learned to occupy herself far too soon, and the contact between us was always inadequate. It was as if we were playing the roles of mother and daughter, and without a doubt we were skilful actresses, both of us. Unfortunately the same sort of relationship applied to father and daughter – perhaps even more so. Throughout the whole of her childhood Synn was in charge of her own life: she looked after her school work and her relationships with her friends in exemplary fashion – or at least without any interference from us – and she kept her secrets to herself. I have no idea when she started her periods, nor when she lost her virginity. Two weeks after taking her school-leaving exam she moved to France, and I remember thinking that I had been a sort of hotel-keeper rather than a mother. I'd had a guest in the same room for nineteen years, and now she had moved on.

I never discussed this with Martin – there wouldn't have been any point. The other hotel guest, Gunvald, had moved out only six months before his sister.

When I write about this it feels as if it isn't true. It can't have been as bad as that, I'm sitting here and making it all up. I lay awake night after night, worrying about it – surely that was the case? I thought about them and was convinced that I loved them.

Ah well, there are some people who believe that telling lies is the only way of getting close to a sort of truth.

★

We arrived at the hotel in Kristianstad at about seven o'clock. It was a grey morning, foggy. I had slept in the car for a few hours, but Martin was so tired that he couldn't see straight. He drank three cups of coffee, and after our substantial breakfast and a shortish walk with Castor we continued to Ystad, where we drove onto a ferry to Świnoujście shortly before lunch.

The crossing took six hours. Martin slept more or less all the time; I sat in a deckchair beside him and tried to solve the crossword puzzle in the *Svenska Dagbladet*, as it was a Friday and I had managed to buy the newspaper in a kiosk on the way to the harbour. Castor lay stretched out at our feet. I recall that there were not many passengers, and I was soon overcome by a strong feeling of being abandoned. Almost a loss of identity. Who was I? Where was I going? Why?

Those are not useful questions for a fifty-five-year-old woman to ask herself, especially in circumstances in which there is no chance of finding an answer. After a while I realized that the best way of imposing a check on my increasing angst would be to ring Christa and exchange a few words with her: but by the time this insight dawned on me we were already so far out to sea that there was no mobile signal.

Instead I started thinking about a speech Martin had once given, in which he declared that there was no great difference between the concepts of 'potato' and 'angst'. There were characteristics that could be ascribed to angst, and characteristics that could be ascribed to potato: some were the same, others were different. And that was that. It was in connection with a dinner to celebrate the awarding of a doctorate to one of his colleagues, a dry-as-dust lecturer in semantics. I recall that the comparison gave rise to much amusement around the table, and that Martin was immensely proud of his ingenuity. Without acknowledging it with so much as a smile, of course. Personally, I had no idea what he was talking about.

We met at the Monkeyhouse a hundred years ago, Christa and I. We worked under the same roof – and as often as not within the same cramped walls – for several years before we got to know each other. Our friendship began at the end of the nineties when she divorced her husband, a not exactly unknown actor with an enormous ego. Christa was far from well, and indeed felt so bad that some days when she came to work she needed to take two sleeping tablets and then go and hide away in order to avoid a complete breakdown.

She used to say: 'Maria, I'm on the edge of complete breakdown – please sit by me and hold my hand until I fall asleep.'

And I would sit there, in one of the Monkeyhouse's small rest rooms, holding one of her hands in both of mine while she wept, spoke, started slurring her words and eventually fell asleep. That would happen several times a week for at least three months, and how on earth we managed to conceal the situation from our bosses is still a mystery.

But you get to know one another in such circumstances, and we have continued to be close. Christa is the person I would like to scatter my ashes when I finally die: I've already chosen her in fact – and she me, but I don't know if she'll remember. About a year after her difficult divorce we went on a trip to Venice together, just the two of us, and one night after a long and wine-soaked evening in a restaurant we stood on one of the bridges over a deserted canal and exchanged promises to that effect. Whichever of us survived longest would look after the other's ashes and make sure they ended up in the right place. I assume that what we had in mind was the black waters in the city where we were at the time, and that by scattering our ashes there we would be assured of eternal life – but we never talked about it afterwards. Obviously, we were a little drunk at the time . . .

Unfortunately I didn't have Christa by my side after that incident in Gothenburg. She was on a reporting mission in South America with her new husband, a photographer, and they didn't get back to Stockholm until August. We had exchanged a few e-mails and spoken on the phone once or twice, but we didn't meet face to face to discuss the matter until a few days after I had been in Gothenburg and interviewed the woman who may or may not have been raped. We had lunch at the Ulla Winbladh restaurant, and sat there talking for three hours. But to be honest, I felt somewhat disappointed when I left.

And to be even more honest I don't really know what I had expected; but we hadn't met for over six months, and if truth be told . . . well, if it were told, our friendship had cooled off a little over the last few years. We had not been colleagues since the autumn of 2008. We had met increasingly infrequently, and kept in touch by e-mail, a few times a month and occasionally more often. Short factual reports, no more than that – ironical and rather playful, which is the simplest way of writing when it doesn't concern real life. Or rather, when it does.

Right now, of course, it concerned rather a lot of important things – or so I tried to convince myself, and if I didn't get in touch for several weeks after leaving Stockholm Christa would suspect there was something fishy going on. Despite every-thing. Or at least would think it was odd – surely there are internet cafes in Morocco just as there are everywhere else in the world? We had spoken on the phone three days before Martin and I left.

As I sat there on the ferry with my unsolved crossword puzzle, I had the feeling that I had drifted away from her, and that it was my fault. The thought made me sad. I had never managed to be the sort of woman who always has half a dozen close friends on call, and I can live with that. But maybe my relationship with Christa had never been for real either? Whatever that means. *For real?* I don't know. Angst or potato?

It's remarkable how geographical changes can stir up so many other different things. It was as if everything I had been and thought and believed had to do with that house in Nynäs-hamn. And with the Monkeyhouse. Gunvald's comments that time and the horrible image of the mirror came to mind in any case, and out there in the middle of the Baltic Sea it sud-denly dawned on me that there was nobody out there who could give a toss. About what would happen to me. Or to Martin. We had lived our lives, had been in the premier league for a few years, danced in the headlines for a few months, and then we had fled. And the rest is silence. Or the big sleep, if you prefer Chandler to Shakespeare. Eugen Bergman had an interest, of course, but that was professional rather than brotherly love. Our children? Huh. Christa? I doubted it.

Perhaps I underestimate the significance of the circle of academic friends that Martin had assembled over the years, but that is not for me to judge. I have been underestimating things and making wrong choices all my life.

The fact that I saw no point at all in exchanging such thoughts with the man snoring by my side spoke volumes, of course. I remember leaning down and stroking Castor for quite some time, and that he responded by licking my right ear clean, as he usually does.

But I venture to suggest that something deep down inside me woke up during that voyage over the Baltic Sea. Something that ought to have been left to sleep in peace. But if you insist on riding your high horses, it no doubt becomes a case of your will versus fate, your choices and motives. Needless to say I can't find the words to pin it down more specifically, apart from what I have already said: so much was left behind in the Monkeyhouse, and that damned family home in Nynäshamn. Thirty years of hard-fought life experiences – how petty they seem on a sunny day at sea.

It took only half an hour to drive from the ferry terminal at Świnoujście to Professor Soblewski's house. It was a large, old wooden mansion in a beech wood not far from the sea. It had been built in the thirties by some Nazi bigwig or other, and during the Communist years had served as a summer residence for party functionaries. This was explained by our host while we were drinking champagne on the terrace. He didn't explain how he had come to acquire the property. He was in his seventies, well-mannered and quite charming. His thirty years younger wife, or perhaps partner, was called Jelena and spoke only broken English and German, and so conversation was somewhat halting. But I was used to that – two academic men talking and chuckling, two wives trying to smile.

I am not sure about the point of our visit to Professor Soblewski. Perhaps Martin had filled me in, but I wasn't listening attentively enough. In any case he had explained at an early stage that we would take this route through Europe rather than the more obvious westerly one: Rødby-Puttgarden-Hamburg-Strasbourg . . . and so on. I know that Soblewski had been a member of the group that used to gather on Samos in the seventies, and in view of Martin's past experiences – and what was the alleged purpose of the whole journey – I assumed that our visit had to do with Herold and Hyatt. In one way or another.

But I may be wrong. Soblewski is a big name in the literary history world, and although I had never met him before, Martin had been in frequent contact with him over the years. We have half a dozen of his books at home in Nynäshamn, one of them even in translation: *Under the Surface of Words*.

In any case we had a long and slightly strained dinner, just the four of us – and needless to say the strained aspect referred only to the two ladies present. The men had no difficulty at all in keeping the conversation going, and two carafes of red wine plus a few glasses of vodka helped matters along. Jelena drank vodka but not wine: the reverse was the case for me. The food and drink was served by a sombre-looking woman with a limp: Professor Soblewski informed us that she was a distant relative who had been ill-treated by life.

After the coffee, I asked permission to withdraw – which was granted. As I lay in the large double bed on the upper floor, waiting for sleep to swallow me up, I could hear the voices of Martin and Soblewski in the room down below for several hours. They were arguing and discussing, and sounded very enthusiastic, occasionally even aggressive: but I have no idea what they were talking about. Not then, and not now, seventeen days later. I think it was almost half past two when Martin tumbled into bed beside me. He was enveloped in a cloud of vodka.

11

The fifth of November. Thirteen degrees. Fog.

We went northwards on our morning walk, towards what is called the Punchbowl and Wambarrows. Wambarrows is one of the highest points on the whole moor, but visibility today was no more than thirty or forty metres and the world was hiding away. We followed a well-trodden path, which was very muddy in parts and difficult to cope with; and in order to avoid the risk of getting lost we turned round after half an hour and followed the same route back. No wild ponies loomed up out of the mist, just the usual screeching pheasants. And the occasional crow. I'm grateful for the fact that Castor has no trace of any kind of hunting instinct: it would be difficult to wander around as we do with a different kind of dog. But he trotted along as usual, ten metres behind on the way out, ten metres ahead on the way home.

We also came upon 'that woman's grave', as Mr Tawking put it. Surrounded by a circle of low, windswept trees is a small metal plate on a wooden stake: *In memory of Elizabeth Williford Barrett, 1911–1961.*

Nothing more. It didn't look like a grave. I thought it was

probably where her ashes had been scattered in this private little memorial grove.

Who was she? And why this barren spot? No more than a hundred metres from Darne Lodge. She only lived to be fifty years old, and I thought I ought to find out more about her. Not today, but in due course. She is my nearest neighbour after all.

I had lit a fire before we set off, and the house was warm when we got back. I had my breakfast in peace and quiet while reading the first thirty pages of *Bleak House*. It's difficult to grasp that the description of a London fog in the opening chapter is a hundred and fifty years old. It could just as well have been written today. I haven't read all that much Dickens, but Martin has always rated him highly. Maybe I'll make it routine to read thirty pages of *Bleak House* every morning: that would make it last for a month, and then I can go to the antiquarian bookshop in Dulverton and buy a new Dickens. Why not? I need to build up my day-to-day existence around practical rituals – now is a time to proceed prudently, not to dismantle everything.

When I look out of the window and compare my Exmoor mist with Dickens's nineteenth-century fog it feels as if it were a living being, just as he claimed. A sophisticated and intelligent enemy intent on encircling, penetrating and swallowing up everything. As patient and methodical as a virus, it needs bodies with as much energy as the sun to defend themselves in the long run, and needless to say the environment Castor and I have done our best to create will submit eventually. But I think that in fact it is just a variation on the old, familiar theory about the incorruptibility of life and death and the forces of nature, and I persuade myself that I should not succumb to passing whims. And concentrate on outliving my dog, as I have said before. Make decisions and stick to them. Fog or no fog.

Shortly after eleven o'clock we got into the car and set off for Exford. That is a village slightly larger than Winsford: two local pubs instead of one, a separate post office and general store, and with plenty of overnight accommodation for passing visitors. We bought a newspaper, then continued north-westwards over the moor: I suspected that this was the part of the moor that Mark Britton had referred to. But there were no views at all of the Bristol Channel and Wales which were allegedly visible on a clear day.

Then the road sloped steeply down into Porlock, before following the coast to Minehead. I had consulted the map carefully before setting out, and stopped occasionally in order to establish exactly where we were.

Minehead is a real town – no doubt a tourist destination of significance in the summer, but comparatively deserted at this time of year. We parked the car, then walked along the main street – The Avenue – to the sea. We found a launderette, where I eventually managed to fill and start two machines after various problems, and not far away was an open internet cafe. I bought tea and scones, and with Castor under the table I opened our mailboxes for the first time since we left Sweden. First my own, and then Martin's. I must admit that my heart was racing. I hadn't taken our own computers with me, but was sitting at one of the cafe's six slightly old-fashioned set-ups: I had the impression that this is what one was supposed to do, even if I had seen youngsters with their own computers linked in to up-to-date connections at Starbucks and Espresso House. But I had failed to find either of these coffee temples in sleepy Minehead.

My inbox contained no fewer than thirty-six new messages, thirty-one of them general and of no interest, but five personal ones. Among the latter were two invitations to autumn parties, one from colleagues at the Monkeyhouse, the other from a friend and former colleague from Skåne who organizes a Martinmas party every year in her home in Söder in Stockholm – I've been receiving the same invitation every year since 2003, the only time I accepted. Since this year's party had already taken place I didn't bother to reply. The other three personal messages were from Synn, Violetta – who is living in our house in Nynäshamn – and Christa. None of them was more than three lines long. Violetta had a query about rubbish collection, that I was able to answer forthwith. Synn just wanted to know that all was well and wondered where we were – the sending date was eight days ago. I wrote a polite but non-committal reply to the effect that we were doing fine, had arrived in Morocco, and hoped that everything was satisfactory in New York. Christa wrote as follows:

Dear Maria. I have the feeling that all is not well. I've dreamt about you two nights in a row. Please get in touch and assure me that I don't need to worry. Where are you? C.

I wrote a reassuring reply to Christa. The journey through Europe had gone very well, we were renting a little house not far from Rabat and from it could see the sea in the distance – or at least could just about make it out. Both Martin and I were well and enjoying ourselves. But I noted how my spirits had been raised by Christa contacting me in this way: we presumably don't dream about people unless they are important to us.

Then I went over to Martin's inbox. It was the first time I had ever read his e-mails, but he had been using the same password for ten years, so it was not difficult to open it. But I did have a sudden rush of guilt feelings – which gradually faded away – while I was reading the messages. Who would deal with his correspondence in future if I didn't?

Thirty-two messages. I opened all of them and was able to discard a third without more ado, but I read the rest carefully, every single one. Most were from colleagues about whom I knew a little, one was from Gunvald, one from Bergman – and one from somebody calling himself G: his address details didn't provide any clues. The content of the message was also a bit cryptic, and when I checked back I could find no earlier messages from him. But as I was going via the internet no messages older than twenty days were preserved. Anyway, this G wrote:

I fully understand your doubts. This is no ordinary cup of
tea. Contact me so we can discuss the matter in closer detail.
Have always felt an inkling that this would surface one day.
Best, G.

I read the text again – it was written in English, and I translated it into Swedish in my head.

Your doubts? No ordinary cup of tea? Discuss in detail? A
feeling that this would surface one day?

What was all this about? I felt a clear stab of worry, and
made a mental note to check up on Martin's address book
when I got back to Darne Lodge, in the hope of finding out
more about this G. But I had no high hopes. Martin has never
understood how to keep a register of that kind, and instead
merely kept all messages for years on end. But that route was
probably blocked now as well, since both of us – for one
reason or another – had acquired new addresses during the
summer.

I clicked away the message from G and instead began writing a reply to Gunvald. I provided the same information as in
my own messages to Christa and Synn, and decided to make a
few notes about our fictive residence – for my own use and so
as to make sure I was consistent in future.

A house not far from Rabat. Self-contained and secure.
Small swimming pool, the sea close by.

I also explained that we were only going to read our e-mails
once a week, so that a delay in responding wasn't something
they should worry about. We had found a little internet cafe
only a few kilometres from our rented house, but one of the

reasons for our journey was of course to keep some distance away from the madding crowd. So we would be grateful if Bergman, Gunvald, Synn, Christa and all the others would respect that.

I spent a minute or so wondering whether I should write a reply to the message from G as well, but I couldn't find a suitable way of expressing it and decided to postpone it. And I also decided to delay an answer to Bergman.

When I had finished dealing with the e-mails I started reading some news from Sweden in the web versions of the biggest newspapers, but after only a couple of minutes I realized that it didn't interest me in the slightest. In any case there were no reports about the missing wife of a professor who had been found dead in mysterious circumstances on the Polish Baltic coast; and although I hadn't expected to find anything of that sort, I noticed that I found it a relief. I thanked the girl behind the counter, paid what I owed and said I would certainly be coming back again.

I returned to the launderette, inserted several one-pound coins and pressed a few buttons to begin the drying process. I took Castor back to the car and let him lie under a blanket on the back seat while I wandered around the town, bought a few necessary provisions and eventually collected my clean and dry washing.

I certainly felt pleased and satisfied after having sorted out these necessary chores, as if I were any respectable and hard-working middle-aged woman you care to name. With a dog.

★

We drove a different route back over the moor. We passed through the medieval town of Dunster, passed by Timberscombe and Wheddon Cross – all the time on the same narrow, winding road that sometimes even passed through tunnels. One has to drive very carefully, and occasionally it is necessary to stop and allow oncoming traffic to pass: but I have the feeling that I'm getting used to it.

I'm getting used to everything, in fact. We arrived back at Darne Lodge at half past four as dusk was falling. The mist had persisted all day without lifting at all. Going out for walks at this time is simply unthinkable: both Castor and I could have done with some exercise, but instead the evening hours were spent ironing the washing and preparing a vegetable soup that ought to last for at least three days.

They were all useful and necessary tasks, but I noticed that my thoughts had a tendency to return to the mysterious correspondent G, and his not really specific disquiet.

12

'We'll go for a walk along the beach first. Castor needs some exercise.'

It was half past ten in the morning. We had just taken our leave of Professor Soblewski and his Jelena, who were still standing on the terrace, waving. We were sitting in the car on the rough gravel road that led up to the house, about to set off.

Martin was obviously hung-over, and admitted that it was a little too early for him to be sitting behind the wheel. I said I agreed. We had a long day on the roads ahead of us, and it wasn't only our four-legged friend that needed some fresh air.

It didn't take long for us to find our way down to the sea-shore. We drove along the coast for five or six kilometres, and stopped at a little lay-by in the beech woods, next to a cafe that was closed for the winter. A walking and cycle track continued over the steep hill down to a pale grey sandy beach that could just be glimpsed through the trees. We followed it, and concluded that the beach continued for ever in both directions. There were no people to be seen, it was misty and quite a strong wind was blowing – from the north-west, as far as I could judge. Without even needing to discuss the matter, we set off in an easterly direction. Castor has always liked sandy beaches, and for once he ran ahead of us with his tail held high. Martin was much more subdued, held his hands dug deep down into his trouser pockets, with his shoulders hunched. He also preferred to walk a pace or two ahead of me, and it was obvious that he wasn't in the mood for chit-chat. I assumed that it was yesterday's vodka that still had him in its grip: I was not unacquainted with the situation.

Perhaps also the conversation with Professor Soblewski, but I wasn't acquainted with that.

After a while, when we had walked five hundred metres or so without having seen another soul, it dawned on Martin that he had left both his wallet and his mobile in the car. I asked if he wanted to go back, but he just shook his head in irritation.

'You can't blame me for that,' I said.

'Have I tried to?' said Martin.

I didn't bother to answer. I found a piece of wood instead and started playing with Castor. He is not usually interested in chasing sticks, but he was in that mood today. I threw the stick, he ran and kicked up clouds of sand, then came back with the imagined prey in his mouth.

'Make sure he doesn't get wet,' shouted Martin. 'Remember that he'll be lying in the car in a smelly state for the rest of the day.'

I made no comment on that either. But despite the sea and the beach and the wind, my will to live started sinking to a dangerously low level. I don't really know what I mean by that expression – a dangerously low level – but they were words that came into my head there and then, not something I fished up afterwards when I tried to analyse and understand what happened later. The mood from the previous day's ferry crossing returned immediately, and the sleepless hours during the night before Martin came to bed – no sooner had he lain down than he started snoring, which meant that it was nearly four o'clock before I got to sleep; and as we continued along that beach, being careful to stay ten to fifteen metres from the water's edge, where there was a wide strip of tightly packed sand that was pleasantly easy to walk on, it dawned on me that despite everything, it had nothing to do with angst.

More to do with futility. A feeling without feelings, a nonchalance that surprised me because I couldn't remember ever having experienced it before. Even if it might have been what Gudrun Ewerts was trying to track down during our conversations. Or is it typical of futility that one *doesn't* experience it? It sounds as if that might be the case. I wondered if in fact it might have been some quite different person walking along this beach with her husband and her dog – or that some cynical supernatural power was amusing itself by substituting a different brain and a different memory bank in my poor head, and that was why I was unable to get my bearings. I had gone astray in my inner landscape, and that was due quite simply to the fact that it had been changed. Or erased. It seemed to me that a person of my age ought not to be exposed to emotions and moods that can't be weighed up and identified: but that was exactly what seemed to be happening. I was a newly born fifty-five-year-old baby.

I am trying to put into words my state of mind that day, and I'm doing that almost three weeks later. It might seem that by doing so I am trying to express a need to understand and justify what happened, but I'm afraid that might also be false. I'm writing in order to avoid going mad – the gradual eroding madness of solitude – and in order to outlive my dog. Nothing else.

We continued walking. A kilometre, maybe one-and-a-half. Without a word. Without a trace of any other people, it was quite remarkable. Just me, Martin and Castor, at reassuring distances away from one another. Each one of us evidently in a world of our own. Three living creatures on a beach, in late October. Castor had stopped chasing after sticks, but was in the lead. It struck me that there was nothing I craved. I wasn't hungry, wasn't thirsty.

And then we came to the bunker.

It was half-buried in the sand quite some way from the water's edge, just below the steep slope up to the edge of the beech woods.

Martin stopped.

'Just look at that, for Christ's sake!'

It was the first time either of us had uttered a word since he instructed me to keep the dog under control. I looked at the bunker – there was nothing else he could have been referring to – and asked what he meant.

He burst out laughing, somewhat unexpectedly, and I thought that the wind and fresh air might in fact be having a positive effect on the vodka.

'I'd like to take a look inside there,' he said, his voice filled with all the boy-scout enthusiasm I have so valiantly coped with for thirty years. 'It must be a left-over from World War Two, I reckon. But I remember . . .'

And as we trudged through the somewhat looser and more difficult to cope with sand – and as he began kicking away the heavier sand that had piled up against the rusty iron door at the back of the bunker – he went on about a novel by quite a well-known Swedish writer in which a concrete bunker just like this one played an important part. I was familiar with the author but hadn't read the book, which Martin evidently had done. And thought highly of it, it seemed, because it was suddenly very important to take a look at the inside as well. He removed even more sand, now using both his hands and his feet, and as he panted heavily he tried to explain to me the precise role played by the bunker in the story. A crucial meeting between two rivals, it seemed, but I was only listening with half an ear at most, and thinking back now I can't recall any details at all. But eventually he had removed so much sand that we were able to remove the bolt from its moorings, and by using all our combined strength managed to begin moving the heavy, awkward door. It squeaked and squealed on its rusty hinges, and opened no more than thirty or forty centimetres – but that was sufficient for us to squeeze in.

Castor thought it was sensible to stand ten metres away, and watch what we were up to with grave suspicion. If we wanted to force our way into a filthy old bunker, that was our business, not his.

It was dark inside, the only light came from the door we had just opened slightly and two small apertures facing the sea. They were located right under the roof, and the size of two small shoeboxes on end: I assumed they were intended for observation duties, and for shooting through.

So there was just one room, about five metres by five. Running along three of the walls was a bench almost a metre wide, also made of rough concrete. Wide enough to lie and sleep on, but also at a height suitable for standing on and keeping a look-out for any signs of enemy soldiers advancing from the sea. And shooting them dead.

The walls were covered in graffiti – names and dates and slogans of various kinds – and the smell of stuffiness and damp concrete was pervasive and stomach-turning. Traces of oil or petrol and cold soot also stuck in our nasal passages, and Martin pointed at the remains of a burnt-out fire more or less in the middle of the floor. These lumps of charred wood plus two tin drums with unknown contents and a few iron hooks in the ceiling were the only objects in the room.

Or at least that was what I had thought until two large rats emerged from underneath the bench, scampered over the floor just in front of our feet and disappeared in a dark corner. But then, perhaps rats don't count as objects. I screamed and Martin swore.

'Bloody hell!'

'Huh, what on earth are we doing in here?'

That seemed to be a very good question indeed, totally justified, and I hurried back to the door. But Martin stayed behind. Climbed up onto the bench and looked out through one of the apertures. His head covered the whole of the opening, and it became even darker inside the room.

'I'll be damned if this isn't almost exactly the same as in the book . . .'

There was a distinct tone of excitement in his voice, and I was overwhelmed by disgust. My field of vision seemed to shrink, and before I knew what was happening I had backed out through the door, summoned up reserves of strength I didn't know I possessed and closed it behind me, then lifted the heavy bolt into place.

Castor was still sitting at exactly the same spot. I hadn't been inside the bunker for more than a minute. I could hear Martin shouting something from inside.

My field of vision regained its normal dimensions, but my disgust remained.

'Come on, Castor,' I said, and we started walking back along the beach, retracing our steps. I assumed that Martin was shouting again, but the strong wind effectively drowned out all sounds.

I checked that I had my car keys in my jacket pocket. And thought about that sticky substance on Magdalena Svensson's stomach.

TWO

13

For the first hundred kilometres or so I was unable to get the rats out of my mind.

Not the rats in the bunker, but those fat creatures the Swedish author E writes about in one of his novels. It's only an episode, but Martin wrote his thesis on that very author and I know that he was always fascinated by the story about a man who secretly breeds a veritable army of large rats in his cellar. When they have become sufficiently fat and blood-thirsty – I don't remember the details, but I seem to recall there were a dozen or more of them – he starves them for several days, then sets up a sort of trap based on his wife needing to go down into the cellar (as he was ill in bed): she slips on the ice on the steps and slides down into the darkness where the rats are lurking, through a door that automatically opens up and then closes behind her.

And those rats are a bit on the hungry side . . .

Readers assume that everything went according to plan, because one day the wife suddenly disappears out of the story. It is an episode I find it hard to imagine a female author writing.

As I drove southwards – heading for Szczecin and Berlin –

I wondered if right now Martin was remembering that episode in E's novel.

And if he himself might be on his way to disappearing out of the story.

But before we got as far as the car and the journey along the E65, Castor and I had to tackle a strenuous walk along the beach, into a headwind, and I can't simply jump over it. *That remarkable walk*; and no matter what we thought about and what we felt during that crucial part of our lives, we didn't turn back. We didn't even stop to think things over, not once. Neither I nor Castor, *we didn't look back*. I could blame that on the fact that after a very short time it would have been too late anyway. What would I have said to Martin?

But nevertheless – and once again – it was as if my percep- tions and sensations were in the control of somebody else. As if I were seeing and experiencing the world for the first time. Words seem inadequate when I try to describe it as I look back on the situation, more inadequate than ever; but it was the sand, it was the sea, it was my footsteps – yes, every single one of them – it was the wind in my face, the cries of solitary seagulls, my breathing, and the fact that my dog glued himself to my side – yes, he really did. These external and internal factors seemed to be unprecedentedly clear and sharp, and at the same time they seemed to be in harmony, to be significant and very much relevant: all these qualities were increasing in strength all the time, and I felt myself growing hotter and hotter, as if in the late stages of a fever attack.

But we kept on walking. It was an hour before we found ourselves back at the little lay-by. We hadn't met a single person on the way this time either, and there was no vehicle apart from our dark blue Audi parked outside the boarded-up cafe. There may have been a hint of rain in the air, but when we clambered back into the car Castor and I felt comfortably uplifted and refreshed. Once I had checked that Martin's mobile, passport and wallet really were in the outside pocket of his briefcase – and after I had spent some time studying the map – we were able to set off and concentrate exclusively on the future.

We reached Berlin at six o'clock in the evening. On the way there I had telephoned and cancelled the hotel rooms Martin had already booked: I explained that we had fallen ill, and we were excused penalty charges. Instead, Castor and I booked into the Albrechtshof in Mitte for six nights. I felt that we needed time to make plans and take precautions without feeling under undue pressure, and that is in fact how we spent the next few days.

That first evening, only an hour after we had checked into the hotel, something took place that, looking back, I have interpreted as a sign. We had gone out for a little walk, and suddenly found ourselves outside a police station. I must have suffered some kind of shock as I found myself standing there outside the entrance, unable to move. I just stood there with Castor by my side, feeling that the imposing buildings were leaning over us and threatening to collapse on top of us. The noises of the city were magnified in my ears to form a bewildering cacophony, but after a few seconds they died away and instead I heard a voice inside my head intoning: *It's not yet too late. He's still alive. You can go in through that green door and put everything to rights.*

And without a second thought I walked up the three steps and opened the door, with Castor at my heels. We came into some sort of reception area, and were immediately confronted by a stern woman in a uniform who informed me that it was not allowed to take a dog with me into the police station. For some reason I couldn't understand she was holding a stethoscope in her hand. Surely police officers don't normally use stethoscopes?

I hesitated for a second, then apologized and left together with Castor.

We continued our walk, and a quarter of an hour later were back in our hotel room. I enjoyed a night's dreamless sleep, and when I woke up early the next morning I felt like an overture.

Or perhaps that's just a peculiar thought I had. It's presumably not possible to feel like an overture.

The Albrechtshof was just over a kilometre from the Tiergarten, and we spent several hours roaming around this attractive park, making necessary decisions. The weather was mild and pleasant all the time – not much in the way of sunshine, but no rain. It was the first time I had been in Berlin for many years, and what I remembered now was my very first visit to that troubled city. It was in May 1973, six months before Gunsan died; and in charge of us was our much admired form master and Swedish teacher, known affectionately as the Beanpole. The whole class was there, with not a single pupil missing: twenty-eight fifteen- or sixteen-year-olds, plus the Beanpole and a couple of parents. It was three weeks before we left our secondary school and some of us proceeded to sixth-form college, and we scurried around like scalded cats, visiting various museums, cafes and monuments, stared in bewilderment and horror at the Wall and passed through Checkpoint Charlie, scribbled our names on walls at the Zoo railway station, shopped at KaDeWe and tried to speak German even among ourselves.

And we visited Tiergarten, then as now. Fifteen years old then, fifty-five now. It seemed to me that the park was more or less unchanged. I decided that life was short, and said as much to Castor at regular intervals. Life is short, a dog's life even shorter. We sat on a park bench and ate a curry wurst. What shall we do with the time we have left? I asked my dog. Eat more German sausages was his suggestion – I could see that just by looking at him, and it seemed to me that I was now seeing the world as it really was. For the first time. I burst out laughing: it soon passed, but that was a moment when the sun came out from behind a cloud and I started laughing, there on a bench in Tiergarten.

The first decision I made was not to go back to Sweden. Going back to a familiar environment, making up some kind of story about Martin having disappeared, directing my sorrowful steps back to the Monkeyhouse . . . No, that felt like an utter impossibility, and I didn't spend many minutes thinking about it.

The second decision was just as straightforward: we would not continue to Morocco. I had never set foot in that country, there was nobody and nothing awaiting us there, and I had no illusions about the prospects of a solitary woman with a dog being able to establish a foothold there.

So what was the alternative? The alternative was to find a suitable place in Europe in which to spend the winter. A suitable country. It was distinctly possible of course that I might have a nervous breakdown, I was the first to acknowledge that. Everything could very easily go to hell, but while waiting for that day and that moment to arrive I couldn't simply sit on a park bench in Tiergarten and eat sausages. Sorry, Castor.

And so there were a number of practical details to be attended to. It was vital that I didn't leave behind any traces that could be followed up. I mustn't allow use of my credit card and mobile telephone to betray routes and stopping places. In case somebody came looking for us – the police, or a husband who had somehow managed to find a way out of the bunker.

During the days spent in Berlin I became increasingly unsure of how I judged the latter possibility. I had no clear idea of how long a person can survive without food and water, but I assumed his worst enemy would be the cold. I recalled having read that some people had survived for more than a fortnight without water, perhaps as long as a month, but they had been isolated in temperate conditions. What was the temperature in the bunker? Hardly more than seven or eight degrees, I estimated, and of course it would get much colder at night.

I tried to refrain from thinking about what role the rats might play – but surely they must have had some way of getting in and out? Or did they use the apertures facing the sea? I was sure they were too small for a grown adult, but of course they were big enough for a rat.

Anyway, what were the realistic chances of a man being able to get out?

How likely was it that some walker would come past and hear somebody crying for help?

And how likely was the other scenario – that the police would start looking for Castor and me? If somebody found a dead body in a bunker on the Polish Baltic coast, how would they go about discovering who it was?

No identification documents. No mobile. Did Martin have anything in his pockets that could indicate Sweden? I didn't know. But in any case the fifty-year-old literary colossus Martin Holinek from Sweden had not been reported missing, and his fingerprints and DNA were not in any register. Unless of course the police had taken his prints that day when he was being interrogated on suspicion of rape. I didn't know. How could I? Would some kind of suspicion crop up in the head of Professor Soblewski if he read in his local newspaper about a macabre discovery on a remote beach? There was surely no reason to fear that it would. Or was there?

Good questions, perhaps. But as early as my third day in Berlin I decided to regard them as irrelevant. The answers had nothing to do with my strategies for the future, and I needed to plan and act as if everything was under control. Whatever happened outside my horizons did not affect our circumstances – Castor's and my circumstances, that is. Make the best of the situation, that was all that mattered, and keep plugging away.

I realized quite quickly that I had a cool, logical brain, and concluded that it was largely because I wasn't in a hurry. Despite everything, I wasn't being hounded, wasn't under stress. There was time to analyse and ponder upon every step and every measure, and if I were to decide that I needed more time there was nothing to prevent me from extending our stay at the hotel for a few days. In any case, Berlin would be the last place where I left any trace of my presence, I made my mind up about that. The last place where I used any of our credit cards, and the place where I finally switched off our mobile phones. All the newfangled inventions that were so easy to track down.

The fact that I would have to keep on using our car was possibly a complication, but stealing another car or trying to change the registration plates seemed to be quite simply out of the question. If I had murdered a president or a prime minister I would probably have considered such actions, but I wasn't guilty of such crimes after all.

For the foreseeable future nobody with conventional resources was going to be able to find us: that was the basic fact that I had to grasp and adhere to.

And I did so.

*

When we left the Albrechtshof early in the morning of the twenty-eighth of October, I had succeeded in withdrawing from various banks and ATMs a total of 45,000 euros, which together with the 10,000 US dollars and the 12,000 euros we already had in our travelling funds ought to be sufficient ready money to keep our heads above water for at least six months. And if we lived frugally, for considerably longer.

And during the misty morning hours on the motorway between Berlin and Magdeburg, I decided on England. I had toyed with the idea of both Spain and Provence – and Italy and Greece as well, to be honest – but in the end what really mattered was not the climate. I wanted Castor and myself to withdraw to a country where I could speak the language reasonably well, could read a daily newspaper without any problems and follow the news broadcasts on the radio and television. I'm not absolutely clear why those factors felt so essential – but God knows, that was not the only thing I was not absolutely clear about.

The following night we stayed in a small hotel in Münster, literally in the shadow of the big cathedral. When we checked in I explained that both my credit cards and passport had been stolen, and asked to pay in advance in cash. No problem. It is a distinct advantage to be a respectable-looking fifty-five-year-old woman: people tend to believe you, whatever you say.

Nor were there any problems when it came to getting Castor across the English Channel – but there would have been if I hadn't bluffed my way through customs. I only became aware of the British regulations regarding the movement of animals when I got to the tunnel terminal in Calais, and after thinking things over carefully I decided to take a chance. I adjusted all my luggage to make room for Castor, and covered him over with a blanket: I prayed to God that nobody would discover him, and my prayers were answered. I had to present my own passport, of course, but as far as I could see it wasn't scanned – and so I'm not sure whether my arrival in the UK was registered at all.

Be that as it may, I have no intention of looking further into the matter. Moreover, if I had spent more time thinking matters through, I might well not have chosen Great Britain as my destination anyway. The border between France and the island kingdom is basically the only manned crossing between two countries in Western Europe. But the fact is that I didn't spend more time thinking about it, and so fate took its course. As I sat resting in the car as the train rattled its way through the tunnel, I concluded that one has to take a few risks and challenge fate and the powers that be now and then, one really does.

We drove off the tunnel train and found ourselves in dirty grey, rather shabby imperial territory. Driving from Folkestone into central London was a veritable challenge. All the way I had the feeling that I would have a collision at any moment, and that Castor and I would spend the evening in police custody. And hence that everything would have been lost. I tried to continue challenging fate and the powers that be, but it was far from easy. During the two-and-a-half hours it took us to get to Marble Arch I was preoccupied with controlling a racing heart and barely suppressed panic, and when I eventually managed to park in a little side-street leading to Queensway in Bayswater I had such feelings of relief that I clasped my hands in prayer and gave thanks to God.

It was half past six, and raining. Unfortunately the entrances to Kensington Gardens and Hyde Park were closed as it was dark, and so we had an evening walk to Notting Hill instead. The rain was thin, to say the least, a kind of drizzle you only experience in London – drops of water drifting around in the air without actually falling. I have never experienced anything like it anywhere else, at any rate. We started asking about accommodation, and eventually found a small hotel in Leinster Square that agreed to take both me and my dog for the next three or four nights. It was a cramped little room looking out onto a firewall; but both Castor and I were grateful for having a roof over our heads. We returned to the car at precisely the right moment to avoid a parking ticket, and the warden actually smiled and waved at us as we drove away. I regarded this as a friendly sign from heaven above, and after having unloaded some of our luggage and a packet of dog food at our hotel, then driven around for a while, I found a multistorey car park not far from Paddington where you could drive in and leave the car without needing to pay in advance. I thought I would let it stand there until it was time to leave London, and that I would be able to explain to the attendant that I had lost my credit card and hence would be paying cash.

Respectable-looking middle-aged ladies don't tell lies in this country either.

And that is exactly what happened in the end. It's not all that easy to remain incognito nowadays, but I had the feeling that I was learning how to do it as a matter of course.

14

Twelve degrees. Lifting mist and a south-westerly wind. The sixth of November.

A fire, a short walk towards Dulverton, breakfast, thirty pages of *Bleak House*. Mornings are easy. We've only slept in the house for four nights, but it seems as if it could have been forty. The way you live one day is the way you can live all the rest of your days – that is a recurrent thought, but I'm not sure how true it is.

A group of wild ponies came to greet us. Shaggy but friendly, they seemed to us. Muddy and wet, one might add – I'm thinking of buying a pair of Wellingtons to wear instead of my walking boots.

At about noon the sun began shining in earnest, and we went for a car ride to nowhere in particular. We drove north-wards and eventually stopped in a little lay-by between Exford and Porlock. Up here the moor is just as barren and extensive as Mark Britton described it. You can see for goodness knows how many kilometres in all directions, and there isn't a single building in sight. No sign of any human activity at all, barely even a tree: just heather, gorse and bracken. Rough grass, moss and mud. The heavens seem very close indeed in such landscapes. We followed a sort of path in a north-easterly direction – I assume it's the wild ponies that have made it – but it seemed to peter out in places and then double back on itself. It was often too wet to walk on, and we were compelled to literally force our way through the rough heather: but Castor regarded it all as a stimulating challenge, and I noticed that his attitude was rubbing off on his missus. I felt possessed by a strange feeling of freedom, of something wild and primitive. *The way you live one day . . .* We skirted around the most water-logged swamps, always looking back over our shoulders to make sure we didn't lose our bearings – always respectful guests in this barren, unspoiled countryside. You don't need to steel yourself to act like that, the feeling simply takes possession of you, the most natural thing in the world. You feel incredibly small.

Then suddenly the sky was cloudless and bright blue. It occurred to me that simply knowing that such days are a possibility, that they are stored away in time and in our calendars, makes it possible to endure our environment in ways that I have frequently found too easy to forget. After a while we came across a large group of ponies some distance away, twenty-five or thirty of them, all grazing on a sunny slope: and I immediately imagined them standing there for ever, in exactly the same place, totally indifferent to world wars, the decline and fall of the Roman empire, and the invention of the wheel. On that sun-drenched slope in the England that was after all the cradle of the modern era.

Five or six hours from now they would be enveloped in mist and darkness, but nothing could worry them less.

As we slowly trudged back towards the car I wondered if reflections such as these were something I would have tried to put into print, if I had in fact been the writer I pretended to be. Or perhaps I should put them into print in any case? But I decided that such thoughts were irrelevant. Why add a few more straws to the rubbish heap of nature observations that . . . that white men have squeezed out of their existential poverty ever since the dawn of civilization? Words, words, words, I thought, and I felt undeniably pleased and relieved over the fact that my writing is no more than a mask.

On the way home we paused in Exford to do some shopping and buy a newspaper. I had barely glanced at a newspaper since sitting with *Svenska Dagbladet* on the ferry between Ystad and Poland, and when we got back to Darne Lodge, after making a new fire, I lay down on the sofa with Castor curled up under my legs and read through the *Independent* from the first page to the last. It was more of a gesture in the direction of reality and civilization as such, I think, and I found nothing that concerned me in any way, or induced me to take any interest in the outside world. I eventually fell asleep, of course, and when I woke up it was dark in the room and the fire was reduced to a barely glowing heap of embers.

I lit two candles on the table, lay on the sofa again and meditated. Listened to the whispering sounds of the rhododendron branches rubbing against the windowsill, and to the wind. It was beginning to blow quite strongly. There are no curtains in the living room. If a person or an animal were standing two metres outside the house and peering in, I wouldn't detect it. I got up and added *torch* to my shopping list. According to Mr Tawkings's inventory tucked away in its folder, there are supposed to be two torches in the house: but I haven't discovered either of them.

Having got thus far on this unremarkable November day, I decided to take my first look at Martin's material from Samos and Morocco.

15

There was no internet connection in my room in The Simmons Hotel, but there was a computer available for guests to use down in the lobby. Much to the annoyance of some younger guests, I spent almost two hours on it that first morning in London. It took me that long to find Darne Lodge just outside the village of Winsford in the county of Somerset. I must have checked up on over a hundred possible places to rent in the south-west of England: my reason for homing in on that area had to do with the fact that many years ago we had rented a house outside Truro in Cornwall – Martin, the children and I. We stayed there for a whole month, and I recall it as the happiest holiday we ever had during all our years together. Gunvald and Synn were in their early teens, but it worked well even so and I know that when we had our evening meals in the cramped little kitchen in our stone cottage after the day's outings, we felt a sense of togetherness and fellowship that I had never felt before. Perhaps it was imagined rather than real, but it's difficult to judge matters like that. I also remember that Martin and I enjoyed a really excellent sex life down there in Cornwall. Incidentally it was the summer before the winter in which Martin had his affair with another woman.

And I can't be certain that the affair hadn't started before the summer.

I'm not sure exactly how I thought that previous holiday could be of significance for the current circumstances, but I suppose I must have been looking out for the possibility of linking up with something in the past that had positive vibrations. In any case it had more to do with emotions than with rational thought, and I was aware that I had visions of a little cottage in south-west England in the back of my mind even before we left Berlin.

The description of Darne Lodge provided no contact information via the internet, only a telephone number. I borrowed the telephone from the sleepy Hungarian receptionist, and Mr Tawking answered after only one ring. As if he had been sitting there, waiting for somebody to phone him. After five minutes we had agreed on a rent for six months, and it was a done deal provided I paid a deposit into his bank account before the day was out.

'Before the day is out?' I wondered.

'Before the day is out,' said Mr Tawking. 'People are generally queuing up for the privilege of living in my house.'

I doubted that, both at the time and later, but I accepted the condition. Castor and I went for a walk through the park down towards Kensington, and eventually found a bank where, after some discussion, I managed to make the payment to Mr Tawking without my needing to produce a credit card or any personal details – well, in fact I gave the new name I had adopted, Maria Anderson, and a fictitious address in Copenhagen.

I also changed some money and acquired £1,500 in sterling; and I thought I ought to do the same in several of the small bank branches along Queensway before we set off on our journey westwards – suitably split up into a number of small-ish transactions which would not raise any eyebrows.

I mustn't leave any traces. Incognito. When we emerged into the sunshine and the hustle and bustle of Kensington High Street I was suddenly possessed by a surprising degree of optimism. I was making decisions and carrying them out. I was coming across problems and solving them. I gave Castor a liver chew, and promised him that I would stay alive at least as long as he did.

My optimism was changed into its opposite about twenty minutes later, next to the Peter Pan statue in Kensington Gardens.

'Maria?'

I saw immediately who it was. Katarina Wunsch. Now working for Swedish Radio in Luleå, but we had been col-leagues in the Monkeyhouse until the turn of the century. We were not all that close, but had been working together for rather a lot of years. She was with her husband: I didn't remember his first name, but we had met several times.

And now here they were in London. A brief holiday visit, perhaps, or maybe to do with work – how could I know? I had half a second in which to react.

'I'm sorry?'

'But . . . ?'

Her surprise was total. She stared at me, then glanced at her husband for confirmation.

Confirmation that the woman with the dog they had almost literally bumped into in Kensington Gardens really was Maria Holinek, who . . . who they had known for many years. Granted that we hadn't met since about 2005 or thereabouts, but still? Surely there couldn't be any doubt about it? The woman wasn't exactly an unknown face, and they had even heard about the dog. No doubt they had read all that awful stuff in the papers in the early summer, just like everybody else. But could it really be . . . ?

I obviously don't know what thoughts were whirling round inside the heads of Katarina Wunsch and her husband, whatever his name was, but it wasn't hard to guess. And it felt as if something inside my own skull was about to burst.

'Are you not . . . ?'

'I'm sorry. There seems to be a mistake here.'

I really did manage to come out with that sentence. I actually told a lie. I didn't faint, and I didn't sink down into the ground. Mr Wunsch cleared his throat in embarrassment and took hold of his wife's arm.

'I apologize. We thought you were somebody else.'

I nodded.

'Somebody we used to know. So sorry.'

They both produced a stiff smile, and continued on their way.

'No worries,' I said to their backs, but they didn't turn

round. I put Castor on his lead and hurried out onto Bayswater Road.

Then I sat down at a pavement cafe in Westbourne Grove and tried to calm down. Tried to analyse what had happened, and to guess what the Wunsches had said to one another after our surprise meeting.

Surely it was her?

Without a doubt, I'd say.

What on earth was the matter with her?

Could it be . . . Could it have something to do with that business of her husband? That we read about last summer. Rape. Good Lord, how little we know about other people!

I simply didn't know. I couldn't make up my mind. Maybe I had got away with it, despite everything? There was a minimal chance. After all, there are duplicates and doppelgängers in this world, people who are almost exactly like other people even though they are not twins. Perhaps the Wunsches had concluded that they were mistaken, and that the woman they had bumped into was somebody entirely different?

But I was quite clear about one thing: if the Swedish police were ever presented with a dead body belonging to the well-known literature professor Martin Holinek, and news of it leaked out into the press – which it would, of course – the Wunsches would have no difficulty in recalling their meeting with that woman in Kensington Gardens. The woman they had no difficulty in recognizing, but who denied she was who she was.

And they would now have a very obvious explanation for it.

I also realized that I ought to be careful when feelings of unvarnished optimism began to overcome me. I needed to raise my guard, to be more cautious. Perhaps I ought to change my hairstyle and dye my hair? But it was a bit late for that now . . .

I left the cafe, urged Castor to stay close to me, and walked back to the hotel under a cloud of irritation and despondency.

We spent one more day in London. I actually did have a haircut, but didn't have it dyed. And tried to understand how I could have been so naive as to think that I – with a face recognizable to half the Swedish nation – would be able to wander around unhindered in a city like London which is visited every day by . . . well, goodness only knows. Ten thousand Swedish tourists? Quite apart from the hundred thousand or so Swedes who live here already.

This final day in the big city was grey and cloudy, with the usual characteristic, drizzly rain: but nevertheless I bought a couple of pairs of sunglasses, each of which covered about half my face.

And also a broad-brimmed hat and a fluffy shawl. I was presumably thinking about that photograph I'd seen of Jacqueline Kennedy Onassis, drinking coffee in a cafe in Uppsala. Or at least, that's what a literature lecturer in Uppsala likes to believe, and has told Martin and me about it at least twice.

I bought pounds sterling for my euros in several small bureaux de change just as I had planned, and amassed over

£8,000 without needing to show any kind of identity documentation. That ought to last for a few months – whatever I got up to when I reached Exmoor, I wasn't intending to be extravagant; and surely it would be possible to change money in other places in this island kingdom if necessary, not just in the capital.

But the night before we set off on our westward journey I didn't sleep a wink. All kinds of old detritus floated up to the surface from the murky depths of my memory: I was without a doubt being attacked by the life I was just taking my leave of. Or had already left, to be honest. It was as if all those memories and all those years were trying to drag me back to places and circumstances where I no longer belonged. Mind you, where I belonged now, to be precise and accurate, was also a question I couldn't just answer and forget about and fall asleep. And how I was going to be able to drive us out of London in one piece the next day without an hour or two's sleep in my body . . . well, that was something that felt more and more difficult for every sleepless minute that ticked by.

In the end – at some point after four in the morning – I was exposed to an episode that drove aside everything else, and refused to leave me in peace: Vivianne's lover. I didn't understand why.

Vivianne was Martin's elder sister. I write *was*, because she has been dead for many years. She threw herself out of a window on the sixteenth floor of a hotel in Singapore – or she might have been pushed, or it might have been an accident. It was the twenty-eighth of February 1998. She had rather a lot of alcohol in her blood, something that wasn't exactly unusual in the final years of her life, and if I understood it rightly the police investigation was put on ice after a few weeks because there were no suspicions of any crime having been committed.

But the story of her secret lover happened twelve years before that, about a month before Olof Palme was murdered.

16

A thousand pages, he had said.

It took some time for me to get an idea of the actual amount, but I was inclined to reduce Martin's estimate by about a half. But of course, it all depended on how you counted the pages. A handwritten page, even if it is A4 size, is not the same as a typewritten or printed page, and quite a lot of what I assumed was his 'material' was handwritten, in four thick notebooks of a kind that I recall Martin being very enthusiastic about when we first met, and for several years afterwards. Thick oilcloth covers with a hundred and forty pages in each book – I think he ordered them specially from Germany. On the unlined flyleaf at the beginning of each one he had noted meticulously the place and the time of writing: *Samos, July–August 1977. Samos, June–July 1978. Samos, July 1979. Taza, July–August 1980.*

The first two books were more or less full. The third was a little more than half-full, and the fourth, from Morocco, roughly a third full. But he only wrote on the right-hand pages, it should be stressed. Martin has never liked writing on one page to leak through onto the other side, as it were. An empty page should be an empty page. I knew that he had taken a portable typewriter with him on his last trip to Samos and the one to Taza the following year, and assume that he had used this at least in part for the sort of diary entries he seemed to have been making on these later journeys.

But this was unclear as yet: before I even started to read the contents, I tried to estimate the scope. If I was going to examine the project as a whole, I had every reason to adopt a methodical approach.

Perhaps I also had Eugen Bergman at the back of my mind; I think so. A situation could well develop in which it would be useful if I knew a little about it, even if I were grateful for the fact that Martin always stubbornly refused to discuss the content of his work while it was in progress. That had been the situation for as long as he and Bergman had been working together: the publisher wouldn't think there was anything odd about his not being informed in detail about how work was progressing while Martin was in North Africa.

But it seemed more or less inevitable that I would have to conduct a certain amount of e-mail correspondence in my husband's name.

With Bergman and with others.

With G? That felt bizarre, and I decided not to think about that in more detail.

In the work chest – the large brown suitcase that contained exclusively books, writing tools and desk utensils – I found a bundle of almost three hundred typewritten pages in a file marked *Writings*. This material was not dated – not systematically, at least – and I had the impression that it comprised both fair copies of diary entries, and original texts. There were no page numbers, but when I leafed through it I saw that there were occasional headings and dates, and here and there also changes and additions made in pencil. There were also copies of photographs in some places, evidently produced by an ordinary photocopying machine on typing paper. I glanced quickly at a couple of them: the quality was awful, and they both depicted a small group of people sitting on chairs round a table. Martin appeared in both of them. It seemed possible that a tall woman standing in front of a white wall in the background of one of them was Bessie Hyatt. A mop of hair, large white tunic and bare legs – yes, I was convinced it was her.

In addition to the handwritten and typewritten material I eventually found a file on Martin's computer entitled *Taza*, and as I knew that he didn't start using a computer until the beginning of the nineties I assumed – without opening the file – that it comprised fair copies of earlier pages, or something he had written later. I didn't find any other documents that seemed to deal with those summers, and didn't bother to look any further into that particular aspect.

Now that I had acquired a certain degree of familiarity with the material, I immediately started to feel distinctly sceptical about the project as a whole. What was the point? What was I going to get out of it? What would *anybody* get out of it? Wouldn't it be better if I spent all my time reading Dickens instead? Or something else, goodness only knows what. Surely I could deal with Bergman in some other way when it became relevant? In so far as there was any point in considering a future. I let Castor out for the evening's last peeing session, and poured myself a glass of port to help me reach a conclusion.

In the end I decided to take the first of the diaries for bedtime reading. As a trial, without committing myself to continuing along those lines, but to give it a chance even so. Perhaps I thought I owed him that in a way, maybe it had something to do with the unhealthy feminine efficiency we women are alleged to have: but I'm quite sure this would not be a truthful description of my motives. Let's face it, one tells lies mainly for one's own peace of mind.

The first obvious problem I came upon was Martin's handwriting. I had been used to it for over thirty years, but sometimes that didn't help. I also know that he himself had difficulties at times in understanding what he had written, especially if it was something he had just scribbled down hastily in a notebook or on a loose scrap of paper. In his diary of the stay in Samos, 1977, it was obvious that he had made an effort to write neatly or at least legibly in the beginning, but after a few pages it was impossible to read some words, even when one considered them in context.

Besides, it was all rather uninteresting – I couldn't help but feel that. The date, getting up, breakfast, the weather, conversations with somebody or other. A walk, a swim, an attempt to describe nature. Name-dropping – there was a distinct whiff of that, even if the people concerned were not anybody I knew about, apart from Hyatt and Herold, and he rarely talked to them, not in the first week at least. And he only refers to them from a distance, as it were. 'Bessie sat in the shade of the plane tree all morning, writing.' 'Tom went off in the boat and there was no sign of him all day. He came back at dusk with a dozen reddish fish.' It is noticeable that he admires them, especially him. In the summer of 1977 Bessie Hyatt's sensational debut novel hadn't yet appeared – if I remember rightly, that is: I think it came out in the autumn or the winter of that year – but Tom Herold was already a sort of icon. Comparisons with the likes of Byron were not uncommon. Somewhat jokily (one assumes) Martin describes him as 'The Childe Herold of our time', and it is presumably not just the similarity in the name he is referring to.

He also describes the practicalities of life in the collective. They sleep on simple mattresses lying on the floor in a large building with about a dozen small rooms: that fits in with what Martin told me when we first met. A shared shower room, shared toilets – he thinks the building had previously been used by the military, and as some kind of children's home or children's holiday camp. The house that Herold and Hyatt live in was evidently where the permanent staff used to live, or people with varying leadership status. It is situated some distance away on a hill, and the famous couple apparently tend to keep themselves to themselves – there is no mention as yet of going to visit them in their home. For all the others there is a large shared kitchen and also a taverna a couple of hundred metres away by the road leading down to the beach. He mentions the rent: apparently they pay Hyatt and Herold a few hundred drachmas a week via somebody called Bruno. A paltry sum, according to Martin.

He also writes that Finn hasn't yet arrived, although he had promised to spend the whole summer there. I know that Finn is Finn Halvorsen, a Norwegian and a good friend of Martin's – and in fact the person who had told him about the notorious collective, and invited him to stay there.

But there is not much in the way of reflections at the beginning of the diary: not pregnant reflections, at least. As I read it I have the impression that Martin feels somehow overwhelmed, despite the fact that he is leaning over backwards to avoid revealing that. By the place itself: the blue Mediterranean, the white beaches, the cypresses, the scent of thyme – but perhaps above all by the people surrounding him: free-thinking hippies and citizens of the world, young men and women who seem to lead a voluntary and unrestrained bohemian existence in the classical Greek island setting without thinking that what they are doing is in the least remarkable. That they seem *to have a right to it.*

And they are all writers of one kind or another. Or practitioners of the liberal arts, at least. Two women – he assumes they are a lesbian couple but never says what they are called – stand up on the hill every morning, painting. 'Until the midday sun forces them down to the sea, or indoors. They are half-naked all the time.'

Eroticism? I think. A place like that must have reeked of eroticism.

But Martin prefers to comment on the conversations. 'Sat and chatted to Hernot and Della for a few hours,' he writes. 'About hermeneutics and Sartre. Bons came and joined in: he must be the most cheerful Nietzschean I've ever come across, but he'd been smoking too much weed and fell asleep after a while.'

The most cheerful Nietzschean I've ever come across? It's not difficult to get the impression that he's writing to impress somebody. Himself, presumably; or maybe some woman who in future happens to glance at the book which he has left open in front of her on their first date, apparently by accident. I remembered that in the summer of 1977 I hadn't yet met Martin at that garden party in Gamla Stan in Stockholm. The summer of 1977 was when Rolf fell over a cliff above Flüeli in Switzerland, and died.

At another point – it's the fifteenth of July and he's been on Samos for just over a week – he writes:

> Two new members arrived at the collective today.
> A German and a Russian, remarkably enough. The German
> is a poet and is called Klinzenegger [I'm unsure about the
> spelling here, we'll see if he's mentioned again later on], the
> Russian is called Gusov but is careful to point out that this is
> only his pseudonym. We had lunch together at the taverna
> – Elly and Barbara as well – just the usual Greek salad and a
> few glasses of retsina, of course, and it transpired that Gusov
> has been living in Greece on and off for several years, and
> among other things has been active in the struggle against
> the military junta. Claimed he spent several months in prison
> on that account, but that he was released when it was all
> over in 1974. I think he regards himself as a sort of honorary
> Greek citizen on the basis of his efforts. He also speaks quite
> fluent Greek with Manolis as the meal is being served. But
> unfortunately he sounds rather cocksure of himself. Too
> much preaching. And a shaggy mass of beard as befits a
> revolutionary and resistance fighter. I tried to talk to him

about Mayakovsky and Mandelstam, but he didn't seem interested. Presumably didn't have anything much to say about them.

I yawned and checked the time. It was a quarter to one. I registered that even if the overall total was only five hundred pages, I had so far read a mere three per cent. I felt tired out, put the book down and switched off the bedside lamp.

For some unknown reason Castor was lying on the floor beside the bed instead of in it. And before I fell asleep I could hear the rain beginning to drum on the roof as the wind grew stronger.

17

It was the twenty-fourth of January 1986.

In the morning I had dropped off the children and was getting ready to travel to the Monkeyhouse. I was due to read the early evening news and didn't need to be in the studio until one o'clock.

The telephone rang. It was Martin.

'We have a problem,' he said.

'Really?' I said.

'My sister. She's made a mess of things again. She'll be coming over this evening.'

'I thought she was in Spain?'

'So did I. But she's evidently been at home here in Sweden since Christmas.'

'I see. And what's the problem this time?'

Vivianne was Martin's only sibling, and if she had a problem now it certainly wasn't anything new. She had been divorced three times – but no children, thank God – and she had lived her life so far on the periphery of the film world. In January 1986 she was thirty-eight, five years older than her brother. It had all begun quite early on, when she was involved in two Swedish films in the sixties while she was still a teenager: one of them was regarded as an excellent example of the new vogue of Swedish sex and was sold to several countries. In connection with that Vivianne had met a rich American producer, married him and moved to Hollywood. She made a few films, met an Italian director, got divorced, married him and moved to Rome. Made a few more films . . . And so on.

She had about five nervous breakdowns and five potential scandals behind her when she met the Spanish film mogul Eduard Castel round about 1980, and a sort of stability entered her life. That is what she claimed, in any case, and what we convinced ourselves. She even made a film that was featured at the Cannes festival, in which she played the role of a woman torn between love and sexual liberation. Martin and I saw it in Stockholm, and agreed afterwards that she had played the part brilliantly.

We had very little contact with Vivianne; it was really only when she was going through one of her crises that she remembered she had a brother. Martin used to sum her up as *the triple m*: a manipulative, manic-depressive mythomaniac.

And now it seemed to be a case of here we go again. I thought hard and concluded that I hadn't seen her for over two years. She had stayed with us for a few days when she was in Sweden after her divorce from Castel. Synn had been born that year, and I was starting to recover from my post-natal depression – but my condition was a summer breeze compared with Vivianne's state. Naturally, we had sat up three nights in a row, talking to her and drinking red wine.

'I don't really know what's going on,' said Martin now, on that freezing cold day in January 1986. 'She was quite reticent.

But she did say that it's a delicate situation, and she'll be coming round to us this evening. If I understood it rightly, she won't be on her own.'

'Not on her own?'

'No, but I'm not certain. She asked if she could stay the night with us.'

'What? Are you saying that Vivianne actually asked?'

'Yes, she did. What's so remarkable about that?'

'Nothing, I suppose. But she doesn't usually ask.'

It was silly of me, and Martin hated the role of protector of his sister. He disliked her just as much as I did, but we both found it hard to say no to her. He said nothing for a while, and I apologized.

'Okay, it'll work itself out, no doubt. When exactly is she coming?'

'I don't really know,' said Martin. 'She's supposed to be ringing again.'

I finished at the Monkeyhouse soon after half past eight, and as I hadn't heard from Martin all day I rang home to find out what was going on.

'I think she's lost the plot,' he said. 'I've never seen her like this before. But I've got the kids into bed at least.'

He sounded tired and worn out, and I couldn't help but feel relieved that it hadn't been my turn to do the domestic chores that evening. He must have done the shopping, collected the children, made a meal, read some stories and done the washing up . . . all the time with his mad sister at his heels. It was of course out of the question that Auntie would have helped out with anything. I asked what exactly was happening.

Martin sighed. 'She's waiting for her lover to appear. Yes, you could no doubt say that's what it's all about.'

'And who's her lover this time round? Why does she have to show him off to us, by the way?'

'I don't think she wants to show him off,' said Martin. 'It's more like the other way round.'

'The other way round?'

'Yes. It's precisely because he mustn't be seen that he's coming to our house.'

'I don't follow you.'

'Well, God only knows,' said Martin. 'What she claims in any case is that he's a national celebrity. A high-ranking politician – a minister, in fact. They've been having a relationship since Christmas. It's absolutely top secret, and nobody must know about it. They couldn't possibly meet in a hotel, for instance – that would be much too risky.'

I thought it over for a minute.

'Do you believe all this?'

'I've no idea,' said Martin. 'But she's in a right flap, that's for sure. He was supposed to appear at about eight o'clock, after a government meeting, but there's been no sign of him yet.'

'Does she remember that I'm a news presenter on the television?' I asked.

'She's relying on our discretion,' said Martin. 'And I've promised her.'

'But we'll be meeting him, will we?'

'I've no idea,' said Martin again. 'But I assume so.'

We didn't, in fact. When the alleged lover and national celeb-rity finally arrived at our house in Nynäshamn – it was almost ten o'clock, I'd been at home for over half an hour – the secu-rity level had been raised to the ceiling, with red alert. Martin and I stood in our living room window and watched the pro-ceedings: Vivianne had gone out to meet him when he parked his car a couple of blocks away, exactly as they had arranged on the telephone shortly beforehand. He was quite a slim man, slightly shorter than Vivianne, wearing smart dark clothes and ordinary shoes despite the fact that it was more than ten degrees below zero: but that was just about all we could make out as he was walking pressed up close to Vivi-anne, staring down at the ground, and with some kind of scarf or jacket hood over his head. It concealed all of his face, and it reminded me of when the police escort an accused into a courthouse so that photographers can't get pictures of him.

A few metres from the front door Vivianne noticed that we were standing in the window, watching them. She stopped dead and waved at us in annoyance – it was obvious that we were supposed to keep out of the way. We looked at one another, shrugged and went to sit down in the kitchen. I recall thinking that it was among the most absurd situations I had ever experienced, and I was on the point of going out into the hall when I heard them hanging up their outdoor clothes. But

Martin saw what I was intending to do, shook his head and placed his hand on my arm.

'We'd better leave her alone. Things will only get worse if we start interfering.'

'This is ridiculous, Martin.'

'I know, but that's life.'

We heard them walking up the stairs to the guest room, then closing the door and locking it.

Yes, they really did lock the door. When Martin and I tip-toed past soon afterwards, on our way to our own bedroom, we could hear them talking. Very faintly. It sounded like a serious, conspiratorial conversation.

He must have left at some time during the night, for Vivianne was alone when she came down for breakfast the next day. It was a Saturday, both Martin and I had the day off. Vivianne looked tired and shaken, and to begin with she had nothing to say about the previous evening. I at least hoped that we would be spared having to listen to her account of it all, and that she would leave everything shrouded in mystery. But after a cup of coffee she had evidently decided to lift the veil of secrecy somewhat.

'It's an incredibly delicate situation,' she said. 'There's so much at stake, and lots of things could go wrong.'

That was not an unusual claim, coming from Vivianne Holinek. Her life had to be littered with drama and perilous situations, otherwise it was not a life worth living.

'So you are having a relationship with a top politician, and you're afraid his wife will get to know about it – is that it?' I asked, and received a dirty look from my husband.

'I can't go into details,' said Vivianne, 'but it's much more complicated than that. And I have to bear the responsibility myself. Perhaps it was unfair to involve you, but the situation was such that I didn't have any choice.'

'Who is he?' asked Martin. 'I thought he looked like—'

'That's enough!' interrupted his sister. 'No names. Don't make the situation worse than it is already.'

'All right,' I said. 'I hope you had a good time anyway.'

'It's not like you think,' said Vivianne.

She left us an hour later, warning that she might well come back. She said she was in a very precarious situation, but given the circumstances her own safety was not the most important consideration. There were much more important things at stake than that. People's lives could be under threat.

We didn't hear from her again until a month later. Or rather, it was Martin who heard from her. She telephoned from a hotel in Copenhagen and according to Martin she was totally hysterical. He spoke to her for ten minutes, but I couldn't hear what was said as I was in another room; however, I could hear that he was doing his best to calm her down. When the call was over, I asked what it was all about this time.

'She's mad,' said Martin. 'I reckon she's ripe for the loony bin. She claims that somebody is going to be killed.'

'Killed?'

'Yes, and that she can't do anything about it. I really do think she's gone off the rails this time.'

Four days later Olof Palme was murdered in Sveavägen in Stockholm. That same day I asked Martin if we ought to contact the police.

'Not on your life,' said Martin. 'Don't you think there'll be enough loonies ringing the police with tips? Surely you don't seriously think that my sister would have anything to do with the assassination of the Swedish Prime Minister?'

I didn't think so, of course, and as we said nothing from the start, we didn't say anything later either. And it was over a year before we heard anything from Vivianne again. She was now living in Austria with a professional skiing instructor, and I think I'm right in saying that we only met her twice more before she died.

The fact that she died on the anniversary of Palme's death was something we discussed briefly, Martin and I. We agreed that it was a coincidence. If it had been ten years later, we might have regarded that as being of some significance: but in fact twelve years had passed.

Nevertheless, I do occasionally think about that mysterious man walking up our drive with the hood concealing his face, I have to admit that.

18

The eighth of November. Clear but windy and cold. Only plus three degrees at eight in the morning.

We had spent the whole of the previous day indoors, due to appalling weather. Rain and gale-force winds non-stop – or perhaps it wasn't in fact rain, but the upper layer of the sea that was being blown in over the land. It seemed suspiciously as if that really was the case, and was coming from that direction. Castor was restricted to three short runs around the garden. It was a difficult day in every respect – the worst one since I came here. I understand that I need to get out briefly every day, irrespective of the weather and the wind: spending thirty-six hours at a stretch in a house like Darne Lodge is not something to look forward to, most certainly not.

Perhaps I had convinced myself that Martin's notes would keep me occupied, but after only a few pages I found myself overwhelmed by a degree of resistance that I neither want nor am able to explain. I put the whole lot of material away, and spent the day reading Dickens and playing patience instead. I hadn't played patience since I was a teenager, but I found two almost unused packs of cards in a drawer, and after a while had remembered four different variations. Idiot Patience, of course, and Spider Harp – I can't remember the names of the other two. I'm sure I learned all four from my father, probably even before I started school: and once I had realized this I simply couldn't get him out of my mind. He was a person who wanted the best for everybody, and did whatever he could to make that happen; but in the last years of his life, after Gunsan had died and my mother had entered a twilight world, well . . . How was he able to sum up his journey through life? As he lay there in hospital and died of a broken heart. What was left for him?

I thought about Gudrun Ewerts, and how she went on about the importance of weeping. If she was gazing down on me yesterday from the heavens above, she would have had every reason to nod approvingly. I cried my eyes out.

But that was yesterday. Today is another day, and having learned our lesson we set off on foot immediately after breakfast and Dickens. We headed southwards to start with, towards Dulverton, and after a while we came to that simple signpost pointing the way into the village. After eyeing one another up and down and thinking it over for a few moments, we set off along that path. It was muddy and difficult to follow at first, but after a few hundred metres we came to a narrow road along which one could stroll without too much difficulty. It wasn't wide enough for a four-wheeled vehicle – I didn't really understand how it had come to exist, or what purpose it could possibly have: but there is a lot about the moor that I don't understand. It was downhill all the way, and the vegetation was abundant: deciduous trees in full leaf even though we were well into November; moss and ivy, holly and brambles.

The road followed a fast-flowing stream, pheasants and all kinds of other birds twittered and hopped around in the bushes, and here and there, on the other side of the thick undergrowth, we could hear the bleating of sheep. It seemed to me that the ground must be enormously fertile – if you lay down and slept for twelve hours, you were bound to be covered in creepers when you woke up: it seemed a bit like a cautionary fairy-tale. A little girl and her dog go for a walk in the woods, and never return to their village. I tried to shake such thoughts off me.

We eventually came to a house. We had been under way for about half an hour, and its sudden appearance was about as likely as the chances of meeting a lawyer in heaven. That was another of my father's expressions, incidentally, and I assume it was a hangover from the previous day's games of patience. Anyway, it was a dark-coloured stone-built house so embedded in the vegetation that it was almost invisible – it was on the other side of the stream we had been following all the way, which at this point changed from being fast-flowing into a stretch of more or less still-standing water. A moss-covered stone bridge ran over the water to the house. We paused and contemplated the building: it was two storeys high, and the walls were covered in ivy and other climbing plants – some of the windows were almost completely overgrown.

It was when I raised my gaze to observe the upper storey that I realized there were in fact three floors: there was a narrow window immediately below the gable gutter, and in that window I could just make out a face.

It was pale, almost white, and it belonged to a young man

who was evidently standing up there, watching us. He must have been pressing his face against the glass – no lights were lit in the house but even so his features were quite clear through the windowpane. It was a thin, colourless face, dark hair with a parting, prominent eyebrows and a long, pointed nose. A grim-looking mouth, little more than a narrow slit.

And completely motionless – my immediate reaction was that it was a doll.

But it wasn't a doll. After we had been observing each other for about ten seconds, he slowly raised his right hand and made a very obvious gesture in front of his neck: a sideways movement across his throat. There was no mistaking its significance.

Then he backed away into the darkness of the room.

I had difficulty in moving away from the spot. Castor was halfway over the bridge to the house, and I called him back. A hen pheasant burst out from a clump of trees, a screeching male just behind her. In the distance I could hear the sound of a vehicle accelerating away, and concluded that we must be quite close to the village. I could also see that below the house the road became slightly wider: it must presumably be possible to drive up to here.

As we stood there, getting on for a minute, the sound of water bubbling away on all sides became louder, sharper, and then a deafening shriek from a bird pierced the air – not a pheasant this time. I glanced up once more at the dark attic window, then began moving away at last. It felt as if something significant had happened, something irrevocable, I don't know what.

It took less than ten minutes to get down to the village – the final section was a muddy but easily passable road suitable for vehicles. There were traces of ponies' hooves, but also wide wheel-tracks looking as if they had been made by a tractor. At regular intervals narrow channels of bubbling water crossed over the road. Where did all the water come from? I asked myself automatically – but then I recalled the previous day's weather . . . Castor was forging ahead all the time now, as if he had already registered a whiff of civilization and the prospect of something tasty to eat.

The Royal Oak had just opened for lunch, and since the plan was to walk all the way back to Darne Lodge, we went in. It had taken us more or less exactly an hour to get here, so it would probably take us about twice as long to get back up the hill.

It wasn't Rosie behind the bar today, but a man past the full bloom of youth. Perhaps he was Rosie's husband. He greeted us heartily, and asked if I wanted some food. I said that I was indeed intending to have lunch, and sat down at the same table as the time before. He came over with a menu, but explained that today's special – chicken breast and broccoli with fried potatoes – was not on it. He had a tattoo on his lower arm: *Leeds United 4ever*. I said I rather fancied the chicken breast. He nodded and asked if I minded if he gave the dog a few treats as well. I had the impression that Castor also nodded, and a couple of minutes later he was fully occupied guzzling down a plate of mixed meat trimmings and drinking half a litre of water before dozing off in front of the fire.

No further conversation took place and no other guests turned up during the forty-five minutes we stayed at The Royal Oak. I tried not to think about the face in the window – and that gesture with the hand over the young man's throat – with only limited success.

Before starting back towards Winsford Hill – this time on the other side of Halse Lane, and over rather more open ground if I had read the map correctly – we went for a short walk round the village. There can't have been more than about fifty houses, but on the other side of the church I discovered a sign pointing to something called 'Community Computer Centre'. It turned out to be a low, modern-looking building with white plaster and featureless office-type windows, and as we passed it I noticed that it was open. We went inside and found ourselves in a room looking like a school classroom with about twenty rather old-fashioned computers. Sitting at a slightly larger table was a dark-haired woman of about thirty, chewing at a pencil and staring at a screen. She looked up and smiled when she saw me.

And smiled even more broadly when she saw Castor.

Good, I thought. A human being.

'Welcome! How can I help you? What a handsome dog! A ridgeback, methinks.'

'He's a very good friend,' I said, without adding that he was the only one I had. 'I gather you have links to the internet here, is that right?'

'It certainly is. It would be a bit much if we called ourselves a Computer Centre and didn't have a link to the web, don't you think? Are you travelling through?'

I hesitated for a second before explaining that in fact I was living just outside the village. At Darne Lodge, if she knew where that was. Everything suddenly seemed very straightforward: I didn't understand why I had been so reticent at The Royal Oak last week. If Mr Tawking wanted to let his house to a foreign woman writer for the whole winter, it was surely not impossible that he might have mentioned it to others, even if he was a miserable old curmudgeon. There was every reason to suppose that my presence up there was well known in the village.

'Oh, so you're the one, are you?' said the woman with a smile. 'I heard that somebody was going to be living there for quite some time. I'm Margaret, by the way . . . Margaret Allen. Welcome to Winsford, the end of the world.'

'Maria. Maria Anderson.'

We shook hands. Castor flopped down onto the floor with a sigh. I took the opportunity to introduce him as well. Margaret knelt down and stroked him over his neck and back. I felt the need to burst into tears, but managed to control it. There were occasions when weeping should be kept under control, even Gudrun Ewerts would agree with that.

'I take it you don't have an internet connection up there,' said Margaret when she stood up again. 'But you can come down here whenever you like. We're usually open between eleven in the morning and six in the evening, but if there's anything urgent you can always knock on the door of that little stone cottage next to the church – it says Biggs on the door. Alfred Biggs and I take it in turns to sit here, and he never says no to anybody, I can promise you that.'

I thanked her and said that I had no urgent need to contact anybody just now, but I would be back in a few days' time.

'Isn't it a bit lonely up there? Forgive me for asking, but . . .'

She burst out laughing, evidently embarrassed by her presumptuousness. 'I speak out of turn. I'm sorry, but we haven't had a single client so far today – most people have a link in their own homes nowadays. It was a bit different when we started this place fifteen years ago. There's been lots of talk about closing it down, but we do get quite a few young people calling in after school. And there are in fact a few families who are still not connected. I don't know if it's because they can't afford it, or for some other reason . . .'

It was obvious that she wanted to talk, and mainly out of politeness I asked if she knew anything about Darne Lodge. When it was built, and why, for instance.

'Oh yes,' said Margaret enthusiastically. 'There's an awful lot to say about Darne Lodge. Didn't old Tawking tell you anything?'

I shook my head.

'No, I don't suppose he would, that old miseryboots. Would you like a cup of tea?'

*

And while we drank tea and ate some biscuits with some black but rather tasty goo evidently called Branston Pickle, I was provided with a fair amount of information about the house I was living in – and would be living in for the best part of six months. I had the impression that despite her comparative youth, Margaret Allen knew more than most about what was what in the village. She also said that both she and her husband were active in the local folklore society, and in addition to her unpaid work at the computer centre she worked as a librarian in Dulverton.

But anyway, Darne Lodge. Well, Margaret recalled that it was built at the beginning of the nineteenth century as the residence of a certain Selwyn Byrnescotte. He was a soldier who returned home as some kind of hero after the Napoleonic wars – the Battle of Trafalgar and two other sea battles that Margaret named, but I didn't recognize. The problem with this Selwyn was that even before he had gone to war he had been disowned by his family – or at least by his father, Lord Neville – on the Byrnescotte estate roughly midway between Winsford and Exford. The background was top secret, but probably had to do with homosexuality. In any case, the Lord had Darne Lodge built so that his decorated but wayward next-oldest son would have somewhere to live (had it been his eldest son, things would have been much more complicated) at a fairly safe distance away from the family seat. However, Selwyn didn't like being isolated on the moor and soon moved to London, where he led a dissolute and debauched life for several years. The war was still raging, but he was unable to return to the battlefield because of some injury or other. He came back to Darne Lodge to die – it was the same year as the Battle of Waterloo – and he hanged himself from one of the roof beams. As a result of his London excesses he also had another serious injury: half his face had been shot away in a duel. Apparently he was not a pretty sight when he was eventually discovered and cut down after several months. Nobody knew that he had returned to Darne Lodge.

I suspected that Castor and I would be spending several hours with Margaret Allen – she didn't leave out many details: but as luck would have it there was a hundred-year gap in the story. After Selwyn Byrnescotte's tragic end, the house stood empty until about 1920 when it was bought by a Londoner who needed somewhere for himself and his household to spend the night while he was out hunting red deer on Exmoor. It was eventually taken over by his son for the same purpose, but after this unfortunate young man – his name was Ralph deBries and he seemed to be of Belgian extraction as far as one could make out – had also committed suicide there, this time with the aid of tablets, the house was sold at auction in 1958 and bought by the father of the current owner, Jeremy Tawking.

Anyway, nobody had died in the house since 1958 – Margaret Allen was careful to stress that fact – and no doubt over two hundred people had been living there as Mr Tawking had been renting it out for at least twenty years. Usually by the week during the summer months, of course, but Margaret recalled that somebody had been living there last winter as well. In any case, it seemed to be well built and insulated, and was able to withstand the winter storms.

I was able to confirm that this was the case. Even if the really hard winter storms hadn't actually occurred yet – an assertion that Margaret agreed with. The worst usually came in January and February.

I thanked her for the tea and the information, and re-affirmed that Castor and I would be turning up again very shortly. Margaret said she suspected she had been too negative about Darne Lodge in some respects, and apologized for going on so long.

We said our goodbyes and left. The walk back up to Wins-ford Hill turned out to be quite difficult, with various gates, herds of bleating sheep and glaring cattle, and when we even-tually came up onto the moor itself we had the wind directly against us all the way to the edge of the Punchbowl, which I could now see, looking at it from this direction, really did look like a crater. Or like the after-effects of a gigantic meteor that had crashed down several thousands of years ago and left behind a hole a hundred metres deep and roughly twice that wide.

Nevertheless, we eventually got home – both Castor and I were equally muddy and exhausted – and even as I opened the garden gate I could see that there was a dead pheasant lying outside the front door.

A magnificent male bird, lying peacefully on its side with its wings and its tail feathers in excellent shape and apparently uninjured.

Apart from the fact that it was dead.

Then Castor did something totally unexpected. He walked slowly up to the bird, sniffed at it from various angles, then carefully grasped it by the head with his teeth. Dragged it gently to one side, just a metre or so, then left it lying there next to the wall.

Then he looked at me, as if to say that it was okay to go in now.

19

In the last-but-one chat show I ever hosted, something happened that I believe was unique in the history of Swedish television.

The theme was quite serious: people who had vanished.

And how family and friends cope with a situation in which somebody has disappeared, and nobody knows what happened. Not even if the missing person is alive or dead.

We had several guests. A psychologist, a woman from the public registration office, a senior police officer who explained how the police deal with missing persons, and three people who had been affected. The latter trio comprised a couple from Västerås whose teenage daughter had been missing without trace for two years, and an elderly woman from Norrland who had reported her husband missing twenty-five years ago.

And there were two of us presenting the programme, to make sure everything went without a hitch. In other words, a normal and carefully planned set-up for twenty-eight minutes of off-peak broadcasting.

The woman from Norrland arrived quite late, just as we had planned. All the others had had their say, and the female half of the pair from Västerås had cried a little. I now turned to Alice, as the new woman was called, and asked her to tell her story. Who was the person who had disappeared from her life?

'Ragnar, my husband,' she said curtly.

'And that was quite a long time ago, I believe?' I said.

'Twenty-five years ago,' said Alice.

'And what were the circumstances when he went missing?'

'Nothing out of the ordinary. It was in the autumn, shortly before the elk-hunting began.'

'And he disappeared from your home, is that right?'

'Yes.'

At this point my male colleague stepped in. He had interviewed Alice on the telephone the previous day, and received a fair amount of information from her.

'When we spoke yesterday you said that he'd gone off on his bike to fetch your newspaper from the post box: is that right?'

'No,' said Alice. 'We'd already collected the paper. He was going to see if there were any letters. It was round about lunch time.'

'And this was twenty-five years ago?' asked my colleague.

'Twenty-five years and one month,' said Alice.

'And you haven't seen him since then?'

'Not since that day, no.'

I intervened: 'So he didn't come back after going to fetch the mail.'

'Oh yes, he came back all right,' said Alice.

I recall that she was wearing a very elegant dress. And high-heeled shoes. Her hair was newly trimmed and dyed in a slightly unusual hue verging on gold. I think I realized that something was about to go wrong, but I couldn't think of anything else to do other than to keep going. I saw a floor-manager holding up two fingers – so there were two minutes' broadcasting time left.

'Are you saying that he did, in fact, come back?' I asked, wondering if I had misunderstood what my colleague had said briefly before the programme.

Alice sat up straight on the sofa and suddenly stared directly at the nearest camera – instead of looking at the person she was talking to, as we had instructed her beforehand, like we did with all our guests.

'Oh yes, he came back all right,' she said again. 'And he's been lying out there in the woodshed ever since.'

For some reason it never occurred to anybody to stop the broadcast.

'Why is he lying in the woodshed?' asked my colleague.

'I killed him with the sledge hammer,' said Alice with something reminiscent of triumph in her voice. 'Then I dragged him into the woodshed and covered him in firewood. I haven't seen him since then. I always fill up with more firewood before he appears.'

Now I realized the seriousness of the situation. Time to cut. I signalled that we would go over to Camera 3 and begin to round off the programme.

'He was an evil person,' our guest from Norrland managed to get in. 'But it's statute-barred now, I can't be prosecuted!'

★

There was quite a hullabaloo after we managed to stop broadcasting – but before that, the very first few seconds, a deathly silence. Everybody was staring at Alice, and it wasn't hard to imagine what was buzzing round in everybody's head.

What exactly had she said?

She had killed her husband.

She had put him in the woodshed and left him there for twenty-five years. And reported him missing.

She had confessed to murder on a live television programme.

Or else she was a madwoman who had succeeded in creating a sensation. How come the programme research hadn't discovered something odd was going on, incidentally?

But then everybody started talking at once. Various studio officials came running up, and the police officer made a call on his mobile. The only person who remained calm in her place on the sofa was Alice. Sitting up straight, with her hands clasped on her knee, she contemplated the chaos on all sides with a slight smile on her lips. Order was restored when the programme's producer came in and announced that we would all assemble in his office for a brief discussion.

The woodshed in question – located on the edge of the village of Sorsele in southern Lappland – was examined by the police the following day. When they dragged out the skeleton of Ragnar Myrman, they tried to keep all the journalists and photographers and nosy parkers at a distance, but there was no chance of that. There were too many of them – a hundred or so – and in the coming weeks Alice Myrman received as much attention in the media as she had evidently aspired to. After interrogating her, the police released her without charges or conditions because, as she had rightly said during her momentous television appearance, the crime was so far in the past that under Swedish law it was now statute-barred.

I met her once again, purely by chance. She was standing in Sergels Torg, Stockholm, handing out leaflets for a Christian organization – The Pure Life. I couldn't resist asking her how things were going for her nowadays: it was three or four years since that memorable evening in the Monkeyhouse.

'I've moved on,' Alice explained. 'I think you should do so as well. Take this – we have a meeting this evening in the City Church.'

She handed me a leaflet, and said that she'd been living in Stockholm for about a year now. She had become too much of a celebrity to stay on in Sorsele, she maintained, and since she had met Jesus – and the pastor in charge of the organization, to whom she was now married – her life had taken on a deeper meaning.

She thanked me from the bottom of her heart for allowing her to take part in that television programme. If she hadn't had the opportunity to tell all and sundry the truth about what had happened to Ragnar, this miracle would never have taken place.

'Never give up,' was the last thing she said to me. 'When things are at their worst and you are walking through the valley of the shadow of death, He is with you, and He will comfort you.'

Her eyes were blazing. I have often thought about her. Especially lately, this last month, since we were walking into the wind on that Baltic beach in Poland and my life branched off in a new direction.

About what it must feel like behind blazing eyes like those.

How she must have felt as she sat there on the television sofa, waiting for her turn to speak.

20

The ninth of November. Ten degrees at half past eight. Grey and misty when we went for our morning walk, but an hour later the sun had broken through. Nevertheless I've decided to stay here working until noon, and then we'll go for a walk by the sea if the weather holds.

When I write 'working', what I mean is reading the material from Samos and Morocco. I have the feeling that we really must make progress with that: I don't know where that feeling comes from, but perhaps it's just a little splinter under a fingernail that one has to get rid of. I've been reading so much Dickens these last couple of days that he can wait his turn now. I've put the packs of playing cards back in the drawer where I found them.

So I made another cup of coffee and sat down by the window with the diary from that first summer on Samos. Bit the head off every feeling of doubt and uncertainty, and started reading. Make decisions and stick to them . . . When Eugen Bergman gets in touch it will be as well if Martin has at least some idea of what he's been doing.

Three hours later I'd got as far as 1 August 1977. There is a week left before he is due to return to Sweden, and it's possible that all kinds of things will happen then. Martin is still writing in his restrained, neutral style – as if he thinks that one day somebody else will read the text, probably a young woman with intellectual ambitions. I can't help having that impression, nor can I help it that here and there some things that he writes are impossible to understand. But it is only occasional words, nothing of significance for the meaning overall.

The most important thing that happened towards the end of July – and there is no need to read between the lines in order to understand this – is that he pays a visit to the Herold/ Hyatt house. It is not just Martin, but the whole of the so-called writers' collective, and it evidently turns out to be quite an impressive occasion. There are about twenty people present, and they eat a succession of fancy Greek dishes prepared by the staff at the nearby taverna, who also act as waiters and waitresses, at least at the beginning of the festivities. The guests sit at a long table on the terrace with views over the pine-clad hillside and the sea. There is guitar- and bouzouki-playing, singing, poems are read in every language you can think of, animated discussions take place, a manifesto written and masses of wine drunk. 'Retsina,' Martin goes out of his way to stress, 'that's the only drinkable wine you can get down here.' He writes that it is absolutely blooming magical, and he's not referring to the wine. Marijuana is also smoked, but not by Martin.

The reason – if there needed to be a reason – for Herold and Hyatt inviting all the guests to their house is that the first reactions to Bessie's debut novel have started flowing in. There is still a week or so to go before the book is due to be published in the USA, but her publisher has informal contacts and can already inform Bessie that the reviews are going to be brilliant. Not to say sensational. Tom Herold gives a speech in praise of his young wife, and declares facetiously that a year from now he will be forgotten, but Bessie Hyatt will be as resplendent as a modern-day Pheme on the uppermost pinnacle of Parnassus.

Those are the exact words that Martin wrote, and then he comments that the choice of that particular goddess is rather odd. Pheme is above all the goddess of scurrilous gossip in Greek mythology: he points out that he seems to be the only person present who reflects on that fact, and that he will take the matter up with Herold in due course. In any case, he adds, Bessie doesn't seem to have taken the reference amiss. On the other hand, she may well not be familiar with all the details of the ancient Greek gods and goddesses. But Martin is.

The party continues until dawn. Martin writes that he eventually joins a little group discussing Cavafy, and Durrell's *Alexandria Quartet*. These learned discussions seem to go on for ever – with the Russian Gusov sitting in a corner and annoying everybody with his ignorance; also present are the two lesbian artists and the French poets Legel and Fabrianny. Plus the cheerful Nietzsche specialist Bons. Martin devotes over two pages to the comments and points of view expressed in these discussions, and concludes his account of this long day and night by describing how a group of eight or ten persons trudge down to the beach and bathe naked as dawn breaks. He notes once again that it is absolutely blooming magical, but then crosses the phrase out when he realizes that it is a repetition.

He also writes – in the same unemotional style – about an outing a few days later to a place called Ormos Marathokambos, if I've managed to decipher the spelling correctly. A trip undertaken on four Vespas. There is a driver and a passenger on each of the scooters, and on the way back home he has the one and only Bessie Hyatt sitting behind him. By now her book has appeared, and the reception was just as overwhelming as her publishing contacts had predicted. In a week she will fly over to the USA for a PR tour. Martin writes that 'he drives along the dusty country road towards the setting sun with the young American genius's arms around his waist,' and that it makes him feel 'remarkably exhilarated'. Good God! I think: but that's exactly what he put.

It is not clear whether Herold was also present on the outing. I decide to save the last ten pages, the rest of the notes about 1977, until the evening, load Castor into the car and set off for a different sea.

We took the attractive route via Simonsbath again, and before we got to Lynmouth we stopped at a place called Watersmeet. We clambered down some steep steps into a deep ravine dug out by the River Lyn: the village gets its name from the fact that it is at the confluence of the West Lyn and East Lyn rivers. I was feeling irritated, thanks to reading Martin's confounded diary. I kept trying to tell myself that it was about happenings thirty-five years ago, and that it was the year before we first met: but it didn't really work. He was twenty-four years old that first summer in Samos, and he ought not to have written like a pretentious grammar school pupil. Is this what he had sounded like when we sat together at that party in Gamla Stan? I couldn't believe that was the case. Or perhaps we were different people at that time, both of us. If I had been able to read these notes then, what impression would I have got? Would I have fallen for them? Would I have even considered marrying him? How much did Rolf's death and my general state of fragility mean for my decision? For my life?

Good questions, I thought as I wandered along with Castor under the green arches of the trees lining the cheerfully babbling brook. There it came again, the *cheerfully babbling* brook, but it didn't give me the same degree of satisfaction on this occasion. Not by a long way. There seem to be moments when one feels in harmony with Jane Austen and the Brontë sisters, but this was not one of them. At the same time, however, there was something inside me that was rather pleased by my irritation. When had I last felt irritated? Not during the past month, in any case; perhaps not for six months. If I were to dress up the situation in a way reminiscent of that twenty-four-year-old I didn't want to think about, I could perhaps maintain that a pile of rotten old junk had been set alight in a forgotten corner of my comatose soul – and there was good reason to feel gratitude for that: something had awoken.

Be that as it may, we walked quite a long way along the bank of one of the two rivers, and when we came to a bridge after about forty minutes we crossed over it and wandered along the opposite bank back to Watersmeet. We climbed up the steep steps to the road and the car, and drove to the little seaside town of Lynmouth.

We had a late lunch at one of the pubs down by the harbour without speaking to a single soul. We bought a few essentials in the neighbouring town of Lynton, including a pair of Wellington boots, then returned home over the moor to Darne Lodge.

A day in the life, I thought once again. I read the old diaries of my husband, who is probably dead. I go for a walk with my dog. I buy a few essentials.

Before long I shall regard cutting my nails or brushing my teeth as an event of significance.

I tried to rekindle my irritation once more – it seemed to have been blown away by the wind. As I had enjoyed it – the irritation, that is – and as it had no doubt been caused by the Samos diary from 1977, I decided to continue reading it. The rest of that first summer. Then a few chapters of Dickens, four games of patience, and then bed.

I duly did all that, and when I was about to let Castor out for his final evening walk, I noticed something lying there just outside the door. It was that dead pheasant again.

Or possibly another one, but just as dead. I dropped the glass I was holding in my hand, it shattered as it hit the stone paving, and I realized that once again I had forgotten to buy that torch.

21

The tenth of November. Cloudy with sunny intervals and a strong wind from the south-west. Eleven degrees in the morning. I took the dead pheasant with us in a plastic carrier bag when we went for our morning walk, and threw it into a clump of thorn bushes on the way to the Roman remains at the top of Winsford Hill. I tried not to think about it – the pheasant, not the Roman monument – but it was not easy. How come that it had ended up outside my door twice? I had convinced myself that it was the same bird, in fact. Some animal must have dragged it there, I thought – on the second occasion at least, at some time yesterday evening. But what animal? There are presumably foxes around here even if I haven't seen one, but why would a fox kill a pheasant and then leave it completely untouched?

Another bird? Various birds of prey soar overhead on the moor, but even if I don't know much about their habits it didn't seem very likely. Birds don't attack other birds, surely? Not in that way, at least.

A person? I dismissed the thought.

Instead, as I struggled into the powerful headwind with Castor hard on my heels, I began thinking about that face in the window. The pale young man and the gesture he had made over his throat. What had he actually meant by that? The significance in itself was obvious enough, of course – but in this case? Was it some sort of bizarre joke? Was there an intention behind it? Something serious? Who was he? Perhaps a madman who lived in that isolated house and made the same gesture to everybody he saw? Or at least, everybody who walked past his home: there were presumably not very many who did.

I also thought about the two deaths that had taken place in Darne Lodge. Two suicides with more than a hundred years between them. Irrespective of how many normal people had lived in the house since the latest act of self-destruction, it felt macabre. But on the other hand, wasn't every aspect of my stay here macabre? Perhaps that wasn't the right word, but something like that in any case. Something on its way out of the real world. But then, where exactly is the borderline between what we call real and what we call unreal? I had only slept in that house for eight nights by this time, and already I was beginning to experience . . . well, what exactly?

Some sort of menace? Something warning of danger, something telling me that if I wasn't careful I would find myself in a right mess?

Rubbish, I thought. Figments of the imagination.

Then again, what had I expected? I had divested myself of my old life on that Polish beach: I had put an end to it just as conclusively as one breaks a bone off a chicken. Absolutely everything had changed, nothing was the same as before. Isn't that the fact of the matter? If you wanted, you could argue that it was Martin who had set everything in motion when he raped that waitress in the hotel in Gothenburg – or left his sperm on her stomach, at least. What I did in the bunker had simply been a natural reaction, albeit a bit on the late side, albeit a bit drastic and very much unplanned – something done in a flash, as they say. But nevertheless one thing had led to another, and there was a clearly linked series of causes and effects for the left side of the brain to revel in . . . Yes indeed, there was a lot that one could maintain and think about in the back of one's mind, surrounded by this open, peaceful moorland with bracken, cheerful-looking gorse and surly-looking heather, mud, grass and wild ponies: but when all was said and done, the biggest problem, the distressing point, was my own mind which simply couldn't calm down and rest. Couldn't stop producing all these words and half-baked analyses, futile and would-be wise, non-stop, every day, every hour and every minute until at the predestined moment my heart stopped pumping oxygen-laden blood into these highly overrated rantings.

The real world, I thought. I need some kind of context, otherwise I shall succumb unnecessarily. A dog isn't enough.

And so I made up my mind to visit the Winsford Computer Centre during the afternoon. What had Margaret Allen said? Between eleven in the morning and six in the evening?

It was Alfred Biggs who was on duty. He was a mousy little man wearing clothes that were too big for him. As if he had shrunk after buying them, or inherited them from an older brother who had died in some war or other a long time ago. His spectacles with black plastic frames were also too big: I had the impression that he was trying to hide behind them, and that his smile was shy and somewhat introverted.

'You must be that writer,' he said when we had introduced ourselves. 'Margaret told me about you.'

'Is she not here today, then?'

'No, Saturdays are mine. Margaret only works here two days a week. She works at the library in Dulverton as well.'

I nodded. 'Yes, she said that.'

'But I live more or less next door. I'm retired, so I have all the time in the world.'

'I'm pleased that I can come here occasionally – I don't have an internet connection where I'm living.'

'You're always welcome. That's the point of this place. If we're not open, all you need to do is to knock on my door – that red one just round the corner.'

He pointed in the direction of the church.

'So this is Castor, is it?'

Castor heard his name and stretched his nose out towards Alfred Biggs, who stroked him cautiously on the head. He smiled again, and I tried to assess it. There was something odd about his teeth. Something his lips did their best to conceal. He showed me where I could sit, and asked if I would like a cup of tea. Just like the previous occasion, there was nobody else in the room; I accepted and made a mental note to bring with me some sort of biscuits the next time I came.

When I had received my cup, I sat down to check our

e-mails – first mine, and then Martin's. Alfred went back to his book. Castor settled down under my table.

There was only one message in my inbox. Katarina Wunsch. The title was: *London?* I swallowed, then opened it.

> Hi there Maria! Something very odd happened a few weeks ago when my husband and I were in London, and I really must ask you about it, no beating about the bush. We met a woman in Hyde Park and I was quite certain it was you. We said hello but she spoke English and said it was some kind of mistake. It was very awkward. My husband and I talked about it afterwards, and I simply can't get it out of my head. Was it really not you? It feels so odd – forgive me if I'm being presumptuous. Love, Katarina.

I don't know how she had got hold of my new e-mail address, but I assume she'd got it from the Monkeyhouse. I don't know how easy or difficult it is to find out information like that, but in any case I thought it over for quite a while before writing the following reply:

> Hi Katarina! Great to hear from you, it's been ages since the last time. But I really have no idea who that woman might have been. One thing is clear, of course: it wasn't me. Martin and I have been down here in Morocco for quite a while now. He's busy with some writing project or other as usual, and I've accompanied him mainly in order to avoid a Swedish winter. We'll be staying here until May next year. I hope all is well with you and yours – let me know if you bump into me again! Love, Maria.

I hesitated for a while before writing that last sentence, but thought I might as well demonstrate that I was taking it light-heartedly. I sent it off and went over to Martin's inbox.

Seven new messages. Four from people who were presumably colleagues of one kind or another, brief messages not requiring an answer – not immediately, at least. One was from a student complaining about the mark he had been given for an essay: it was several pages long, I'd had more than enough after about half of it and trashed it.

The two remaining messages were from Eugen Bergman and from G. I waited with G and read what Bergman had to say – I needed to write to him today as I hadn't replied to his previous message.

> My dear friend, I hope you have arrived safely and that everything comes up to expectations. Stockholm is grey and miserable: I must say I'm a bit envious of you. Any old halfwit should be able to cobble together something readable while spending winter in a nice warm place like the one you two have ended up in. The only news from the publishing world is that we've got our furry-gloved hands on a couple of so-called celebrity memoirs – an ice hockey legend and a reformed murderer – but they're not the kind of thing you'd want to hear more about.
>
> Do keep me informed: if nothing else let me know that all is going to plan.
>
> All the best, Eugen B.
>
> PS – by the way, some woman by the name of Gertrud something-or-other is keen to get in touch with you. Can I give her your e-mail address?

Before replying I tried to trace some previous messages Martin had sent to his publisher, but as I was doing everything via the internet this wasn't possible. Old messages are kept for such a short time, and as usual I hadn't taken our own computers with me this time either. Anyway, I bashed out a few lines to Bergman to say that we had indeed arrived, that all was well and that he didn't need to worry. I was writing six to eight hours every day, and everything was proceeding as it should. The nearest town of any size was Rabat. I also said he was welcome to give my e-mail address to Gertrud, and that I thought I knew who she was.

When I was satisfied with this basic stuff and had sent it off, I opened the message from G.

> Where are you? What are you up to? No reply to my last
> message, it's a week and I'm getting frustrated. Please
> contact me. ASAP. G

ASAP? That meant 'as soon as possible', unless I was much mistaken.

'*What are you up to?*'

I felt a little bit worried, but just then two young girls came in through the door. They greeted Alfred Biggs politely, glanced at me and Castor, then each of them sat down at a computer with their backs towards us. Alfred Biggs got up and went to help them with something.

I took a drink of my tea, and tried to concentrate. Stared at G's message and did my best to convince myself that there was no need to worry. Without much success. I cursed the time we lived in, when it was possible for people to contact each other whenever they felt like it, no matter where they were in the world and what the circumstances were. And that people seemed to think they had a right to expect a reply no matter what. That you could contact anybody at all and demand a response more or less immediately.

And that you could even do so anonymously. Things used to be different, I thought. In the old days you could batter somebody to death in Säffle or Surahammar, or indeed in both those places, and then escape to Eslöv where nobody would be able to find you.

No doubt this G wasn't anonymous as far as Martin was concerned, but that didn't make the situation any easier. There was no mistaking the threat in the background, and if I didn't reply it would presumably only make matters worse.

Or was I making a wrong judgement? I went back and looked at G's previous message.

> I fully understand your doubts. This is no ordinary cup of tea. Contact me so that we can discuss the matter in closer detail. Have always felt an inkling that this would surface one day. Best, G

That was hardly any less worrying. I sat there thinking and trying to formulate something for at least twenty minutes before managing to produce the following response:

> No worries. Everything is fine, trust me. I am off to a secret place to work for six months. Will not read my e-mail on a regular basis. M

I sent it off, and just after my index finger had pressed the send-key – or perhaps just as I was doing so – I had a sudden impression of having done something rather different. That it was not a question of a centimetre-square button on a key-board, but the trigger of a gun. It was such a totally surprising and disorientating image that for a few seconds I was not sure whether or not I was awake.

But then one of the girls laughed in front of her computer screen, and everything rapidly became normal again. Castor raised his head, looked at me and yawned. I switched off the computer and resolved to steer well clear of all inboxes for at least a week.

Just as I was about to leave the premises something occurred to me. I turned to Alfred Biggs and asked if he was well acquainted with Winsford and its surroundings.

'I certainly think I can claim that,' he said with his usual faint smile. 'I wasn't born here, but I've lived here for nearly forty years. Why do you ask?'

I hesitated for a moment, but couldn't see that there was anything presumptuous in what I had in mind.

'It's just that I went past a house the other day, along the path that goes from the top of Winsford Hill down into the village – on the other side of Halse Lane, that is – and I saw a boy, or maybe a young man, standing in a window. A few hundred metres before you get to the pub – do you know which house I'm talking about?'

'Just below the waterfall?'

'Yes.'

'An old, dreary-looking stone house standing all by itself?'

'Yes.'

He sighed. 'Ah yes. You must be referring to Heathercombe Cottage. It belongs to Mark Britton, poor chap.'

'Mark . . . ?'

'Mark Britton, yes. He lives there with his son. It's a sad story, but I don't want to spread gossip.'

He fell silent, evidently feeling that he had said too much already. If he didn't want to spread gossip. I hesitated once again, but decided not to ask any more questions. Not to allow Pheme her say here as well. Instead I thanked him for the tea and the internet and said I would no doubt be putting in an appearance again a week or so from now.

'Remember that you only need to knock on my door if there's nobody here,' he said again. 'The red door, with the name Biggs on a plate.'

I promised not to forget. And so Castor and I left the Winsford Computer Centre with another question mark in our pockets.

Mark Britton, poor chap?

22

'I think we ought to talk a bit about Rolf. What do you think would have happened to the pair of you if he hadn't died?'

A year or so had passed. We had a nanny for Gunvald, and Synn was on a waiting list for a day nursery place. I had started working again, and generally met Gudrun Ewerts on Thursday evenings at her surgery near Norra Bantorget.

'Rolf? I don't know . . . Why should we talk about him?'

'If he hadn't had that accident and died when he did your life would have been quite different. Do you never think about that?'

I thought for a moment, and realized that I had occasionally thought along those lines, but decided that life was life. 'Of course,' I said. 'But isn't that always the way it is? If this or that hadn't happened, things would have been different . . .'

'That's not what I was wondering about. Did you have visions?'

'Visions?'

'Yes. Did you sometimes imagine you and Rolf having a family? Having children, and living together for the rest of your lives?'

'Yes . . . No . . . I don't know. I don't see the point of dragging this up.'

Gudrun leaned back in her soft leather armchair and her face took on that expression indicating she had something important to say. That it was time for me to sit up and take notice. I had had a long working day – perhaps she was assessing my ability to cope with things. She clasped her hands under her chin as well: that was usually a definite sign.

'It's because this is a characteristic of yours that it worries me. You have no vision of your future.'

'No vision of my future?'

'No. You sometimes give the impression of not caring about your future, and I think that has been the case for a very long time.'

I thought again, and said that I didn't really understand what she was talking about.

'I think you do,' said Gudrun. 'It has to do with the way you switch off. That was how you reconciled yourself to the death of your sister, and that was how you managed to survive Rolf's death. And those of your parents. What you really felt on each and every one of these occasions when somebody close to you died was so overwhelming that you couldn't cope with it. But when you switch off your emotions you unfortunately short-circuit other things that you ought to continue dealing with. Would you say that you love your husband, for instance?'

'I beg your pardon?'

'I asked if you love Martin.'

'Of course I love him. What has that got to do with it?'

'Do you keep telling him you do?'

'Of course. Well . . . no.'

'Do you often cry?'

'You know that I don't often cry.'

'Yes. And I also know that you ought to do so.'

'Wouldn't it be better to laugh?'

Gudrun smiled, but soon became stern again. 'If you can't do one, you can't do the other. Not properly. But you're extremely good when it comes to smiling on the television.'

I said nothing for a while, and she waited for my next move. The intention was that I should become angry, that was part of her method and I understood that; but I felt too tired to offer her any resistance on this occasion.

'Why did you want us to talk about Rolf?' I asked eventually.

'Because I'm interested in when it started.'

'Really?'

'If it was there before he came along. If it began with your little sister, perhaps.'

We sat there in silence again, and I suddenly felt an urgent need to burst into tears. But I also knew that she was right: it was buried so deep down inside me that I couldn't possibly get near to it. An iceberg of tears.

'I cried a year ago,' I said. 'When I had my depression. When you began treating me.'

Gudrun nodded. 'I know. And it passed after two weeks. Think now: have you ever cried again since then?'

I suddenly felt most unwell. There was a sort of suppressed panic inside me that was trying to break out, like an itch in a leg in plaster, and it was stuck so fast underneath that iceberg that all I could do was to grit my teeth and confirm that she was quite right.

'Not that I can remember,' I said.

We talked about a lot of things during those years, Gudrun Ewerts and I. About Göran, for instance, my brother, and my relationship with him. Why hadn't we supported one another when our little sister died? she wondered. Why hadn't the family closed ranks and mourned as a unit? Why had my mother and my father slowly succumbed, one after the other?

They were horrendous questions. Gudrun wondered if I was scared of the answers, and that was why I preferred to keep them under wraps. I said I didn't know, and she suggested that perhaps it was the *imagined* answers that I was afraid of. By now I already had a considerable collection of dead bodies in my emotional baggage – but it had all begun with just one. Isn't that the case? she asked. *Isn't that the case?*

I said yes, of course it was. It had begun with Bengt-Olov the Football Star backing his bus over Gunsan in that car park, and since . . . well, since something like that could happen in just a second, then . . . then goodness knows what else could happen in the same way. Just as quickly and with just as little warning. You could lose your grip and fall off a cliff face, for instance. Darkness and death were lurking on all sides, she knew that as well as I did, and asking unpleasant questions simply created openings for them to force their way through.

Was that how I saw the circumstances in the lives we live?

my therapist wondered. Was that why I was unable to lift up the lid and look more closely at the relationship between me and my brother, if we were to restrict ourselves to that particular question for the time being?

'I sometimes find it more or less impossible to listen to your exaggerations,' I recall protesting on one occasion when we were discussing such matters. 'You are fishing in murky psychological waters. Göran and I are very different fish, and you'll never be able to catch us using the same hook. The fact is that some siblings simply are that different.'

The imagery was nothing special, but I sometimes tried to counter-attack her in that way and Gudrun always used to smile at my faux pas.

'I'll tell you what I think, in order to save some time,' she said on another occasion. 'One shouldn't really take this kind of shortcut in therapeutics – after all, it's the patient who should find the answers, discover them deep down inside and all that . . . But I wonder if the basic fact is simply that you loved your little sister above all else, and that after she was snatched away from you, you have never dared to love anybody else. Not in the whole of your life. You just haven't dared to take the risk.'

'That sounds rather banal to me,' I said.

'Who on earth has ever suggested that life isn't banal?' asked Gudrun Ewerts.

We never got very far in questions associated with my family relationships. They cropped up, we talked about them, I agreed that there could well be a fair amount of truth in her suggestions – but even if that was the case I had no idea what I could do about it now, so long afterwards. She pointed out, of course – the way therapists do – that we needed to sort out the past in order to cope with the present, and that it was essential if I was going to be able to deal rather more successfully with crises in the future. My post-natal depression was a clear sign, but I was the only one who could decide whether I was going to take it seriously or not. Surely I wasn't so naive that I thought this was the last of the crises?

And so on . . . Towards the end of our conversations, the last three or four months, we only met every other week, and Gudrun admitted that our sessions were beginning to be reminiscent of chats between old friends rather than some kind of therapy. Old friends who had different points of view on some matters, and who liked to discuss them now and again in congenial circumstances.

'I can't accept payment from you any longer,' she said at our last meeting. 'It would be unethical.'

We didn't meet again after that. Those friends with the different points of view went their different ways, and I assume that's the way it is as far as therapists are concerned. They meet people who have lost their footing, help them back to their feet, support them, then take the props away – it can take time, months and years, but when it's over the patient staggers off and the therapist goes to the waiting room where other lost souls are sitting and suffering.

I could have done with Gudrun Ewerts after that business with Magdalena Svensson at the hotel in Gothenburg, I know that. But she died at the beginning of 2006; I actually attended her funeral. There were at least three hundred people in the church, and I wondered how many of them were former patients.

Anyway, I have thought quite a lot about my relationship with Göran, my elder brother: that was a button Gudrun often pressed. If siblings don't have much in the way of contact when they are young, they are not going to have much when they are grown up: that is not exactly a contentious conclusion. And when I occasionally manage to transport myself back to my young days, to the feelings and moods that might well have possessed me at that time, they are as elusive and unreliable as feverish dreams; but if I try to penetrate them even so, all these years later, the only conclusion I can draw is that I didn't like him. No, I didn't love my elder brother, I really didn't.

But that is all there was to it. There is nothing more sinister behind it, he never did me any harm, he never bullied me. He was just irrelevant to me. Presumably because I was irrelevant to him. I have no special memories of him, nothing we did together, nothing he said on a particular occasion, nothing at all. He was present more or less like those distant relatives who usually appear on the fringe of old family photographs. He was always there, he was always in the vicinity, but nothing he ever said or did or got up to is preserved in my memory. I realize that it is a bit remarkable. Perhaps it is even *most* remarkable, which is what Gudrun always used to say.

Anyway, nowadays he is a secondary school teacher with two children and a wife he will never leave. She might leave him, but I don't think that will happen either. In May, when those headlines had started appearing, he telephoned me and stressed that I knew where to find him if I needed him.

He rang again when Magdalena Svensson withdrew her allegations of rape, and expressed the relief of both himself and his family.

That was a bit much.

It's understandable that Martin and Göran have never had much to say to each other. We celebrated Christmas twice with his family when the children were small, once at our place and once at theirs.

The experiment was never repeated.

And if Rolf hadn't died? If I'd never become pregnant with Gunvald? I don't know, how could I know?

When I ask myself just what it is that has gone so wrong, I can find no answers. Perhaps it's just that things were meant to be that way. Maybe it's as simple as that. Martin once said that the main reason why human beings have been provided with such big hearts is so that they can feel unhappy.

I contemplate Castor as he lies stretched out in front of the fire and think that on that point – for once – I'm inclined to think that my husband was right.

23

The seventeenth of November. Eight degrees. Rain and wind in the morning.

Several days have passed now. And more especially nights, as it's getting darker. Light can't manage more than eight hours per day in these parts at this time of year, while darkness holds sway for sixteen.

It's the anniversary of Gun's death. I sat for a while with a burning candle this morning, thinking about her. It all seemed very distant, almost an old illusion. I don't know if I really remember her now, or if it's no more than images of my remembering her in the past. Copies of copies.

Anyway, I have begun to settle down into a sort of rhythm. The good thing about habits is that as you follow them, you don't have to make decisions. We go for a walk every morning, Castor and I, either southwards towards Dulverton or northwards, up towards the Punchbowl and the abandoned stone quarry. If it's not too windy we sometimes go on up to Wambarrows, the highest point of this part of the moor – 426 metres above sea level, according to the map – where those scanty, overgrown Roman remains are to be found.

But we don't normally go such a long way before breakfast;

instead we save the longer walks until the early afternoons. Often two hours or more. The other day, for instance, we went as far as the remarkable church in Culbone: St Beuno's, named after a Welsh saint from the seventh century. It is said to be the smallest parish church in the whole of England, and it is hidden away among dense greenery close to a waterfall in a place where you wouldn't expect to find any buildings at all. It took us an hour to get there: we started from Porlock Weir on the coast, and followed the path tended by the National Trust, which runs alongside more or less the whole of the coast of Somerset, Devon and Cornwall. Incidentally, it was somewhere in Culbone parish that Samuel Coleridge wrote his poem *Kubla Kahn* – after an evening spent high on opium, according to legend – and if Martin had been with us we would no doubt have spent several hours looking for the farm where the great poet spent that remarkable night.

A bit further inland is Doone Valley, where we have also explored quite a lot and visited pubs in all three of the old villages Oare, Brendon and Malmesmead. A woman and her dog: we are welcome wherever we go. I have also succumbed to temptation and bought R. D. Blackmore's *Lorna Doone – a Romance of Exmoor* and started reading it instead of Dickens, despite the fact that I'm only halfway through *Bleak House*. *Lorna Doone* is a must, I was told by the hundred-year-old lady in the antiquarian bookshop in Dulverton: you can't possibly live on Exmoor for more than a week without starting to read John Ridd's 'A simple tale told simply'.

So when we get back home after the day's excursion, irrespective of which muddy paths we have been plodding along, we spend a few hours in the late seventeenth century: it feels remarkably close, in contrast to my dear departed sister. I have no difficulty in imagining the lives and motives of John Ridd and Lorna Doone, no difficulty at all. But as I don't have a television set and have very little idea of what is happening in the world out there, time takes on a different character. Dawn-daylight-dusk-night; minutes and hours become more important than days and years. There is an old radio in the cottage, but I've only tried once to switch it on – and found myself tuned into a station reproducing something strikingly scratchy by Elgar, that was all.

Cooking has been somewhat neglected, I must admit. This last week I have had dinner at The Royal Oak in the village three evenings out of seven. I'm already regarded as a regular there: Rosie or Tom always go out of their way to bid me welcome, Castor always gets a saucer of treats, and the few customers who are already there when we arrive – usually Henry, always Robert, and two evenings out of four an elderly gentleman whose name I don't know who is disabled and has his Permobil parked outside the entrance – all smile at me and wish me good evening and comment that the weather has got worse.

I've got into the habit of taking with me Martin's notes from Samos when I go to The Royal Oak. Doing so no doubt confirms my status as a woman writer. I sit at my usual table, eat away and concentrate hard on my reading while Castor snoozes at my feet. It's not a difficult role to play, either for me or for him, and the others leave us in peace. I feel that I am respected and I always drink two glasses of red wine, not enough to prevent me from driving back up Halse Lane through the autumnal darkness. I think I have managed to create around me an appropriately protective layer of egocentricity. We get home between a quarter to ten and ten, and I always switch off the bedside lamp before eleven.

I read a bit of the Samos material in the mornings as well, and as I write this I'm within a few days of finishing the second book, describing the summer of 1978. I don't like it.

It's about the month after I met Martin in Stockholm's Gamla Stan, and it's possible that the increasing unease I feel as I read it has to do with this fact. It is before our life together began, but I recall thinking back to the garden party and that man Martin Holinek during the summer that followed. I'm sure I never imagined things would progress so far that we would get married and have children, but I had the feeling that there would be some kind of continued contact. However, I am never mentioned in *Samos, June–July 1978*: but there are references to lots of other women.

For the first time he admits in writing that he has had sex with somebody. With two women, in fact, about a week apart. One is called Heather and is a 'red-haired Celtic nymph'; the other is American and is simply referred to as 'Bell'. The intercourse is described in roughly the same tone as a Vespa ride to Ormos to buy groceries, or a discussion of receptivity aesthetics with a Danish philosopher by the name of Bjerre-Hansen.

But what makes me feel uneasy is neither the intercourse

nor the receptivity aesthetics. It is something else, something that isn't actually mentioned.

Or perhaps it is just imagination, I can't be sure yet. I have two diaries left to read, plus the typewritten material and what is on the computer; but I have no idea what Martin had in mind when he told Bergman that he was sitting on material such that anybody would go down on their knees in order to get permission to publish it.

Well, perhaps I do have a suspicion: but I don't dare to spell it out yet.

Anyway, his Norwegian friend Finn Halvorsen – the one who originally told Martin about the collective on Samos – has turned up this second summer, and they spend quite a lot of time together. In the middle of July Tadeusz Soblewski from Gdansk also puts in an appearance: he is a poet, a doctor of philosophy and the editor of a literary magazine, and he soon becomes a highly rated participant in conversations. These three – Martin, Finn and Soblewski – are also invited to private get-togethers at Tom Herold's and Bessie Hyatt's house, on more than one occasion, and I have the impression that they are forming a sort of inner circle. That would include those mentioned – including Hyatt and Herold of course – plus the two German women writers, Doris Guttmann and Gisela Fromm.

Holinek, Soblewski and Halvorsen. Guttmann and Fromm, Herold and Hyatt, yes, those are the ones. Plus Gusov: the annoying Russian muscles in on the get-togethers, and they evidently find it difficult to get rid of him. Martin writes that he can't understand why Herold persists in tolerating him.

But he doesn't have sex with Doris or Gisela – or at least, he writes nothing about any such activity. They like to sunbathe in the nude – but then all German do, is all he says.

On one occasion, and as far as I can ascertain it is the only time, he finds himself alone with Bessie Hyatt. It's only for an hour, but he devotes four pages to that hour. One doesn't need to be an exegete in order to understand why.

They go for a short walk together. Bessie Hyatt is going in search of a certain herb that grows quite some way up the mountainside, and Martin goes along to keep her company. He never mentions which herb they are looking for, but he describes Bessie's movements as 'her girlish enthusiasm', and her mop of long hair fluttering in the evening breeze is described as 'a sail that has finally caught sight again of its Ithaca'. On the way back home, with a bunch of herbs in each hand, Bessie treads awkwardly on a stone and twists her ankle: Martin has to support her during the rest of the walk. When they return to the terrace darkness is falling and lanterns have been lit; Herold and Gusov are involved in a game of chess which is apparently a fight to the death. Whoever loses must drink three glasses of ouzo without blinking.

And Doris and Gisela are singing a Cohen song, accompanied on the guitar by Finn Halvorsen.

'Sisters of Mercy'.

It was not until this evening that Mark Britton turned up again at The Royal Oak. I have just left there, I can't get to sleep, and that's why I'm sitting here writing this. I had just been served my starter, grilled salmon with capers – it has become a favourite of mine – when he came into the room, and just as on the previous occasion I was reminded of my old religious studies teacher, Wallinder. I seem to recall that the similarity occurred to me later rather than at the time, but in any case the impression was even stronger this evening, due to the fact that he'd had his hair cut. Mark seemed more neat and tidy than I remember him looking, and Wallinder was always neat and tidy to his very fingertips. I remember his name now.

He caught sight of me immediately, gave me a friendly smile and hesitated for a moment. Then he came over to my table, and asked if I was busy working or whether he might join me. I felt grateful for the fact that he hadn't gone to sit somewhere else. It was more than a week since I'd had something that could be called a conversation with another person: Alfred Biggs at the Winsford Community Computer Centre, and to be honest that hadn't been much of a conversation either.

'Of course you may. Please sit down.'

'You're sure I won't be preventing you from enjoying your meal?'

'Of course not. Are you going to eat as well?'

He said that he was; and then he added that he was pleased to see me here again. I explained that I was now in the habit of sitting here most evenings, but I hadn't seen him since that last time.

He shrugged, and gestured towards my notebook, which I had closed when my starter was served. 'So you work even when you're eating, do you?'

'Revising and checking,' I said apologetically, and he nodded seriously as if he knew what I was talking about. As if he had seen into my mind again. He stroked Castor, then went over to Rosie at the bar and placed his order. I finished my salmon and realized that I was feeling a bit nervous. I assumed it was because of that face in the window, but wasn't sure. Nevertheless, I took up the matter when he came and sat down again.

'I think I walked past your house the other day.'

He looked at me in surprise. I noticed that he was wearing the same pullover as last time, but with a lighter coloured shirt underneath it. His eyes were the same shade as his jumper, and I thought I could detect a trace of unease in them.

'You don't say. And how do you know it was my house?'

I suddenly felt in a bit of a quandary. Ought I to explain that it was Alfred Biggs who had told me? Admit that I'd been talking to him about the face in the window?

'It's a bit further up the hill towards Halse Farm, isn't it?' I asked by way of diversion. 'There's a path going past it from the part of the moor where I'm living, and we walked along it one morning. Castor and I. I must say . . .'

'What must you say?'

'I must say it's very beautifully situated. And . . . remote.'

He didn't repeat his question about how I knew it was his house, and I was grateful for that.

'That's true,' was all he said. 'We live there, Jeremy and I.'

'Jeremy?'

'My son.'

I wondered if I ought to mention that I had seen him, but Mark had suddenly become subdued, as if he had no wish to talk about his personal circumstances. Or at least as if he were wondering whether he ought to. I had a clear memory of Alfred Biggs saying that it was 'a sad story', and began regretting the fact that I had said anything at all about the house. I felt that I had been tactless, and that it was because I was becoming increasingly unused to talking to other people.

But then he cleared his throat, leaned forward over the table and lowered his voice.

'If I tell you a bit about my personal circumstances, can I reckon on something similar from you in return?'

'If you start the ball rolling,' I said without giving myself time to think it over. 'So you live alone with your son, do you? How old is he?'

'Yes, Jeremy and I live on our own,' said Mark, taking a klunk of beer. 'We have been doing for quite a few years now. That's the solution I chose in the end, and not a day has passed since then without my regretting it.'

He smiled briefly to indicate that it was a truth with modification. 'But I would have regretted it even more if I hadn't taken care of him.'

'Taken care of him?'

He nodded. 'He's twenty-four. And not exactly normal, to make a long story short.'

'If you make long stories short I shan't tell you anything about myself.'

He smiled again. 'All right, if that's the way you want it. It happened one winter evening nearly twelve years ago. On the way between Derby and Stoke – we were living just outside Stoke at that time.'

I nodded and waited.

'Me and my wife Sylvia and Jeremy were on our way home late one evening. We crashed with a lorry. I was driving. Sylvia died in hospital a few hours later. Jeremy was badly injured and was in a coma for two months. I escaped with a broken wrist.'

'I'm sorry. Please forgive me, I didn't know . . .'

He assumed a facial expression I couldn't pin down. Somewhere between resignation and confidentiality perhaps, I don't know. In any case, at that moment Barbara came in with our food – Mark had given the starter a miss, and so we were neck and neck in that respect at least.

And then, as we slowly worked our way through our boiled cod with potatoes, asparagus and horseradish sauce, he continued the tale. Jeremy eventually came out of his coma at the hospital after eight weeks – while he was lying there unconscious he had somehow managed to celebrate his thirteenth birthday. His bodily injuries eventually healed, but something had also happened to his brain. He could hardly talk, his motor functions were almost non-existent, he had frequent fits and seemed not to understand any but the simplest of instructions. He couldn't read, couldn't write, didn't seem to know whether he was coming or going. Nevertheless Mark took him home and survived the first two years with the aid of an assistant who came to help several hours every day. Jeremy had improved, Mark explained, but only very slightly. He continued to have fits – it was apparently some kind of epilepsy – and on several occasions Mark was forced to take him to the hospital in Stoke. The doctors recommended that Jeremy should be placed in some kind of institution; Mark was very much against that, but by the time Jeremy reached the age of fifteen and started showing signs of aggressive resistance he felt obliged to give way. The boy was placed in a home not far from Plymouth, and was moved after a year to another home near Lyme Regis in Dorset, where he stayed until he was nineteen. Meanwhile Mark had bought and moved into that house on Exmoor: he didn't explain why, merely said that he wanted to get away from the Midlands. He stressed that there was no question of Jeremy being ill-treated at the home, but 'in the end I just couldn't bear seeing him sitting there. And so I took him home once and for all.'

I found myself breathing a sigh of relief.

'Anyway, that's the way it is,' he said. 'He hardly ever goes out. He sleeps fourteen hours a day, and sits in front of his computer for ten. But it seems to work. Who says that people have to go to the cinema, go shopping for food and go on holiday? Eh? Read books? Mix with other people? Who says that?'

But there was more hope than resignation in his voice.

'And I can leave him on his own. He doesn't do silly things any more.'

'You mean he used to?'

He shrugged. 'It happened. He could be a danger to himself. But that's not the case any more. I'm sitting here now, for instance, as you may have noticed. And I often go for walks over the moor, as I think I said last time. No, he needs help with practical things such as washing clothes and preparing food, that kind of thing, but he doesn't mind being left on his own.'

'Do you talk to him? I mean—'

'He understands what I say. Not everything, but as much as is necessary. He never answers, of course, but he understands that it can be helpful if he does as he's told. If he's been a good boy when I get home this evening, for instance, he'll get a reward. A Crunchie.'

'A Crunchie?'

'Yes, a chocolate bar. It's his absolute favourite. I have a secret store in the car. If he ever found it he'd probably eat himself to death.'

I thought about all that while Barbara came to clear away our used plates.

'But that means you can never go away, does it? Not for more than a short time.'

He shook his head.

'Not without help. But luckily I have a sister. And if necessary I can arrange for him to spend a week at that place in Lyme Regis. But I try to avoid that . . . Although I have to admit that I spent a week in northern Italy last year. I managed both Florence and Venice. Anyway, that was my life in thirty minutes. May I offer you a glass of wine while I listen to yours?'

I didn't need the stipulated half an hour, but managed to occupy twenty minutes. While Mark had been talking I had managed to think up a story I thought sounded quite credible, and that I ought to be able to remember in future.

I had been married and I had two grown-up children. I had

been divorced for seven years, had worked behind the scenes at Swedish Television for over twenty years, and had started writing books around the time I got divorced. Three novels so far: they had sold sufficiently well in Scandinavia for me to take a year off and devote myself exclusively to writing. Which I thought was an enormous boost. What were my books about? Life, death and love – what else?

He laughed good-humouredly at that, then asked if any of them had been translated into English. I told him they hadn't – Danish, Norwegian, Icelandic, but that was all so far.

But what I talked about more than anything else was my childhood – and in some strange way, after only a short while, I almost felt as if I were sitting in Gudrun Ewerts's old room in Norra Bantorget again. Mark was leaning forward over the table on his elbows, watching me speak all the time with his piercing blue eyes almost the same colour as his pullover. And I spoke. About Gunsan. About my home town. About my poor parents. About Rolf and Martin, although I used a different name for the latter, and I recall that for a moment – no longer than that, but even so – I was convinced that I would be able to tell him the truth. That I could tell him what had really happened.

I didn't do so, of course, but I knew that beyond all doubt there was something about this man and his restrained sorrow that attracted me. When we said goodnight outside The Royal Oak shortly after ten o'clock, I found it difficult not to give him a hug.

But I didn't do that either, and now, a few hours later as I lie in bed with Castor over my legs and am about to put a full stop after the evening, I think about how I talked so much about me and my life. I must have had a great need to do so. The story about his son and that tragic accident was still lingering on inside my mind, of course, but I also realized that we hadn't discussed something we had talked about on the previous occasion. His ability to see what was hidden. The missing husband, the shadow, the sun-drenched house in the south and all the rest of it.

Once again it had become quite stormy during the evening. The wind was howling around the eaves, and there was a hint of snow in the air. I felt a little depressed, more depressed than I had been for several days, I don't know why.

THREE

24

I left the Samos material untouched for over a week. I also wondered whether I ought to get rid of it all, take it out onto the moor with a can of petrol and burn it up somewhere; but I decided that would be a bit overhasty. Perhaps it would be useful eventually, even if I wasn't at all sure what was meant by 'useful' and 'eventually'. Another couple of concepts had been robbed of their usual meaning, but that's the way things seemed to be going. I was now living within the framework provided by the hours of the day and the borders of Exmoor. I carried on reading about John Ridd and Lorna Doone, and I went for walks with Castor for three or four hours every day, all over the moor, but especially in the region of Simonsbath and Brendon, where heaven and earth kissed. At least, that's what it said on a little memorial stone where I parked the car one day: *Open yer eyes, oh, ye lucky wanderer, for near to here is a playce where heaven and earth kiss and caress.*

The weather was consistently pleasant, several degrees above zero, relatively gentle winds and hardly any rain. I made my own dinner every other evening, and every other evening drove down to The Royal Oak Inn. There was no sign of Mark Britton, and even if that made me a little disappointed every time, there was nothing I could do about it. I exchanged a few words with Rosie, Tom and Robert about the weather and about Castor, but that was usually about all. When I got back to Darne Lodge I lit the fire and played four games of patience. Switched off the bedside lamp before eleven and slept until I was woken up by the dawn. Castor would be by my feet, under the covers.

No more dead pheasants appeared in front of the door, and I had gradually got used to thinking that we would go on living like this until one of us had an attack of thrombosis during the night and died in our sleep. Either me or Castor, but preferably both of us the same night. Why not? Why was it necessary for one of us to outlive the other? Would it be possible for me to convince Mr Tawking that I could rent this modest dwelling indefinitely?

But on the twenty-fifth of November I visited the Winsford Community Computer Centre once again. Something had told me that it was high time. Over a month had passed since that remarkable walk, but it could just as easily have been a year. Or several, it seemed so far away in the past.

Everything that wasn't here and now seemed to be so far away in the past, and I suppose that's how it must feel for any-body who only takes account of hours that pass and walks that are undertaken. I hadn't even realized that it was Sunday when I stood rattling the door of the centre, but I was duly informed by Alfred Biggs when I took him at his word and knocked on his red-painted door just round the corner a few minutes later.

That was no problem, no problem at all. Alfred Biggs un-locked the door for me, and helped me to set up links with the outside world. Then he apologized and said he had a job to do in the church, but he promised to come back again in about an hour. If I wanted to leave before then, all I needed to do was to switch off the lights and make sure the door was locked behind me. If anybody else wanted to come in and access the web, I should let them in so long as they signed their names in the visitors' book.

Before leaving, he naturally made sure that there was a cup of tea and a plate of biscuits on my table. And that Castor had a bowl of water and a handful of treats that his missus could give him as she considered appropriate. I thanked him for his kindness, and when he had left I sat absolutely still with my eyes closed for half a minute before opening our mailboxes.

Mine first, that already seemed to be the routine.

Just one message. I couldn't pin down the precise reaction I felt. Relief or disappointment? It was Katarina Wunsch again, in any case. In three lines she apologized for upsetting me with her doppelgänger story, and hoped that I would enjoy a pleasant winter down in Morocco. I wrote an equally brief reply, closed the box and feeling somewhat uneasy I turned my attention to Martin's e-mails.

Ten new messages: I could ignore seven of them straight away. The remaining three were from that student about that incorrectly marked essay again, from Bergman and from the person calling himself G. After a little thought I decided to ignore the student as well, and instead looked to see what Eugen Bergman had on his mind.

He said thank you for my (i.e. Martin's) previous message, wished me all the best with regard to the work and the time down there in general, and he had a question. A journalist from the Swedish magazine *Svensk Bokhandel* was on a journey through north Africa and would very much like to call on me for an interview. Bergman didn't think Martin would be interested, but had promised to ask. I wrote a response in which I (Martin) confirmed that we were totally uninterested in any kind of contact with journalists, and that work was going according to plan. Then I drew a deep breath and opened the message from G.

> Your last e-mail made me more than confused. Did you have a stroke or are you just trying to avoid the issue? I'm coming down. What is your address? G

I just sat there for a minute or more, trying to absorb the implications. My last message had obviously not calmed G down at all. He was *more than confused. Trying to avoid the issue?* But what was the issue that Martin was trying to avoid? What was so important that he needed to meet Martin?

And who was he?

I realized of course that Martin must have told G about our plans for spending six months in Morocco, and presumably also that the purpose was to write something involving Hyatt and Herold. Something to do with the years before her suicide. And that this had disturbed G so much that he felt he must put a stop to it. Isn't that the case? I asked myself. Surely that's the way the land must lie?

Unfortunately I was unable to dig out the message Martin must presumably have sent him, and as I nibbled away at my biscuits and sipped my tea I wondered how hard it would be to sort out something like that. My knowledge of computers and IT had always been as limited as my interest in such matters, but I could see that it shouldn't be too difficult for anybody with a bit of competence in the field.

But I was also only too aware of the fact that I would never be able to bring myself to take that step. It was not certain that Martin's old message would in fact throw any light on the matter, and in any case it was distinctly possible that I would find the key anyway. Surely it must be somewhere in the remainder of the material from Samos and Morocco, the two-hundred-and-fifty pages or however much it was that I hadn't yet got round to reading. If there was something as important as G was alleging, it could hardly escape my notice, provided that I could raise enough strength to sit down and read the stuff. It seemed highly likely that G himself would feature in the material, but if he wasn't in fact the Russian Gusov, I didn't think I had come across him yet. Where I got that feeling from was not something I could answer for.

On the other hand, wasn't it possible that there would be no risk involved in simply ignoring G? I had already tried to give him a reassuring reply, which had obviously not worked, and if I now simply ignored him, what might the consequences be? Why should he be so important? What was it that shouldn't see the light of day? In any case, so long as he didn't have our address in Morocco he couldn't very well go there looking for us. What other possibilities were open to him? Contact Bergman? That couldn't be excluded, of course, but I needn't worry about such an eventuality as in that case Bergman would certainly be in touch with me.

Wouldn't he? I sat there for quite a while, trying to think up various strategies and assess their validity, and in the end I chose a sort of middle way. I wrote a brief reply to G, thinking that it ought to calm him down a bit at least temporarily – there is nothing that annoys hot-tempered individuals as much as not receiving replies to their questions, that was something all my years at the Monkeyhouse had taught me. Any reply at all was better than no reply, and my impression of this unknown G was that without doubt he was an impatient devil.

My dear friend. When I tell you not to worry I mean it.
There is absolutely no reason for us to meet. Best, M

That would have to do. I sent it off, closed Martin's mailbox and spent a few minutes glancing through the Swedish news. There was nothing of interest, and nowhere did I find any reports of a missing professor or the discovery of a dead body on the Polish Baltic coast. With a sigh of relief I switched off the computer and left the centre.

We went for a short walk through the village, and as we walked through the thin drizzle, stopping every ten metres or so for Castor to give himself a good shake, it occurred to me that I hadn't read a single e-mail from Morocco. Wasn't that a bit odd? I wondered. Martin had said that he had contacts down there, and it was these contacts that would help him to arrange our accommodation for the winter. Hadn't he made any preliminary arrangements before we left Sweden? Hadn't he contacted anybody at all, somebody who by now ought to be wondering why we hadn't turned up and hence been in touch with a question or two? This was surely very odd, and perhaps something that ought to have occurred to me some time ago? Despite the fact that I had so much more to be thinking about.

But so what? I thought when we had both installed ourselves in the car next to the war memorial. So much the better if there wasn't a Moroccan complication to keep an eye on and take into account.

Apart from that old one, that is – that Taza business which it seemed was lurking inside a suitcase in a wardrobe in Darne Lodge, and which by now had been lying there undisturbed for over a week. I started the car and began the now familiar drive up the road to Winsford Hill. There seemed to be enough daylight left for us to undertake a fairly substantial walk, but I was well aware that afterwards, during the long evening hours when darkness held sway over the moor, I would have to sit down once again with those confounded notes.

Those summers that had long since disappeared from a life that didn't concern me, and never had.

25

It took me nearly seven hours to go through the rest of the handwritten material from Samos. The week that still remained from 1978, and the whole of the summer of 1979.

It was turned one by the time I was finished, and when I snuggled down into bed with Castor, exhausted and with my eyes aching, I said a silent prayer hoping that I would remember enough to write a summary the next morning.

My prayer was answered. After Monday's morning walk (plus six degrees, quite a strong northerly wind, a greyish-white sky and only thin streaks of mist) I sat down in the rocking chair remembering and noting down what I considered to be the most significant things. As I did so I had a distinct feeling of being watched. That I was performing some sort of task that I had been instructed to carry out, and that the instigator – whether it was Martin or somebody else: Eugen Bergman perhaps, or the elusive G, or why not the two dead main characters, Herold and Hyatt? – was sitting like a raven, or even more than one, on my shoulders, making sure that nothing was overlooked.

Because something was afoot. Something was happening

down there on that Greek fairy-tale island: one didn't need to be a raven to understand that.

Nothing sensational happened during the rest of the 1978 stay. Martin describes the final week in his usual restrained manner: Hyatt and Herold are only mentioned in passing, Halvorsen and Soblewski rather more often. The day before Martin travels back to Sweden he and those other two go for quite a long walk along a ravine in the mountains, and Martin really does his best to record his impressions. The recurrent theme is that it is strenuous and terribly hot. And that Halvorsen has chafed feet and has to be more or less carried the last part of the homeward trek.

By the following summer, July–August 1979, the situation has changed somewhat. Martin is no longer living with the so-called collective. Instead he is lodging in a small house just a stone's throw away from Herold's and Hyatt's villa. He lives there for five weeks with various different people who come and go, but Soblewski arrives after a week and is still there when Martin goes home, and not long after Soblewski somebody called Grass turns up. I guess that he might well be the person hiding behind the pseudonym G – well, I suppose in fact I decide that is the explanation, and for some reason it comes as a relief. He is a writer and media researcher, originally from Monterey in California, but currently based in Europe.

The house they share seems to accommodate up to eight people: couples or women live in two of the rooms, and after

Soblewski's arrival he and Martin share a room for the rest of their stay. There is a kitchen, a toilet and outside shower: on the whole the place is an improvement on where they lived in previous summers.

The fact that they are closer to Hyatt and Herold is obvious, and it is not just Martin skewing matters to give that impression. By this time the couple are famous and worldwide celebrities, and the main reason for this is Bessie Hyatt's debut novel. Her second (and last) book, *Men's Blood Circulation*, has been edited and proof-read and will be published in the English-speaking world in October. Martin writes that all kinds of journalists and paparazzi 'are crawling around the pine-clad hillsides like cockroaches,' but that Tom Herold in particular makes sure that 'not so much as a bloody autograph-hunter crosses over the bridge.'

Grass turns out to be an old acquaintance of Bessie Hyatt's. They evidently come from the same part of California, went to high school together, and there might even be closer ties although Martin doesn't succeed in uncovering them. In any case there is a lot of socializing with the hosts: I gather that there is a group of six, in addition to Hyatt and Herold, who generally spend the long evenings on that famous terrace 'with views over the pine trees, the cypresses, the beach, the sea, the setting sun: if it is true that human beings are the creatures the Creator produced so that they could observe and admire one another, this is the right place and we are the chosen people' (sic!). The half-dozen comprise: Martin, Soblewski, Grass, the German women writers from the previous year (Doris Guttmann and Gisela Fromm) and the inevitable Russian Gusov.

Occasionally also Bruno, who is still playing the role of a sort of caretaker and hence seems to be degraded to a kind of second-rate citizen. That is not something stated by Martin, but a conclusion I have reached. Other people occasionally also appear on the terrace, of course: for two evenings the icon Allen Ginsberg is a house guest, and a week later Seamus Heaney joins the party – the Irishman who is awarded the Nobel Prize sixteen years later.

And these lengthy sessions, with Greek snacks served up in a never-ending stream by the housekeeper Paula, with boutari wine and retsina, with ouzo and tsipouro and beer, with witty discussions on Existentialism and hermeneutics, on Kuhn and Levinas, Baader-Meinhof and Solzhenitsyn and the Devil and his grandmother, with guitars and bouzoukis, these orgies in hyper-intellectual exuberance and Gauloise cigarettes with or without extras – well, as far as I can judge these happenings take place every evening, week after week, and usually end up with a group of participants trudging down to the beach about an hour or so after midnight for a session of skinny-dipping. For Christ's sake, this is heaven for a streber like Martin Holinek, a twenty-six-year-old research assistant from Stockholm in the backwoods of ultima Thule. For Christ's sake.

And on the heavenly throne the couple themselves: the British poet that everybody was talking about, and his fifteen-year-younger American wife. 'If anybody around this table might be considered to have come from Olympus, if any one of us were a reincarnated goddess,' writes Martin in a moment of poetic inspiration, 'she would certainly be the one.'

Whence Tom Herold had been reincarnated was less clear:

Martin found it difficult to describe him in words. It is quite obvious that this is connected with almost histrionic respect, but it is three weeks later before a note suggests that something is not really as it should be.

'There is something about Herold that makes me pause and think,' he writes on the thirteenth of July. 'There is no doubt that his temperament is a handicap, both for Bessie and for himself. Last night he stood up and left the table in a fit of anger – it was after something that Grass had said and that I didn't catch on to, and afterwards Grass was reluctant to discuss. Bessie remained in her seat and tried to keep up appearances, but I could see that she was upset. After a while she apologized and withdrew: Soblewski and I took the opportunity of doing the same. This was the first time since I'd been on the island that I'd got to bed before midnight. Every cloud has its silver lining.'

A few days later he writes about another controversy on the terrace. A young American poet is visiting; Martin writes that he and Bessie Hyatt evidently find a lot to talk about, but that Tom Herold, after having consumed a sufficient amount of retsina, is unable to contain his irritation. Bessie apparently defends her table companion – his name is Montgomery Mitchell and Herold makes fun of the name: it all ends with Herold taking his wife by the arm and dragging her away from the table. They return after a while, 'Bessie seems cowed and helpless,' Martin writes. The mood feels subdued and uneasy, it's only Gusov who fails to register the situation. He encourages all present to sing Theodorakis songs in Greek, and before long has most people joining in.

Many of the later diary entries for this last summer on Samos deal with this topic: how Martin interprets the man-oeuvring between Herold and Hyatt. He speculates quite a lot as well. Is there an illicit affair in the background? Is there something going on between Bessie and Mitchell – he stays on for more than a fortnight after all? Or between Bessie and Grass? Martin talks quite a lot to this Grass character (without using the abbreviation G, however), who claims to have known Bessie inside out from his childhood onwards, and he confirms that the facts are what Martin has suspected. She is not happy with her considerably older husband, who wants to control her more and more. Grass maintains that there is both jeal-ousy and envy involved: from a literary point of view Herold feels that he is being outshone by his beautiful wife, and no matter how much he pretends to enjoy her success, there seem to be different emotions lurking in the background. But Bessie says nothing at all about it, not to Grass or to anybody else. 'This is going to be a disaster, that pompous poet is a bloody big time bomb ticking away,' Martin notes that Grass commented in early August. 'We ought to rescue her,' he says at another point, 'but how the hell do you rescue somebody who doesn't want to be rescued?'

There are other things discussed in the diary notes, of course, but I find myself skipping over all the more or less strained Hellenistic observations and all the complicated dis-cussions about life, politics and literature. Although Martin comments on Tom Herold's moods, it is clear that he is full of admiration for the great poet. 'What would he be without that restless, creative ocean thundering away inside himself?' he wonders. And 'After having read *Ode to Ourselves* I can see that he is presumably the greatest living poet in Europe just now. Quite simply, Herold's poetry has a significance and a richness which is unmatched in our continent and in our century.'

But he is never on intimate terms with the great poet – or at least, there is no mention of that and I'm sure that Martin wouldn't fail to write about it if it existed. On one occasion he has an opportunity for a rather more private discussion with Bessie Hyatt: they happen to find themselves together on the beach one morning when a group has gone swimming 'before the heat is such that every rational person retires to the shade'. 'Are you happy?' she asks him out of the blue, and Martin is inspired to respond that any man would consider himself happy if he found himself sitting on a Greek beach with a Greek goddess. She evidently laughs at this, but then she asks if he thinks that she is happy. Martin says he doesn't think so in view of the fact that she asks such a question, whereupon she nods thoughtfully and just for a moment 'looks so sad that one would willingly sell one's soul to save her'. Hmm. I read this somewhat obscure comment again, but that is in fact exactly what he writes. He would willingly sell his soul for Bessie Hyatt's sake. I note that this is August 1979, and that Martin and I have been in a relationship for over six months by that time.

A few days later on the terrace Tom Herold lets slip the fact that they are going to move. All good things come to an end, he says, but they have sold their Greek paradise and will settle down in Taza in Morocco. The new owners will be moving in in September, 'so I am afraid the bell tolls for all of you!' Quite a lot of emotional reaction erupts all round the table: nobody is sure if they ought to congratulate or commiserate or both, but Martin writes that he happens to glance at Bessie Hyatt and that she seems anything but pleased. There is even more smoking and drinking than usual that evening, and for once Herold is at his wittiest and most cheerful. Martin writes that he 'produces a perfect sonnet from up his sleeve, just like Cyrano de Bergerac: but instead of stabbing an opponent after the final rhyme of the fourteenth line, he pours a glass of retsina over the head of Montgomery Mitchell and kisses his wife.' Enthusiastic applause breaks out, and not even poor Mitchell seems to have anything against it.

Needless to say there are discussions the following day about the reasons for the imminent departure of Herold/Hyatt, including one between Martin and Grass. The latter maintains that it is a coup engineered by the deeply egotistical Herold, and that Bessie has been presented with a fait accompli. It is not clear on what grounds Grass is able to make this claim, but Martin refers to him as if what he said was 'the whole truth and nothing but the truth'. Once again Grass expresses his worries about the fate of his childhood friend, and maintains that things will never end up satisfactorily between the ill-matched couple. Grass has evidently also read a proof version of *Men's Blood Circulation*, and declares that when it is published 'everybody with more than one brain cell in their body will realize the facts about this English verse-monger'. One might well wonder about the term 'verse-monger', and Martin reflects at length about Grass's aggression. He suspects that he can smell a rat, or possibly several, and wonders if Grass is arguing the case for Mitchell, whatever that might be.

Martin leaves Samos together with Soblewski: they take the ferry to Piraeus, spend two days together in Athens, visit the Acropolis, eat and drink in tavernas in Plaka and eventually part at the airport on the fifteenth of August. Martin devotes almost nine pages to these final days, but nevertheless he concludes his 1979 diary with the words: 'It feels as if something has come to an end. I shall never return to Samos, perhaps I shall never again meet Tom Herold and his goddess, which is a thought that suddenly feels like a millstone.'

Oh yes, I think more than three decades later. And within a year you have a goddess of much lower significance to take care of. Pregnant to boot. But even so you go off on another journey.

There are forty more handwritten pages from Taza.

Not to mention the typewritten pages. Nor the computer files. I decide to wait for a few days. I don't feel too good when I heave myself up out of the rocking chair: walking along hand-in-hand with young Martin Holinek like this is not exactly without its problems.

26

'And do you know why our church is painted white?'

It's early afternoon on the second of December. Castor and I are in and around Selworthy, a village quite high up in the hills, between Porlock and Minehead, quite close to the sea. We have joined forces with an elderly lady and her considerably younger dog, an energetic labrador. We parked the car next to the church, and are on our way up to the Selworthy Beacon: it's a bit on the chilly side but otherwise fine, and we hope to be able to see for miles from the summit.

'No,' I say. 'I don't know why.'

The old lady chuckles with pleasure. 'I assume you're a foreigner, if you don't mind me saying so; but it's very unusual to find white-painted churches in this United Kingdom of ours. They are supposed to be grey, the colour of natural stone, both in towns and in the countryside . . . Unlike in some other parts of the world – Greece, for instance.'

'Yes, I have noticed that,' I say. 'That the churches are usually grey.'

'That's right,' says the lady, pausing for a moment to adjust the woollen scarf she has wrapped around her head. 'But we had a vicar here who painted the church white. He had good reason for that – or at least, he thought he had.'

We turn round and confirm that we can still see the church quite a long way down below us, through all the wintry green foliage of the trees. There is no doubt at all that it is white-washed.

'He was very fond of hunting, you see – this was a few hundred years ago – and while he was out hunting for deer or pheasants or whatever, down there in Porlock Valley . . .' She points in that direction with her walking stick. '. . . It's called the happy valley, and they say it really is that, and it certainly is the most beautiful valley in the whole of England . . . Anyway, while he was wandering around looking for prey, he would take a swig now and then from his hip flask to keep up his body warmth and his good humour . . . and then, you see, as dusk began to fall and it was time for him to go home, he hadn't a clue where he was or which direction he should be heading in . . . And so he had the church painted white. So that it was clearly visible, and so that he'd be able to find his way home no matter what state he was in. And it really worked – you can see it wherever you are in the valley. You can't miss it.'

'Is that really true?' I ask aghast.

'Of course it's true,' says the lady. 'Do you think I'd make up stories to impress a visitor from a long way away?'

We part company shortly afterwards. She and her Mufti turn off along a path to Bossington – it's too steep for an eighty-year-old to get to the summit, and in any case, I'm told, all there is there is a pile of stones and masses of wind.

But Castor and I keep plodding along. I think for a while about the lady's farewell words – *a visitor from a long way away* – and how appropriate they are. It's exactly a month since I moved into Darne Lodge – I have a copy of *The Times* in the car that confirms this; and even if I no longer regard the passing of time like I used to, even if I'm now a sort of desert dweller and an emigrant from all normal life, I couldn't avoid noticing that they had started decorating for Christmas in Dulverton. We drove through the village on the way here, and as I stood in the queue to pay for my newspaper I saw a poster advertising 'Dunster by Candlelight' the coming Saturday – a big event, it seemed.

For normal people.

We trudge up the last long slope to the cairn at the summit, and I entertain the thought that I will never return to Sweden. No, that's wrong, I don't entertain the thought because I've been doing that to excess for a very long time: it's the feeling that I entertain now, the discomfort that swells up relentlessly in my midriff. This must be the first time since I came to live on the moor that I have felt such pangs of homesickness, such longing for home.

But longing for what, exactly? If I'm not really longing for anything any more, if I don't even want to carry on living, why should I long for home? A feeling of belonging, perhaps, of being well known – is this the link I'm fumbling for? Context and security and the reassuring presence of somebody else? But why are such emotions attacking me now on this windswept hillside? We have no future, Castor and I: I shall outlive him and then die, that is the contract we have agreed upon. That we sign up for every day, my dog and I, is that not the case?

I try to shake it off me, whatever it is, but it's not easy and I know that it was the old lady's words that started it all off.

A visitor from a long way away.

It could just as well be a description of what is involved in being a human being in this world.

On the way back to Selworthy – we are following a different path now, there are lots of them – we come across a little stone monument. According to an inscription it was raised for a man who liked to walk up to this summit with his children and his grandchildren, talking to them all the time about the beauty and richness of God's nature surrounding them on all sides. According to the same text, the monument is intended to be a haven where a tired wanderer can rest, protected from the wind: as Castor and I have both coffee and liver chews in our rucksack, we sit down in the lee with the pale but nevertheless warming sunlight shining into our faces. I read a poem on the wall:

> *Needs no show of mountain hoary,*
> *Winding shore or deepening glen,*
> *Where the landscape in its glory*
> *Teaches truth to wandering men:*
> *Give true hearts but earth and sky,*

And some flowers to bloom and die.
Homely scenes and simple views
Lowly thoughts may best infuse.

Even these lines touch me deeply. I really don't understand why I am so affected and why so many doors to my soul are standing open on this lovely December day, but that's the way it is. I'm suddenly reminded of the novel *A Happy Death* by Albert Camus, which both Rolf and I read during the short time we were together and the theme of which we discussed: choosing the time and the place of one's own death. That dying is the most important moment in life, and hence that one shouldn't leave its circumstances so casually in the hands of others, as most people do.

Would I like to die here and now? Is that the question that should be occupying my mind? I don't think so, but perhaps I would like to die on a day like this in a place like this. Perhaps even this very place?

I contemplate Castor as he lies stretched out on the ground in the sunshine. I contemplate England's most beautiful valley in all its glory. I listen to the wind in the treetops, and it occurs to me that as long as we live we shall never be able to ignore the passage of time, nor the Christmas decorations in Dunster, nor what we are guilty of having done.

That is why we need the door of death through which we can take our leave.

The sun is swallowed by clouds. Castor sits up and stares at me. It's time to go back to the car.

★

There are two vehicles in the car park next to Selworthy's white-painted church. One is my rather dirty dark blue Audi, the other is a silver-coloured Renault with a badge indicating it is from the rental firm Sixt. Despite the fact that there are at least ten empty spaces, the driver has parked it so close to my car that I can barely open the driver's door and squeeze my way in.

It is while I am performing this difficult manoeuvre that I notice the newspapers lying on the dashboard just above the steering wheel of the rental car – it is right-hand drive, whereas mine is left-hand drive. There are two papers and I recognize both of them: one is the Swedish *Dagens Nyheter*, and the other the Polish *Gazeta Wyborcza*.

I manage to sit down in the driver's seat and close the door behind me. I look around. No sign of anybody. I start the engine and drive away. My heart is beating fast: I know that this is one of my vulnerable days, and I hope the fear that took possession of me in a flash will fade away provided I don't feed it with unnecessary thoughts. As long as I concentrate on other things.

On the way home we drive once again through the narrow medieval streets of Dunster. I stop and buy four bottles of red wine and two of port. It will soon be Christmas, after all.

27

I leaf through the Morocco material before starting to read it carefully.

Martin seems to have spent thirteen days in Taza in the summer of 1980. Or at least, that is the number of days there described in the diary, but he doesn't pack up and travel back home, nor does he even say goodbye to Herold and Hyatt. I seem to recall that he was away from Stockholm for at least three weeks, but of course it's possible he took the opportunity of visiting Casablanca and Marrakesh, not just the notorious couple in Taza, having already gone all the way to Morocco. Perhaps he told me about it when he got back home, but when you're in the eighth month of pregnancy with your first child, other things don't register.

Maybe he realized that it was time for him to leave Taza. Maybe something happened that caused him to stop writing – something of which he didn't want to have a written record, for whatever reason. Perhaps I'll find the answer in the typewritten material, or on the computer.

I no longer know if there really are ravens on my shoulders, and if I am obliged to continue with this undertaking I have embarked upon. The thought of a big nocturnal bonfire out on the moor, with all Martin's belongings, has become increasingly attractive this last week, but that might be overhasty. Why it should be overhasty is something I still don't understand: there is a difference between burning clothes and burning bridges, but perhaps it's not as great as I'd like to think. I really am ambivalent about it, but think that I might as well read these irritating notes to the end – just as well as I should play patience or become acquainted with Lorna Doone's and John Ridd's exploits on seventeenth-century Exmoor. What is important and what ought to be done are questions that become less obvious for every day that passes. I assume that is the legitimate price of isolation.

In any case, the situation in Taza in 1980 is different from what it had been on Samos the three previous years, and I can't help wondering why Martin has been invited at all.

Or why anybody has been invited, come to that. *Have* they been invited in fact? By whom? Seven people have come to visit the big house outside the town of Taza this summer: Grass, Gusov and Soblewski, one of the Germans, plus a much older French novelist called Maurice Megal and his wife Bernadette. And Martin. Nobody else is mentioned, apart from Hyatt and Herold. On checking I confirm that this charmed inner circle comprises six men and three women; in addition there is also a female chef, a gardener and a swimming pool supervisor. So if one were to write a play about the goings-on, one would need a dozen actors.

Why on earth would anybody want to write a play about it?

But why on earth would anybody *not* want to write a play about it? Good Lord, I haven't had much to do with drama at the Monkeyhouse, but I have been involved in four or five productions and think I can claim to know the rules of the game. *Evenings in Taza?* It sounds almost like a classic already.

Martin arrives in the evening of the twentieth of July, and his last handwritten note is dated the first of August.

Bessie Hyatt is pregnant, that is the hub around which everything else revolves. Martin doesn't discover this fact until the third day of his visit, and her body shows no sign of pregnancy. But it is a fact even so. She is in the beginning of the third month, and the same evening that Martin hears the news he is in a private conversation with Grass and is informed of a possible complication. Martin has underlined the word 'possible' twice, because Grass is not yet certain of the circumstances – namely that the father of the expected child is alleged to be someone other than Tom Herold.

I stop reading at this point because I am suddenly reminded of that comment Martin made about Gunvald when we were driving through the night to Kristianstad before continuing to Poland. His suggestion that he wasn't the father of his son. Is this where he had got the idea from? He had been talking about Strindberg's play *The Father*, and said it was a question all men asked themselves, fairly seriously. But if the problem had been a key point in the drama between Hyatt and Herold, perhaps it had a special sort of relevance for Martin? A heavier weight? But so what? I thrust the thought to one side and continue reading.

Before the question of Bessie's pregnancy crops up in the notes there are quite a lot of descriptions of the surroundings and the house; but from the twenty-fourth of July onwards everything is about events and relationships between people at Al-Hafez, as the palace-like creation is evidently called. It is built in Moorish style and is owned by a Swiss billionaire, Martin writes. Tom Herold has rented it for two years, and since it is so incredibly hot in the middle of summer, residents and guests rarely venture outside the white stone wall that encloses the property. Inside this wall, topped with broken glass, there is everything one could possibly want: shade-providing trees (oleanders, tamarisks and a generous plane, according to Martin), a large kidney-shaped swimming pool, stimulating conversation, food, drink, a certain amount of mild drugs, and the three aforementioned servants.

And so we have the stage setting and scenography – that thought keeps on recurring, despite everything.

'Had a long conversation with Grass,' writes Martin on the twenty-fourth of July.

> I find it hard to judge if there is anything in what he says, or if he is just paranoid. He drinks too much, and has presumably popped some kind of pills, I don't know what, but they make him exceptionally intense and insistent. Words come flooding out of his mouth, and he pays absolutely no attention to objections – not when you are talking privately to him at least. When Herold is present, on the other hand, he usually sits there in silence and keeps his thoughts to himself.

What Grass keeps coming back to and stressing is that his

childhood friend (childhood sweetheart? Martin wonders) Bessie is in danger. She is on the brink of a nervous break-down, and it's her pregnancy and her husband's interpretation of it that are the key causes of the rapidly escalating crisis. Martin can see with his own eyes that the successful young author is clearly in a state. Grass is not imagining things: any-body can see that Bessie Hyatt is unwell, she staggers between a state of manic exhilaration and almost catatonic introver-sion. She is always present at the obligatory, prolonged meals – which begin as soon as dusk and cool evening air begins to descend on Al-Hafez, and usually continue into the early hours – but from one evening to the next it can seem as if Bessie is two different people.

All nine of them sit there, and it is Tom Herold who holds court. Martin uses that expression several times. It's Herold who is very definitely the main character, and to stress this role he likes to dress up and act like a sort of Arab prince. He has a long beard now, wears a white ankle-length djellaba and a red fez. He likes to hold forth about Arabic culture and how superior it is to that of the West; he quotes Sufi poets and at every meal recites something of his own invention, often just a few intense lines composed that morning – he spends a few hours every morning shut away in his cool study. He likes to repeat these lines several times during the course of the evening, and calls it 'tattooing the souls of the cretins'.

Martin doesn't describe the others present in much detail, apart from the French couple whom he hasn't met before. He compares the novelist Maurice Megal to a short-sighted goat, but he also calls him 'an over-cultivated snob who is careful never to say anything comprehensible, and so it is not possible to comment on it or oppose it'. His wife Bernadette, who is a good twenty-five years younger, is a 'dark-haired, slim and mysterious woman who plays with Tarot cards and has a reputation as a hypnotist'. She demonstrates her latter skills one of the first evenings she is present, when she persuades Doris Guttmann to undress and in her naked state to perform some kind of snake dance for the rest of those present, convinced that she is a harem lady from the fourteenth century.

'It's also entirely possible,' Martin notes, 'that she wasn't hypnotized at all but didn't want to miss an opportunity of dancing naked before an audience.'

I assume Martin must have felt both stimulated and somewhat embarrassed in this company, even if he never admits to either of those reactions. He tries to make it sound as if it is nothing very unusual, in the early days at least, but as time passes (he devotes at least four pages of text to each day) his account acquires a special focus: Bessie Hyatt. On the morning of the twenty-eighth of July he has his first (and only, I think) private conversation with her, and what she says to him in one way strengthens Grass's case, but in another way it demonstrates how extremely dependent this young American woman is on her husband. She swears that she worships him, literally *worships*. She laughs and cries indiscriminately, behaves 'with a level of controlled hysteria that is so close to the surface that you can detect it even when she is sitting still and saying nothing. Like a bridge over dark water, her face is.' (sic!) Obviously Martin can't ask her outright about her pregnancy, about who is the father of the child she is expecting, but the question is answered as loudly as a trumpet call as early as the following evening. In the play *Evenings in Taza*, we have reached the first highlight – even if that term is inappropriate in every respect as far as those present are concerned.

To sum it up: thanks to a combination of potent recreational drugs and the efforts of the hypnotist Bernadette Megal, Tom Herold, in full view of all present, has a vision in which he discovers the rapist Ahib, who has clandestinely placed an unwanted olive-coloured bastard foetus in Bessie Hyatt's swelling stomach. Ahib is clearly possessed by a demon, or several demons, and must die. It is a duty to kill him, and more especially it is a duty to kill him before the child has grown too big and strong inside Bessie. This performance is enacted with a series of remarkable pirouettes and poetic outpourings over twenty minutes: Madame Megal accompanies it all on the bongo drums and some sort of native stringed instrument, and the drama ends with Tom Herold howling in pain and anger like an injured lion, and Bessie throwing herself into the swimming pool.

I stop reading after this description. Martin has three more days in Taza, but a thought has suddenly occurred to me: what is there to indicate that he wasn't sitting in a hotel room in Copenhagen or Amsterdam, making up the whole story? What proof is there that the whole rigmarole is not an invention?

None, so far as I can see. Why haven't I heard anything about all this before? Why has he kept quiet about these bizarre happenings for more than thirty years? Why hasn't he written about it? I decide to check that there really is a place in Morocco called Taza. That will have to be the next time I go to the Winsford Community Computer Centre – I realize that it's over a week since the last visit, so it's presumably high time.

But then I recall that e-mail from G.

Have always felt an inkling that this would surface one day.

And the promise to Bergman and the conversation with Soblewski in his big house that night . . . No, there must be a reality behind these notes, I have to accept that. It actually did happen.

Which of course doesn't necessarily mean that every word is true. I decide to put the whole business on ice for a few days, put the notebooks back in the suitcase and the wardrobe, and think that if nothing else I should try to get hold of Bessie Hyatt's two novels. For reasons I don't really understand I haven't read either of them: they are no doubt on the shelves in Nynäshamn, but those shelves are a long way away. Perhaps that nice lady in the second-hand bookshop in Dulverton can help?

I look at Castor, lying there in front of the almost dead fire. Ask him if he wants to go for a walk. He doesn't answer. Through the window, on the other side of the wall, I can see a whole herd of Exmoor ponies grazing in the gathering dusk. At least twenty of them. In an hour we shall be swallowed up by darkness, both us and them.

28

The seventh of December, a Friday. Rain during the night, but fine the next morning. A cloudy sky, but no mist. A south-westerly wind, hardly stronger than five to six metres per second.

I have been sleeping badly for several nights, and during the day have felt restless, neglecting the usual routines. The lack of sleep has left me feeling sluggish whenever there is still a bit of daylight: I lie in bed, try to read, but instead end up in a sort of semi-torpor. If I didn't have the obligatory daily walk with Castor to think about I would probably allow dawn and dusk to merge, and thus sink into a state of absolute lethargy. But our walks become shorter for every day that passes, and when I looked at myself in the mirror this morning, I had the impression of a woman on the downward path. I have also drunk two of the bottles of red wine I bought in Dunster, and half a bottle of port. All I have managed to do is to buy the basic necessities at the general stores in Exford. No excursions, not to Dulverton, Porlock nor anywhere else.

In the afternoon, after a short stroll down towards Tarr Steps, I pulled myself together even so: took a shower, washed my hair and had a complete change of clothes. Wrote in my notebook that I really must drive to Minehead on Monday to see to some laundry. I persuaded Castor to jump into the passenger seat of the car and drove down to Winsford and the computer centre.

It was already five o'clock by the time I got there, but there were lights in the windows and Alfred Biggs immediately bade me welcome. At one of the tables towards the back of the room were the two young girls I'd met on my first visit – or at least, I thought they were the same ones. Castor went over to greet them, they asked what he was called and spent some time playing with him before returning to their screens. I felt a surge of gratitude towards them.

'It's pretty bleak at this time of year,' said Alfred Biggs.

'You can say that again,' I said.

'How are things going for you up there?'

'Not too badly, thank you.'

'It must be hard, being a writer. Keeping tabs on everything.'

'Yes, it's not always all that easy.'

'I mean, all those words and people and things that happen.'

'Yes, exactly,' I said. 'Not all that easy.'

'But I assume you keep a notebook?'

'Yes, I do. You have to keep making notes all the time.'

'I must say I admire you. For keeping tabs on everything. But forgive me, I mustn't distract you with my chit-chat.'

He indicated where I could sit down, and went to make tea.

E-mail from Gunvald to Martin:

Hi. I hope all is well in Morocco. Work has been keeping me

pretty busy, but virtue has its reward. My book has gone to the printer, and over New Year I'm going to a five-day conference in Sydney. I'll stretch it out of course with a week's holiday. Greetings to Mum, and have a Merry Christmas if we're not in touch again before then.

E-mail from Soblewski to Martin:

Just a quick note to say that I've talked to BC and there is no problem. Let's stay in contact. My best to your lovely wife and dog.

E-mail from Gertrud to Martin:

What are you up to nowadays? I got your e-mail eventually. Lennart and I have split up, so I'm as free as a bird. It would be great to meet and pick up the threads again, don't you think?

Nothing from Bergman, nothing from G. I was grateful for that, especially the latter. The message from Gunvald could just as well have come from a cousin or a distant acquaintance. And as for Soblewski – greetings to your wife and dog?

Gertrud aroused suspicions, of course. Who is she, and what the hell does she mean by picking up the threads again? And why had I given her Martin's e-mail address so casually when Bergman asked for it? But I couldn't really get het up about it – whatever might have taken place between her and Martin belonged to a different life. For a few seconds I considered sending her a reply, just to amuse myself: but I let it pass. And didn't write to Gunvald or Soblewski either.

E-mail from Synn to me:

> Hello, Mum. I hope all is going well in Morocco. I'll probably stay in New York over Christmas and the New Year – I assume you won't be going home either. Business is going well, I've applied for a green card and expect to get it. I agree with Woody Allen: there's hardly ever a good reason for leaving Manhattan. Greetings to the old bastard.

E-mail from Christa to me:

> Dear Maria. Dreamt about you again. I think it's odd, I hardly ever remember that I've been dreaming, never mind what about. This time you really were in danger, you cried for help and I was the one who would be able to help you. But I didn't understand what I could do. There was a man in a car chasing you. You ran like mad to get away, and I really wanted to save you but I was so far away all the time. In another country, or something like that. Never mind, but it was both very clear and very horrible in any case. Write and let me know that all is well. Love, C

I thought for a while, then wrote to both of them. I wished my daughter a Merry Christmas and reported that both I and the old bastard were in good shape, all things considered. Christa was duly informed that everything was under control down in Morocco, and that I would try hard to behave myself rather better in her next dream. I took the opportunity to pass on season's greetings, and asked her to pass on greetings to Paolo.

I didn't bother to chase up the latest news from Sweden –

nor news from anywhere else, come to that. Instead I thanked Alfred Biggs, and went with Castor to The Royal Oak for dinner.

Six days have passed since my last visit.

And it feels like a month since I sat here talking to Mark Britton that last time, which just shows how my conception of time is going off the rails. When he now comes in, less than a minute after I've ordered my food and got a glass of wine on the table, I suddenly feel grateful – and just as suddenly uneasy as well, in case he is only going to sit at the bar, drink a pint of ale and then leave.

But I needn't have worried. When Mark sees me he gives me a broad smile and sits down at my table without even asking.

'How are things? How's it going with the writing?'

'Fine, thank you. A bit up and down, but that goes with the territory.'

'It's nice to see you again. You brighten up my mealtimes, if you don't mind my saying so.'

'All right, I'll allow it. But you'd better hurry up and order or we'll get out of step.'

And so we are sitting here again. I think that either I'm so starved of everything to do with human relationships, or that it has something to do with this man. Most probably a combination of the two. I can feel butterflies in my stomach, and am relieved that I smartened myself up before coming here. Mark looks very smart, a little darker under the eyes than I remember, but newly shaved, well combed and wearing a wine-red pullover instead of the blue one. Corduroy trousers and a Barbour jacket that he's hung over the back of his chair. Indeed, I think he could well be a sort of semi-noble country squire after a successful afternoon's shooting, and I can't help smiling to myself when I realize that I've given him a title that my father used to like using. *Country squire.*

'I gather you don't come here all that often,' I say, 'or is it just that we happen to have missed one another?'

'I don't know,' he says. 'I usually come here at least twice a week – but I like cooking, so that's not why I come. I reckon you need to see somebody else's face besides your own occasionally. Don't you agree?'

'Mine, for instance?'

He leans forward over the table. 'I prefer your face to Rosie's and Henry's and Robert's, I'll admit that. And I'm grateful that you can put up with me now and again.'

I manage to shrug and assume a neutral smile. Being a television hostess for a quarter of a century does leave its mark. 'You're welcome,' I say. 'Being with you doesn't cause me pain.'

'But you have done,' he says, suddenly becoming serious. 'Suffered pain, that is. Things are a bit rough for you up there in your house when darkness descends to gobble us up. I'm right, aren't I?'

'What do you mean? You're not sitting there again and reading my mind, are you?'

'Only a bit,' he says. 'I see a bit and guess the rest. Who could spend a whole winter up there and survive with their mind in one piece? The moor is best for people who are born on it. In the winter, at least. Cheers, by the way.'

We each take a sip of our wine and look each other in the eye for a second too long. Or maybe I only imagine that extra second: it's not the kind of judgement that is part of my repertoire any longer. Good Lord, I think, if he stretches out his hand over the table and touches me I'll wet myself. I'm as emotionally unstable as a fourteen-year-old.

The new young waiter, who is called Lindsey and is undoubtedly as gay as the Pope is Catholic, comes with our food and we start eating. A couple arrive with an elderly terrier, and there is a pause while the dogs greet each other and we indulge in doggy talk before our four-legged friends settle down under their appropriate tables. I am grateful for the interruption, as it gives me time to get a grip of myself. Mark wipes his mouth.

'Good, but not five stars. What was yours like?'

We had both chosen fish: me cod, him sea perch.

'Pretty good. Five stars plus or minus a half.'

'I would have cooked it more slowly at a lower heat,' he said, nodding at his plate. 'But of course, then the customer needs to be patient and wait a little longer. Would you like to try it?'

I don't understand what he means. 'Try what?'

'My cooking. You could come round to my place for a meal one evening, and see what I'm capable of.'

I'm taken completely by surprise, but at the same time must ask myself why. What is so remarkable about a single man inviting a single woman to dinner?

'You're doubtful?' he has time to say before I can squeeze a response out of myself.

'No! Of course not . . . I mean, obviously I'd love to go to your house for dinner. Forgive me, it's just that I'm a bit socially retarded.'

That makes him laugh. 'We're in the same boat, then. I . . .'

He pauses and looks embarrassed for a moment.

'Well?'

'I really wasn't at all sure if I would dare to invite you. But anyway, it's done now.'

'Are you saying it was planned?'

He smiles. 'Of course. I've been thinking about it all the time since we first met. If you think I'm some sort of village Casanova, I'm afraid I'm going to disappoint you. But I'm pretty good with fish, as I've already said.'

'Thank you,' I say. 'Thank you for being so bold. But how is Jeremy going to take it? Will he accept that you are being visited by a stranger?'

Mark gestures with his hands and looks apologetic. 'He's not going to hug you enthusiastically. You'll probably think he's being antagonistic, but he will leave us in peace. He has plenty of private business to be getting on with.'

I think about the gesture Jeremy made when I saw him looking out of the window. I wonder if I ought to mention it, but decide that it can wait. 'And dogs? Does he like animals? I won't come without Castor, I hope you understand that.'

He bursts out laughing. 'The invitation is for both of you. As for Jeremy, I think he prefers animals to humans. I've thought about buying a dog, but haven't got round to it.'

And so we start talking about breeds of dog, about loneliness and the particular kind of darkness that embraces the moor at this time of year. He maintains that some nights, when there are no stars visible, heaven and earth can take on exactly the same shade of black – it's simply not possible to distinguish between them, it's as if one were living in a blind universe. Or as if heaven and earth had actually merged. Such nights can be dangerous for your state of mind, Mark says, even if you don't go out on the moor to experience it. The phenomenon creeps into your house and under your skin. He remembers it from his childhood in Simonsbath – people just went out of their minds overnight.

'And it's at times like that you need to visit a good friend and have a bite to eat, is it?' I ask.

'Exactly,' says Mark. 'See a different face, just like I said. Shall we say next Friday? A week from now?'

We agree on that. Why wait for a whole week, I wonder, but I don't say anything. He explains that I can drive right up to the house even though that doesn't seem possible from a distance, and when we leave The Royal Oak Castor and I accompany him a short way up Halse Lane so that he can show us where we must turn off.

'A mere three hundred crooked yards,' he says.

'I know,' I say. 'Castor and I have already walked them, but in this direction, not towards the house.'

Then we shake hands and part.

★

I wish I could regard that as the end of the day, but unfortunately that is not possible. When we come down to the war memorial, where we have parked the car as usual, there it is again: the silver-coloured hire car. I can't see the silver colour, of course, because this little central spot in the village is only lit up by a single street lamp which is hanging over the memorial, swinging back and forth in the wind, and its dirty yellow beam is inadequate – but there is no doubt that it is the same car. The same newspapers are lying on the dashboard, one Polish and one Swedish, and this time he has parked so close that I have to get into my car via the passenger door.

He? Why do I write *he?*

29

I must get to grips with this.

Must bring my fear out into the daylight. It's the unformulated apprehensions that are the worst, and once you have dared to put a face on the monster you are halfway to overcoming it. I recall that Gudrun Ewerts used to use images like that, and when I get up on Saturday morning after a chaotic night, I realize that it's high time.

What exactly is it that is scaring me? What am I imagining? My goal is simply to outlive my dog, after all. Isn't it?

But first the routines, otherwise chaos will take over. I must make a fire and have a shower. Wake Castor up. Make the bed. Note down my meteorological observations.

Five degrees at nine o'clock. Moderate wind, misty, visibility fifty metres or so.

We walk in the direction of Dulverton: those are the fairly dry paths we know best, and where we meet the ponies three mornings out of four. And as we are walking I think through everything in detail. Or at least try to formulate the apprehensions. Put a face on the monster. Return to Międzyzdroje.

★

So:

More than six weeks have passed. One-and-a-half months. If he did manage to get himself out, he must have done so that first day.

Otherwise he'd have frozen to death.

Been eaten up by the rats.

Or?

Okay, two days. Two days maximum. I decide on that.

So, assume that Martin has been free since the twenty-fifth of October. Alive. What would he have been doing all that time? Would he have spent over forty days looking for me? I erased all traces of my movements after Berlin. Was there something I overlooked?

Has he been looking for me without making his presence known? Is that a possibility? Surely it sounds impossible. Or is it in fact as impossible as that?

Has he somehow found a trail leading to England?

Rented a silver-coloured Renault and followed a new trail to Exmoor?

Found our car? No doubt it's possible that the registration number is on a data list at the tunnel terminal in Calais – but how could he have got hold of such a document?

And Winsford?

Rubbish. It simply doesn't add up.

But if he really did get out of the bunker – I think, hypothetically – he must have kept everything secret. Somehow or other. There's no doubt about that: he must have chosen not to have revealed the truth. Everybody thinks we are in Morocco. Everybody I am in touch with, that is. Gunvald. Synn. Christa. Bergman. Soblewski. G, whoever he is.

Other people as well – colleagues in the Monkeyhouse, colleagues in the Sandpit, Violetta di Parma and our neighbours with whom we never socialized . . . The fact is that every man jack who knows who we are also knows that we chose to leave Sweden because of certain improper goings-on at a hotel in Gothenburg. *Together*. Surely . . . Surely there would have been some sort of mention in the e-mails if Martin had suddenly turned up and put a stop to all the illusions and circumstances I so carefully cobbled together? In Stockholm or somewhere else. Surely?

Surely?

I pause briefly at this point because a little bird appears from nowhere and perches on the back of a pony. Only ten metres away from us. It sits there wagging its tail for a few seconds before flying away. I don't know if it's an especially remarkable event, but I don't think I've ever seen it before. The pony paid no attention to it in any case, just carried on grazing calmly.

I shake my head and pick up the thread again. How . . . *How* could he possibly have traced me to the edge of an obscure little village in Somerset? We were supposed to be going to Morocco, after all.

It's a more or less rhetorical question. I haven't used a bank card or a mobile phone since I left Berlin, I am using an assumed name, there are no connections between the fictitious writer Maria Anderson and the former television personality Maria Holinek. None at all.

In the relative light of day during a familiar morning walk it is not difficult to reach this conclusion. The fact that I'm fighting against figments of my imagination. If Martin were alive, I would know about it. Everything else is out of the question. Everything else is fantasy.

Unless . . .

I pause again and think. *Unless this is exactly the strategy he has decided to follow.*

This sort of revenge, to be more precise: to slowly, extremely methodically and cunningly let me know that he is on my heels . . . *Revenge is a dish best served cold* . . . Letting me know that he knows where I am, and then, nudge nudge, scaring me over the edge into a nervous breakdown before finally . . . Well, before doing what exactly?

Would he be capable of acting like this?

I have to ask myself that question in all seriousness. Would Martin Holinek, the man with whom I have shared house and home for the whole of my adult life, be capable of doing something like that? Would it be in line with his character?

To my horror I realize that I can't answer no to that question without reservations.

Especially if I consider the fact that the person he is after is his lawful wedded wife who tried to take his life by shutting him into a bunker full of hungry rats – and I really do have to take that circumstance into account, no matter what.

I start walking again. I feel sick. I can feel the first drops of what promises to be a heavy rain shower, and speed up in order to get back indoors as soon as possible.

But would it be possible to do that? I ask myself. Even theoretically possible? All he had with him when I left him there was the clothes he stood up in. How could he possibly have managed it?

An accomplice.

That thought strikes me just as we are clambering over the wall that separates Darne Lodge from the moor, and I realize immediately that it is a legitimate conclusion. Ergo: if Martin somehow managed to extricate himself from that confounded bunker and is still alive, he must have acquired an accomplice more or less immediately. There is no other possibility.

Somebody who assisted him with his plans, and helped him in every way necessary. Silence, money, support.

But how? I wonder. How could he possibly have found somebody like that?

Who?

When we had come indoors I tried to look at the situation from the other direction, from my point of view. What indications do I have? What exactly is there to suggest that these might be the facts of the situation? That the professor of literature Martin Emmanuel Holinek is in fact alive, and has a plan.

A silver-grey hire car with two daily newspapers in it?

Dead birds outside my front door? But it's several weeks now since the pheasant appeared there: would Martin really have been on Exmoor for as long as that?

No, I think. It doesn't add up. It's too implausible for it to be true. He would already have killed me if he had been here.

I don't know how convinced I really am about the correctness of this conclusion, but I curse myself for my stupidity. Curse myself for not having had the sense to make a note of the registration number of that car on either of the two occasions I've seen it. Armed with the number, it shouldn't be impossible for me to find out who hired the car from the Sixt rental company.

If I have a third opportunity I certainly won't waste it.

When we've been back at home for a while another thing occurs to me. If Martin Holinek is alive, he has exactly the same opportunity as I have for going into an internet cafe and checking his e-mails. For example . . . For example, reading the messages he himself is alleged to have sent to various recipients.

And surely he must ask himself who is looking after his e-mail correspondence so efficiently in his absence. Is there more than one candidate?

Using computers with their own unique IP addresses – for I haven't used our own computers, not in Minehead, and not in Winsford. If you have that number, that address, surely you must also be able to find out exactly where in the world that computer is located?

Could that be how it happened? Is that what he has done?

But I reject the idea. Martin has always been just as ignorant about and uninterested in computers as I am.

Perhaps it was that accomplice, then?

I reject him (her?) as well. Put two pieces of firewood on the fire and pour out a glass of port. Take two large swigs and feel my unease receding.

I take out the playing cards – I feel too unfocused to be able to read. Not even about John Ridd and Lorna Doone, 'a simple tale told simply'.

I reject the hazy hypotheses of fear.

Martin Holinek is dead. We met one day in June thirty-four years ago, at a garden party in Stockholm's Gamla Stan. We lived our lives together, and now he has gone. Naturally. Eaten up by rats and impossible to identify when some curious walker wandering along the beach on the Baltic coast of Poland feels moved to take a look inside a filthy old bunker.

That's the way it is. It's just that I have chosen not to spell it out previously with such brutal clarity. I've done exactly the same as the author E, and let it hide itself away between the lines: please forgive me for that detail, Gudrun Ewerts, when you read this up in your heaven.

I check that I have locked the door. Empty my glass of port and pour myself another, and set out the game of Spider Harp.

30

When Martin celebrated his fiftieth birthday, his present from me was a long weekend in New York. It was in September 2003: we arrived on a Thursday afternoon and left four days later. We stayed at a hotel in Lexington Avenue quite close to Grand Central Station, and I never set foot outside our room from start to finish.

The cause was a major stomach upset which had begun to make itself felt as our flight was approaching Newark, and which forced our taxi driver to stop twice on the drive into Manhattan.

I needed to be within easy reach of a lavatory, it was as simple as that. I suppose I thought it would pass after a few hours – or a day at most – but it didn't. I couldn't keep down a crumb of food until the Sunday evening, and as we boarded the plane the next morning for the flight home I was extremely grateful for the fact that I'd treated ourselves to business class in view of the journey's significance. If I'd been in economy I'm quite sure I would have been sick again.

Martin was loyal that first evening, just went down to the hotel bar for an hour and spent the rest of the time with me in room number 1828. The room was on the eighteenth floor, and so we had a splendid view. To the south and the east, downtown and over the East River towards Brooklyn on the other side. From the very beginning, that first evening, I made it clear to Martin that this was to be his trip and it wasn't the intention that he should sit twiddling his thumbs in a hotel room on my account. Neither of us was especially familiar with the city (Synn hadn't yet moved there, that happened about three years later and in any case didn't increase the frequency of our visits), so he ought to get out and about.

It wasn't too difficult to persuade him of that. On Friday he went out after breakfast, came back at six o'clock, had a shower and a whisky, then went out again. If I remember rightly he eventually tumbled into bed at about half past two.

On Saturday Martin woke up at about eleven and asked if I still had the stomach problem. I admitted that unfortunately that was still the case, he went back to sleep, got up an hour later and after another shower wondered if, given the circumstances, I didn't fancy going out for lunch.

I confirmed that unfortunately that was also the case, and he left me soon after two.

He returned thirteen hours later in a new but somewhat soiled suit. I asked him where it had come from, and he explained that it had come from Fifth Avenue and was his fiftieth birthday present to himself. I wondered what had happened to his old clothes, the ones he had been wearing when he went out, and he said he had given them away to a down-and-out in Union Square.

He fell asleep still wearing half his suit, without asking me about the state of my stomach infection.

I woke up early on Sunday morning, went to the bathroom and was sick. I realized it was due to the banana I had eaten during the night, and wondered if it was going to be possible for me to board a plane the next day. I also felt rather annoyed about Martin, and wished we had had separate rooms. But at the same time I felt a bit guilty: here he was, for once, in the city of cities, and of course it was only right that he should go out and enjoy himself.

But you can't deal with annoyance using reasonable thoughts of that kind, and when he had left me alone again, a few hours into the afternoon, I was merely glad to be rid of him. I didn't ask him to tell me what he had been up to the last couple of evenings, nor what he had in mind for the third and last one. And he didn't seem all that interested in informing me either, so in that respect I suppose you could say that we were on a par. I was also so exhausted after all my visits to the toilet that I reckoned as far as I was concerned he was welcome to go and drown himself in the Hudson River.

Or why not the East River – then I could watch it happening from my window.

The phone rang at a quarter past one in the morning. It was from the police station in 10th Street in Greenwich Village. Somebody called Sergeant Krapotsky.

He asked if he was talking to Mrs Holinek, and I confirmed that he was. What was it all about?

Was I perhaps married to a certain Martin Holinek? Sergeant Krapotsky wanted to know.

I confirmed that as well

'Very good,' said Krapotsky. 'We have your husband locked

up in a cell at the police station here. Could you perhaps be so kind as to come and collect him?'

'What has he done?' I asked.

'I'm sure you'd rather not know that,' said Krapotsky. 'But if you were to come and fetch him we could draw a veil over the whole business.'

'Is he drunk?' I asked.

'Is the earth round?' said Krapotsky. 'Is there water in the sea?'

'I understand,' I said. 'But I'm afraid the fact is that I'm ill and would have great difficulty in travelling from one end of the town to the other. We're flying back home to Sweden tomorrow, so you'll be rid of him in any case.'

'I know that,' said Krapotsky. 'He says he has to catch a plane early tomorrow morning. That's why I want to get him out of here.'

'Has he said anything else?'

'He says he's been trying to follow in the footsteps of Dylan Thomas, and it was going very well. I don't know if that makes any sense to you, but those were the exact words he said before he fell asleep. The footsteps of Dylan Thomas – I've no idea what that means.'

'I think I understand,' I said. 'But the fact is that our flight doesn't leave until tomorrow afternoon. Couldn't you let him sleep it off in his cell, and I'll pick him up in our taxi on the way to Newark?'

'Just a minute,' said Sergeant Krapotsky. 'I need to consult my boss.'

The telephone was silent for about half a minute. I looked

out over the skyline of south Manhattan – you can't avoid being impressed by it. Then the sergeant spoke again.

'Okay,' he said. 'My boss says that's okay. What time will you be calling in?'

'At about two o'clock, is that all right?' I asked.

'That would be absolutely fine,' said Krapotsky. 'Make sure you have his passport with you, assuming you have it, and tell them I've told you to collect him then. The address is 112 West 10th Street, but I won't be on duty then. Thank you for your cooperation.'

'Thank you for your help,' I said and hung up.

'I don't want to talk about this. Not ever, not with anybody.'

That was the first thing – and generally speaking the only thing – that Martin said during the taxi ride to New Jersey the following afternoon. I could see that he was on the point of bursting into tears and had the impression that if I hadn't had my sensitive stomach to think about I ought to have taken hold of his hand and said that I had forgiven him, irrespective of what there was to forgive him for. But I didn't. He was still wearing the suit from Fifth Avenue, but it was hard to tell that it was only two days old. It looked more like twenty years old, and it also concluded its short life in a rubbish basket at the airport. Later I found a receipt indicating that it had cost 1,800 dollars, which was roughly the same as the price of the hotel room. But I took it for granted that this was also a part of our agreement: that we shouldn't keep going on and on about the whole affair.

But the remarkable thing, the reason why I keep recalling those four days in New York, is the sudden feeling of tenderness that overcame me with regard to Martin. When I collected him from that police station in Greenwich Village, when we sat in silence on the back seat of the taxi, looking out through our respective windows, when he was in the toilet at the airport, changing his clothes. I ought to have been absolutely furious with him, even if it's not for me to require people to live up to great heights; but the feelings that actually filled me were the precise opposite. True enough, this hung-over wretch was a fifty-year-old literature professor; but he was also a little boy who had gone astray, and if I hadn't still been plagued with the after-effects of my stomach upset, I might well have told him so. That I really did feel sympathy for him. That there was something there reminiscent of what is called love – during those brief hours of our long marriage.

Perhaps it might have made him feel happy if I'd said something.

Perhaps it might have changed something.

Anyway, I told Christa about it a few days later, of course I did. Not that feeling of tenderness, just the rest of it. I remember her laughing, but I noticed that she did so because the situation demanded it, and I suspected she had been through similar experiences in her own life.

'I expect you know the difference between a fifteen-year-old and a fifty-year-old man?' she asked rhetorically in order to maintain the arms-length tone of the conversation. 'Forty kilos and enough money to put their daft dreams into practice.'

I have sometimes felt that life is in fact about as half-baked as that summary suggests. And that we really shouldn't go on and on about things.

I myself celebrated my fiftieth birthday a few years later. I travelled to Venice without Martin – that was a present I had asked for, and the family duly obliged. When my daughter asked why I wanted to go there on my own, I told her I'd had a secret lover in Venice for many years, and that shut her up.

I could see that she wasn't a hundred per cent sure that I was joking.

I could also see that she *hoped* I wasn't joking. That made me sad, extremely sad.

But I didn't go there alone in fact. Christa was with me for four of the five days I spent in that magic city, and I've already mentioned that business of ashes in the canal.

But that feeling of tenderness in New York: where did it come from? Where did it go to?

31

Rain is pelting against the bedroom window, and dawn is the colour of old meat. Castor is fast asleep down by my feet; I wish it were possible to teach a dog how to light a fire, so that I could for once get up without almost freezing to death. We have fallen asleep and then woken up for forty nights in Darne Lodge by this time, and I no longer wonder where I am when I open my eyes in the morning.

I live here with my dog. In a remote, stone-built cottage that was once built for a wayward son who needed a roof over his head. He enjoyed it so much that he eventually hanged himself. I lie in bed for a while, wondering exactly where. There are substantial roof beams both here in the bedroom and out there in the living room: perhaps he hung up there, swinging back and forth, from a beam directly over his bed? In which case the bed must have been located somewhere different from where it is now, which is not impossible. The room is quite large in fact, at least thirty square metres. It is the ridiculously low ceiling that makes it feel smaller: it strikes me that he must have used quite a short length of rope, otherwise his feet would have been touching the floor.

On the other hand, I think eventually . . . on the other hand

I've read about people hanging themselves from door handles and radiators. Nothing is impossible for a chap with an inventive turn of mind. And the fact that no more than two people have hanged themselves in this house in over two hundred years is a circumstance one ought to regard as something positive. Bearing in mind the moor. Bearing in mind the rain, the mists and the darkness.

I get up. Light a fire, sit down at the table and note down today's weather details in my diary. Tuesday the eleventh of December. Six degrees at a quarter to nine in the morning. A strong wind from the south-west and rain looking as if it's never going to stop falling.

A group of ponies suddenly appear some way away on the moor as the darkness begins to lift. They seem to have got stuck in the mud. I sit watching them for a while, but they don't move at all. I go for a shower, then get dressed. My last-but-one pair of knickers – I really must go to Minehead today and do some washing. I lift the cover off Castor and explain the situation to him.

He gives an enormous yawn, and licks my ear. I remind him that I love him. I keep my fear under lock and key.

About ten hours later all the day's chores have been completed, and I take out the brown suitcase. Maybe this will be the last time. In any case, I must work my way through the rest of the diary this evening. It's no more than ten pages. I have no idea about the typewritten pages or what is on the computer.

The last I read about Taza was that final act from the twenty-ninth of July: Tom Herold was roaring like a wounded lion and Bessie Hyatt had thrown herself into the swimming pool.

I thumb my way through to the thirtieth.

'It's beginning to feel ominous,' Martin writes.

> I can't help acknowledging that. This morning I discussed yesterday's events with both Grass and Soblewski, and they are just as worried as I am. Moreover something new emerged which makes the situation even more tense. Soblewski has had a private conversation with Herold and been informed that the great poet is sterile. He's incapable of creating children, which is why his first marriage collapsed. Which also means . . .

He doesn't go into what that means because it is obvious anyway. Herold is not the father of the child that is growing in his wife's stomach, Bessie really does have a lover – or at least has had sex with another man. Martin doesn't believe there is any truth in the suggestion that she was raped by the Arab Ahib, nor do Grass and Soblewski, it seems. It's too much like a back-to-front *Othello*, and all three seem to recall noting several loans from that Shakespearean drama in yesterday's performance.

Martin summarizes the conversation with Grass and Soblewski in one-and-a-half pages, then comes a blank line and the rest of the entry of the thirtieth of July is about what happens during that evening.

Which is not very much, it seems. There is none of yesterday's drama. Herold and Hyatt act almost like a newly married couple: she sits on his knee for most of the meal, or at the very least extremely close to him, and they caress and kiss each other with a total lack of modesty. Martin writes that 'they behave like a pair of turtle doves, it seems they just can't wait to get undressed and crawl naked between the sheets together – I really don't know what to think.' The atmosphere seems to be infectious, for Martin notes that Doris Guttmann appears to have fallen for the ever-present Russian Gusov. The evening is characterized by an affectionate, not to say erotic mood, and they leave the table unusually early. Even the French couple seem to be besotted with each other, and the same trio as during the morning – Martin, Grass and Soblewski – are left alone at one corner of the table. They sit there for a while, drinking single malt whisky and chewing olives, evidently disappointed by the events of the evening. Needless to say Martin doesn't write that he feels disappointed, but I can tell by the tone of what he puts that he is. In his final free-standing line he sums it all up:

'Our senses never betray us, it is in our heads that we get lost. Always in our heads.'

I read that line over and over again, trying to understand precisely what he means. But I don't reach a conclusion, apart from the thought that it might well be a quotation, and possibly that it smells of Scottish distilleries.

The following day, the thirty-first of July, is dominated by a visit to Al-Hafez. The Belgian artist Pieter Baertens has delivered a large oil-painting they have commissioned and Martin describes in detail how the canvas is unrolled, spread out, gaped at, admired and commented on. It depicts Salome with John the Baptist's head on a dish, and is at least six square metres in size. Baertens is accompanied by his wife, 'or mistress or whatever she is': she is Japanese and it is obvious that she posed as Salome. By all accounts Baertens is quite a famous and successful artist, and Grass states in an aside for Martin's benefit that a commissioned painting like this would certainly cost around 100,000 dollars.

But then Herold has never had a reputation for being poor. Needless to say they indulge in an especially extravagant dinner during the course of the evening – the anonymous servants really deserve their wages, 'whatever they may be' – and no serious incidents occur. As midnight approaches they all go skinny-dipping in the swimming pool, apart from Megal whose excuse is that he's too old, and Bessie who is reluctant to display her widely discussed stomach.

This would have been an appropriate point at which to reflect on swollen stomachs: back home in Stockholm there is one in Folkungagatan – much larger than Bessie Hyatt's, if I'm not much mistaken – but it doesn't occur to Martin to make any such comparisons.

Instead he states that he simply went to bed with a mysterious hypnotist and an extremely pleasant Japanese lady in his mind's eye. In his mind's eye, note . . .

One day left. Only four pages, thank goodness.

*

The first of August begins with the sentence: 'I ought not to write about this.' As I understand it, he is sitting in his room and doing just that. In which case it is about five o'clock in the morning, and hence the second of August in fact, and he is sitting there because he is waiting for dawn to break.

This is because at first light he will embark on a short walk into the desert-like countryside that begins immediately outside the walls surrounding Al-Hafez. He will do so along with the other five actors of the male sex. I'm the one who uses the word 'actors', not Martin, because at this stage the thought that the whole procedure is pure theatre seems very obvious. I read twice over everything that Martin writes about the day and the evening, to make sure that I haven't misunderstood anything.

In broad outline, this is what happens. The Belgian artist Baertens takes his Japanese Salome with him and leaves the stage at some point in the afternoon. Martin allows himself an hour's siesta in his room, and soon afterwards the usual group is sitting round the table on the terrace. Martin states that Bessie Hyatt 'is having one of her dark days'. He describes her appearance as that of 'a wounded hind' and 'a bird that has flown too close to the sun and burnt itself'. (I decide not to write any more 'sic!'s, and continue.) She also leaves the party after less than an hour – and does come back again a little later, but only to say goodnight, and wish the men good luck.

At this point Martin doesn't yet know why she is wishing them good luck – but later he remembers this and realizes that she must have been involved, or at least known what was going to happen. When the meal can reasonably be considered over and done with, Tom Herold explains that he expects the men present – as a gesture of appreciation and thanks for the hospitality that has been lavished upon them – to take part in a scientific experiment. He goes into no detail about what the experiment involves, nor what its purpose is – that will become obvious later. He assumes they will all trust him and behave like upright and civilized gentlemen. When they have all said that they are willing to accept these conditions – only Gusov tries to wriggle out of it for some reason or other, but is soon talked round – Herold produces three hookahs which they divide among themselves, two by two. Martin is sitting next to Soblewski. It is not clear from Martin's text what the ladies present get up to while these preparations are taking place.

And so they light up a mixture of tobacco and something else. Martin tries to describe what happens inside his head, but isn't quite up to it. In any case, he must have fallen asleep after a while because he writes that he wakes up at about two o'clock, still on the terrace but now, like the others, lying on the ground. Lanterns are still burning here and there, but the three ladies are no longer present. Tom Herold and Grass are awake, the others are just regaining consciousness. When they are all back in the land of the living they are offered water to drink. Martin writes that he feels more thirsty than he has ever done in his life before. When they have all drunk their fill of water and returned to their places around the table, Herold produces six revolvers from a black box on the table in front of him. He asks how many of the gentlemen present are familiar with guns. It seems that everybody is apart from Grass –

Martin assumes that the others, like himself, have undergone some sort of basic military training. Without actually firing a shot, Herold demonstrates how a revolver functions. Martin notes that all six seem to be identical and are evidently of the same make. When everybody says they understand how the pistols work, Herold loads them, with six bullets in each revolving chamber. 'Some of these bullets are live, the rest are blanks,' he explains. 'It's not easy to distinguish between them, as they all sound equally loud. Unless we look into the effect they have had, of course.'

Martin repeats that last sentence, and underlines it in his text. *Unless we look into the effect they have had, of course.*

When the explanation and demonstration are completed, Tom Herold wonders if anybody has any questions.

Nobody does.

That really is what he writes. Nobody has any questions, and Martin doesn't even comment on that fact. I assume that the brains of both him and the others are overfull of what they smoked, and what sent them to sleep.

'Okay,' says Tom Herold. 'We shall go out into the desert at dawn. You will be collected from your rooms at exactly six o'clock.'

And that is where the diary from Taza ends.

32

Perhaps there are authors who would be pleased to write a conclusion like that to a play, but I find it difficult to imagine that an audience would applaud.

I check to make sure that no pages have been torn out. It's easily done, and incidentally Martin's text ends halfway down one page.

Then I take out the typewritten pages. Sit and read through them for half an hour. It becomes clear that about three-quarters is typed-up material from the diary. There is nothing about Morocco, only Greece. Plus a few short free-standing texts: nature descriptions from Samos, a short essay on Cavafy and Odysseas Elytis, and something that looks like the beginning of a short story. Five pages of short poems, some of them in haiku form.

That's all. Nowhere is there any continuation from Al-Hafez in Taza. Not a single page, not a single line about that. There is good reason to assume that all the typewritten pages were composed before the summer of 1980.

I put the pages away and check the clock. It is a few minutes past eleven. I let Castor out to do his business, and think:

Should I start examining the computer material now, or wait until tomorrow?

Bessie Hyatt committed suicide in March 1981 – I have checked that. Eight months after the goings-on in Taza. She never gave birth to a child, I've checked that as well. Martin indicated to Bergman that he had material he had been sitting on for thirty years. It seems to me that it must be this stuff I have been working up towards. It must surely be about what happened at dawn on the second of August 1980, when six men went out into the desert with their revolvers.

Which resulted in Martin ceasing to keep a diary, and leaving Al-Hafez.

I can probably offer you eight translations of this without further ado, Bergman had said. How could he be so sure? Had Martin told him something about it? Or had a few vague hints been sufficient?

Castor came back. I put three new logs on the fire, and took out Martin's computer.

I hadn't opened the folder marked 'Taza' before, but when I did so now I saw that it contained two separate documents. I opened the first one, and it soon became obvious that it was the written-up diary entries. From all four summers, if I was not much mistaken. It occurred to me that I had been an idiot: I could have read it all on the computer instead of having to struggle with Martin's messy handwriting. There might have been differences between the two versions of the text – he had naturally revised and rewritten some bits – but when I read carefully the first two days I couldn't find any significant differences.

I scrolled down to the end. Bit my lip when I discovered that the text on the computer stopped at the same point as the handwritten diary.

But no, not quite. He had added a few lines. Five short sentences.

> I'm sitting here, waiting. I feel very odd – the stuff we smoked is still hanging around, no doubt about it. The first signs of dawn are appearing. I don't know what's going to happen. It feels like a dream.

Then the document comes to an end. *It feels like a dream*. I closed it down. Went back to the folder to open the other document, the one he had entitled simply 'At Dawn'.

I clicked on it.

It didn't open. Instead I was informed that a password was needed.

Password? I thought. Martin Holinek? Well, knock me down with a feather (my father again).

I repeated the procedure with the same result. The document 'At Dawn' could only be opened if you typed in the correct password.

It didn't say how many figures or letters were required. I could feel the irritation growing inside me – Martin had difficulty in remembering the code for his debit card. He could just about manage his own social security number, but not mine nor those of our children. He hated all PIN-codes. But nevertheless, he had locked access to this document.

You could see when it was created and when he had last opened it – the twentieth of September 2009 and the fifteenth of October 2012 respectively. It wasn't all that old, only three years, so I assumed there had been an original version. And that he had opened it and looked at it – perhaps edited and added to it – as late as the week we left Nynäshamn.

The size was also given: no more than 25K, which as far as I knew could mean anything at all between three and fifteen pages of text. And I was convinced that the file comprised pages of text.

But what could the password be?

I started with *Castor*.

Was informed that was incorrect, and tried *Holinek*.

That was also wrong. I tried *Martin*.

Same again, and this time I was also informed that I couldn't have any more attempts. I closed the document, and the folder as well, and started again. Surely it can't be the same as with debit cards and mobile phones? I thought. That you only have three chances, full stop?

But it was.

Well, not quite. Another message appeared: *Try again tomorrow*.

Try again tomorrow? What did that mean? That it was okay to try different passwords the next day? Could it be so . . . so damned cunning? And above all, could Martin have invented anything so damned cunning? Three attempts per day?

Perhaps he could, I thought. If there was something especially serious involved. Something that had to be concealed at all costs.

There was good reason to think that this criterion might apply.

I cursed and looked at the clock. It was ten minutes to midnight.

Midnight? If I could manage to restrain myself for ten more minutes, that should mean I would then have three more chances. Surely that must be the case?

Fair deal, I thought, and suddenly felt like the skilful female hacker in a traditional American thriller. Or why not an English war film? What was it called? . . . Ah yes: *Enigma*.

I shook off all my film thoughts and tried to think straight. To put myself inside Martin's head. If I had been married to a man for thirty years, surely I ought to be able to work out what password he would use to prevent anybody from penetrating his secrets?

When I formulated that question I tried to convince myself that it was rhetorical. That of course it could be answered with 'yes', certainly: a gifted hacker wife ought to be able to sort that out, and it was only a matter of time before I gained access to the document. I started writing down possibilities in my notebook, and by the time the clock said it was the twelfth of December I had decided on three.

Emmanuel. His second name.

Maria. His wife.

Bessie. For obvious reasons.

I opened the folder and clicked on the document for the third time. I expected the little light-blue window to appear, but instead I was confronted by the same message as last time. *You have given an incorrect password. Try again tomorrow.*

But it is tomorrow, you stupid berk, I hissed at the computer – shut down and opened up once again. It's turned midnight, for Christ's sake.

I was surprised to find myself sitting here like this, talking to Martin's computer: Castor raised his head from the fleece rug and looked enquiringly at me. He's usually the one I talk to, at least since we've been living here in Darne Lodge.

I explained the situation to him, and assured him there was nothing he needed to worry about.

Then I noticed the little indication of the time up in the top right-hand corner of the computer screen. *Wed 01.06.* And various seconds ticking away.

Swedish time, in other words. 01.06 there would be 12.06 in England. What did that mean? Unfortunately it was not difficult to work it out: I had wasted my first three attempts during the first hour of the new day, not during the last hour of the previous one as I had at first assumed. I would have to wait . . . for twenty-three hours. Until eleven o'clock the next evening.

Emmanuel. Maria. Bessie.

Unless I hit upon something better in the meantime.

I swore at the computer and switched it off.

Took Castor with me and went to bed.

Irritation – wasn't that supposed to be an indication that you were healthy? I seemed to remember that it was, as I switched off the light. That had been the thought that struck me some days ago – and just now I can't remember when I had last been as irritated as I am now.

Not since I came here, in any case.

Not since I closed that heavy iron door on the beach in Poland and thought I had become somebody else.

So I'm still alive?

I decided on that interpretation.

33

I think I realize it's a mistake the moment I turn off onto the road leading to Hawkridge.

We've been shopping in Dulverton. Had lunch at The Bridge Inn and visited the second-hand bookshop. There was no book by Bessie Hyatt on the shelves, but the obliging owner, who reminds me of a dying dandelion every time I see her, has promised to have acquired both of them if I call in on Monday or Tuesday next week.

'They're quite good, actually. I read them thirty years ago – then things didn't go so well for her, poor girl. But I've never come to grips with that Tom Herold character, I'm afraid . . . Is there anything else I can tempt you with?'

I explain that I'm only halfway through *Lorna Doone*, but thank her for being so helpful.

In fact it's Lorna Doone who makes me want to take a look at Hawkridge: the place is mentioned in the book, and we pass the worn-looking signpost every time we drive between Winsford and Dulverton. If nothing else, we could do with a walk, both Castor and I: that's the real reason, and there are a couple of hours of the day left.

Not much in the way of daylight, however, but at least the

rain that fell all morning has now stopped, and no doubt we shall find some public footpath or bridleway. But even after a few hundred metres I realize that I must tone down my expectations.

The road to Hawkridge is gloomy and full of bends. It's also sunk down several metres below the surrounding countryside, and I have no idea where we are as I've left the map behind at Darne Lodge. We are like two blind rabbits in a deep ditch, and we edge our way forward with extreme care – but that is a poor image: Castor would never agree that he is a rabbit. We are a half-blind beetle – or rather, two of them of course – that's better, on our way under the earth, on our way to . . . No, enough of all these silly images that flicker away unbidden inside my head, I think: to hell with you, for this is serious.

And fear is sitting beside me in the passenger seat: I don't know how to cope with this, it's new to me.

New dirty signposts pointing along even narrower roads to even more dreary places. *Ashwick. Venford Moor. West Anstey.* I don't recall any of the names from the map, and we don't meet any other vehicles at all. That's just as well, bearing in mind that the road is at no point wider than three metres. Blackmore writes that the wheel didn't reach Exmoor until the end of the seventeenth century: people moved around on horseback without carts, and it is evidently those bridle paths and winding tracks between ancient villages and dwellings that were eventually tarmacked over several centuries later to create what are now called roads. That must surely be what happened: these lanes have been trodden down by the hooves of weary horses over thousands of years.

We eventually get to Hawkridge. There is no sign of any people in the village, which seems to comprise about ten houses and a dark grey church on a hill. At the only crossroads is a red letter box and an equally red telephone kiosk. And a tiny little parking area where we stop alongside a deserted tractor. We get out of the car and look round. It's not only the tractor that looks deserted.

I catch sight of a sign pointing down to Tarr Steps. I gather the path must lead to Barle from the opposite direction to ours, and that it's not possible to get there by car. I recall John Ridd's comment to the effect that as everybody knows, the big block of stone in the *merrily flowing* river was placed there by the Devil himself, and that it is somewhere to avoid unless you have urgent business to do there.

Despite the fact that we don't really have any urgent business to do there, we start walking down the steeply sloping road. Car drivers are warned that the slope is one in three, and that there are no possible turning places for a mile and a half. But it strikes me that a woman walking with her dog must be able to turn round whenever they feel like it, and so we head down the slope in determined fashion. There is no direction to look in apart from downwards, as the embankment on both sides of the road is more than two metres high. I assume there are muddy fields on either side of the road, but it's simply not possible to leave it.

All of a sudden Castor decides that he has no yearning to go any further. He sits down in the middle of the road and looks at me with an expression that makes it clear he's had enough. I explain to him that we've only been walking for ten minutes, and we'd agreed to walk for twenty minutes before turning back

But it doesn't help. I argue with him for a while, but he refuses to budge. I take a couple of liver treats out of my pocket, but he's not interested. He merely turns his head and looks back up the hill towards Hawkridge. The sky is low up there, leaden-coloured and heavy. I think things over for a while, and decide that there really are places that God seems to have abandoned. It must have been this very road that the Devil walked along when he carried the stones down to Tarr Steps in order to cross over the river to the brighter side – there seems no doubt about it.

And then I see the raven. It's sitting on the top of the left-hand embankment ten metres ahead of us, and I understand straight away that this is the reason why Castor has refused to go any further. You simply don't pass underneath a raven that is sitting there staring at you. Most certainly not, that's something every dog learns in its first class at school.

And at that very moment, as I am standing there, staring at the raven while the big, black bird sits glaring at us with one eye and Castor looks studiously in another direction, it starts raining. Not the familiar, pleasant and gently caressing rain that usually falls over the moor, but a veritable cloudburst from directly above us. Fistfuls of hailstones clatter down on the asphalt. There is nowhere to shelter. I shout to Castor and tell him he is absolutely right, and we start hurrying back up the Devil's road. Behind us I can hear the raven croaking a threatening message as it flies away. If we could, we would run all the way back to the car: but it's too steep. My heart is pounding away in my chest as a result of the effort, and perhaps for other reasons as well, and I assume that Castor's is pounding similarly. He is staying close by my side all the while, and he doesn't usually do that.

It takes us much longer to get back to the church than it took us to get down to the raven, and the rain persists all the while. Aggressively and stubbornly as if it were intent on destroying something: that seems to be the kind of rain it is, and we can't avoid it. Not for a metre, not for a second.

But it hasn't managed to make our filthy Audi look much cleaner. At least not the front door on the driver's side, which has been slightly screened by the abandoned tractor – and somebody has written in very clear letters rubbed out of the dirt: DEATH.

Probably with an index finger inside a glove, by the looks of it.

I stand and stare at it.

I look round. No sign of anybody. Darkness is falling fast. No lights are lit in any of the houses round about us, not a single one. The church seems to be leaning over us.

Can that message have been there earlier, when we left Dulverton? Can somebody have written it when we were in The Bridge Inn? Death?

Or has somebody written it during the half-hour we left the car in this remote place?

What difference would it make? What kind of an idiotic question is that to ask? I rub out the letters with my jacket sleeve. Castor is whimpering by my side: I let him into the back of the car, and I clamber into the driver's seat. Soaking wet dog, soaking wet missus. But at least we have a roof over our heads now. The rain is pounding away. I lock the doors and sigh deeply.

Turn the ignition key: but the engine doesn't start.

I close my eyes and repeat the procedure.

Nothing happens. Not a sound from the engine.

I whisper a desperate prayer.

Third time lucky. The engine starts, I back out quickly from the parking area, and drive away.

I've no idea in which direction I'm heading, but that doesn't matter. I must get away, I think. Away from here.

No, it was a mistake to go to Hawkridge.

34

The thirteenth of December, a Thursday. St Lucia's Day, the day when Swedes burn candles to celebrate the light in the middle of winter. It continued raining all night, growing less heavy during the next morning but not ceasing altogether. The usual westerly wind, the morning walk up to Wambarrows and the same route back. Six degrees. It's getting muddier and muddier for each day that passes, and you need to be careful not to get stuck. In the afternoon we drive to Watersmeet, walk up towards Brendon and are back in Darne Lodge by early dusk soon after four o'clock. No previously unexplored paths, no strolls along steep roads used by the Devil.

Generally speaking, I feel more on edge. With a fear lurking in the background that I would prefer not to look more closely into. I'm grateful that we are going to have dinner at Mark Britton's place tomorrow evening. Extremely grateful. I only wish it were this evening.

I play sixteen games of patience, but only solve three of them; I read a little but find it hard to concentrate. When it has become midnight in Sweden, albeit only eleven o'clock in this country, I try three new passwords: *Grass*, *Soblewski* and

Gusov. They work just as badly as yesterday's *Herold*, *Hyatt* and *Megal*. Perhaps I shall have to think along different lines.

But what lines? I ask myself. I have no idea. In any case I have noted down the names I've already used, so that I don't risk repeating the same mistake twice. Names? It occurs to me that there's no reason why the password should be a name. It could just be a word, any word at all. *Doubt. Bunker. Raven.*

It doesn't even need to be a word in any language: a combination of letters or letters and numbers would be sufficient. How on earth could I possibly hit upon the correct combination? How could I imagine that I knew my husband so well that I could work out what password he would choose from hundreds of thousands of possibilities?

Presumptuous.

Presumptuous and stupid.

But I must open that document – it seems more of a burning necessity with every hour that passes. I don't know why. Or do I? *At Dawn.*

Is there a short-cut? How would a Lisbeth Salander approach the problem?

A silly question. Lisbeth Salander would already have solved it. For an ordinary person it's a question of finding a Salander.

Or somebody of her calibre, at least. Or half of it. A tiny fraction of it.

Alfred Biggs?

Margaret Allen?

Mark Britton. That thought feels like a lump of ice in my throat. No, not Mark Britton, as . . . as Mark Britton has no part to play in this business. I'm not at all sure where he does have a part to play, whatever I mean by that, but in any case I don't want to involve him in Greece or Morocco.

On the other hand – during today's walk alongside the East Lyn River, a pleasant and quite dry route that I could walk five times a week – I have started to toy with another thought involving Mr Britton. So far it is no more than an undeveloped foetus, maybe I shan't develop it any further, but it's that experience in Hawkridge that lies at the bottom of it.

Hawkridge together with the other things. The hire car and the pheasants. But as I said, I don't want to spell it out yet, nor even to think about it. We go to bed instead, my dog and I; we switch off the light and lie there under the covers, listening to the wind and another sound that comes whining over the moor. I don't know what it is, it's the first time I've heard it: a metallic, almost mournful noise; I can't decide if it's coming from an animal or from something else.

Something else? What might that be? It's two miles down to the village. One to Halse Farm.

The curtains are not quite tightly closed, as usual. I roll over onto my side, with my back towards the moor. Place the pillow over my head so that all sounds are eliminated. I think about Synn. About Gunvald. About Christa and about Gudrun Ewerts.

About Martin.

Rolf.

Gunsan.

People I have met during my life. One more week, and it's the shortest day of the year.

*

We wake up late on Friday. I feel sluggish and listless. If I didn't have a dog to think about I would presumably stay in bed all day.

No, that's not true. If I didn't have a dog I would kill myself. I would become the third case of suicide in Darne Lodge – perhaps Mr Tawking could turn the place into a tourist attraction on that account. Our names on a plate on the wall; but I have forgotten the names of my predecessors. Selwyn something, and the man with the Belgian name. Maybe he could include Elizabeth Williford Barrett on the other side of the road, I remember her name because we pass her grave nearly every day. It occurs to me that I still haven't found out who she was, and why she is lying where she is. Maybe I can ask about that at the computer centre: I remind myself to pay a visit there later today. Perhaps I can ask about the password as well, if there is some way of getting round it. In principle, that is: I could make it seem that it's one of my own documents and I've simply forgotten what the password is because it's so long since I thought it up . . .

As I lie there in bed it also occurs to me that I haven't heard a squeak from Mr Tawking since we sorted out the rental contract and I received the keys to Darne Lodge. That was some six weeks ago. Shouldn't he have been in touch to ask how things were going? Or at least to check that I hadn't burnt down his house?

All the thoughts and questions have gradually scraped the sluggishness out of my body, and I get up. It's a quarter past ten. Eight degrees and patches of blue sky here and there. I haul Castor out of bed and tell him he'd better get a grip – a missus shouldn't need to wake up her dog.

He doesn't understand what I'm talking about, but a quarter of an hour later we are out on the moor in the sunshine. And so the unhealthy pallor of those worrying thoughts is transformed into the healthy tan of decisiveness.

Two e-mail messages of a certain importance. Or at least, they need an answer. The first is from Bergman to Martin:

> Hi! I had dinner with Ronald Scoltock from Faber & Faber yesterday evening. We got round to talking about you, and he seemed to be very interested. He would like to get in touch with you, and perhaps even pay you a visit. As I understand it he has a house in Marrakesh. Is it okay if I give him your e-mail address? Keep your nose to the grindstone, I hope all is going as it should. Greetings to your wonderful wife, of course. Eugen

I think it over for a while before replying that we would prefer not to have any visits at the moment, that I (Martin) am in the middle of a spell of very intensive work, and that perhaps it would be best if we were to make contact with Scoltock after the New Year.

The other message is from Violetta di Parma:

> Dear Maria, I'm feeling very much at home in your house. It really does feel like a privilege to be able to live here. I'm sorry I haven't been in touch sooner, but everything has been working as it should, so there has been no reason to contact

you. I'm extremely busy as well, but that is stimulating and so I'm not complaining. The only thing I wonder is whether I ought to forward post to you. There has been quite a lot, in fact, and perhaps you ought to take a look at it, to be on the safe side. But I don't have your address. If you let me know what it is I can send you everything without delay.

A Merry Christmas! There is no snow yet here in Stockholm, but it seems to be in the air. It's very cold and windy in any case. I hope all is well with you – no doubt it's much warmer down there where you are!

With best wishes from Violetta

I recall that I had promised to send her our address as soon as we had settled down in Morocco, and that it really was high time I did something about it. There shouldn't be any invoices to pay in the post that had been delivered to Nynäshamn: we changed everything to direct debits before we left, but of course you never know . . . In any case, I must answer her message, and the best response I can come up with is to ask her to forward post to *Holinek, poste restante, Rabat*. I explain that this is the safest way to proceed, add that we are in fine shape, are pleased that she feels at home in our house, and that we send her our very best wishes for a Merry Christmas and a Happy New Year.

I don't attempt to read any news on this occasion either, and since Margaret Allen seems to be rather busy at her own computer I decide not to take up with her that business of solving the password problem. I merely thank her for the tea, and say that I shall probably call in again before Christmas.

'Surely you're not going to spend Christmas all alone up there?' she asks, looking somewhat worried.

I tell her that I shall probably be going to visit a friend in Ilfracombe, but that in any case I have my dog to keep me company. That makes her smile, and she gives Castor a pat on the head.

'I'd like to read one of your books, I really would.'

'If you can hang on for another fifty years, no doubt one of them will appear in English translation.'

We leave Winsford Community Computer Centre, and walk down to the war memorial to collect the car and drive back to Darne Lodge and spruce ourselves up before dinner at Heathercombe Cottage.

Just as we are about to get into the car, a silver-coloured Renault drives past. It turns off to the left at the crossroads, in the direction of Exford and Wheddon Cross. I have time to see the logo saying it is a Sixt rental car, but not to catch the registration number.

And nothing more of the driver than a glimpse of his outline from behind. It is a man, that is quite clear, but that's about all that can be said.

For a brief moment I toy with the thought of following him, but drop it almost immediately. Instead that vague plan about spinning a yarn to Mark Britton suddenly takes on a new reality.

35

It was Jeremy who opened the door.

He must have been sitting there waiting for us, as I didn't have time to knock. Quite a slim young man, an inch shorter than me – he had seemed bigger than this when I saw him in that upstairs window.

He looked hard at me with his dark, almost black eyes – a little worried, perhaps, but not threatening as I had feared he might be. The inspection took five seconds. Then he looked down at the floor and took a pace backward so that I could go in. He was wearing black, scruffy jeans, big fluffy slippers and a multicoloured jersey with the name Harlequins embroidered on the chest.

'That used to be his favourite rugby team,' explained Mark who appeared in the kitchen doorway.

'I see. Rugby.'

Used to be? I thought. When he was twelve?

'Welcome. I think he wants you to shake hands and introduce yourself.'

I did as I was bidden. Jeremy's hand was cold and dry, and he let go of mine after only a second: but nevertheless I detected something positive in his attitude. A feeling that he was at ease in the situation. That I was okay. Mark placed a hand on his shoulder.

'You can go up to your room if you like. I'll give you a shout when the food's ready.'

Jeremy stood there and seemed to be thinking things over, then turned on his heel and went off upstairs. He had paid no attention to Castor at all, who had been sitting discreetly just inside the door, waiting his turn.

'Welcome, both of you,' said Mark and took my jacket. 'Come into the kitchen and you can have a drink while I finish off the delicacies.'

He smiled, and patted his black apron to illustrate how seriously things were being taken. I thought a drink was exactly what I needed, and followed him along a short corridor that led into a large, cosy kitchen. A dark oak table in front of a mullioned window looked as if it could accommodate at least a dozen people; a fire was burning in a hearth, and it occurred to me that without much in the way of rearrangement one could shoot a cookery programme in here.

I told Mark I thought it looked lovely, and he threw wide his hands. 'The heart of the house,' he said. 'I spent all the money I had on this when I moved in. The rest of the cottage is in nowhere near the same class, I'm afraid; but I'm glad you like it. I'm going to have a gin and tonic. What about you?'

'A gin and tonic sounds splendid,' I said, sitting down at one corner of the table. 'But not too strong – I have to drive home eventually.'

'Don't worry about that,' said Mark. 'I've already taken care of that detail.'

I didn't ask what he meant by that, presumably because I badly wanted a drink and a few glasses of wine.

'With a kitchen like this you ought to have guests every evening,' I said instead. 'Especially if you're as good a cook as you claim to be.'

'You're my first guest for a year,' said Mark. 'My sister was here with her husband and children last Christmas. Since then it's just been Jeremy and me.'

He handed me a glass, and we sipped at our drinks.

'Good.'

'A donkey can make a gin and tonic. Has Castor had something to eat?'

I nodded and received a surprised look from my dog. He has a tendency to forget that he's eaten the moment he finishes doing so.

'He's had his evening meal. But maybe you could give him a bowl of water?'

Mark stroked Castor and provided a bowl of water that he naturally turned up his nose at. Went and rolled up in front of the fire in passive protest.

The starter was scallops. Fried in butter with a pinch of cayenne pepper and a touch of black sauce that I would have called piquant, were it not for the fact that I can't stand that word. But it was good in any case, just as good as I'd hoped it would be.

That's what Mark and I had – Jeremy sat beside his father and ate fish fingers with chips and mayonnaise. 'There's no point in making fancy stuff for him,' Mark had explained. 'There are four or five dishes he condescends to eat, and they're all in the same class as fish fingers. Preferably some yellow Fanta to wash it down, as you can see, but he only gets that on special occasions.'

Jeremy didn't seem to mind Mark speaking about him like that. He was too busy concentrating on eating. Very carefully, almost scientifically, he cut up the fish fingers with his knife, speared a piece on his fork, added a suitably sized piece of potato, dipped it into the mayonnaise, tasted the result and then put it into his mouth. As he chewed away at length, he sat motionless with his eyes closed.

Then he washed it all down with a mouthful of Fanta. I tried not to look at him, and Mark noticed that. 'I know,' he said. 'He eats like a robot. But he tended a bit that way even before the accident, so perhaps it has something to do with his personality . . . Whatever is left of it.'

I thought about that gesture Jeremy had made in the window. It didn't seem at all appropriate to the impression I had of him now. But as I hadn't mentioned it before, I didn't bring it up now. I just felt surprisingly well disposed towards this boy who had never had a chance to learn how to behave in social circumstances. He looked so well groomed and harmless, and I wondered if he was always like this, and how much training he had needed in order to get him to behave in such a civilized manner. Lots of medication, perhaps? Good days and bad days?

'He'll leave us as soon as he's finished this course,' said Mark. 'He never has a starter or a dessert.'

'Not even a Crunchie?'

'He'll get a Crunchie up in his room.'

Mark's prediction turned out to be correct. When Jeremy had eaten his six fish fingers he stood up and looked at his father. Mark nodded, Jeremy shook my hand again then went back up the stairs to his room.

'I hope you didn't . . .'

I paused, but it was too late. Mark raised an eyebrow. I could see that he had expected me to ask the question I wanted to put. So I asked it.

'I hope you didn't instruct him to go away and leave us in peace, did you?'

We both had a drop of wine left in our glasses. Sancerre, dry and full-bodied, and a much better accompaniment to the scallops than yellow Fanta would have been. Mark raised his glass and gave me a slightly reproachful look.

'Certainly not,' he said. 'I'd like you to be clear that I would never do anything like that. He is worth that respect. He's out of his depth wherever he goes in the world, but not in his own home. This is the only place where he will ever be fully accepted.'

'Was that why you took him home?'

'Yes.'

'Forgive me.'

'Of course,' said Mark, with a smile. 'I have a bit of a hang-up with this. I stress it too much and when it's not necessary,

I know. But now we're coming to the real fish. Could you see your way clear to continuing with the same wine?'

'I can most certainly see my way clear to continuing with the same wine. Is there anything I can do to help?'

'You could stack the plates away in the dishwasher while I see to the halibut. Cheers once again, and thank you for coming. It's going pretty well, don't you think?'

'So far I've nothing to complain about,' I said, and Mark burst out laughing.

That must have been the first time for goodness knows how many years that anything I'd said made anybody burst out laughing.

I don't know what expectations I'd had for his halibut, but whatever they were there is no doubt that Mark's dish exceeded them, and he repeated what he'd said at The Royal Oak: 'It's the low cooking temperature that does the trick, nothing else. You turn the heat right up for a few seconds so that it doesn't lose its moisture, then no more than sixty to seventy degrees for an hour.'

You could hear that he really was interested in this kind of thing, and I wondered how pleasant life might have been if I'd been married to a cook rather than a professor of literature. It was presumably as a follow-up to such thoughts – and also the fact that by now we had drunk almost two bottles of wine – that I decided to put my little problem to him.

'To change the subject, I have a bit of a problem,' I said. 'I think I'm being pestered by a stalker.'

'What?' said Mark. 'What do you mean?'

'A bloke who's following me around. I think he is, at least . . .'

'Well, that is what a stalker does,' said Mark. 'He follows people around. I'm not surprised, in fact.'

'Now you've lost me.'

'It's obvious that a woman like you is going to get a stalker sooner or later . . . No, I'm sorry . . . Are you serious? You don't mean here and now, do you?'

'Yes,' I said. 'Unfortunately I do mean here and now.'

He gave a laugh, and looked confused for a moment. As if he couldn't make up his mind if I was joking or not. 'A stalker in Winsford? That sounds like . . . No, surely it can't be true?'

I recalled what he had said about reading other people's minds, and wondered if he really could see that I was lying. But emboldened by the wine I went on:

'If it's who I think it is, it's an old story. It's rather unpleasant, to be honest, and I can't help feeling that I'm being got at. The fact that I'm not absolutely sure almost makes it feel worse.'

Now I could see that he was taking me seriously. He moved his elbows up onto the table and leaned forward. 'Huh, you'd better tell me about it. You're not going to get a dessert until we've sorted this out. A stalker? A loony who's after you . . . ?'

I took a drink of wine, cleared my throat, and started my tale.

'It's an old story, as I said. I think I mentioned that I have a past as a television presenter?'

He nodded.

'Everybody knows it can be a bit risky, always appearing on the box. Lonely loonies sit on their sofas, imagining all kinds of fantasies . . . I suppose it goes with the territory, unfortunately. Anyway, there was a bloke some years ago who started to get all kinds of strange ideas. He managed to get hold of both my address and telephone number, and . . . well, he kept pestering me quite a lot until we managed to put a stop to him.'

'You put a stop to him? What did he do? Ring up and do some heavy breathing?'

'That happened, yes.'

'Were you on your own by then?'

'Yes. It started about six months after my divorce. At first I actually thought my ex-husband was mixed up in it somehow or other.'

'But he wasn't in fact?'

'Certainly not, no.'

I suddenly realized I couldn't remember how many children I'd said I had. I hoped he wouldn't ask – but then, why would I lie about something like that? I decided to say there were two.

But he concentrated on the stalker, thank goodness. 'What happened? I've read about such characters, of course, but this is the first time I've met somebody who's actually been pestered by one.'

I swallowed, and followed the plan I'd worked out. 'He used to ring, and also to follow me around. Sat in his car, keeping an eye on me. Keeping watch outside my house, and turning up on all kinds of occasions. But he never attacked me, he never came up to me and said anything; he was just there all the time, in the background. To start with, at least.'

'Did you feel threatened?'

'Yes. When you don't know what he's thinking, it's threatening.'

'You said to start with . . .'

I nodded and took another mouthful of wine. 'It carried on like this for about half a year. I reported it to the police, but they weren't much help: they just gave me a number to ring if he overstepped the mark. They reckoned they couldn't do much if he didn't actually threaten me.'

'But they identified him, did they?'

'Yes. They took him in once for questioning. Then they released him because he hadn't done anything illegal. That's what they said, in any case.'

'Silly so-and-sos,' said Mark.

'Maybe, but they have a lot to do. And they kept stressing that they were understaffed.'

'But it, er, escalated, did it?'

'Yes. I came home one evening and he was lying in my bed.'

'Lying in your bed?'

'Yes. He was naked. I still have no idea how he got in. He told the police we'd had a date and I'd given him a key. Luckily they didn't believe him.'

'Good God,' said Mark, slapping the table with the palms of his hands. 'But what happened when you found him naked in your bed?'

'I rushed out. Rang the police on my mobile, and they came to fetch him a quarter of an hour later. He was still naked when they dragged him out into the street – I don't know why they didn't give him time to put his clothes on, he was carrying them, trying to use them to hide his modesty.'

I noticed that I was beginning to enjoy my tale, and realized that I ought to keep myself in check. It wouldn't be very clever to give him a mass of facts about all kinds of things that I might then forget about.

'I don't need to go into detail. He ended up with a year in jail in any case. But the problem is—'

'That he didn't stop there.' Mark finished off the sentence for me. 'He carried on pestering you after he came out, did he?'

'Exactly,' I said. 'He waited for a few months, but before I came here a few things happened that I'm sure he was mixed up in. There was nothing especially remarkable or threatening, so I didn't contact the police. I was going to leave Sweden anyway, so I didn't think there was any real danger. But now . . . Well, now it seems that he's found me again.'

'Here on Exmoor?'

'Yes, I think so.'

Mark shook his head. 'How on earth did he manage to do that? But I suppose you've had your mail forwarded and so on . . . Perhaps it isn't all that difficult if you really put your mind to it?'

I shrugged, and wondered if I ought to start going into speculation. I decided it wasn't necessary. No point in getting bogged down in details, as I'd already thought.

'I think I've seen him in a hire car,' I said instead. 'Both here in the village and in a few other places.'

'Bloody hell,' said Mark. I think that was the first time I'd heard him use a swearword.

'And there are a few other things he might have done as well,' I added.

'Such as?'

'Somebody has been leaving dead pheasants outside my front door.'

'Dead what . . . ?'

He paused and sat up straight. Looked at me with a new expression in his eyes that I couldn't make out. Had he seen through me? But how could he have seen through me? The pheasants were not an invention, nor was the hire car. Or was it just that ability to read other people's minds that he claimed he had? I decided not to mention the Hawkridge business in any case.

'Dead pheasants?' he repeated thoughtfully, scratching at the back of his neck. 'That sounds really odd. Do you know . . . Well, I suppose you can't very well know what that means, can you?'

'Means?' I said. 'What do you mean?'

'What it *could* mean,' he said, correcting himself. 'But it seems pretty far-fetched when I think about it. Anyway, it's just a matter of an old superstition.'

'Superstition?' I repeated, feeling rather silly.

He laughed and held his upturned palms towards the ceiling to indicate that what he was about to say was not something he believed in.

'In the old days,' he began, 'out here on Exmoor in any case, it was seen as a way of warding off death. If somebody was lying ill in their house on the moor, for instance, people would sometimes place a dead animal outside their front door during the night.'

'Really?'

'The idea was that when Death came to knock on the door and harvest a life, he would make do with the animal and go away. A sort of primitive sacrifice, you might say, and inevitably there are countless stories to suggest that it really worked. The animal had disappeared by the next morning, which meant that Death had been sent packing and the sick person could recover in peace and quiet. It didn't have to be pheasants, of course, but there were plenty of them around. You come across them everywhere, and the males especially make very handsome sacrificial offerings – assuming you haven't run them over with your car, of course.'

'They were males,' I said. 'Both mine. And they seemed to be completely uninjured.'

'Apart from being dead?'

'They were most certainly dead. They could have been just the same one, incidentally.'

'But nobody came to collect them? Or it?'

I shook my head. 'No, I threw them away.'

Then we sat in silence for quite some time. Mark poured out what remained of wine bottle number two. I thought that if I had still been a smoker this would have been an obvious moment to go out onto the terrace for a ciggie.

But I wasn't a smoker any longer. Nor was Mark. He really did seem to be sitting there thinking over what I had said.

'I'm sorry,' I said. 'I should never have brought this up.'

'Rubbish,' he said. 'Of course you needed to mention it. What are our fellow human beings there for?'

That sounded a little theatrical, and he noticed that himself.

'Anyway, I shall obviously do whatever I can to find out who this character is. But I don't understand that pheasant business. You don't have customs like that back in your country, do you?'

'Not that I know of.'

'Do you happen to have the registration number of that hire car he drives around in?'

'I'm afraid not. I've boobed there. But it's a silver-coloured Renault. The rental company is called Sixt, and they have their logo on both sides of the car.'

'A silver-coloured Renault from Sixt?'

I nodded.

'Right,' said Mark, standing up. 'I'll do what I can. But now it's time for afters. Just a simple pannacotta, but you'll get a full-bodied Sauternes to help it down. What do you say to that?'

I said it might be possible to force it down, and as he stood pottering about by the refrigerator I wondered how on earth he thought I was going to get home.

I certainly wasn't going to try to walk home with Castor through the dark.

36

'A boy may only make love to his girlfriend when the gorse is in bloom. That's an ancient rule here on Exmoor – are you familiar with it?'

'No. But I'm not exactly a girl.'

'I won't pretend that I regard myself as a boy,' said Mark. 'But the point is that gorse blooms all the year round. Even now, in December – perhaps you've seen it?'

We were lying under the feather duvet in his wide bed. We really had made love. I couldn't believe it, but I didn't want to deny it either. We were both naked, and it had gone really well. Before we removed our clothes I told him that I was fifty-five years old and hadn't been in bed with a man for over two years. He responded by saying that the figures were not far off identical for him: fifty-two and two-and-a-half respectively.

A cluster of scented candles was still burning on the window ledge. It was half past one. The door was ajar, and had been all the time. Castor was presumably still curled up in front of the fire in the kitchen downstairs. I assumed that Jeremy was asleep in his room on the next floor up. I thought it felt remarkable, and said as much to Mark.

'You ought to know that this is among the most unexpected things that have happened to me for a very long time.'

'For me too,' said Mark, stroking my cheek with the back of his hand. 'I stopped thinking about this kind of thing ages ago. If you live in a village like Winsford that is the only sensible attitude to take. The number of available women has been rather less than zero for the last sixty years.'

'I thought lots of tourists come to Exmoor every summer?'

He snorted. 'If you're looking for a man you don't put on Wellington boots and a waterproof jacket and go out on a moor.'

'But I would like to go walking over the moor with you.'

'You are different. Presumably you're not quite right in the head, but that suits me down to the ground. Where would you like to go?'

I thought for a moment. 'Simonsbath and on towards Brendon, I think. Isn't that what you recommended? Where you went walking as a child?'

'Whenever you like,' said Mark, yawning. 'Yes, that's where the moor is at its most beautiful . . . And its most desolate. It'll be as windy and rainy as hell at this time of year, but that's a risk you have to take. As long as you have the right clothes it's not a problem.'

I explained that I even had a waterproof jacket for my dog, and he promised that we would go there as soon as an opportunity arose.

'But not before Christmas,' he said.

'Why not?' I asked, more as a joke than anything else. 'There's a whole week left yet.'

'I'm going to be busy at the beginning of the week,' he said. 'A chap I work quite a lot with is coming here. And then Jeremy and I are off to my sister's over Christmas – the main holidays, that is.'

'I see. Where does she live?'

'Scarborough, if you know where that is. It takes half a day to drive there, and I don't know how it will go. How Jeremy will react. He doesn't really want to leave this house at all, as you've probably gathered. I suppose you could say it's an experiment, but I've set my mind on going through with it. In any case, we'll be back before New Year, and then I promise to go walking over the moor with you until you drop.'

I said I was looking forward to that. Then added that what I wanted more than anything else just at the moment was to sleep for a few hours.

'I thought you were never going to stop talking,' said Mark, and so we rolled over on our sides and fell asleep.

It was eleven o'clock the next morning before Castor and I left Heathercombe Cottage. Jeremy joined us for breakfast – for twenty minutes, at least: that was the time he needed to eat his meal which comprised two eggs fried on both sides, a cup of tea, and two slices of toast with apricot jam. Mark said he had eaten exactly the same breakfast every single morning for the last two years, and the only place you could get the right sort of apricot jam was a little health food shop in Tiverton. If ever it closed down there would be a major problem.

Three spoonfuls of sugar in the tea, and lots of milk.

Jeremy measured the dosage himself, concentrating as if he were placing the final card in a house of cards. He was wearing the same Harlequins jersey as yesterday, but his jeans were blue rather than black; and just as the previous day he shook hands with me once again. As I sat at the table, watching him more or less counting the grains of sugar in each spoon, I felt overcome by a feeling of tenderness towards him that I found difficult to explain.

'What does he do up there in his room with his computer?'

Mark hesitated. Jeremy had just left us, and I found it difficult to talk about him when he was present. Castor had been given a portion of scrambled egg and bacon that he gobbled in less than five seconds.

'You don't really want to know that.'

'Yes I do,' I said. 'I really do.'

He sighed. 'Okay. Only two things, in fact. Recently, at least. He watches violent films and solves sudokus.'

'Violent films and sudokus?'

'Yes, I'm afraid so.'

'And he . . . I mean, why violent films?'

'I don't know. But he doesn't seem to be adversely affected by them. And he gets into a much worse humour if he's not allowed to look at them. I've tried restricting him, believe you me.'

I thought about that gesture he had made in the window, but yet again decided not to mention it.

'I'm sorry, I didn't mean to . . .'

Mark shrugged. 'That's okay. He sits watching those films . . . He does watch other films as well, not only ones in which people kill one another, but I just don't know what he gets out of them. Either sort. He sometimes watches the same film three times without a pause – maybe he needs to do that for it to sink in. He's not exactly a star at solving sudokus either.'

There was a trace of bitterness in his voice, and I wished I hadn't asked in the first place. 'I suspect sudokus aren't the easiest of puzzles to solve,' I said, 'but I've never tried so I don't know.'

Mark laughed. 'He understands the rules. I tried telling myself that he's better with numbers than with letters, so I spent a few weeks teaching him . . . Well, he understands what you have to do, but the problem is that he has no idea how to distinguish between right and wrong. I've checked up on him, and instead of working something out he tries pot luck, and it's wrong more or less all the time. When he realizes it's wrong, he goes back and tries pot luck again. I think it takes him about half a day to solve a sudoku of the easiest sort.'

'Hmm,' I said. 'But it keeps him occupied, I suppose.'

'Yes, it does,' said Mark with a sigh. 'And who's to say what the rest of us do to occupy ourselves is so much more sensible? Manufacturing weapons? Selling shares? Advertising rubbish that nobody wants?'

He was certainly starting to sound gloomy, and I thought it would be best to let the matter drop. Once again I'm not at all sure what I mean by 'let the matter drop'.

'I dreamt about it again last night,' he said after a few seconds of silence.

'About what?'

'About what I said when we first met. That absent husband

and the house in the south. Perhaps it was because you were lying beside me . . .'

I was totally unprepared for this, and it came as a bit of a shock. I had almost succeeded in repressing his clairvoyant abilities, or whatever they were. In any case, I hadn't spent much time thinking about it, and that business about reading other people's minds felt more like an in-joke by this time.

But perhaps that was an over-hasty conclusion?

'Really?' I said, sounding more doubtful than I would have liked.

'It was the same thing, really. A group of men around a table dressed in white, wondering where somebody had disappeared to. A white house as well . . . somewhere a long way south, as I said before.'

'And what about me? Was I there in a corner somewhere?'

'That might be what was new about it,' said Mark, looking thoughtful. 'You were walking along a beach – it must have been quite close by, because I saw you at the same time as I saw the house. Yes, you were walking along a beach with your dog . . . There was no more to it than that.'

'That's quite enough,' I said, trying to laugh. 'I don't want you to be limitlessly supernatural.'

Mark cleared his throat and apologized.

'But I'm really pleased that Castor and I could come here,' I said after a short pause while I got a grip on myself. 'I'd like to invite you up to Darne Lodge, but that somehow feels like a move in the wrong direction . . . And I assume it would be hard to persuade Jeremy to come there. It really is a rat-hole.'

He smiled. Reached over the table and took hold of my

hands. 'I'm sure you've made it very cosy up there,' he said. 'But even so I think we should blame Jeremy and continue to meet here.'

'Continue?'

'Yes.'

'We must go for a walk above Simonsbath first.'

'Certainly,' said Mark, looking serious. 'First Christmas, then a walk over the moor, then Heathercombe Cottage part two.'

'Okay,' I said. 'I'll go along with that. The entire programme.'

'By the way, that stalker – what's his name? In case I happen to come across a certain Renault . . .'

Castor and I were already on the way to our car, which I'd parked on the other side of the bridge.

'His name's Simmel,' I said. 'Yes, he's called John Simmel.'

That was just a name that happened to come into my head. I've no idea where it came from: perhaps from a book or a film.

'Good,' said Mark. 'John Simmel. I'll remember that. Look after yourself. It's possible that I might be having dinner with my colleague at The Royal Oak on Wednesday . . . Just in case you fancy meeting two nice Englishmen instead of just one.'

'I'm perfectly happy with one, thank you,' I assured him as I let Castor into the car. 'Thank you for everything.'

'I'm the one who should be thanking you.'

I glanced up at Jeremy's window, but he was evidently sitting at his computer. A violent film or a sudoku?

And as we sat shuddering and shaking on the bumpy and muddy road down into the village, it occurred to me that I'd forgotten to ask for help with that password.

Something told me that was just as well.

Something else told me that I should forget all about all those silly threats and thoughts. No doubt it is the moor and the solitariness of my existence here that gives rise to them.

37

The nineteenth of December. A Wednesday. The moment I wake up I remember that it's Yolanda Mendez's birthday.

Yolanda Mendez was my best friend for two years at primary school – year four and most of year five. She came from Peru, had big brown eyes and a horse of her own. If the family hadn't moved she might well have been my best friend at secondary school as well – I think so, as there was never the slightest hitch in our well-oiled friendship.

And her birthday was so close to Christmas: I recall being a bit sorry for her on that account.

I get out of bed and wonder why she has suddenly come into my head. And then I remember that she always does on this day, every year. Just for half a minute or even less. I usually wonder what became of her, and I do today as well.

Is this what old age is like? I wonder as I check the thermometer and observe the sky through the window. People crop up then disappear, crop up and disappear. In a never-ending stream and with no apparent order or reason. Not just on their birthdays, I assume. The older we get the more vulnerable we become to our memories.

I feel listless today again. Come to that, I have done so every morning since that evening and night with Mark Britton. I can't make up my mind if it's because I miss him, or if there is some other reason – even if it's the opposite of missing him. But why should that be so? I note down that it's only four degrees, and looks wet and windy. It's not exactly foggy, but it's as if a thick but quite translucent cloud were drifting over the moor. Three ponies are chewing away just on the other side of the wall, with two more not far behind them. The sky is dark.

It strikes me that everything is going awry.

I start crying.

Then stop crying after a few minutes and light a fire instead. Castor comes sauntering in from the bedroom. I don't think I'd be setting foot outside the house today if it weren't for him.

I can't even decide what is worst about sitting in prison like this. You leave no impression on the world. You are outside time. If you somehow managed to cease existing for a day it wouldn't make any difference. Nobody would notice anything at all. Is that why some people become pyromaniacs? Or break into schools with their gun and shoot children? In order to make the impression that is so terribly important?

Is this a peculiar question? I don't know; but the reason why I am here – isn't it precisely so that I can avoid making any impression? And why am I suddenly enquiring about a reason?

We go for a morning walk instead. The same rough heather, the same grass and moss and thorn bushes. Bracken, pheasants and mud. After ten minutes there is a hailstorm: we turn back and hurry home.

*

Halfway through breakfast I realize that I fell asleep before eleven last night, and that I haven't yet used today's words. I read through my list and decide to have one more go with literary figures. The last two days I've tried Russians and Americans, so if I spread myself out a bit in Europe today, I can try three Swedes tomorrow.

Fagin. Quixote. Faust.

No luck, I note as usual, but I thought I detected a little bit of hesitation on the part of the computer when I tried Quixote. There was a slightly longer pause than usual before it stated that I had provided an invalid password. Could that be because some of the letters were correct?

Or is it just that I'm losing my grip and imagining things?

I start playing patience instead, but only eight games. I'll save the rest until this evening.

I go to the centre after a long, difficult walk up to Dunkery Beacon, the highest point on the whole moor. We started from Wheddon Cross, in accordance with instructions in the guidebook, and almost all the time we had our destination in view, apart from when it was partially obscured by mist and clouds. But after having struggled up through soaking wet pasture land, difficult to negotiate, for what seemed like many hours, and forcing our way past aggressive herds of very fat cows – they were worryingly reminiscent of surly uniformed officials at border crossings into totalitarian countries – we came to the narrow road that encircles the summit in an irregular circle, and decided that we would attempt the final five hundred metres some other day. The wind was blowing straight at us, and there was good reason to think that the view would be restricted on a day like this one. We hadn't seen a single person on the whole way up, and in fact the only real plus was a group of stags some way away from the path.

So we turned back, and walked down along a sheltered path through a valley – wet and muddy, but protected from the wind – and were back at the car park outside The Rest and Be Thankful Inn after two-and-a-half hours in all. This was the very pub I had called in at when I first arrived on the moor fifty days earlier: I remembered the big-bosomed blonde barmaid, the crossword-solving woman and the peripatetic plumber, and thought that it seemed as if had happened a year ago.

But I didn't consider even for a moment popping in again. Instead we got into the car and began driving along the now familiar A396 back to Winsford. And as we were doing so, I decided it was high time to check the e-mails again.

Both Alfred Biggs and Margaret Allen are on duty for once. And there are two young girls and two young boys, sitting in different corners and lost in a world of their own of which I have no conception. I think in passing of Jeremy Britton, and exclude him from my thoughts just as quickly.

'Welcome again,' says Margaret Allen.

'Ah, it's our lady writer,' says Alfred Biggs.

I apologize for the fact that Castor and I are so dirty, and explain that we have just been climbing up towards Dunkery Beacon.

'On a day like this?' exclaims Alfred.

'That was brave of you,' says Margaret. 'I'll put a cup of tea on for you. You can have your usual computer.'

I take my own e-mails first this time. Answer three Christmas greetings from colleagues at the Monkeyhouse, one from my brother and finally one from Christa. She says nothing about me appearing in her dreams or that she is worried, and I'm grateful for that. Violetta di Parma writes and says that she has forwarded our post in accordance with my instructions, and that she must now rush off so as not to miss the performance of Handel's *Messiah*. I write a brief thank-you, and hope she enjoyed the concert.

Then Martin's inbox. As always, I open it with a degree of dread. Offer up a silent prayer that at least there won't be anything from G.

And my prayer is answered on that point. I read through the six messages that might require an answer: the first five can safely be ignored, the sixth and last is from Professor Soblewski:

My Dear Friend,
A Merry Christmas and a Happy New Year to both of you.

That was in Swedish, but then he goes over to English and writes about an anthology of short stories that he and Martin evidently intend publishing – in Sweden and Poland simultaneously, half of them by Swedes and the other half by Poles. Young and promising writers, no old, established authors:

they aim to promote the avant-garde. Soblewski suggests that they should replace one called Majstowski by somebody called Słupka, and promises to send the story in question as soon as he receives the translation. Then he wonders if young Anderson, whose story *Carnivores* he has just read in translation, is really all that outstanding. He would like Martin's views on both these points. And to conclude he writes:

> By the way, a curious and slightly macabre thing has occurred just a few miles from here. The police have found a dead body, they suspect foul play but are apparently unable to identify it. We live in a dangerous world, dear friends. Take good care of each other.
>
> Sob

A sound rings out in my right ear, and I suddenly have difficulty in breathing.

A dead body. A few miles from here. The police are not able to identify it.

I notice that the room I'm sitting in, and which Margaret Allen has just left, waving goodbye from the doorway, has started swaying. I feel sick, and for a brief moment I think I'm going to throw up over the computer.

Or faint. Or both.

I cling tightly onto the table with both hands as the feeling slowly passes over. I close my eyes for a while, and hope Alfred Biggs hasn't noticed the state I'm in. The sound is still there, but is not quite so loud now and has moved over into my left ear, for some reason. I open my eyes and read the text again.

Not the part about the anthology. Only the section about the dead body. Three times.

Foul play? Take good care of each other?

It's almost dark when we leave the computer centre, despite the fact that it's only five o'clock. This is the evening when Mark Britton will be at The Royal Oak with his friendly IT colleague. Until now I haven't been able to make up my mind whether or not to go there and join them. But Soblewski's e-mail has made the decision for me.

Castor and I will spend the evening alone at Darne Lodge.

We might not even play patience. We might simply lock the door and sit there with our thoughts and assess the remainder of our lives.

38

Julie. Wrong.

   Markurell. Wrong.

   Berling. Wrong.

   We go to bed. Lie there in the darkness, listening to the rain and the wind – or at least, I do. I don't know how much of all that Castor is aware of as he lies by my feet under the duvet. Or how much he cares. I have said missus to him several times: at first he cocked his head in order to hear better, but then he lost interest.

   I feel disorientated. Not so much by my surroundings, for they have been constant for several weeks now, but inside me. I have difficulty in remembering thoughts, or linking one thought with another: this might be something I've been experiencing for quite a while, but it feels especially intense this evening. I suspect it must be Soblewski's e-mail that has brought it on – acted as the amplifier or catalyst. *The police have found a dead body.* Perhaps I would emerge unscathed from a mental examination, perhaps not: I have personal experience of the concept of Angst, no doubt about that – mainly during the time when I was suffering from depression, and it really doesn't have anything to do with potatoes. But what I am feeling now has nothing to do with Angst: it's more a question of total rootlessness, or connectionlessness, if such a word exists. I don't know. The process of cause and effect has vanished, or at least I no longer understand it. I can't pin it down.

I hope it is due to the fact that the year is coming to an end. The day after tomorrow is the year's shortest day – I notice that I keep coming back to that fact with the stubbornness of a lunatic: but then all of a sudden everything changes. Light arrives. When the new year has established itself I shall be able to think ahead, not merely to outlive my dog but also to make decisions that imply . . . that imply that I shall be able to live a sort of real life. Connections will emerge and then fade away. I think I can see this ahead of me: all I need to do is to allow a few days to pass, a Christmas to come and go; to wait for Mark Britton to come back from Scarborough perhaps, to enter a new, untried year and somehow to progress . . . Like a book you have on the bedside table but haven't yet had the strength to start reading. But you can imagine how interesting it is going to be. And what you can imagine exists, it really does – in a certain way and to a certain extent it really does.

I lift up the duvet and ask Castor if he understands my way of thinking, because I have actually been speaking aloud about all this. He doesn't move a muscle. I suddenly hear that metallic sound out there on the moor again. It's coming in waves, rising and falling. I wrap my pillow around my head and do my best to fall asleep. I think I'm ready to cope with most things, but I'd rather not dream about Martin. I start mumbling the only quotation from the Bible that I know off by heart, the Twenty-third Psalm:

The Lord is my shepherd; I shall not want.
He maketh me to lie down in green pastures:
  he leadeth me beside the still waters.
He restoreth my soul: he leadeth me in the paths of righteousness
  for his name's sake.
Yea, though I walk through the valley of the shadow of death . . .

Before I get to the end I've started to dream about rats. No, I realize that I'm still awake, so it's not a dream. In which case I don't know what it is: just a notion, perhaps, or a mirage. But this evening it is something that risks complete collapse.

  . . . apparently unable to identify it.

Huh, I suddenly thought. What had I expected? What other message could have been more desirable? *Which?*

Well, then . . .

The twentieth of December. Thursday, eight degrees and a clear blue sky. Virtually no wind at all. From the overgrown cairn where Roman legionaries must once have stood and gazed out over the countryside after having killed Caratacus, it is possible to see for miles in all directions on a day like this.

  Dunkery Beacon, for instance, that we tried to reach yesterday but didn't quite manage it: if you were an eagle or a falcon you would easily be able to fly there in five minutes in today's clear weather. Everything is extremely beautiful: charming and undulating moorland, with the blossom on the gorse bushes striving up longingly towards the sun. It's allowed for a boy to make love to his girlfriend – almost obligatory, in fact.

After a late breakfast we set off for Porlock Common. High above Exford we park in a tiny lay-by and then walk over the open countryside for several hours without a map. We see stags again some distance away, and maintain the high spirits of the morning until dusk begins to fall. By the time we get back to Darne Lodge it is half past four, and we arrive at our simple cottage at almost exactly the same moment as Mark Britton. We haven't even entered the house, and we stand outside in the yard, talking. He hands over a bouquet of roses and a bottle of champagne.

'Just a little Christmas Box,' he says, and his smile is slightly unsure. 'I intended to give it to you last night at the pub, but you never came.'

'Something else cropped up, I'm afraid,' I say, and he is civilized enough not to ask what.

'Jeremy and I will be setting off early tomorrow morning,' he says. 'To Scarborough, that is. So I thought I'd wish you a Merry Christmas slightly in advance. If you . . .'

'If I what?'

'If you save the bubbly maybe we can share it on New Year's Eve?'

I promise to think about that, and give him a hug. 'But I hope I can look at the roses before then? When will you be back?'

'That depends. In good time before New Year in any case. Do you have a mobile so that I can get in touch with you?'

I shake my head.

'I must say you keep yourself pretty isolated. Can I call in on you when I get back?'

I promise that he will be welcome, and then we say good-bye. Wish each other the compliments of the season again. I remain standing there, watching as he negotiates the twists and turns of Halse Lane. I think it's odd that we actually made love only a week ago.

But then, the world's an odd place.

Then we are on our own.

I manage to read another chapter of *Lorna Doone*, and note that people were much more courageous in the old days.

Sixteen games of patience, four go out.

Dylan. Wrong.

Cohen. Wrong.

Coltrane. Wrong.

I look closely at the roses. They are not quite red. I drink two tumblers of wine before bed, and that helps to some extent.

39

The shortest day.

At The Stag's Head in Dunster, where we have a simple lunch – a ploughman's and fizzy water – we get into conversation with a local fudge maker. I'm grateful for every form of human contact, and it seems the fudge maker is as well. He tells me that his ex-wife runs a little delicatessen shop in the town, and although it's fifteen years since they divorced he is still responsible for making the fudge. Selling it is still the cornerstone of the whole business, he stresses: people come from as far away as Taunton and Barnstaple to buy Mrs Miller's Home-Made Fudge. Occasionally they even get customers from as far away as Bristol, and during the weeks leading up to Christmas she sells as much as during the rest of the year put together.

I promise to call in and buy a few lumps.

'Vanilla,' he says. 'Take the classic stuff. Or possibly coffee, but don't go for any of the newfangled fancy tastes. Fudge ought to taste like fudge, for God's sake.'

Then he asks where I come from. I tell him I'm a Swedish writer but I'm spending the winter on Exmoor and writing a novel. He asks where I'm living, and I tell him I'm renting a house just above Winsford.

'Winsford!' he exclaims, and his expression becomes distinctly dreamy. 'I had a girlfriend there once. I should have married her instead of Britney. She runs the pub there, by the way – perhaps you've seen her?'

'Rosie?'

'Rosie, yes! She's a fine-looking woman, isn't she? Not as attractive as you, of course, but pretty good by my standards.'

I make a non-committal response and we chat for a while about Exmoor and the way that life makes up its own mind about how it's going to proceed. When we say goodbye I can't avoid thinking what a small world it is, here on Exmoor. The fact that a fudge maker in Dunster was once sweet on a pub landlady in Winsford is nothing remarkable. I also remember clearly Mark Britton's estimate of the number of marriageable women on the moor. Rather less than zero.

And that makes me think about something else as I sit chewing fudge in the car on the way back to Darne Lodge: how many people actually know that there is a mad Swedish woman author sitting writing in that old house, the scene of several suicides?

One or two, presumably.

The evenings are the worst. Unless I think about going to The Royal Oak Inn, and I've decided not to do so today. Better to save it up for a day or two. Once before Christmas Eve, once afterwards, and then Mark Britton will be back and as the new year dawns I shall be in a fit state to make plans. To create a future for myself.

I try to convince myself of this as I wander around the house, as I make a fire, as I put stuff into the refrigerator and sip at a glass of port. It's five o'clock and already pitch dark, impossible to move around outdoors. I recall that the moon was shining the evening I came here, briefly at least, but I don't think I've experienced a moonlit evening since then. Ten metres away from the house is the overgrown stone wall, I know that, but there's no chance of seeing it from my window. Tonight it's foggy as well: it's usually possible to detect the borderline between heaven and earth, where the rounded hill with a handful of trees on the summit can be seen to the south; but not the way things are this evening.

Not in the evening of the year's shortest day.

I manage to make the hours pass with the aid of routines. I avoid thinking about Soblewski. Avoid Samos and Taza and all that. I make some soup instead, working at snail's pace so that time can pass unhindered. I eat half the soup, put the remainder into a plastic container then stow it away in the tiny freezer compartment.

Wash up.

Give Castor some food.

Another chapter of Blackmore.

Sixteen games of patience. At last it's eleven o'clock.

Three more attempts – that's also a part of the routine now. I've spent the last half-hour sifting out this evening's words.

Garbo. Wrong.

Monroe. Wrong.

Novak. Wrong.

I write them all down in my notebook. Put more wood on the fire to keep us warm during the night. Let Castor out to do his business while I brush my teeth.

I go to let him in. It really is impossible to see more than two metres out into the darkness – the faint light that seeps through the door opening seems afraid of venturing too far out. As I stand there I can feel that it has become colder, and I remember my fudge-making friend going on about the frosty nights we had in store.

No sign of Castor. I whistle twice, have no desire to stand there getting cold.

He still doesn't appear. That is odd. I hope he hasn't found something and is busy chewing it. His stomach can be rather sensitive, and half-rotten meat is not what he needs. Come on now, you blasted mongrel, I think.

But he doesn't. I whistle again.

I look at the clock. He must have been out for five minutes. At least – perhaps seven or eight. He usually needs only one or two. I almost close the door. Then change my mind and open it again.

Shout for him.

Once. Twice.

I feel frightened, suddenly and overwhelmingly. I shout again. My voice sounds weak and terrified, and is gulped down by the darkness.

But I shout once more even so.

Again and again.

It's the longest night of the year, and there is no sign of my dog.

40

I put on two more jerseys under my jacket and go out again. Walk round the house several times, shouting and whistling. To the south, where light from the two windows produces a slight trace of illumination, I can see for about three metres; but nothing at all in any other direction. It seems that my eyes have not yet grown accustomed to darkness. Nothing can be darker than the darkness that surrounds me now.

A faint whine from the wind can be heard from the moor, but nothing of the metallic sound that I had noticed on several evenings. In the far distance, in the direction of Exford I think, I hear the sound of a car accelerating, but it lasts no more than a second.

I walk over to the wall. Shout three times before climbing over it. The chances are that he must have gone in this direction, I think. In the other direction is the fence and the gate. Needless to say he could have negotiated those if he had really wanted to, but I have to make a choice.

I am breathing very heavily now. When I've climbed over the wall I stand quite still, partly in order to calm down, partly to give my eyes the chance of seeing something.

After a while I can make out my feet and a metre or so

around them. *Make out*, not see: the nearest to any light in the darkness is the mist that is floating around and seems to be oozing forth out of the ground itself. I remain standing there, wondering about this silent and fluid movement as I continue to hold on to the wall and shout at regular intervals.

My voice still sounds very feeble, and it doesn't penetrate many metres out into the emptiness. But Castor's hearing is better than mine. He ought to hear me if he is around – hear me and bark in response.

I don't dare to leave the wall. After five, perhaps ten minutes of shouting and listening I go back into the house. I fetch my torch and check that the batteries are working, then dig out two spares before going out again.

Walk round the house a few more times. Shout once more. My fear is like a tightly tied scarf around my neck.

Back to the wall. Three more shouts, and then I remain silent and listen to the faint whispering of the wind. Observe the dancing of the mist once more, and decide to head in the other direction.

Over the road and up towards the top of Winsford Hill. If I can find my way there. If it's at all possible to work out where I am at any given time.

I find a familiar path and then lose it. I decide to adopt a plan and stick to it. Walk twenty paces. Stop, shout, listen. Wait there. Shout again.

The mist becomes more dense and less mobile the higher I get. The wind has faded and is no longer audible. I soon find myself in the middle of a patch of rough heather which is very difficult to negotiate, and I have already lost my bearings. The light from the torch is swallowed up by the mist – there's not really any point in having it switched on. It almost makes it more difficult to make progress.

But I keep following the plan. Twenty paces. Stop, shout, listen.

I don't know how long I've been following that pattern when the torch suddenly flickers and then goes dead. It doesn't really matter. I don't bother to try to make it go again, I just check that the spare batteries are still in my jacket pocket.

Twenty paces. Stop, shout, listen.

It's when I'm standing still and listening that panic creeps up on me. It's better to keep moving, better to be active: when I stand still I can't avoid hearing my heart beat and my blood rushing around in my veins at much too fast a pace.

I am soon completely disorientated. I can't work out what is up and what is down, what is south and what is north. I'm in the middle of quite a flat stretch of ground – or at least my immediate surroundings are flat, it's not possible to be sure of any more than that. When I fumble around with my hands I can feel dead ferns on all sides. I seem to be following something resembling a trodden path, but when I take my eighteenth pace I find myself in a thorn bush. It smacks me in the face, and a twig brushes against my eye.

Good Lord, I think, please help me. Where are you, Castor?

You have never been a hunter. You merely glance with a minimum of interest when you come across a rabbit. We can walk through a flock of sheep without your raising an eyebrow.

I stand next to the thorn bush and for the first time try to understand what has happened. Rather than simply allowing panic to take control of me.

Why on earth would my dog want to disappear into the night?

I try to answer that question: why?

The problem is that I can't find an answer. Perhaps I *don't want* to find an answer. Instead I stand motionless beside that anonymous thorn bush and shout a few more times. Close my eyes and listen. Your hearing becomes more acute when you close your eyes.

But there's nothing; all the time nothing. Hardly even any wind. Well, maybe there is something in fact, something that feels like a slow movement, as if . . . as if the moor was *breathing.*

Something inside me stiffens at that thought. I realize that I must return to the house. Of course . . . Of course, Castor is there already. No doubt he is wandering around the garden but can't get into the house because I've closed the door. And then maybe he'll set off to look for his missus.

Never go looking for your dog. Remain where you are and let the dog do the searching – they are much better at it than you are.

We didn't get much benefit from that course we attended, Castor and I, but I suddenly remember those words very clearly. *Never go looking . . .*

But there are sinkholes on the moor. Depressions full of water covered by a thin layer of soil that won't carry anything heavy. Even ponies can sink into them and drown – I've read about such incidents, and we have passed close by such places.

I leave the thorn bush and start heading back home willy-nilly – I'm far from sure that I am in fact heading back home. I stumble into another cluster of thorn bushes, my heart is pounding, my blood is racing, but soon I come upon a path that seems to be heading downhill at least in places. I can't see it, I have to fumble with hands and feet every time I take another step forward, and there are mounds of rough, razor-sharp heather on both sides. I have started crying – I only realize that when I taste the salty tears on my lips.

And then I can hear that breathing sound again. It's louder now, and it suddenly dawns on me where it's coming from: the ponies.

The ponies. Without warning I find myself in the middle of a group of them. Six perhaps, maybe twelve. They are so close to me that I can smell them, and feel the heat coming from their heavy, substantial bodies. I reach out my hand and touch the one standing closest to me, it doesn't bother him in the slightest – and as I hold the palm of my hand against his warm haunch I can feel another one sniffing at the back of my neck. With my eyes I can barely make out the contours of their bodies – dark, blurred silhouettes – but their presence is so strong that just for a moment I can feel what it must be like to be a little foal. A newcomer to the world, but already embraced by the powerful bond that holds the herd together. It is a remarkable and an overpowering feeling. We stand there, breathing together in the blindness of the night and the mist. Only for a few minutes, and then one of them – a leader no doubt – gives a snort and the whole herd starts moving.

They leave me, and their absence seems just as sudden and

natural as their presence had been. I stand there alone. All the breathing has ceased, silence has descended over the moor like a cold shroud.

I manage to make the torch work, not that it helps much but at least I can see my feet. I set off walking without worrying about the direction I'm taking. Walk, stop, shout, listen. After quite a while, half an hour perhaps, I come to a road. I decide it must be Halse Lane and start walking along it to the right. Slightly uphill. And soon it becomes clear that I have guessed correctly. I continue shouting at regular intervals, stand still and listen. I don't give up. It's so cold now that there are occasional thin patches of ice on the asphalt.

Stop. Shout. Listen.

Nothing.

Over and over again nothing.

When I go through the gate into Darne Lodge I see that the time is twenty past one. I've been out for almost two hours.

No Castor.

I walk around the house several times before I have to accept this as fact.

I spend the rest of the night standing and shouting, sometimes through the window, sometimes in the doorway. When I fall asleep on the sofa as dawn begins to break, I have drunk five or six glasses of wine. I am almost unconscious, but perhaps I have outlived my dog even so.

FOUR

41

All children disappear.

In every family there's a story about Tommy or Charlie or little Belinda who disappeared and were not seen again for a whole hour. Or two or three. We made a programme about that – in addition to that one in which Alice Myrman became notorious for having hidden her dead husband in the wood-shed – about those kinds of disappearances. With happy endings – or at least I assume that was the intention. It was never broadcast for various reasons, but together with a colleague I met at least twenty parents who told us about similar experiences.

It's all about fear, of course. The unparalleled worry a parent feels when they don't know where their child is. They clasp their hands and pray to God, despite the fact that they haven't prayed or been to church since they were confirmed at a summer camp with horse-riding a hundred years ago.

And it happens to everybody, almost everybody. Those desperate minutes and hours when Death is an unwelcome guest standing in the porch. We all have memories like that: there must be a reason.

In my family it was Gunsan who disappeared. It was a few

years before Death actually came for real, and so it was a fore-
taste. I recall it with almost photographic accuracy.

In fact it's my mother I remember most clearly in that context, not so many of the other details. We were on holiday in
Denmark and had rented a house for a week, or perhaps two,
not far from a place called Gut – we joked a bit about the
name. It was not far from the North Sea, albeit not adjacent to
it. My brother Göran wasn't there, presumably he was at some
summer camp or other.

Me and Gunsan, my mother and my father. Four of us. And
one afternoon we couldn't find Gunsan. She was only five at
the time, and it may well be that I was supposed to keep an
eye on her. Made sure that she stayed in or around the house
and didn't go running off somewhere. There was a busy road
not far from the house.

But it was only my father and I who went looking for her.
My mother stayed at the kitchen table claiming that she was
incapable of standing up. He legs simply couldn't carry her,
she impressed upon us, but we must make sure that we came
back with Gunsan, otherwise she wouldn't be responsible for
the consequences.

That's exactly what she said: 'I won't be responsible for the
consequences if you come back without Gun.'

I can see her now at that table in the well-lit kitchen, sitting
on her hands for some reason and staring out of the window.
I have never seen her looking like that before. My father tries
to explain to her that nothing serious will have happened, and
there is nothing to be gained by her not joining in the search.

It would be better for all three of us to go out looking, each in a different direction – surely that's obvious.

Then my mother turns her head and stares at us, at my father and me: that is the brief sequence I remember most vividly. She looks at first one, then the other of us, and says once again: 'Go and find Gun. I won't be responsible for the consequences if you come back without her.'

Her voice sounds like a knife scraping at the bottom of a saucepan, and both my father and I realize that there is something wrong with her. But we don't have time to worry about that now, and hurry out to go looking for my younger sister.

When I find her she is walking towards me along a path coming from some sand dunes where we have been playing several times before. She is totally unconcerned about the trouble she has caused, is singing a song and even carrying a bunch of flowers that I suspect she might have found in a churchyard that is also not far away. All in all she has been missing for about an hour – at least, that's the estimate I make afterwards.

I ask my mother why she behaved in that strange way. I'm only thirteen years old, but I've been in secondary school for a year and begun to have my eyes opened to the way the world works. I want answers to most things.

But I don't get an answer to this question, my mother merely gives me a look that says it's not possible to explain everything to a thirteen-year-old. I remember feeling annoyed with her for several days. When I take up the matter with my father, he looks worried but simply says: 'That's the way it is, Maria. Somebody always has to stay at home, and the one who does so knows that in a way that you and I simply can't understand.'

If we hadn't found Gunsan, my mother would have taken leave of her senses: that is the fact of the matter that both he and I try to avoid spelling out.

When it eventually happens for real, it's as if my mother has had time to prepare herself. Gunsan stays alive for quite a few more years.

I follow my mother's example two days before Christmas forty-two years later. I stay inside the house, or only just outside it, for the whole day. Go no further than the yard and the garden. It's a cold day, and there is even a light snowfall in the early afternoon. I investigate the little stable building, something I haven't done before – all I've done is fetch firewood from the bunker at the gable end. But there really isn't much to investigate and certainly no trace of a dog. Just junk, and more junk – it must be very many years since a horse last stood in here. The only thing I might find useful is a lantern; I think it is designed to burn some kind of oil, and despite the fact that it's filthy and rusty I take it into the house to examine it more closely.

How I could possibly be interested in something like that, now that darkness has fallen again, is way beyond my comprehension. I have a headache that is getting worse, and realize that it is due to the fact that I haven't eaten or drunk anything all day. Perhaps all the wine I drank yesterday is also making its presence felt. I take out the remains of the soup, but the mere sight of it makes me feel sick and I put the jar back in the fridge. I drink a glass of apple juice and eat a few dry biscuits instead – it's simply not possible to force anything else down. Apart from two headache pills and another mouthful of juice. By seven o'clock Castor has been away for twenty hours . . . I remember letting him out just after making my attempt at finding the passwords last night.

Twenty hours on a moor. The temperature has been round about zero all the time. How long is it possible for . . . ?

Nevertheless I shout and I shout. And shout and shout.

Why shouldn't I shout?

About an hour later I am possessed by some sort of urge to act logically. I sit there with paper and pencil and try to put things into perspective. I write down the following facts and try to find a thread linking them together – it seems to me that there must be one:

> The dead pheasants
> The silver-coloured rental car
> The man calling himself G
> *Samos*
> Taza
> Professor Soblewski's e-mail
> Mark Britton
> Jeremy Britton
> Death
> Castor's disappearance

I eventually cross out several of them. All that remains is the pheasants, the rented car and Castor. And Death, although I would prefer to cross that out as well. I decide that the rest are irrelevant, at least in the current situation. After a while I add two questions:

Is Martin really dead?

In which case how do I know that?

And after having sat perfectly still for several minutes, staring at my piece of paper, I manage to revert to a thought I recall having had several days ago, before I read that last e-mail from Soblewski:

An accomplice?

Might it be that . . . ?

Would it be possible that . . . ?

It takes quite some time to make these trains of thought comprehensible, and that has no doubt to do with my state of mind. Castor has gone missing and I'm on the edge of a nervous breakdown: there's no point in my pretending otherwise, and I don't do so.

But if I do go back to that question about a possible accomplice that I raised some time ago – the only possible way for Martin to keep himself incognito if he did manage to get out of that rat-filled bunker – what exactly do I think? Well, I think that realistically there is only one possible accomplice.

Professor Soblewski.

Isn't that the case? I ask myself. What other scenarios would be possible? In what other way could Martin have reacted without it being known that . . . that his wife left him to die in an old bunker from the Second World War? Who would he have trusted to be his confidant if he decided to take the matter into his own hands and get his own back? As he walked along that beach, shuddering and filled with hatred. Because that surely has to be when he decided to solve the problem.

Soblewski, of course. The professor's house is not far away – certainly no more than a three-hour walk. He and Martin had sat talking and making plans for half the night, so even if Martin wasn't actually looking for a comrade-in-arms, Soblewski's must have been the first name to occur to him, and his first move after getting out must have been to return to Soblewski's house.

What would the implications of that be? What exactly are the implications of this way of thinking?

Despite my predicament it's not all that difficult to answer that question. It would quite simply mean that Martin and Soblewski are fully acquainted with all the e-mail correspond-ence that has taken place since I came to Exmoor.

Furthermore: that Soblewski's own messages to Martin are fictitious, invented with the aim of not making me suspect anything. In particular I am not supposed to suspect anything when Soblewski, almost in passing, mentions that a dead body has been found not far from his home.

Surely this must be a possible set-up?

Yes indeed, I'm forced to concede that it is indeed a possible set-up.

And it also produces a link – a series of threads – between the various facts I scribbled down on that sheet of paper.

How many people in the world would Castor voluntarily go off with if they shouted for him?

I crunch up that sheet of paper and throw it into the fire. There is thunder inside my head. Are there any more false e-mails in addition to those from Soblewski? What's the situation with those more or less aggressive messages from G, which have dried up over the last few days? Might they also have been written by my husband and his accomplice?

It dawns on me that I haven't been out to shout for Castor for quite a while, and – to demonstrate to myself that there is a credible and possible alternative to the conclusions I'm close to drawing – I get dressed and go out to shout for him for at least half an hour.

In various directions, but without leaving the garden.

In my mind's eye I can see how he has sunk down so deep into a quagmire out on the moor that only his head is still above ground. He's trying to turn it so that he can see from which direction his missus is coming to rescue him: but in the end he accepts that any such solution simply isn't going to happen. It's better to just close your eyes and give up your miserable dog's life. It's better to abandon any such vain hope.

Or else . . . Or else he's lying and licking his chops on a bed in a guest house somewhere not far away. Dunster or Mine-head or Lynmouth, why not? Lying there and watching his master, the man sitting over there in the armchair with a glass of beer and a newspaper, who has just materialized out of nowhere . . .

In neither case is there much point in his missus standing out there in the dark shouting for him in a voice that increasingly resembles that faint scraping of a knife on the bottom of a saucepan.

But you go on shouting even so. You do that. As long as you have something to do, no matter how useless it is, you carry on doing it: because that's how you stop yourself from going out of your mind.

You shout and shout.

And when I've finished shouting I fall asleep on the sofa yet again.

42

There's a knocking on the door that wakes me up.

I pull the blanket off me and sit up. Check that I am dressed, and run my hands through my hair. Confused images are helter-skeltering through my mind, hammer blows are pounding away behind my eyes. I probably look like a witch, and am not sure if I should go and answer the door or not.

Then I recall the situation and decide that it doesn't matter if I look like a witch. Nothing matters any more – most probably nothing has mattered for a long time now, but it is time for me to face up to that fact. To take it seriously.

More knocking. I stand up and go to open the door.

It's Lindsey, the new waiter at The Royal Oak: several seconds pass before I manage to identify him. It's been snowing during the night, just a thin layer that is no doubt starting to melt away already: but the landscape is still white, and that comes as a surprise.

As does Lindsey, of course. Nobody has never knocked on the door of Darne Lodge while I've been living here. He is stamping in the snow rather nervously with his low shoes, and apologizes.

'Tom asked me to drive up here. I have to return straight

away – we'll be opening for lunch shortly and we're expecting a biggish group . . .'

'What's it all about?'

'Your dog, madam,' he says. 'We have your dog at the inn. He was sitting outside the door when Rosie came downstairs. So we let him in and have given him something to eat – I assume he ran off from here earlier this morning, did he?'

I stare at him but can't produce a word. He shuffles uncomfortably and throws out his arms as if he still wants to apologize for something.

'I must be getting back. But you can come down and fetch him whenever it suits you. Rosie and Tom asked me to tell you that.'

'Thank you, Lindsey,' I manage to say at last. 'Thank you so much for coming here to tell me. He's been missing ever since yesterday evening, in fact. It's so worrying . . .'

I don't know why I reduce the length of his absence by a whole day.

'Anyway, that was all I have to tell you . . . He's a lovely dog, madam.'

'Yes, he is lovely. Tell Rosie and Tom I'll be there in an hour.'

'Thank you very much, I'll do that,' says Lindsey and returns to his Land Rover that is chugging away on the road.

I get undressed, stand in the shower and reel off the whole of the Twenty-third Psalm. This time without being interrupted.

★

He comes to meet me as I walk in through the door. I sink down onto my knees and throw my arms around him – I had been determined to retain my dignity and not do any such thing, but there was no chance of that. He licks my ears, both my right one and my left. He smells a bit, not absolutely clean but not the way you would stink after spending two nights and a day out on a muddy moor.

'The prodigal son has returned, I see.'

It's Robert, sitting in his usual place with a pint of Exmoor Ale in front of him.

'Dogs,' says Rosie from behind the bar. 'They're nearly as bad as men.'

'I don't follow you,' says Robert.

Rosie snorts at him. 'If you can't find them at home, you'll find them at the pub. But it's great when they come to the right place. He's had a bite to eat and he's slept for an hour in front of the fire. Lindsey says he's been missing since yesterday evening.'

'That's right,' I say, standing up. 'I don't know what got into him. I let him out to do his business, and he was off before you could say Jack Robinson.'

'No doubt he picked up the scent of something that took his fancy,' says Tom, who appears next to his wife behind the bar.

'That's exactly what I'm saying,' says Rosie. 'Just like a man.'

'Haven't I stood by your side for thirty years?' sighs Tom, winking at me. 'I don't know what you're talking about. A

Merry Christmas, by the way! It looks as if it might be a white one – but you're used to that, I suppose?'

'I certainly am,' I say. 'But I don't suppose this will stay.'

'The main thing is that you do,' says Rosie.

I don't understand what she means, and they can tell that by looking at me.

'To eat lunch here, that's what I mean. We have a carvery today. There'll be a big crowd coming in about half an hour, but you'll be able to take the best bits if you sit down now.'

'You promised me the best bits, have you forgotten that already?' protests Robert, raising his glass.

Life goes on as usual, despite everything, I think, and sit down at the table nearest the fire. Castor lies down at my feet.

It really does. Life. It goes on as usual. And Castor and I will continue to wander around together as before.

I sit wallowing in that grandiose but perceptive thought as we drive to Dulverton after our lunchtime gluttony at The Royal Oak. As a tribute to this eternal truth and practical process we are going to buy some Christmas food. If we can find any: it's the twenty-third today, and high time . . . The road is rather bumpy and slippery after the snow, but even so Castor sits in the front passenger seat without a safety belt, so that I can keep stroking him.

Where have you been? I think. Over and over again. Where have you been? Where have you been?

But I don't really care just now. Perhaps I don't really want to know, and the main thing is that he's back. I'll never let him go out again on his own in the darkness. Not as long as we're both alive.

I manage to keep such speculation at arm's length – presumably the season of the year helps in that respect. Christmas Eve, Christmas Day, Boxing Day. We don't go anywhere, we stay in Darne Lodge and go for long walks over the moor, one in the morning and one in the afternoon: down towards the village, but only halfway – it's too muddy to go all the way; uphill towards Wambarrows with long detours in the direction of Tarr Steps. Tarr Steps from the good side, not the Devil's road.

And I don't let Castor out of my sight for a single second.

I read about John Ridd and Lorna Doone, almost to the end. I called in at the second-hand bookshop and collected Bessie Hyatt's two novels when we were doing our Christmas shopping, but they can stand next to Dickens and wait for a while. I cook and keep the fire going. We eat, we cuddle on the sofa and exchange our thoughts. We've nothing to complain about. Nothing at all.

The weather is so-so. The temperature is close to freezing, but there's no more snow: what did fall has melted away. Even so, Castor wears a dog jacket when we are out walking. We don't meet a soul out on the moor, not a single one for three days. The ponies don't seem to be celebrating the birth of Jesus: we come across groups of them here and there as usual. It looks as if they move around during the night, and you never know where they're going to appear the next morning.

But not a day passes without our seeing them somewhere or other. It seems to me that they regard Darne Lodge as a sort of hub, a central point that they can keep an eye on and keep within range.

Just like Castor and I do, of course. This two-hundred-year-old stone dwelling on the moor is our home, for better or worse. It's not yet time to start thinking about roads leading away from it. For now it's somewhere to stay and make the most of.

To stick to routines.

Menelaus. Wrong.

Agamemnon. Wrong.

Achilles. Wrong.

43

During the thirty or more years we have spent together we have socialized with lots of people – of course we have.

But we don't have many lasting friends. I don't feel especially worried or frustrated about writing that, it's just a statement of fact. When we have attended private dinner parties or sessions in pubs, it has nearly always been a case of meeting colleagues and their associates. My colleagues or Martin's colleagues. Mainly the latter. Indeed, I think I can say that I've been introduced to about three times as many academics as he has been to television folk of one kind or another, colleagues who in response to my smiling introduction have felt obliged to shake hands with my husband, the literature professor Martin Holinek.

But of course colleagues can also be friends, and there was one couple who were quite close to us. Whom I didn't hesitate to confide in during the whole of the eighties and into the nineties. They were called Sune and Louise. Sune and Martin had become acquainted at grammar school, and had begun studying literary history at the same time at the same university. Incidentally, Sune is that lecturer who maintains he saw Jacqueline Kennedy drinking coffee at a cafe in Uppsala.

Louise entered Sune's life at about the same time as I became intimate with Martin, and they moved into a shared flat in Åsögatan in the Söder district of Stockholm about six months after Gunvald was born. Louise was working at a bank in those days, and as far as I know she still does – or at least still works in the bank world.

Sune had a very poverty-stricken childhood. He grew up as the only child of a single mother who managed to just about make a living as a cleaner in a little village in Värmland. Thanks to a woman teacher who realized how gifted he was, he had a decent education: she supported both Sune and his mother financially while he was at grammar school as a boarder, and continued to finance his advanced academic studies. Sune always referred to this teacher, whose name was Ingegerd Fintling and had been dead for about a year when we first met, as an angel in human guise. In the seventies both Sune and Martin were naturally very left-wing, and I think that Sune was a sort of political alibi for Martin. Martin himself came from the upper middle-class, but it would be hard to imagine anything more lower-class than the son of a cleaner. For several years Martin was almost jealous of his friend.

But as time passed, needless to say the red paint faded away from Martin, even though he liked to insist for many years that he was a social democrat. In any case, we socialized with Sune and Louise quite a lot during those decades: after all, we lived only a few blocks away from them in the early eighties; and they had their first and only child, Halldor, about halfway between our two.

I remember being very fond of Louise without really

understanding why. She was an unusually quiet and friendly person – perhaps that was why. She didn't seem to expect much from life, and was always satisfied with herself and her circumstances. Whenever we met she was happy to allow Sune and Martin to make the elaborate gestures, lay down the political manifesto and go on about politics – but not in a submissive sort of way. She often laughed at them, and we sometimes did so in partnership; but there was never any trace of malice or irony in Louise, just a sort of mild and amused tolerance. Boys will be boys, after all.

It was several years before I realized that she was religious. Deeply and privately so, without any fuss. When the penny dropped I asked her why she hadn't told me, and she said it was because I had never asked.

And she added that she felt no need to advertise her beliefs. Nor to discuss them. She didn't go to church, and she didn't believe in organized religion. She and God had a relationship of their own, it didn't need any augmentation.

I wanted to know how she had achieved that relationship, if it was something she had experienced ever since she was a child: she explained that she had a revelation when she was fifteen, and it just went on from there.

I wondered how she reconciled her faith with all the left-wing chatter, and pointed at our living room where Martin and Sune were absorbed by an analysis of some radical political subtlety or other. Louise and I were standing in the kitchen, preparing the dessert as the gentlemen had been responsible for the main course. We were both stone-cold sober as I was pregnant with Synn and Louise was breast-feeding. Halldor and Gunvald must have been fast asleep in our warm bed-room.

'It's not a problem,' said Louise. 'I have no desire to sit there debating Our Lord and socialism with Martin, but inside my head everything is straightforward. God comes first, if you understand what I mean.'

'And what about Sune?' I asked of course. 'Opium for the masses, or whatever it is they say?'

'Sune is number three,' explained Louise, and giggled – she really could giggle like a thirteen-year-old. 'Halldor is number two. Sune knows the ranking order, and accepts it.'

For some reason I never mentioned Louise's religious beliefs to Martin, and long afterwards, when we no longer met, I sometimes wondered why. It wasn't as if it were a secret she had trusted me with. Louise and I didn't talk about it between ourselves either, not even when she was holding my hand during the difficult period after Synn's birth. I guessed of course that she was sitting there praying for me in her own quiet way, but I never asked nor commented on it.

Perhaps I kept it to myself simply because I had no wish to hear Martin's exposition and analysis of the circumstances: yes, that was probably the top and bottom of it.

Sune eventually got a post in Uppsala and they moved there. We visited them several times: they had managed to buy a house in Kåbo, the district of Uppsala where high-ranking aca-demics are supposed to live – Martin used to tease Sune for what he called a betrayal of his lower-class roots, but I always had the feeling that there was a grain or two of jealousy in his comments. Sune had completed his dissertation before Martin, and hence at this stage was probably a step or two ahead of him in his career. I recall Martin occasionally – especially when we were still living in Söder – confiding in me comments on Sune's so-called research which suggested that he really wasn't up to standard.

But even if we didn't meet so often we were still in touch throughout the nineties. They occasionally came to visit us in Nynäshamn and we went to Uppsala. Our children were friends, and I think they regarded themselves as sort of cousins. Halldor turned out to be extremely talented, and he completed sixth-form courses in maths, physics and chemistry while he was still in the fifth form. As far as I know he's now a researcher at a university somewhere in the USA – in any case he won a scholarship and went there shortly after taking his school-leaving examinations.

Anyway, both Martin and Sune applied for the same professorship. It was just after the turn of the century, and for some reason I don't know about there was a delay before a final decision was made. As I understood the situation, it was clear early on that one of the pair of them would get the chair: none of the other applicants could match Sune's and Martin's qualifications.

It was a strange time. For several months in the autumn it was as if war was in the offing. As if something major and unstoppable was on its way, and there was no way of avoiding it. Martin had submitted various extra items to the appointment committee after the closing date – I never asked what it was all about as I preferred not to know, and sometimes when I observed him at the breakfast table, or when he was absorbed by the television, I had the impression that he was somehow half-paralysed. As if he had suffered a cerebral haemorrhage but the only after-effect was this numbness. This sudden emptiness, or absence – I don't know what to call it and didn't know at the time, but at least it was clear to me that if it didn't pass soon I would have to contact a doctor.

But it did pass. One day at the beginning of November it was announced that Martin had been awarded the chair, and almost immediately everything was back to normal again. The paralysis lifted, war was called off. We celebrated, of course, but not excessively. We went to a pub in the Vasastan district of Stockholm with a few of his colleagues, and sank a glass or two.

A few days into December Louise rang and hoped we could meet for a brief chat – she was going to be in Stockholm the following day, and wondered if I had some time to spare.

Of course I had. We met at the Vetekattan cafe in Kungs-gatan: I recall that she was wearing a brand new red coat and that she looked younger than when we had last met, which to be honest was a few years back. I also thought that she radi-ated a sort of glow – that really was an unusual thought for me to have, which is probably why I remember it.

'Anyway, there's something I want to tell you,' she said when we had found a quiet, out-of-the-way spot and started sipping our coffee. 'I wasn't at all sure that I ought to, but Sune and I spoke about it and he thought the same as me – that you ought to know.'

She smiled, and shrugged as if to indicate that it wasn't the most important thing in the world despite everything. Not in her and Sune's world, at least. I expect I probably raised an eyebrow, and asked what it was all about.

'He cheated,' said Louise. 'Martin cheated. He got that professorship because he lied about something. Sune could report him, but we've agreed that we're not going to do so.'

I stared at her.

'That was all. But I think you ought to know about it. Nobody else knows, and Sune isn't going to say anything.'

I opened my mouth, but couldn't find any words.

'We've agreed about that. You don't need to worry. You know that you can trust Sune.'

I ought to have taken the matter up with Martin, of course I should; but yet again, as if it had become a sort of golden rule in our relationship, I chose to say nothing.

Or perhaps that was the very moment when I lay down the golden rule. In any case, I soon realized that my silence meant that I was also guilty. I wasn't sure of what, but it was simply not possible for me to doubt anything that Louise had told me in confidence.

Anyway, I became an accomplice. I had buried something and cemented over an injury that would have needed light and air in order to heal. It seems to me that it is very much in keeping with so much else that I have failed to do during my journey from the cradle to the grave.

That really is the story of my life.

44

The other person who makes history by knocking on the door of Darne Lodge is not Lindsey from The Royal Oak, but Mark Britton who has come back from Scarborough.

It is in the morning of the twenty-ninth of December. I invite him in – I have in fact been expecting him, and the house is in as good a shape as it's possible for it to be. A fire is burning in the hearth, and two candles are lit on the table. Castor is snoozing on his sheepskin, I have showered and look a little bit less like a witch now. Mark seems rather tired, and I suspect that the stay in Scarborough was not entirely without its problems.

'We got back yesterday evening,' he says. 'It wasn't exactly the most idyllic Christmas I've ever experienced, but at least nobody needed to go to hospital.'

'Jeremy?' I ask.

'He wasn't exactly on top form.'

'I thought you got on well with your sister?'

'There's no problem with Janet – but she has a husband and three kids as well. And Jeremy is all at sea as soon as he leaves his room. Or is away from our house, at least, but I knew that already. Anyway, it's over and done with now. It was an experiment and I prefer to skip the details. How have things been with you?'

I have already decided not to tell him that Castor went missing. I'm not sure why, and if he's already heard about it at the pub I intend to try and make light of it. I just say it was okay although we were a bit lonely.

'That's precisely what I intend to put right,' he says, brightening up a bit. 'I have two suggestions: a walk over the moor tomorrow, and a New Year's Eve dinner at our place the day after. I take it you haven't drunk all the bubbly yet?'

I lapse into a sort of feminine routine and pretend to hesitate, then say yes to both suggestions. I also explain that both Castor and I have managed to steer clear of the champagne, but that we're looking forward to tasting it. I ask if he'd like a cup of tea, and of course he would – and then we sit over my opened-out map while he explains in broad outline the route he has in mind for tomorrow's walk.

'Three hours: have you the strength for that? And a rucksack with coffee, sandwiches and dog chews on the way.'

I confirm that both I and my dog can cope with such exertions. We're in good condition. But if it looks as if it's going to pour down or snow we'd prefer to put it off until January.

'Of course,' says Mark. 'But I've already thought of that. We'll have decent weather, a bit windy perhaps but unless I'm much mistaken we might even see a bit of sun.'

'I'll believe that when I see it,' I say.

'Don't forget that I can see into the future,' he says.

He gives me a big hug before he leaves. I have the impression that I am not without significance for him.

'I'll call round tomorrow at about this time. You don't need to worry about the food, I'll fix that. Is that okay?'

'That's okay.'

'And you have suitable clothes?'

'I've been living here for two months.'

'Fair enough. See you tomorrow, then.'

'Mark?'

'Yes?'

'I'm looking forward to it. To both things.'

'Thank you. I'd like to read what you write one of these days.'

You'll never do that, I think when I've closed the door. And there's quite a lot of other things you'll never get to know as well.

There's a lot that's not relevant. A lot that has to remain hidden, even from you. It suddenly feels difficult; I think that I'm never going to be able to sort everything out. But then, I've already decided to put that off until another year.

It feels great to be a woman with a man and a dog – not just a woman with a dog. Sorry about that, Castor. We set off from the edge of Simonsbath soon after half past eleven. We head straight up over the boundless moor into the headwind, and after twenty minutes have crossed over a ridge and find ourselves in a place where there is no sign of civilization wherever you look. Only this bare, undulating landscape in every direction. Heather and grass in dark and light patches: it's the heather that is dark, and where it is growing too densely it is almost impassable. Here and there are isolated clusters of thorn bushes being battered by the wind, and here and there small flocks of sheep. The sky is obscured by a thin band of cloud – perhaps the sun might break through it eventually. Below is a gulley with a beck running from east to west, then turning off northwards and disappearing between two gentle slopes. Mark points in that direction with his staff.

'Where we're standing now is Trout Hill. Down there is Lanacombe, the site of Mrs Barrett's bolt-hole. I thought we could pay it a visit. We'll be sheltered from the wind for most of the way. And then round and up the other side towards Badgworthy. What do you say to that?'

I say that sounds good, and that I seem to recognize the name Barrett from somewhere.

'Of course you do,' says Mark. 'You live cheek by jowl with her daughter, as it were. No, I beg your pardon, I'm jumping over a generation: it's her granddaughter. That grave you must have seen.'

'Yes. Elizabeth Williford Barrett. 1911–1961. I go past it almost every day.'

He nods. 'Unless I'm much mistaken, she was born down there.' He points with his staff again. 'In Barrett's bolt-hole, yes, I think that's right. Her mother – Elizabeth's mother, that is – gave birth to her child in her own mother's house because it was illegitimate; and it was Elizabeth's grandmother who was the real, the original Barrett. Are you with me?'

I nod. I'm with him.

'She was skilful in various black arts, you could no doubt say. Prophecy and magic and all that kind of thing. She operated here in the second half of the nineteenth century, and the fact is that Exmoor lagged behind the rest of England in many respects – in any case in various tiny places on the moor. In certain hidden-away little nooks and crannies.'

He laughs, and I link arms with him. It seems like the most natural movement in the world.

'There are lots of stories about Barrett the witch,' he says. 'But she must have died shortly after becoming a grand-mother, and nobody moved into her bolt-hole after she'd gone. I used to sit there smoking secretly fifty or sixty years later, I have to admit, and there wasn't much of the place left by then.'

He likes telling stories like this, and I like listening to him.

'The Barrett daughter – I think her name was Thelma – gave birth to her daughter in her mother's bolt-hole, presumably because she had nowhere else to go. She had been thrown out of the farmhouse where she worked as a maid – no doubt the owner of the house was the father. Not all that unusual a story, in other words.'

'No,' I say. 'Most things were not better in the old days. Especially if you were poverty-stricken and a woman.'

We set off down the slope. Castor takes the lead: presumably he has been listening and knows where we are heading.

'That stalker of yours,' Martin asks when we have come a short way down the slope. 'Have you seen any more of him lately?'

I shake my head. 'No, he's been lying low.'

'Isn't that odd? I mean, if he's tracked you down and managed to find you in the back of beyond, surely he would . . . well, continue to pester you somehow or other?'

'I don't know,' I say. 'I haven't really managed to understand how his mind works. I've no idea how he thinks or acts. But maybe you are right: if he really has found me, I ought to keep seeing him.'

'But you're not sure?'

'No, I might have been imagining things, of course. It's easy to be a bit paranoid when you think you are being pursued.'

'I can well imagine that,' says Mark. 'But I'd like you to get in touch with me if anything else happens, can we agree on that? If you give me a ring I can be with you in ten minutes.'

I laugh. 'Telephone?' I say. 'Is that what you mean? I don't have a mobile that works up here, I thought I'd told you that. And I don't really want one . . . The point of sitting here writing on Exmoor is that I don't need to have any contact with the outside world.'

'Apart from what you yourself want?'

'Apart from what I myself want.'

I feel sure that I sound absolutely sincere when I say that, and why should he have any reason to doubt it? He continues walking in silence for a while, thinking.

'I know what we'll do,' he says eventually. 'You can borrow a mobile from me. I have an old Nokia in a drawer that I never use. It's pay-as-you-go, and nobody else has the number. It works up here. You can have it as . . . well, as a safety meas- ure.'

I can't think of a reasonable objection, and thank him.

★

371

We drink coffee and eat teacakes in Barrett's bolt-hole. It really is a hole: you can see the overgrown remains of some sort of building, apparently only three walls – the fourth must have been the steep hillside into which the house was built. A few metres further down is a narrow stream; Mark says it's called Hoccombe and that it runs into Badgworthy Water a bit further on. He used to go fishing there when he was a boy. I say it all sounds a bit like Huckleberry Finn: sitting in Barrett the witch's bolt-hole, smoking and waiting for a bite.

'That's more or less how I felt as well,' says Mark. 'But I didn't have a Tom Sawyer, I suppose that's what was missing. Still, I certainly miss all that, it's odd that it should be so difficult to hark back to . . . well, to one's origins, I suppose. I turn into a philosopher when I come here, I suppose you've noticed that.'

'Yes, of course,' I say. 'But I've also noticed that the sky is blue. Although the sun doesn't penetrate as far down as this.'

'Quite right,' says Mark. 'The sun never gets as far as Barrett's bolt-hole. But we're going to go up along that little slope,' he points with his staff again, 'and then we'll be in sunshine all the way back, I promise you that.'

'I'll believe it when we get there,' I say again. 'So, this is where Elizabeth Barrett was born, is it?'

'According to legend anyway,' says Mark, looking thoughtful. 'Maybe not the best of places in which to begin your journey through life, but let's assume that it was in the summer. I know where she got her middle name from in any case. Williford, isn't that what it says on her grave?'

I confirm that he's right about that.

'That was a name she started using after he'd died. She wrote quite clearly in her will that the name should be on her grave. And she wanted to be buried in that little copse where so many people come walking past . . . Everybody should see it, that was the point.'

'What point?'

'The name Williford. That was the name of her father, the farmer who made her mother pregnant and then threw her out. Quite an effective way of getting her revenge, don't you think? There are still people on Exmoor called Williford, and they're not exactly thrilled by that grave.'

He laughs.

Revenge is a dish best served cold, I think. As I've thought before. But it's not something I like remembering.

Mark's weather forecast proved to be absolutely correct. Two hours later we are sitting in The Forest Inn in Simonsbath, having lunch. I feel both worn out and warm. Castor is lying on the floor like a dead body, and what strikes me is that I just don't know how I'm going to sort this whole business out.

Should I tell Mark Britton everything? Literally everything?

What would happen if I did?

I take a drink of fizzy water and think I must be suffering from sunstroke. Simply asking questions like that suggests I must be.

Sunstroke on the thirtieth of December? Presumably pretty unique in that case, in these latitudes at least. I give Mark a television smile and thank him for such a nice day. He belongs to the present, not the past, and that's the whole point. I try to insist on paying the bill, but come up against a brick wall. Never mind, I think, I'll have time to drive to Dulverton tomorrow and buy a few bottles of decent wine at least.

But as we are sitting in Mark's car on the way back to Winsford, I realize that tomorrow is Sunday and everywhere will be closed – so that's another plan that comes to nothing.

'Seven o'clock tomorrow, okay?' he says as he drops off me and Castor. 'You know the way – and remember to bring a bit of dog food with you, because I don't think I'll be driving you back home afterwards. I'll dig out that old mobile phone as well, and make sure it's working.'

I feel like protesting, about several of the implications, but I can't think of appropriate ways of putting it. I nod and try to look enigmatic instead.

45

And so I wake up in that bed yet again.

The first of January. For the second time within the space of two weeks I have made love to a man. A stranger, whom I met in a pub in a village at the end of the world.

Is there anything wrong in that? I ask myself. Not as far as I can see. I assume that my former husband is dead, and I assume that if despite all expectations he is in fact still alive, he wouldn't want me anyway. And so I am a free woman.

My new lover isn't lying beside me in bed, but I can hear him pottering around in the kitchen downstairs. We have a new year, and we have a new situation.

Jeremy was allowed a sip of champagne at the stroke of midnight, but he didn't like it. He spat it out, and washed away the unpleasant taste with a large glass of Fanta. As I lie here in bed I have the feeling that he might actually like me. In any case, he seems to accept that I associate with his father in this way, and if I have understood Mark rightly it would not be routine for Jeremy to do so. He admitted yesterday that he was taking a considerable risk in inviting me to dinner that last time: he didn't know how Jeremy would react, but decided to chance his arm. The last time he was visited by a woman, two-and-a-half years ago, everything went wrong – but he hasn't given me any details.

I look out at the dense foliage outside the window. It doesn't allow much light in. The house really is hidden away from the world, and it feels as if you are both protected and inaccessible here. Mark told me yesterday that the house had been empty for nearly ten years when he bought it, and that putting it into decent shape nearly drove him mad. The middle floor, where I am currently lying in bed, contains Mark's bedroom and study: I've only glanced into the latter, as he was reluctant to show me what a mess it is in. There are piles of papers and files all over the place, and computers, and a stuffed parrot in a green wooden cage that he claims has magical powers. The bird, that is, not the cage. In any case, it can apparently solve difficult computer problems if you know how to ask it properly. I was on the point of asking him – Mark, that is, not the parrot – about my little password problem, but I managed to check myself. It wouldn't be a good idea for him to be aware that it was somebody else's computer, not my own; and if he eventually managed to open the document I shudder to think what he might conclude.

Now that I come to think of it, it strikes me that I could maintain that it is just something I'm writing about: a main woman character who has that little problem. But I decide not to push it. Another day, perhaps, but not today. Despite everything, I might well not want to know what happened when six men, each of them armed with a revolver, went out at dawn one day thirty-two years ago.

I can smell that he's frying bacon downstairs. Perhaps he intends to serve me breakfast in bed, but I'm not keen on eating in bed, so I throw the duvet to one side and go out into the bathroom.

A new year, and a new situation, I think again.

I look for Castor, but realize that he is downstairs with Mark. Let's face it, a kitchen is a kitchen after all. Castor has never had the problems of prioritizing that have troubled his missus.

We decide to walk back up to Darne Lodge and leave Mark and Jeremy at about noon. We can walk back again tomorrow and collect the car – we don't need it for the rest of today.

In my pocket I have a mobile phone that works. Orange instead of Vodaphone, that's the key difference. Mark rings to check before we've gone more than a few hundred metres. I answer and say that it seems to be working, and we close the call. It feels remarkable: I realize that I could hear Synn's or Gunvald's voice within a few seconds simply by pressing a few buttons. Or Christa's? Or Eugen Bergman's?

I put the mobile back into my pocket and promise myself not to press any such buttons. Not in any circumstances. Instead, when we are back in Darne Lodge I sit down at my table and try to sort out what I have been putting off for such a long time.

Planning. Accepting once and for all that there is a whole

ocean of days, weeks and months ahead of me. Perhaps even years. It's high time I took that into account. A new situation?

The fact is that I have an idea, and I sit there the whole evening playing around with it. It is in fact no more than a very primitive thought, a sort of whim that I have purposely left undeveloped inside its shell, intending to give birth to it in the new year.

Yes, I like to imagine it all in that way: you conclude things in December, and you start anew in January. It's feeling more and more like a hang-up, but if it's all to do with magical thoughts, then so what? It doesn't disturb me in the least.

The equation has only one unknown – at this point, just for a moment, the image of my old maths teacher Bennmann comes into my mind: he was anything but magical, and used to pooh-pooh any problem that didn't have at least two unknowns. Toss his head and adjust his bow-tie that was always askew underneath his pointed goatee beard, and either red with white dots or blue with white dots. But I don't want to be disturbed by him at this stage, and I send him back to the cemetery in central Sweden where no doubt he is lying by now.

One unknown, then, and this is the question I must sort out with both patience and precision. If my suspicions turn out to be justified, and my husband in some miraculous way or other managed to crawl out of that damned bunker, that hell-hole I can't bear to think about any more . . . if against all the odds he survived both the cold and the rats, then the fact is that the game is up. More or less in any case, depending on exactly what one means by the word *up*.

But enough of that. Let me go on instead. If the conclusions I have drawn from various experiences – pheasants, hire cars, missing dogs, written messages on filthy car doors, false e-mails and all the rest of it – if those conclusions are really true, then I can state that . . . Well, what exactly can I state? Mr Bennmann rolls over in his grave and tries to fix me with his gaze through six feet of solid earth – there's something for you to think about, you berk, I think, and remember now that I had him in philosophy as well: logic and argumentation analysis, for Christ's sake.

Away with Bennmann for the last time. In any case, there is . . . yes, that's the fact of the matter, and I can feel something positive and hopeful stirring in my mind as I come to this simple and obvious conclusion: there is only . . . there can be only two beings who know the truth, the solution to the equation – apart from Martin himself, of course: my dog and Professor Soblewski not far from Międzyzdroje in Poland.

Castor and Soblewski.

That's right, isn't it? That really must be the fact of the matter. These are the two paths to clarity that are being offered to me. A dog and a professor of literature.

I start with the dog and an acceptable dose of magical thinking. Kneel down on the floor in front of him, look him straight in the eye and say: 'The boss?'

He puts his head on one side.

'Have you been with the boss lately?' I ask. 'The boss? You know who I mean.'

He leans his head on the other side.

'If you've been with the boss, hold out your right paw.' This is magical thinking of a calibre I've never tried out before.

He thinks for a while, then holds out his left paw.

I can't make up my mind what that means. I try another approach.

What would be the point of my undead husband stealing Castor from me, keeping him for a couple of days and then returning him? Where's the logic in that?

Where's the logic in silver-coloured hire cars and dead pheasants and prowling around in the background all this long time? Where's the logic in anything at all?

But I brush this aside as well. Shove it down into Benn-mann's grave and return to square one. I try to think of what point there would be in stealing Castor.

It takes a while, but then the penny drops.

A message.

Some sort of indication on my dog that makes me under-stand where he's been.

Precisely, I think, and feel the buzzing inside my head change key. That is exactly how Martin Emmanuel Holinek would think. I look hard at Castor. Why haven't I thought of that before? It's more than a week since he went missing and then came back.

How do you leave an indication on a dog? What would I do?

It's not many seconds before the thought strikes me. His collar. That's the only possibility. You attach something small to his collar, perhaps a rolled-up scrap of paper under a piece of Sellotape . . . Or you write something.

I remove Castor's collar. Examine it closely. I can't see anything new and different on it. Nothing taped onto it, or fastened in some other way. I examine the inside, check it meticulously centimetre by centimetre: this is how I would do it, I think, just like this. Write *Death* or whatever I would want to note down and pass on, and that is also what Martin would do. I know him. We've spent a lifetime together.

Nothing.

No letter, no sign of any kind.

I slide the collar back over Castor's head and thank him. Tell him to go and lie down in front of the fire and think about something else. To forget the boss.

I move on to Professor Soblewski.

The buzzing inside my head has died down: instead a sad little creature raises its head and tells me that I'm mad. And that I should be grateful that I don't have to submit to a mental examination today.

I tell the creature to shut up, and that I need to concentrate.

'Mark Britton?' it says even so. 'And how do you intend to deal with that little problem?'

'Shut your gob,' I tell it. 'Crawl back to wherever you've come from. Mark Britton has nothing at all to do with this. He's just a way of spending the time.'

'Huh, kiss my arse,' says the creature. But then it has

enough sense to keep quiet. I wish I had a cigarette, which is not a good sign of course, and it soon passes.

Then I get no further. Not a millimetre further.

Much later that evening:

Bach. Wrong.

Handel. Wrong.

Brahms. Wrong.

46

It's Alfred Biggs who's on duty. It's morning, and there are no other customers in the centre, tapping away at their keyboards. He brightens up when I come in and wishes me a Happy New Year. I return the compliment. He goes out into the kitchen to make tea without even asking if I want any. I've forgotten to bring biscuits with me yet again.

I start with Martin's inbox and find that I'm in luck: there actually is a message from Soblewski, just as I had been hoping. He wishes Martin a Happy New Year and attaches the short story he had mentioned in his previous message. 'Change of Wind' by Anna Słupka. He points out that the translation probably needs a bit more revision, but he wants Martin to read it and give his opinion of it.

And he asks Martin to pass on greetings to fru Holinek.

I read the ten lines twice, very carefully, and open the attachment: it strikes me that sending the text of a short story like this suggests that my theory about Soblewski being an accomplice is over the top. Why would they need to go to such lengths if it is all a fake?

Change of Wind? I drop the idea – at least until I've read fröken Słupka's text properly. I also recall that the Swedish short story they had talked about had been written by a young author called Anderson, Anderson with only one *s*, but I make up my mind not to overdo the interpretation. The world is full of possible messages, and one way of going mad is to try to read all of them.

Nevertheless I have to be very careful of course when it comes to my (Martin's) reply to Soblewski's message, and it takes a whole cup of tea and twenty minutes before I'm satisfied with what I've written. I wish him a Happy New Year and say thank you for the short story. I promise to read it as soon as possible, and get back to him with a judgement within a week (Alfred Biggs helps me to print out the twelve pages); and with a minimum of fuss I describe how we have celebrated Christmas and the New Year down here in Morocco. In the end I write:

> And I sincerely hope no new bodies have turned up in your village. Have they identified the last one yet?
> Best, Martin

I was going to put 'on your beach' but I changed it to 'in your village'. There was nothing about a beach in the previous e-mail – and nothing about a village either, come to that, but I can't think of a better way of expressing it. I also think that my (Martin's) tone is exactly right: a bit jokey but even so sufficiently serious for him to answer the question in his next message.

The fact that the body hasn't been identified is of course the only possible answer.

As for the rest of Martin's e-mails, the only one I bother to respond to is a brief greeting from Bergman. In accordance with my plan I write that I (Martin) have fallen a bit behind with my writing, but I hope that things will buck up in the new year. 'A few problems have cropped up and I can't see a satisfactory way round them just yet,' I add.

That is all I need to say at this stage. I think my plan is working well.

My own inbox, which I don't open until I've finished dealing with Martin's, produces something unexpected – totally un-expected. Violetta di Parma writes that her mother back in Argentina has fallen seriously ill, and that her family wants her to come home as soon as possible. They say it can be a matter of months, possibly even weeks, and Violetta writes that she has made up her mind. Her contract with the Opera Ballet runs until the middle of April, but most of the work will be finished in January. The première will be in the middle of February, and she has already been given the okay by the powers that be to leave at the end of January.

And so Violetta writes that she wants to leave our house on the first of February, three months earlier than intended, and that is what she would like to discuss with us. How should we go about it? Would we like her to find a new tenant to look after the house for the remainder of the period? What shall we do about the money she has already paid in rent for the remaining three months? If we can't find any other solution she realizes that she will have to abide by the contract as originally agreed.

It is a long and emotional message: she apologizes for causing us problems in this way, but she can't see any other possibility for herself apart from going back home to Córdoba.

My first reaction is also that fate has been most unkind. I really need these months, this spring, in order to pull this off. As so often recently, I have no idea about what I mean by pulling this off: but after sitting and brooding over the e-mail – and being served another cup of tea by Alfred Biggs – I begin to see things in quite a different light.

What is there to stop me speeding things up a bit?

Why shouldn't I be able to carry out my plan in one month rather than three?

In fact, might that even improve the outcome?

I spend the whole of the afternoon's walk round Selworthy Combe and Bossington thinking about this new situation, and by the time we shut ourselves into Darne Lodge as dusk falls I am quite clear about what to do next.

We shall leave Morocco a month from now. It will work all right, and even make everything more credible if I handle it correctly. It needs more activity on my part, of course: but if there is one thing I have missed during my stay on the moor, it is active involvement in something.

As if to confirm that this conclusion is absolutely correct, this is what happens late in the evening:

Signe. Wrong.

Vivianne. Wrong.

Ingrid.

The screen flickers twice, and then the document 'At Dawn' opens.

Signe is his mother. Vivianne, as I have already explained, is his dead sister. His mother is also dead, incidentally.

Ingrid, on the other hand, is the woman with whom he was unfaithful in the middle of the nineties. She is most probably still alive, and he has evidently not forgotten her.

And I will not forget the password.

47

At Dawn

But I'm on the wrong track already. The distance between darkness and light is short, and there is hardly any dawn as such. The sun is rising over crests of the mountains in the east like a gigantic red balloon, while we are still standing outside the wall, waiting for H and Gusov. I don't know what we are letting ourselves in for, but there is something I can't explain driving us on.

Me and Soblewski. Grass and Megal. The Frenchman looks to be near the point of collapse, there is no trace left of his air of superiority. He's older than the other three of us, considerably older: perhaps he suspects what this theatrical performance is all about. Perhaps he's been through it before – I have that impression. None of us says anything, I am feeling more and more the after-effects of that drug we smoked. Both Grass's and Soblewski's pupils are very dilated. Megal is wearing sunglasses.

When we have been standing there waiting for about five minutes H comes out of the front door. He is on his own, one of us asks about Gusov and H explains that he will join us later.

Before we set off we have something to drink. It is a dark red, strong drink that almost burns your throat, and it seems to contain a mixture of tastes: I can identify anise, mint and bitter almonds. H serves it from a bottle into plastic mugs which we eventually leave in a pile next to the wall. H hands out our revolvers, explains that they are loaded but the safety catches are on, and asks us not to speak during the short walk that lies ahead of us.

'Twenty minutes,' he says. 'We'll be there in twenty minutes. Let me thank you already for taking part.'

And so we set off along a well-trodden path. It slopes gently upwards, and we are heading out into the desert-like countryside, directly towards the sun. Lizards scamper back and forth in front of our feet, and in the far distance an ass is braying. It's getting warmer by the minute.

We come to a little copse of trees, halfway up the slope, and make a short pause in the shade and relative coolness. I check my watch and see it is still only half past six. H explains that we shall soon reach our destination, and asks us to have our guns ready. We drink some more of the red liquid, this time directly from the bottle. There is no doubt that doing so helps to reinforce our feelings of solidarity. I haven't had a wink of sleep all night, and feel that most of all I would like to lie down here in the shade and doze off. I can see that the others feel similarly. All we want is to lie down and close our eyes, that would be for the best. When we set off again Grass has to support Megal, who hasn't the strength to walk unaided.

But the drink is burning in our throats, and in our minds as well: and it is speaking a different language. The same language as H, presumably: keep going, keep going!

We follow a path that seems to be leading round the mountain, and after a while we have the sun directly behind us instead of in front of us, which makes matters a bit easier. Then the path suddenly *heads downwards, into what looks like a dried-out ravine, and we stop when we come to a little plateau. I check my watch again and see that we have been walking for twenty-five minutes in all. It feels like longer. H serves some more of the red drink, but also produces some water from his rucksack and gives us some to drink. My head is spinning, and I have the feeling that I have no idea what is going on.*

Then he points at a clump of bushes not far in front of us on the plateau.

'The monster,' he says. 'That's where the monster lives. Get ready to kill the monster.'

Soblewski bursts out laughing, he obviously thinks it sounds too absurd. H goes up to him and punches him in the chest. Soblewski stops laughing and apologizes. I look at Grass and see that he has raised his revolver, but is just standing there, trembling. I feel an urge to run away, but another impulse yells at me that if I do so I'll get ten bullets in my back. I really have no idea about what's going on.

We stand in a line about ten metres away from the bushes. They are parched and covered in grains of sand which have turned them grey: it's impossible to see through the branches. I have the impression that I can see something black inside there, but can't make out what it is.

'The monster is the rapist,' says H. 'He must die. We shall all share the responsibility for the rapist's death. That's why we've come here.'

He pauses. Nobody says anything.

'Cock your guns,' he says. 'Stand by.'

We release the safety catch and aim into the bushes. The clump is no more than four metres wide, the vague black outline is exactly in the middle.

'Fire!' shouts H.

And we all fire every bullet we have into the bushes. Thirty in all. The sound echoes around and lingers on for several minutes.

Then we all go over to the bushes and pull out that black thing. It's a few large pieces of cloth, now riddled with bullet holes and covered in blood. Inside is a body. It's Gusov.

We have killed the monster.

We have killed the rapist.

48

There is a postscript, evidently added later. I don't know when exactly he wrote 'At Dawn', but in the postscript he discusses what actually happened. It's only two pages long, and he makes no attempt to justify his actions – nor those of the others. What he mainly writes about is how far he knew the point of the dawn excursion before they set off – or if he didn't *know*, whether he ought to have *realized*. Should he not have been able to work out that Bessie Hyatt and Gusov had been having an affair – an affair that might well have been going on for a long time? For several summers? He also wonders how Herold had managed to get Gusov to his place of execution, and concludes that he must have drugged him and driven him there in the dark in his jeep. In that case he would surely have had an accomplice, and when he discusses that with Soblewski and Grass they come round to thinking that the accomplice was Bessie herself. That she played an active role in the plot. It is Grass, above all Grass, who pushes that interpretation, and he evidently does so on the basis of conversations he had with Bessie. Martin recalls that they have known each other since they were children, and it doesn't seem impossible that she might have confessed to him.

It also says in the postscript that he, Soblewski, Grass and the Megals leave Taza the following day. Doris Guttmann seems to have stayed on, however. Martin writes that Bessie Hyatt had an abortion a little later that same summer, something that he also learns via Grass a few months later, and that the story comes to an end when she commits suicide in April 1981. That is exactly how he puts it: 'The story comes to an end when . . .'

By the time I have read the whole document it is a few minutes past midnight. I switch off and put some more wood on the fire, which has almost gone out. I feel that I have many questions, and yet don't have any.

Hyatt is dead. Herold is dead. Martin is presumably also dead, but I wonder what he intended to do with it all. Soblewski and Grass are alive, but I would be surprised if Megal is. His younger wife – the hypnotist – might be still alive, but she isn't involved in the finale itself. Or is she?

Finale? I think, and then once again I have the uncomfortable feeling that it is all made up. But that can't be the case. The e-mail from G (there is no doubt that it must be Grass) together with Martin's meeting and nocturnal conversation with Soblewski are clear indications that those things really did happen. A dark secret. And Bessie Hyatt's suicide in 1981 is also indisputable.

So this is what Martin had intended writing a book about? I sit there for a good long while thinking intently about everything, try to work out how I am going to make it fit in with my own plans, and eventually, when I return to that idea of a play – *Evenings in Taza*, but that isn't a very good title, despite everything – I think I am beginning to get somewhere. I eventually go to bed with this creative thought in my mind: five acts, of course, two or three on Samos and the climax in Morocco . . . But the same dinner table, the same guests, the same story . . . Yes, I decide to sleep on it and examine the idea again in the cold light of morning.

The third of January. I'm woken up by the telephone; it feels like a signal from another world. I answer it because I suspect he will jump into his car and drive here if I don't.

'How are things?'

I say that we are doing fine, both Castor and I, and ask how he is. And Jeremy, I add.

'Excellent,' says Mark Britton. 'When can we meet?'

I note that less than two days have passed since I crawled out of his bed, and that I evidently mean more to him than he does to me. How has that happened, suddenly and without warning?

It is Thursday today. 'How about Saturday?' I suggest. 'I need a few days to work.'

'Has something happened?'

I can hear the concern in his voice. Concern at the fact that I am on the defensive.

'No, not at all,' I say but regret my words immediately. It would be as well for me to give him a warning. 'It's just that I might have to change my plans a bit,' I say.

'What plans?' he wonders. 'You've never mentioned any plans.'

'We can discuss that on Saturday,' I say. 'Shall we meet at the pub?'

'No, certainly not. I want you to come here, of course. Don't start playing hard to get, we're too old for that.'

He tries to make it sound a little ironic and jokey, but doesn't quite manage it.

Huh, that really is the case, I think when I close down the call. I mean too much to him already.

But I shall have to deal with that on Saturday. Today I have other things I must think about and come to terms with as best I can. I might also have a whole play to write, but I spend most of the morning writing messages. After lunch we go for quite a short walk up to the Punchbowl and back, then drive down to the computer centre. Today it's Margaret Allen on duty. We wish one another a Happy New Year, and chat briefly about the weather and the wind and the Queen's speech. Needless to say it's only Margaret who has anything to say about the Queen's speech, since unlike all real English people I haven't even listened to it.

Then I sit down in my usual place. I'm the only customer today: the centre seems more outdated than ever, but I'm grateful that it exists. Grateful for the cup of tea that Margaret serves up, and just for a brief moment I have the feeling that I could live here.

Really live here. In the village of Winsford, far from the madding crowd. On this moor where the sky and the earth kiss each other. For one more brief moment I wonder if that would be feasible to fit in with the rest of the plan, but decide not to get carried away by that thought. I have enough to think about already.

I write as follows from Martin to Eugen Bergman:

> My dear friend, I don't like having to give you bad news at the beginning of a new year, but it can't be helped. The fact is that I'm having big problems with my material, I'm not getting anywhere with it. I don't know what I really want to do, and it's making me feel dejected.
>
> I thought matters would resolve themselves in time, but now I'm beginning to realize that they might not. In any case it's not going to be the bulky documentary novel about Herold and Hyatt that I may have given you reason to expect. If it becomes anything at all, it's going to be on a much smaller scale.
>
> Just as worrying, at least for me, is that I'm feeling extremely depressed. I've been feeling that way for more than a month now. Maria has been doing all she can to get me back on my feet, but it's not enough. Anyway, I'm only writing this because I want you to be aware of the situation, and to prevent overblown expectations at your publishing house and elsewhere. I'm sorry about this development, but I can't do anything about it, believe you me.
>
> With my very best wishes, M

That is more or less word-for-word what I wrote in my notebook this morning. I read it through twice, then send it off.

There has been no response as yet from Soblewski, so I put the draft of my message to him on one side and go over to my own mailbox.

I write to Synn:

> Dear Synn. I hope the New Year has begun well in New York. We have had a quiet and relaxing time down here in the relative warmth, but I have to tell you that your dad isn't all that well. He's been downcast since quite a long time before Christmas and says he simply can't concentrate and do any work – I think he's sinking into a state of depression, more or less. Being so far away from home doesn't make things any easier, and I've begun to wonder if we ought to cut short our stay here in Morocco. I just wanted you to know that – we haven't made any decisions yet, we're taking each day as it comes.
>
> Best wishes, Mum

And to Gunvald:

> A Happy New Year, Gunvald! I hope all is well in Copenhagen – or are you still in Sydney? I can't remember what your dad said. In any case we're having a calm and relaxing time in Morocco, but I have to tell you that your dad is having some problems. I know he would never admit as much to you, but he's simply not able to work at all and

I think he might be depressed – clinically depressed, I mean. If you write to him you don't need to mention that I've told you this, but I know he would appreciate a few uplifting lines from you. Look after yourself wherever you are, and very best wishes from Mum.

I send both messages, then scribble a few lines to Violetta, assuring her that of course she doesn't need to pay rent for the months when she won't be living in the house. I say I'm sorry to hear about her mother's illness, and understand completely that she feels she must go home. She doesn't need to do anything about finding somebody to live in the house – we might well decide to go home rather earlier than originally planned. Martin hasn't been feeling very well lately.

Feeling satisfied with these carefully worded messages, I tell Margaret Allen I hope she has a pleasant weekend, and say that I might well drop in again on Monday.

49

Friday the fourth of January. A sunny day with the temperature a few degrees above zero – when we leave Darne Lodge that is, halfway through the morning. I've consulted the map and decided to head for Rockford. Castor hasn't expressed any objections.

It is a hamlet comprising about fifteen houses, stretching along the bank of the East Lyn River. We get there after walking alongside the river from Brendon, and it has felt like a spring morning from the first stride: small birds are fluttering around in the bushes, and the ground seems to be swelling. It's a few minutes past one, the pub is open and so we go in for lunch.

We find that the pub is hosting an art exhibition: there are twenty or so small oil paintings hanging on the walls, all of them depicting the moor. Ponies in the mist. Gates. Gorse bushes. The artist herself is also present, sitting at a table with her paint brushes and tubes, carefully dabbing paint onto a little canvas on an easel in front of her.

'Jane Barrett,' says the landlady when I place my order at the bar. 'She lives here in the village. She's pretty good – what she doesn't manage to sell herself we usually buy for the pub.

Mind you, she sells more or less everything. If you're interested in a painting of the moor, now's your chance to acquire one. She's not very expensive either.'

Castor and I sit down at the table next to the artist's.

We introduce ourselves and I say that I recognize her name.

'Really?' she says. 'I suppose you must know a bit about Exmoor, then?'

'I don't know about that,' I say. 'But there's a little grave almost next to where I'm living. The lady lying there is called Elizabeth Williford Barrett.'

'Well, I'll be . . .' Her face lights up and she puts down her paintbrush on a rag. 'So you must be living in Darne Lodge. It's my grandma lying there. What an amazing coincidence!'

She smiles broadly. She is a powerfully built woman about forty-five years old, the type my father would no doubt have said was full of go. A mop of red hair, tied up with an even redder ribbon. A paint-stained woollen jumper reaching down to her knees. Lively eyes. She looks every inch a creative artist.

'Yes, we live there,' I say. 'My dog and I. We've been there for a few months, but we'll probably be leaving at the end of January.'

'It's a lovely place to live,' says Jane Barrett, stroking Castor. 'You couldn't have found anywhere better. No matter what your work is, I have no doubt that you are . . . well, protected.'

'Protected?'

'Yes. For one thing you have my grandma on the other side

of the road, and for another she has made sure that the house is disinfected.'

I smile somewhat tentatively. 'Do you mean that . . . ?'

I simply don't know what to say next, but it doesn't matter. Jane Barrett likes talking. 'Maybe you don't know what kind of women we are in my family. There must always be a witch on the moor, and nowadays it's me. My grandma's grandmother is the most notorious – the witch in Barrett's bolt-hole . . . Have you heard of her?'

I say that not only have I heard of her, I've even visited the bolt-hole.

'Really?' exclaims Jane, astonished once again. 'But they haven't put the place in the tourist leaflets, have they? Although it wouldn't surprise me . . .'

'I went walking around those parts with a friend who was born in Simonsbath,' I explain. 'He was the one who knew about her, and explained it all to me.'

She nods and takes a drink of tea from the cup on her table. 'I'll tell you one thing: I'm pretty sure my mother was conceived in your house.'

'Your mother? . . . Elizabeth?'

She laughs. 'No, Elizabeth is my grandmother. But she's the one who was responsible for the conception. Half of it, at least. She lived in Darne Lodge with a young man at the end of the thirties, before he was conscripted for service in the Second World War. Grandma was pregnant with my mother, and gave birth in the spring of 1941. And at about the same time the man died somewhere in Africa. Killed by a German bullet. Mother and daughter Barrett continued living in Darne

Lodge until they were thrown out by the owner, or whatever it was that happened . . .'

It strikes me that Margaret Allen must have missed out the odd chapter in the history of Darne Lodge, unless I wasn't listening intently enough.

'Anyway,' says Jane, 'Grandma Elizabeth made sure that the house was properly protected. No dodgy goings-on were going to make it difficult for people to come to Darne Lodge. All right, I know that people have died there and that things have happened, but that's another story. Have you felt safe, living up there?'

I think that over, then say that yes, I have.

'What do you do for a living?'

'I write books. I'm an author.'

She shakes my hand. 'I thought you were an artist. You can sense things like that – especially if you are a witch.'

She leans back, sticks her thumbs in her armpits and laughs. 'It runs in the family, and things keep repeating themselves,' she says slightly mysteriously. 'We Barretts only give birth to girls. One for each generation. And we keep the name Barrett. But you've probably seen that it says Williford on Grandma's grave.'

I say that I have seen that, and think I know the reason for it.

'Exactly,' says Jane. 'That rich farmer bastard who raped her mother. My great grandmother. And do you know, I also have a daughter . . . she's only seventeen. As pretty as the dawn, and shortly before Christmas she came home and introduced me to a boyfriend. His name is James Williford . . . The choice here on the moor is a bit limited, you might say. It smells of incest, don't you think?'

She laughs again. I think for a few seconds, then I tell her about the pheasants.

'Lucky you,' she says when I've finished. 'Just as I told you, you can't hope for better protection than that. Nobody put those birds outside your door. They came there of their own accord when their time was up. They lay down and died there because Death isn't allowed in. I can tell you that we witches are on unusually good terms with birds. But perhaps that's an indication that . . . well, it might mean that you need some protection. Is that true, perhaps?'

She looks at me pretending to be serious.

'Who isn't in need of protection?'

'Very true. But where do you come from? Forgive me for saying so, but I can hear that you don't come from Oxford.'

'Sweden. And as I said, I'll probably be going back home at the end of this month. But thank you . . . Thank you for the protection. I think I'd like to buy one of your paintings.'

'If I can have one of your books, we can make an exchange – but perhaps you don't write in English?'

'I'm afraid not.'

'Never mind. You can have a painting even so. Witches don't need money.'

I choose a picture with some ponies drinking water out of a beck. It's not big, maybe twenty by thirty centimetres or thereabouts: I like it very much, and insist on paying her for it.

'Not on your life!' says Jane Barrett. 'An agreement is an agreement. Pass on greetings to Grandma, by the way.'

I promise to do so.

As if I really were an author, I sit at home writing all evening. The whole of the first act and the first scenes of act two. I'd love to insert a witch into the action, but of course that's not possible. Madame Megal will have to suffice. Work on the script seems to flow with hardly any problems: I know Bergman will be surprised by the result, but when he has read it all he will presumably understand. I remember that I have had time to prepare him for what's coming, and I feel pleased that things have worked out in the way they have. Before I write acts three and four I must make sure I read Bessie Hyatt's two novels: she isn't really the main character in the drama as yet, but once we've moved from Samos to Taza she will undoubtedly be that.

While I'm sitting writing, the mobile phone rings several times. Only one person has the number, and so I refrain from answering. Mark Britton is a problem I don't have time to deal with just now. We're going to meet tomorrow evening after all, so why does he have to ring now?

On the other hand he probably doesn't regard a telephone call as a serious event, which I have got round to doing because of the circumstances. Maybe he just wants to know if I like coriander?

But even so, I don't answer. That thought about the

possibility of my coming back here eventually crops up again, however.

Once everything has gone according to plan. In six months or so. Coming to live permanently here on the moor? Protected by witches and all the rest of it. Not in Darne Lodge, of course, but there are plenty of houses around here to rent or buy. Every village has adverts put up by estate agents.

What is the alternative? Ten more years at the Monkey-house?

I start wondering how much the house in Nynäshamn might be worth. A couple of million at least . . . Maybe three? I would be able to get by.

Yes indeed, I'd be able to get by.

50

Sunday, the sixth of January. Cloudy, not much wind, a bit colder.

Mark Britton really is a complication, and I don't need any complications just now. Or maybe that's exactly what I do need?

For the third time I've had dinner and stayed the night in Heathercombe Cottage, and for the third time we've made love. When I write 'complication' I don't mean quite the same thing as I did the other day – that I mean too much to him already, and that he isn't as important as that for me.

I feel that I have to reconsider matters somewhat. I'm fifty-five years old, I'm pretty well preserved – but where on earth would I find a better man? Always assuming that I decide not to live alone once I've outlived my dog.

Incidentally that dog shows no sign of growing old: perhaps I should try to find a different yardstick? Reconsider matters in that respect as well. I told Mark last night that I would probably be leaving Darne Lodge at the end of the month, and part of the complication is that I have to put together a plausible story. I've tried to do so: I said I would have to step in and take the place of a friend who has gone up the wall in connection with the production of a play. She has simply been working too hard, and I've more or less agreed to be assistant director and quite a few other things for six weeks from February onwards.

'And then what?'

I said I didn't know. That I really didn't know – at least that is one truth that I haven't kept from him.

But it's not enough, of course. Castor and I are back in Darne Lodge, it's afternoon and I'm sitting in my usual place at the table and feeling a certain degree of shame. Or shame-facedness, at least.

It's as if I'm exploiting him. He invites me to one fantastic meal after another, we drink decent wines, we make love in straightforward fashion without any hang-ups, and Jeremy shakes my hand increasingly as if it were the most natural thing in the world.

Martin used to have a literary hobby horse when it came to love affairs – I thought for ages that he was referring to other people's love affairs. Either it is a fantastically good short story, or it's the promising first chapter of a novel which might keep going at the same high standard, or get out of control. The trick is knowing which it is. Or perhaps it's a matter of making up your mind which it is.

If I hadn't kept hearing that ad nauseam I might have agreed with it. And there is something sad about the short story format, is there not? The primitive tale that doesn't have the strength to grow up.

I put all such questions to one side in order to make pro-gress with my play. Act two: I have decided to let Maurice

Megal play a slightly different role from the one he seems to play in Martin's notes – something of an observer and story-teller, even in the scenes that are set in Greece – and I notice that I am enjoying this work. I really hadn't thought that I would do. My fictitious role as an author is beginning to get a foothold in the real world.

I really do put act two together in three hours – obviously I shall have to look at it again and rewrite parts, add bits here and there and cut a few things, but that goes with the territory. The important thing is that I can envisage the whole thing inside my head – the whole thing and how to get there – and as it's now time for Bessie Hyatt to take on the role of tragic heroine, I must start reading *Before I Collapse*. It's not long before I'm totally absorbed in it, and I don't understand why I didn't read the book during the years when the rest of the world did.

Mark Britton rings shortly before eleven to wish me good-night.

'I'm missing you already,' he says, and I say that in fact I'm missing him as well.

'We must put our relationship on a solid footing,' he says.

'Yes,' I say. 'I suppose we must.'

When I've closed down the call I remember that I also ought to read that short story by Anna Słupka – 'Change of Wind' – although I don't fancy the prospect.

The very fact that it's only a short story goes against the grain – isn't that what I had decided not long ago? A bit like

Bessie Hyatt's life. And my sister's. I promise myself to turn my attention to fröken Słupka tomorrow. I mustn't cut corners when it comes to contact with Soblewski.

An e-mail from Eugen Bergman to Martin, dated the seventh of January:

> My dear friend, I'm very sorry to hear that you are having problems. But writer's block is a phenomenon that affects lots of authors, not just you; remember that. Bear in mind also that there are antidotes: which is best depends on the individual of course, but the most important thing is that you mustn't go around worrying about it. Nobody benefits from sitting and staring at a blank sheet of paper or at a computer screen when the words are hiding away or tying themselves in knots. My dear Martin, give it a rest for a while and try to enjoy something else instead. Go to Casablanca and Marrakesh – simply writing the names of those places gives me goose pimples. Stockholm is sheer hell at this time of year, thank your lucky stars you're not stuck here.
>
> Say if there's something you'd like to read and I'll send you it.
>
> I really hope you can recover your usual good humour eventually, but there's no rush. Taking things slowly is not to be scoffed at. My best wishes to Maria, and write to me whenever you feel the need. I know that I'm your publisher, but I'm also your friend: don't forget that.
>
> Eugen

From Gunvald to Martin:

> Hello! I'm sitting at the airport outside Sydney, waiting for a delayed flight. I've had an absolutely marvellous time down here: both the conference and my free days have been extremely rewarding. I've even tried surfing, but that was just a one-off. The Opera House. Manly Beach. Oysters and chardonnay at The Rocks, Blue Mountains . . . You name it. I hope you two are having at least a fraction as much fun in Morocco as I've been having here. How long will you be staying there? My very best wishes to Mum. Gunvald

From Synn to me:

> Huh. I have to say I find it hard to feel sorry for him. You'll have to take care of him – after all, you're the one who's married to him, not me. I can't help it if you think I sound cold and indifferent, you know I hate conventions and false outpourings. Anyway, we have had a very successful season over here, and we gather there's lots of work lined up for the spring so it looks as if it will be some time before I fly over the Atlantic again. In any case, I hope he doesn't spark off any new scandals: the last one was quite enough to be going on with. Pass on some kind of friendly greeting from me that you can invent. Greetings from a freezing cold Manhattan, small nails are pelting down over the Hudson. Synn

From Violetta di Parma to me:

> Dear Maria. Very many thanks for your sympathetic response. I've booked a flight for 31 January. I'll make sure

the house is clean and tidy. I'll be happy to pay a bit more than just the January rent, but perhaps we can reach an agreement on that in due course. It's cold here around Stockholm, very cold – I assume your weather will be a bit warmer in Morocco. When I get back home to Argentina it will be the middle of summer of course. Many greetings to Martin, please tell him I've really enjoyed living in your house and that I'm very sorry to have to leave it like this. Hugs and kisses, Violetta

Nothing from Soblewski. I assume he's waiting for my (Martin's) views on Anna Słupka, but even so I hope I hear from him before he gets them. I can't very well take up that unidentified dead body again, but if he forgets about my (Martin's) question I suppose that suggests I don't need to worry about it. That's how I decide to interpret the situation in any case, and I also decide not to respond to a single message from today's crop: they can just as well wait for a few days, and by then I reckon it could be time for me to contact Eugen Bergman personally. With a message in my own name, that is.

I leave the centre and turn into Ash Lane. When I'm standing in front of Mr Tawking's front door with its flaking blue paint, it occurs to me that I haven't heard a single squeak from him all the time I've been here. I've been living in his house for over two months: surely that's a bit odd?

I wonder if he might be dead and nobody has thought to inform me, but I knock on the door even so.

He opens after a while and looks more dead than alive, but he did last time as well. I have the impression that he doesn't recognize me, so I begin to explain that I'm the person who has been renting his house up on Winsford Hill since November.

'I know,' he says, interrupting me. 'It's just that my eyesight isn't very good. Come in.'

I don't get any tea this time, and it takes quite a while to reach an agreement. An agreed contract is an agreed contract, Mr Tawking insists, and if I'm daft enough to pay half a year's rent in advance, that's my problem.

I point out that it was he who insisted on that arrangement if I were to move in at all, and we sit there negotiating for a while in his gloomy living room. I don't really care how the negotiations go, I'm not all that hard up in fact; but in the end he agrees to pay back two hundred pounds if I've moved out by the beginning of February. I'm welcome to call in and collect the money in a few days' time, and we can sign a new document then. It strikes me that he is the only genuinely unpleasant person I've come across since coming to live on the moor.

That's that, then, I think when I've left him and am walking back down to the monument with Castor at my heels. That means I have three weeks in which to see to everything. That should be long enough.

51

'That stalker of yours,' says Mark Britton. 'What's happened to him? You haven't mentioned him for a while.'

We are out walking in Barle Valley. The astonishing thing is that Jeremy is here as well: he's walking about ten metres behind us with enormous earphones on his head and his hands dug deep down into his pockets. Mark says he can hardly ever persuade him to leave the house. Castor is walking just behind Jeremy, but when we turn back shortly afterwards and head for home, they change places.

'No,' I say. 'I haven't seen him for several weeks. Not since I told you about him, I think.'

It's the fifteenth of January, and that's about right. It must be nearly a month since I last saw that silver-coloured Renault.

'Hm,' says Mark, kicking at a stone. I can see that he has more to say on that subject.

'Why do you ask?'

He hesitates. Turns round to check that Jeremy is keeping up with us. Adjusts his scarf.

'I think I might have seen him,' he says in the end.

I stop dead. 'What do you mean? Did you see him? Where?'

'It was a few days ago,' says Mark, trying to look apologetic for some reason. 'In Dulverton. His car was parked outside the butcher's, and he came out of there while I was watching. Got into the car and drove away.'

'He?'

'Yes, a man. In his sixties I'd say, or thereabouts. I didn't get much of an idea of what he looked like, I was on the other side of the road. And he was wearing a hat. But it was a hire car from Sixt, and I noted down the registration number.'

'Really?' I suddenly feel all of a tremble. As if I couldn't possibly take another step forward. He can see there's something wrong.

'Are you feeling all right?'

'Yes, I'm fine. It's just that I suddenly felt dizzy.'

'Dizzy? You don't usually have attacks of dizziness, do you?'

'It's over and done with now. What did you do with the registration number?'

I can hear that he didn't leave it at that.

He clears his throat. 'I chased it up,' he says.

'Really?' I say. 'How?'

'I phoned the rental firm and spun them a yarn. I said I thought the driver of that car had reversed into mine, and I wanted to contact him. They were a bit hesitant at first, but when I told them I was a police officer in Taunton and that they should come to the point they backed down. They checked the documentation, and it transpired that the car had been rented on a long-term contract by a person of Polish origins.'

'By a person of Polish . . . ?'

My field of vision shrinks to a tunnel. I clench my fists and take a deep breath.

'Yes. But surely your stalker doesn't have any Polish connections, does he? Didn't you say his name was Simmel? The fact was . . .'

'What was it?'

He laughs. 'The fact was that they couldn't read his name. It was long and Polish and awkward. But if I wanted to seek compensation I should just send them a notification of damage form. Then they would chase him up via his passport number – that appears to be the routine. I thanked them and said I would think it over. What do you think?'

'What do I think?'

'Yes. Surely this must suggest that it isn't him.'

I look at him and try to take a grip of myself. 'You're right, of course. It's just that I was so surprised . . . I haven't thought about him for so long.'

But just now there's no room for anything else in my mind. That's what happens, I tell myself: once the lid is lifted far too much comes rushing out. What would Gudrun Ewerts say about this?

I put the lid back on and we start walking again. We continue walking along the river bank, but stop when we realize that Jeremy is no longer following behind us. We retrace our steps and soon find him. He's stopped in the middle of the path for no obvious reason. He's standing there with his hands in his jeans pockets, staring into space. Castor is sitting beside him, just a metre away.

'Good Lord!' says Mark. 'I must get myself a dog, I really must.'

I'm spending too much time with Mark Britton. It's not for my sake I say that, but for his. I have lost count of how many times I've woken up at Heathercombe Cottage, but soon I'll be leaving here. I know he hopes that our relationship will continue, even if we don't talk about it. And a continuation must involve my returning to Exmoor. It's naturally out of the question for him to consider moving anywhere else with Jeremy. He has made that decision some time ago, once and for all.

But I don't want to encourage him to think I shall return. Not yet. My feeling for magic thoughts forbids it: you mustn't be over-hasty, mustn't jump into square seven when you are in square three. It's possible that Mark understands this – not in detail, of course, and not expressed in that way; but he seems to have an instinct that tells him he mustn't rush things. Not to make agreements and force me to make commitments, there would be no point. I'm grateful for that: if I had to cobble together any more detailed lies it would be difficult. What isn't spelled out is more vital: I only have two more weeks in Darne Lodge, and after having had all the time in the world this past late autumn and winter, the days have suddenly started to become crammed full of all kinds of tasks that need seeing to.

I must finish the play. I must send off a series of carefully worded e-mails to a series of people: Bergman, Gunvald, Synn, Christa and last but not least – Soblewski. I haven't heard from him for ages, but the day after tomorrow I shall send my (Martin's) comments on Anna Słupka's short story (which I'm going to read this evening at long last) together with a quite gloomy report on my (Martin's) writing, and masses of depressing thoughts. I obviously can't bring up that unidentified body again, but I hope that he remembers my question and doesn't leave me in the dark.

If he doesn't give me any kind of answer, I must seriously wonder if something is not as it should be. Or am I thinking along the wrong lines?

It's Tuesday today, Mark and I have agreed not to be in touch until Saturday, when it's my turn to treat him to dinner at The Royal Oak. I think we both take it for granted that we shall end up at his house, as does Castor, and perhaps even Jeremy.

Incidentally Jeremy is a welcome excuse for me not having to provide dinner in Darne Lodge. Mark has done no more than pop in through the door, and I intend to leave it at that. I have quite a few items of men's clothing and other things difficult to explain away hanging around the house, and of course I can't get rid of them. It is essential for me to get home with all Martin's belongings intact.

The thought of me actually sitting down in the car and driving away from here together with Castor fills me with equal doses of exhilaration and dread. No, that's not true: at this point the feelings of dread are greater, significantly greater; but I hope the balance will be roughly equal when the time actually comes.

★

E-mail from me to Christa, the seventeenth of January:

Dear Christa, I hope all is well with you and Paolo. Down here in Morocco, I'm afraid things are not all that good. Perhaps it was daft to come here in the first place: I'm beginning to think that Martin and I should have done the sensible thing and gone our separate ways after all those goings-on. It's not that we quarrel, but Martin is suffering from a terrible attack of depression: he doesn't want to talk about it because he's such a pig-headed individual, but I'm beginning to fear that he might do something silly. I don't want to burden you with all this, but I've got nobody to talk to down here. I'll just say that it's very hard going, and ask you to keep your fingers crossed on our account. Luckily something has turned up: the woman who is renting our house in Nynäshamn is having to break the contract because her mother has fallen seriously ill in Argentina, so there's nothing to stop us going back home. I'm trying to persuade Martin we should do that: there's nowhere here in Morocco where he could get decent treatment, and I really do think he should go into an appropriate institution or at the very least get professional psychiatric help. He hasn't been able to cope with the work he hoped to do down here, and that is of course a significant cause. But as I said, please keep your fingers crossed for me, Christa, and hope that I shall be able to persuade Martin to go back home with me. Love, Maria

E-mail from Martin to Soblewski:

Dear Sob. Let's go ahead with Miss Słupka. No doubt a real talent. As for myself, though, I have huge misgivings regarding my talent. My work is going to pieces and so am I. Fuck Herold and Hyatt. I will give it a last push by trying to write a play about it, but not sure it will work. Sorry to have to tell you this but it is unfortunately the truth. I drink too much, have taken up smoking again and Maria is very worried about me. So am I. M

E-mail from Martin to Eugen Bergman:

Dear Eugen. Thank you for your kind thoughts. I've gone to the dogs, and have even started smoking again. I think we'll have to go home, I can't go on like this for much longer. M

That will do for today. But if I haven't got a response from Soblewski by Monday I shall have to take steps different from those I had planned. I sit there in the centre for some time thinking about that while reading news from the rest of the world without much in the way of enthusiasm. If in fact I am now going to crawl out of my hideaway, I had better make an effort to inform myself about what's going on out there. But it's a pretty depressing thought.

I also try – for the twentieth time since he told me about it – to come to terms with what Mark said he had seen outside that butcher's shop in Dulverton, but only come to the same conclusion as I have reached nineteen times before.

I have never seen Martin wearing a hat.

Mark said the man was in his sixties. Professor Soblewski must be at least seventy.

I already knew that the person who had hired the car was a Pole, bearing in mind that newspaper on the car dashboard.

The fact that there was also a copy of the Swedish *Dagens Nyheter* . . . well, I decide to leave it at that.

I have no desire to dwell on the fact that these are precisely the conclusions I *want* to draw. The time for hesitation and doubt has passed.

And in that depressing short story by Słupka there was just one line – one single line – that jarred. The suggestion that women don't realize they are more cold-blooded than men until after they have passed the menopause.

That was written by a young woman. How does she know? I leave the Winsford Community Computer Centre, skirt round the church and walk up Ash Lane towards Mr Tawking's house in order to collect my two hundred pounds. It's beginning to get dark, and is drizzling slightly. I note that this is my last Thursday evening but one in Winsford, and the village is displaying itself in its gloomiest possible guise.

I knock on the door but nobody comes to open it. I can see that lights are on in two windows, so I think this is a bit odd. To make things worse, Castor is standing beside me and growling, something he never normally does. I knock several more times and think I can hear a noise inside the house. I pause for a moment, then turn the handle.

It's not locked, and we go in.

'Mr Tawking?'

He's lying on the floor on his stomach with his arms underneath him. I can see his left eye as his head is turned to one side. He gives me a terrified look, so it's obvious he's alive. Castor growls and keeps his distance.

'Mr Tawking?'

His head moves slightly and he blinks.

A stroke? I wonder. Cerebral haemorrhage? Heart attack?

Or is that just three different names for the same thing?

I realize that it's not a question I need to think about, hurry back out and ring the neighbouring doorbell. A woman in her forties answers. I explain the situation.

'Ah well,' she says. 'It's just a matter of time. But I'm a nurse, I'll take care of the situation. Bill, take that bloody chicken out of the oven, we'll have to eat later!'

She smiles at me and is already ringing for an ambulance. I can see that the chances of my ever getting back that two hundred pounds are very small.

52

'They said at the pub that Castor had gone missing. You never told me that.'

I think for a moment. 'No, maybe I didn't mention it.'

'Why not?'

'I don't really know. It was during the Christmas holiday period when you and Jeremy were in Scarborough.'

'It's still odd that you said nothing about it.'

'Do you think so? I thought I had done, in fact.'

What is all this? I think, and for the first time I feel a pang of annoyance directed at Mark Britton. Or maybe it's aimed at me. I ought to have told him about those awful days when Castor was missing: instead I'm keeping quiet and telling lies and holding information back when it's quite unnecessary, and in the end I won't be able to keep it up.

'At least nobody can accuse you of being an open book,' he says. 'I'm not scared of mysteries, and sooner or later I'll get to read all the pages, won't I?'

He laughs, and I choose to do the same. After all, this is one of the last occasions we shall meet. At least for the foreseeable future. I take a piece of cheese and a mouthful of wine, and he does the same. We are sitting in his kitchen, and I feel rather upset when I think the thought: the thought that I won't be sitting here any more.

'It's not even possible to Google you,' he adds. 'It's a stroke of genius, using a pseudonym.'

I nod. 'Genius is the right word.'

'And you're not going to tell me what name you're using?'

'Not just yet. Sorry.'

Does he suspect something? Is Mark beginning to understand that there are hidden and worrying motives behind my veil of secrecy? Perhaps. I can't make up my mind. He likes casting out flies on the water like this, in the hope of getting a bite: and he didn't do that a month ago. But I can't say that I don't understand why he does it.

Especially if I mean as much to him as I suspect I do.

But this isn't going to be the very last time we meet. We have another weekend left, assuming I really do leave here on the twenty-ninth as planned. I've looked into my diary and put a cross by that day. I must remember to get rid of that diary, but there are quite a few other things that must be disposed of as well.

'I'm in love with you, Maria – I take it you realize that?'

That shouldn't have been an unexpected declaration, but I nearly drop my glass even so. I don't recall hearing such words since . . . I try to remember if Martin ever said anything like that. I'm damned if I know. But Rolf no doubt did.

How many people are there in the world who never hear such words: an assurance that somebody loves them?

'Thank you,' I say. 'Thank you for saying that. I like you an awful lot, Mark. My life out here on the moor has become so much more meaningful since I met you. But I can't make any promises . . . if that's what you are after.'

He sits for quite a while, weighing over what I said – I would do the same if I were him. Then he nods and says: 'You know, I feel pretty confident regarding our relationship. There must be some reason for you turning up in this very village.'

'Yes,' I say. 'No doubt there was a meaning.'

'We are grown-up people,' he says.

'We are indeed,' I say.

'We know what it means to be in denial.'

'We're experts at that.'

He leans forward over the table and takes hold of my head with both hands. 'In love with you, did I say that?'

E-mail from Martin to Gunvald:

> Hi Gunvald. Thank you for your message – great to hear that you're enjoying life down under. The situation in Morocco isn't nearly so enjoyable, I have to admit. I have total writer's block, and to tell you the truth I feel utterly dejected. We might go back home to Sweden sooner than intended: I know it's a bloody awful time of year and all that, but what can one do? Anyway, take care of yourself – we'll keep in touch. Dad

From Eugen Bergman to Martin:

> My dear friend! Come home at once if you've run into a brick wall. There's no point in wandering around in a foreign

country and suffering. And a play might be just the right thing, don't you think? You've never written anything for the theatre before. But we'll see how it goes with that, the main thing is that you keep your head above water. My very best wishes – to Maria as well, of course. Eugen

From Soblewski to Martin:

My dear friend! You are far too young for depressions! But I can imagine how sitting in that very country with that very story could make anybody go crazy. I suggest you leave it and try to find other distractions – and if you really are on your way home, you are more than welcome to stay a few days in my house, which might enable us to talk things through properly. Your lovely wife and your dog are welcome too, of course. No new bodies have been reported and I have no idea whether they managed to identify the old one. I have heard nothing more about it. All the best, Sob

I read Soblewski's message very carefully, especially the last sentence. *No new bodies have been reported and I have no idea whether they managed to identify the old one.*

I think it over. Surely, I think, surely this must be the most positive piece of information I could have wished for? I sit there for a minute or so, considering it from every conceivable point of view, but I can find no other possible assessment.

What happens next is up to me, of course.

E-mail from Martin to Eugen Bergman:

We shall see, my dear Eugen. It's hard, but maybe we'll do as you suggest and head northwards. Don't have too high expectations of the play, though. All the best, M

From Martin to Soblewski:

Thank you for your concern. We shall see what happens. M

From Christa to me:

Damn and blast! I knew there was something about those dreams! But of course you are the one on the spot down there and will have to take care of the breakdown. I can't say I'm surprised, I'm afraid. As you know I've had my share of depressed menfolk. They're worse than three-year-olds with earache if you ask me – sorry to have to say that. But for God's sake make sure you come home so that we can meet and talk everything over. I'll be staying in Stockholm until the middle of February, so there's time. Then a month in Florida, thank the Lord. Keep in touch and come home! Christa

From me to Christa:

I'm afraid things are no better here. I think we'll probably do a runner in a week or so's time. So if you are still in Stockholm maybe we can meet at the beginning of February. I'd like to put Martin on a flight home and drive all the way myself, but of course that's not possible. In any case, thanks for your concern. Love, Maria

From me to Gunvald and Synn:

> Dear Gunvald and Synn, just a line to let you know that your dad's not very well at all. We plan to start our long journey back home a few days from now. I don't know if he's written to either of you, but it's pretty unlikely. He is very depressed, and hardly speaks to me at all. Keep your fingers crossed that we get home safely and can get some help. Love, Mum

Well, I think to myself, that's the foundation for what comes next done and dusted, and it's with a feeling of relief and cautious optimism that I leave Winsford Community Computer Centre for the last time.

53

We spend the last few days repeating everything.

We go for our favourite walks one more time: Doone Valley, Culbone, Selworthy Combe, Glenthorne Beach. We manage to find our way back to Barrett's bolt-hole and to the pub in Rockford where Jane Barrett's exhibition is still taking place, but she happens to be out when we go there. I'm a bit annoyed to find she's absent: there are a few things I'd have liked to ask her, but I suppose I'll get by even so. The main thing is to dare to get that feeling of confidence she talked about, and rely on Darne Lodge being protected. We call in at the second-hand bookshop in Dulverton one last time and say goodbye to the hundred-year-old dandelion. We also say goodbye to Rosie, Tom and Robert at The Royal Oak Inn. It feels odd to note that it's only three months since I set foot in here for the first time. I remember that sofa the cat had been peeing on for so long. How was it doing now, and how was Mrs Simmons?

And I carry on writing. It's surprising to find how easily I make progress with 'At Sunrise' – that's the working name I've given the play. I'm writing on Martin's computer, of course, and perhaps that's the reason why I don't feel I need to accept responsibility for it all, and the dialogue flows so smoothly. In parallel I'm reading Bessie Hyatt's two books, and with Martin's reports on them at hand it's not difficult to work out the references.

The setting is the same all the time: the big table on the terrace. It's explained that we are in Greece during the first two acts, and in Morocco for the last three. It's important for the audience to understand that time has passed. Eleven roles, of which two are servants. I use Megal – and in a few places his hypnotic wife – as a narrator. They address the audience directly, and describe the off-stage circumstances – exactly as in classical dramas. Their roles are especially important in the closing scenes, when they are together with Bessie Hyatt in the house, watching what happens to Gusov from some distance away. How the murder takes place.

But it's all about Herold and Hyatt, of course. I've changed the names of all the other characters, and I stigmatize Herold as much as I dare without turning him into a caricature. Hyatt is the innocent party, albeit not absolutely so; all the rest are fellow travellers who act in such a way that Herold can assert himself continuously. Which makes it possible for him to crush both Gusov and Bessie Hyatt. For instance, I locate Bessie's abortion in a room adjacent to the terrace: the audience will know what is happening, but the other characters pay no attention: they sit eating and hear her cries through the open window without bothering about them. Her suicide is announced in a sort of prologue before the curtain rises. I know that my play is brutal and harsh, without mercy or reconciliation; but I think a little rewriting can make it more mild and sophisticated. If such adjustments need to be made. I also toy with the idea that at some point in the distant future I can explain to Eugen Bergman that I have worked on the text together with Martin, so that perhaps I can take another good look at it and produce an amended version. At some point in the even more distant future I can envisage the play being performed at the Royal Dramatic Theatre in Stockholm, and picture myself saying a few brief words about Martin from the edge of the stage before it starts. There is no limit to my fantasies.

Two days before we leave I complete the script. Five acts, a hundred and twenty pages of dialogue. Tom Herold and Bessie Hyatt placed under the microscope: I'm surprised by the euphoria pounding away inside me. This must be what it feels like to be a real writer, I think. When you come to the point at which a project has been successfully completed.

My taking leave of Mark Britton turned out to be less emotional than I had feared, and it occurs to me that I have underestimated him. As usual Castor and I spend an evening, a night and a morning in Heathercombe Cottage: when we part on the Sunday, we have checked carefully one another's telephone numbers and e-mail addresses, and I am sure that we shall meet again. Nothing, not even the most awful short story imaginable, can end like this.

'We'll meet again,' says Mark. 'I know we shall.'

'You can read my mind, can you?'

'There is no end of ways in which I know. If I haven't heard from you in a week's time, I shall come looking for you. But of course it's best that you sort out what has to be done, and then come back here. Any questions?'

I laugh. 'So this is plan A, is it?'

'Exactly,' says Mark. 'And you'd rather not know about a plan B, I can assure you. I'm in love with you, have I said that before?'

I give him a big hug and say that I probably feel more or less the same. He doesn't need to worry.

'I'm not worrying,' says Mark.

I shake Jeremy's hand – he's wearing a yellow Harlequins jersey today, with blue and red text – and then Castor and I leave Heathercombe Cottage. In the car on the way up towards Winsford Hill I start crying, and I let the tears flow freely until they dry up of their own accord.

Early in the morning of the twenty-ninth of January I close the gate of Darne Lodge. Drive down Halse Lane for the last time and park by the war memorial. It's a foggy morning, grey and gloomy. I take Castor for a short walk up Ash Lane and knock on the door of Mr Tawking's neighbour. It's answered by the same nurse as last time: she tells me that old man Tawking is in hospital in Minehead, and probably doesn't have much longer to live. I thank her and hand over the key.

'So you're leaving now, are you?'

'Yes,' I say. 'I'm leaving now.'

'You should come back at another time of year,' she says. 'Winter is so damned awful.'

I nod and say that I shall certainly be coming back.

We walk past the computer centre but it's so early in the morning that it isn't open yet. I knock on Alfred Biggs's door, but there is no answer. For once he's not in – but then I've already said thank you and goodbye to both him and Margaret Allen.

And I intend to come back after all.

I do, don't I?

Then we walk back to the car, and drive off.

The A396 via Wheddon Cross, the same road as we came on. We don't go into The Rest and Be Thankful Inn for a glass of red wine. Besides, they're not open.

FIVE

54

I'm sitting at a round table set for six people. The other places are empty and so is the whole dining room come to that. An elderly, bald waiter in a red jacket comes in with my main course: Wiener schnitzel with potato cake and mushroom sauce. He fills my red wine glass without even asking.

It's nine o'clock in the evening. The hotel is called the Duisburger Hof, and the city is Duisburg. Castor is lying on the bed in our room upstairs, having a snooze – we have been for quite a long evening walk. It's a big hotel and in a room adjacent to the dining room a Rotary club is having a meeting: I can occasionally hear laughter and shouting from in there, which underlines my loneliness in no uncertain way. I think the waiter has caught on to that fact as he keeps coming over to ask if everything is to my satisfaction. Every time I tell him it is. *Jawohl, alles gut.*

The journey has gone smoothly and according to plan so far, but everything has felt more strange the further away from Exmoor we have come. The further away from England. I had to show my passport before we drove onto the train taking us through the Channel Tunnel from Folkestone, but a half-asleep policeman merely glanced at it. I didn't even have to hide Castor away – it's when you're travelling in the other direction that checks are thorough. When you are about to enter the United Kingdom.

And then we drove through France, Belgium and Holland before eventually ending up in Germany. Trouble in finding the ring road around Antwerp, trouble in getting coffee out of an automatic machine at a petrol station just outside Ghent, but apart from that, no problems.

Apart from a nagging conviction that everything was unreal, that I was out of touch with the surroundings.

And as a consequence, a feeling of frailty that I haven't experienced since the first few days on the moor. But I tell myself it is a weakness that can be transformed into a strength, in view of the role I have to play in the days ahead. A nervous breakdown wouldn't be a minus – on the contrary. All I need to do is to postpone it for a day: as long as I don't allow it to affect me too soon, it wouldn't be a bad thing. Not a bad thing at all.

After finally succeeding in extracting coffee from that automatic machine in Ghent, I devoted half an hour to finding somewhere to spend the night as there was a link to the internet at the petrol station, and I found this hotel. I rang them from the mobile I'd been given by Mark Britton and explained that I was travelling with a well-behaved dog, that my credit card had been stolen and that I would like to pay in cash. All that was accepted without question, and I am relieved to think that this is the last time I shall need to resort to that cheap trick. As soon as I land in Denmark I shall be able to resume my real identity and re-enter the real world, a fact that leaves me with mixed feelings. There is something attractive about the thought of booking incognito into a comfortable hotel, with or without a Rotary club party, with or without a Wiener schnitzel, but with red wine and a red-jacketed waiter, for the rest of my life.

I also realize, of course, that if anybody were to start checking up on all the details – our address in Morocco, the route we had travelled, our stops and overnight stays en route – then everything would collapse like a house of cards. But why would anyone want to start checking? Why?

This is in fact a stroke of genius in my plan: I can't resist congratulating myself on it as I sit here in this secure German hotel dining room, chewing away at my well-earned schnitzel. All the focus will be on what has happened to Martin, nobody will question our stay in North Africa. It is too well documented in all the incoming and outgoing e-mails. All that is in store for me is sympathy and understanding, no impertinent questions. No checks.

I take a swig of wine. Think once again that I can allow myself a minor – or major – nervous breakdown: it would be regarded as perfectly natural.

Yes, very natural indeed in view of everything that has apparently happened. The poor thing, just imagine what she has had to put up with.

I smile, I can't resist smiling in all my loneliness. All that remains is for tomorrow's little bit of play-acting to be successfully concluded, and that isn't going to be too difficult. I shall no doubt pull it off.

I drink the rest of my wine slowly, and since my waiter

suggests that I might like a coffee and a cognac I drink that as well. I feel slightly drunk, and through the thin veil this creates in my mind I am able to observe everything from a convenient and comfortable distance. My life consists of so many different components: perhaps the whole of my stay on Exmoor is a closed chapter – and Mark Britton a short story, despite everything – and perhaps in the future I shall be able to look back on it in that way. In a year or so's time these three months will be no more than an ingredient, a series of circumstances connected with Martin's death . . . Perhaps also I might recall with regret how vital and significant that period seemed to be while it was actually happening, but also how quickly it faded away.

Or perhaps I might actually return there. I twirl my glass of cognac in my hand, and try to imagine such a development. Perhaps what I partially suggested to Mark might in fact happen, perhaps I really will sell the house in Nynäshamn and leave Sweden. Tell the few good friends I have that I have been thinking of going to live in England for a few years: I need a change of scene now that I have become a widow. What could be more natural than that? Who would suspect that there was something odd about such a thought? You can't continue trundling along as before when one wheel is no longer turning. I smile once more, this time at the formulation of my thoughts. I wonder if I made it up, or if it's something I've read. *When one wheel is no longer turning.*

For some unknown reason, while I'm still sitting here in my splendid isolation and still have a drop of cognac in my glass, I start thinking about all the people I've met who are now dead. Wondering if they can actually see me and can follow my thoughts as I sit here in a slightly tipsy state in between two chapters. In between the fourth and the fifth act. Rolf. Gudrun Ewerts. My father and my mother. Gunsan of course, she was the first in line. Vivianne, the loony. Elizabeth Williford Barrett – I've never actually met her, naturally, but I have passed by her grave at least a hundred times during the last three months: what is she lying there and thinking about? And Martin. What is he mulling over, lying in his bunker? Or possibly in a Polish mortuary. Or is he sitting on a cushion of cloud, watching what I'm up to with a furrow in his brow, a deep and very familiar furrow?

At this point I feel a pang of discomfort and drink the rest of my cognac. I wave to my red-jacketed friend and explain that I'd like to pay. He asks if I want him to add it to my hotel bill, and I say that he might just as well. I leave him a ten-euro note on the table as a tip as I don't have anything smaller, and take the lift up to my bedfellow.

Having come up to my room I make the mistake of switching on the telly. Apart from an occasional flickering image on a screen some distance away in various pubs, I haven't watched any television for three months: and now when I see some sort of heavily made-up panel sitting bolt upright in front of an enthusiastic audience I feel an urge to throw up. A compère, who looks as if he's combed his hair with a pitchfork and is wearing a glittering jacket, struts around in front of and behind the panel shouting out incomprehensible assertions that they have to respond to by pressing either red or green buttons. Then the one who pressed first comes out with something funny and the audience roars with laughter. Over and over again. I watch the appalling display for five minutes before switching off. And this is what I've devoted my life to, I think.

It is clear to me that whatever happens, this is not a path I shall continue to trundle along. Not this lonely path.

When I eventually collapse into bed I fall asleep more or less immediately and dream about a large number of people – living and dead – who simply won't fit into set patterns: Mark Britton and Jeremy. Jane Barrett, Alfred Biggs and Margaret Allen. Tom Herold and Bessie Hyatt. Professor Soblewski. And the vicar in Selworthy, the one who painted his church white so that he would be able to find his way home no matter how drunk and disorderly he was. All of these characters wander into and out of my consciousness without ever stating why they are there or what they want; but they are insistent, as if they wanted to give me credit for something, and when I wake up in the morning it feels as if I haven't slept a wink. Or a blink or a moment, or whatever it is one doesn't sleep for.

But in many ways this is the last day, and it seems to me that as long as I don't get involved in a crash on the autobahn, everything is going to turn out for the best. Thanks to patience and tact I have managed to negotiate every obstacle so far, and there's no reason why I shouldn't overcome the final little stumbling block as well. All I need to do is to make sure I drink enough coffee.

I have a shower and then take Castor for a walk round the

block: it's drizzling, and he does his business on the first stretch of grass we come to. He then has a bite to eat in our room while I go down and sit at the same table as last night for breakfast. The waiter is different though: thirty years younger, but he is wearing a red jacket as well.

We leave the Duisburger Hof at half past nine and continue our journey northwards.

55

I'm kept awake by coffee and the fear of getting involved in a crash. It's a windy and rainy day, and the autobahn north-wards through Germany – A2, then A43, then A1, via Münster, Osnabrück, Bremen and Hamburg – is jam-packed with heavy traffic. I don't think I have ever driven so slowly and carefully in the whole of my life, but the thought of something nasty happening – something that could ruin everything within the space of just a few seconds – feels at times like a noose around my neck. After a few hours the rain develops into sleet, and there is even more need to proceed with caution.

By six o'clock, however, we have passed Hamburg and it has stopped raining. I think it would be as well not to arrive at the ferry terminal too early, and so we allow ourselves an hour-long stop at an Autohof. We go for a little walk, share a bratwurst in the car, and then missus has a coffee in the bar. After filling up with petrol we continue up towards Fehmarn and Puttgarden.

There are about fifty cars waiting at the dock, and it strikes me it's good that there are so many people wanting to cross over into Denmark. Our ferry is due to depart at 21.00 – departures are a little less frequent as late in the day as this. We start boarding at about ten to. I end up at the very back of a long line of cars next to a wall: that couldn't be better.

We make our way up to the commercial deck. There are a few restaurants and cafes, shops selling perfumes and spirits and cigarettes, and lots of people who seem to know exactly how they are going to spend the hour or so the crossing will take. Castor and I wander around aimlessly until we walk up a flight of stairs and sit down on a banana-shaped sofa in a sort of lounge. There are about twenty people ensconced in there, and several more coming and going all the time. I check my watch and see that we have been under way for twenty-five minutes.

And right now, I decide, at this very moment as we are sitting here in this most anonymous of places, me on the sofa and Castor on the floor, I shall re-assume my real identity. From now on everything is authentic. My heart starts pounding as I register this fact, but of course none of my fellow passengers notices anything unusual.

Shortly afterwards there is a loudspeaker announcement to the effect that car passengers should return to their vehicles but not start their engines until instructed to do so. I look around somewhat nervously and check my watch again. Then Castor and I make our way down the stairs, and pay a brief visit to one of the restaurants: I look inside and shake my head.

I look at my watch again. Shrug, and find the door leading down to the car deck.

I let Castor into the back seat but don't yet sit down behind the wheel. A few minutes later the stern ports open and the cars start driving ashore. But not our queue as yet. I remain standing by the car, looking around ostentatiously. I keep checking my watch.

Then I sit down in the driver's seat, but change my mind and get out again.

The vehicle in front of me, a large German-registered van, sets off. I remain where I am. The queue next to us starts moving. Before long I'm the only one left on the whole of the car deck. A member of the crew wearing an orange jacket comes up and asks if there is anything wrong. Won't the car start?

I tell him that there's nothing wrong with the car, but I'm waiting for my husband. I don't know where he's got to.

He looks a bit put out.

'You were supposed to meet at the car, were you?'

He speaks very clear Danish.

'Yes, I just don't understand . . .'

There's no fear in my voice yet. It's too early for that. A trace of worry, perhaps, mixed with a dose of irritation.

'Just a moment, I'll fetch my boss.'

Half a minute later an elderly official appears. He has a reddish-brown moustache that looks as if it weighs half a kilo.

'Your husband's missing, is that right?'

'Yes.'

'And he knows where the car is parked, does he?'

'Yes . . . Yes, he does.'

'Could he have gone ashore with the foot passengers that don't have cars?'

His moustache bobs up and down. I say I don't know.

'You'd better drive off the ferry – I'll come with you. Don't worry, we'll find him.'

He sits down in the passenger seat. I start the engine and we drive ashore. He points to a low building on the right.

'Drive in there, and wait for a moment or two.'

He takes out his mobile and talks to a colleague. Then he instructs me to drive to a door where foot passengers are still leaving the ship and taking their seats in a green bus waiting just outside. There are not all that many of them, I notice. Not more than half a bus-full. The driver is standing outside, smoking.

The moustache-man gets out of the car but tells me to stay inside.

'Sit here and see if your husband comes out through that door. You could take a look into the bus if you like.'

He points, and I nod. I get out of the car and peer into the bus. No sign of Martin. I go back to the car and wait.

After about ten minutes the terminal is empty. No passengers, and the bus has left. The moustache-man comes back accompanied by a man in uniform – I assume it's a police officer.

'You haven't seen him?'

'No . . .'

My voice is barely audible. I'm really shaken now.

'Come along with us, please, and we'll look into the matter.'

It's the police officer who says that. I notice that he is almost speaking Swedish.

'Can I take my dog with me?'

He nods. 'Of course.'

We sit in a small, brightly lit room in the terminal building. Me, Castor, the policeman who almost speaks Swedish and a young female police officer with a ponytail who looks so Danish that she would be a suitable model for a recruitment campaign. I am deeply shaken and hardly need to put on a show. I'm trembling so much that I have to lift my coffee mug with both hands.

'Let us now take it calm,' says the female police officer. 'I am called Lene.'

She is also trying to speak some kind of Scandiwegian.

'Knud,' says her colleague. 'If you are wondering why I almost speak Swedish, it's because I worked in Gothenburg for ten years. Can you tell us what has happened?'

I take a few deep breaths and try to get a grip on myself. 'My husband,' I say. 'I don't know what's happened to him.'

Knud nods. 'What's your names? Both yours and your husband's? You're on your way home to Sweden, I gather.'

I say that's correct. That we've been in Morocco for a few months and are now returning to Stockholm.

'Your names?' says Lene. She is sitting with a notebook and pencil, ready to write down everything I say.

'My name's Maria Holinek. My husband is called Martin Holinek. We—'

'Do you have your passports?'

I shake my head. 'Martin . . . My husband has them. He took both of them because . . . Well, he just took them.'

Knud nods, Lene writes.

'Some kind of identification perhaps?'

I produce my driving licence. Lene notes down various details, then hands it back.

'What happened on the ferry?' says Knud.

'I don't know. We went our different ways for a while. He went to the restaurant for a meal, but I wasn't hungry and so I stayed with Castor . . . Our dog. He said he might smoke a cigarette as well. But . . . But he never came back.'

At this point I start sobbing violently. Lene produces a box of paper tissues. I take one and blow my nose painstakingly.

'I'm sorry. I sat waiting with Castor until they announced that it was time to return to the car deck, and when Martin didn't appear . . . well, I suppose I thought he would go straight to the car.'

Knud clears his throat. 'Perhaps we must take things a little easy now. You seem very upset, fru Holinek.'

'Yes . . .'

I don't know what to say. All three of us sit there in silence for a few seconds.

'What do you think might have happened?'

I shake my head. I feel panic building up inside me – no wonder.

'What state was he in?' asks Lene. 'It's important we discover how things are and we keep our calm. What do you think, fru Holinek?'

I don't answer, just stare down at the table.

'Was your husband depressed?' asks Knud. 'Had you quarrelled?'

I shake my head, then nod. Without looking at either of them. I clasp my hands together.

'Yes, he was depressed. But we hadn't quarrelled.'

They exchange looks.

'Could it possibly be that . . .' says Knud slowly, scratching at a stain on the sleeve of his shirt with the nail of his index finger. 'Could it possibly be that your husband has jumped overboard?'

I stare at both of them, one after the other. Feel that the whole of my body is shaking. Then I nod.

Knud stands up and leaves the room, clutching his mobile tightly. Lene stays with me and Castor.

'Let us now take it calm,' she says again.

We get a room at the Danhotel in Rødbyhavn. It's past midnight when we go to bed. Police officer Lene is in the room next to ours, in case I might need her assistance. We have sat talking in a corner of the hotel dining room for over an hour. I have told her all about Martin's depression, how he couldn't work, how he had started drinking too much and started smoking again, having given up over fifteen years ago. That I was worried about him, and that . . . well, that it is not impossible that he chose to jump overboard rather than going back to Sweden with the millstone of a major failure round his neck.

Lene has explained that they are searching for Martin with

the aid of both boats and helicopters, but of course it is an almost impossible task in the dark. They will increase their efforts as soon as it gets lighter, but I must probably prepare myself for the worst. You can't survive for very long in the water at this time of year.

I broke down and cried several times, and I didn't need to make much of an effort to do so. Gudrun Ewerts would have been proud of me. Lene asked whom I would like to be informed – our children, for instance – but I said I didn't want to tell anybody until a bit more time has passed. Tomorrow, perhaps.

When we said goodnight outside my room door, she gave me a hug.

'Just knock if you want something,' she said. 'I can sleep in your room if you want, you know that.'

'I have my dog,' I say. 'I'll be all right. But thank you.'

56

We go for an hour's walk before breakfast. It's a grey morning with light rain showers that come and go. We can occasionally see a helicopter out over the sea: I assume it's searching for Martin's dead body.

We walk along deserted streets and eventually come down to the water, and a stretch of sandy beach: I take out of my pocket the plastic bag containing our cut-up passports. I have spent quite a while before we set off, tearing them into small pieces, none of them bigger than a couple of square centimetres – and now I spread out the confetti in about ten different places. Dig it all down and remove all traces as far as possible. I throw his mobile telephone and wallet into the sea – I should probably have done that from the ferry, but I simply didn't have the nerve.

When we get back to the Danhotel, Lene is sitting waiting for us in the breakfast room. She has an elderly colleague by her side. Knud has been working throughout the night and is now at home, catching up on sleep, she explains.

Her colleague greets us and introduces himself as Palle – I wonder if Danish police officers only have first names. He explains that he and Lene need to speak to me for a while, but that of course I can have breakfast first.

Morgenmad – he uses the Danish word for breakfast, which reminds me that the Danish word that sounds like the Swedish word for breakfast actually means lunch . . .

'That's a lovely dog you've got,' he says. 'Rhodesian ridge-back. A neighbour of mine has two of them.'

He strokes Caspar in the right way, and I immediately decide that I trust him.

We spend the whole of the morning in the Danhotel in Rødbyhavn. Palle tells me that the sea searches last night and this morning have been fruitless, and he asks me to repeat yet again exactly what happened on the ferry crossing. They also want some more background, and I tell them about our stay in Morocco and about Martin's depression.

'Did he talk about committing suicide?' Palle asks.

'No,' I say somewhat hesitantly. 'I don't recall him mentioning it openly.'

'Are you surprised? Or can you see that the situation we now find ourselves in has to do with his state of mind?'

I say that I don't know. I mention that his sister took her own life. Palle nods and Lene notes that down.

'Is it possible that he considered it a defeat to have to come home early without having achieved what he set out to do? His writing, I mean.'

'Yes, I assume so.'

I burst into tears on several occasions – the attacks just

come and I don't need to fake them. As usual when I cry, Gudrun Ewerts comes into my mind again. I am bombarded with so many confused thoughts and impulses as I sit talking to the two Danish police officers. For instance, I get the feeling that I have been swimming for ages under water, and that what has now happened is that I have at last managed to raise my head above the surface. It is a strange image, of course, in view of the fact that we are talking about Martin's body which went the opposite way. Or so the police think, at least.

When they have run out of questions to ask about what happened, they wonder what I am going to do next. Do I want to stay on in Rødbyhavn a bit longer – in case a miracle happens – or do I want to go back home to Stockholm?

I say I want to go home.

'Have you been in contact with relations and friends?'

I shake my head.

'Who would you like to get in touch with?'

I say I would like to contact our children, and shortly afterwards I compose an e-mail message I send to both of them. Only a few lines, but it's not easy to find the right words. I tell them I'm on my way up to Stockholm, and that I'll have my mobile switched on all afternoon.

'Do you think you'll be able to drive all the way to Stockholm?' Lene asks.

I say I do. I'm used to driving, and it's better than sitting still.

'Do you have somebody to look after you when you get there?'

'Oh yes,' I say. 'That's not a problem.'

'And you're sure you'll be able to drive?'

'Yes, I'll be okay.'

At noon I take my leave of the two police officers. They tell me they've been in touch with their Swedish colleagues, and they also say that they don't intend to inform the media about what has happened – neither the Danish nor the Swedish hacks. It's up to me to decide how to make the accident public knowledge.

It seems they have been told by the police on the other side of the Sound that Martin and I are not exactly unknown in Sweden.

'Look after yourself,' says Lena. 'Feel able to ring me when you like.'

I thank her. I have her business card in my purse.

And so we get into the car and set off on our journey northwards through Denmark. When we reach the Öresund Bridge an hour and a half later, it starts snowing.

It's Gunvald who rings first. I've stopped at a petrol station just outside Helsingborg, and am about to get out of the car and fill up when I see the call is from him, so I drive over to a parking bay instead.

'Hi,' he says, 'Is it true?'

'Yes,' I say. 'I'm afraid it's true.'

'Good God!'

'Yes indeed.'

'Where are you?'

'On the E4 north of Helsingborg. I'm on the way home.'

'When did it happen?'

'Last night. We came on the ferry from Puttgarden.'

'And he . . . ?'

'Yes.'

'Did you see it?'

'No. But he didn't come to the car when we were instructed to drive ashore.'

'I didn't know . . . I mean, he did write . . . And so did you.'

'I had no idea, Gunvald. I didn't realize it was that bad. I thought going home was the right thing to do, but . . .'

'You can't know things like that.'

'No.'

'But they haven't found him, have they?'

'No.'

'Is there any chance that—'

'No. It's too cold.'

'Good God.'

Then we have nothing else to add, neither I nor Gunvald. But we don't close down the call. I sit staring out at the swirling snowflakes for a while, listening to Gunvald's breathing. I recall lying awake at night when he was newly born, listening to his breathing. Now I'm sitting at a petrol station and his dad is dead.

'I'll try to get up to Stockholm tomorrow,' he says. 'Does Synn know about it?'

I say that I've e-mailed her as well, but of course they are several hours behind us in New York.

'You don't need to come tomorrow,' I add. 'Wait a few days,

let me come to terms with it all first. We can keep in touch by telephone.'

'Okay,' says Gunvald. 'Let's do that. Mum . . . ?'

'Yes?'

'I'm so sorry . . .'

'So am I, Gunvald. We'll just have to try and get over it.'

'Yes,' he says. 'We'll have to try.'

Then we hang up. I drive back to the pumps and start filling up.

The snow persists. I buy an evening newspaper which says that it will continue all evening and all night as well. Drivers are warned to be careful.

When we are somewhere in the Småland hills Synn rings. She has just got back from a jog in Central Park and is crying loudly. That surprises me.

'I'm so sorry that I wrote what I did, Mum,' she sobs. 'I didn't realize he was that bad.'

'No, but he did,' I say. 'I never told him what you wrote, so you don't need to worry about that.'

Then we say more or less the same things as Gunvald and I had said an hour earlier, and suddenly the connection is lost without warning. Perhaps it's the snow, perhaps it's something else. She doesn't ring back until after we have passed Gränna, and she announces that she is looking for flights home.

I tell her to wait for a bit. It's better to take things easy for a few days and try to come to terms with what has happened.

And there's no body – without one there's no hurry when it comes to the funeral.

'I didn't realize,' says Synn, and starts crying again. We finish the call just as I'm passing the slip road to Ödeshög.

It's half past nine in the evening when I park outside our house in Nynäshamn. It's minus eight degrees according to the thermometer in the car, and the snowfall has eased off a little. Judging by the snow in our street the snow ploughs have passed through not long ago.

I remain sitting in the car for a while before I feel up to opening the door and getting out of the car. Castor remains on the passenger seat, and doesn't move a muscle.

57

The sixteenth of February.

Twelve degrees of frost. It's half past five in the evening, I'm in the kitchen preparing roast fillet of beef. I've browned it on the outside and am now wrapping it in foil: then it will go in the oven for an hour on low heat. I can hear Chet Baker from the living room.

Just a salad and a mushroom and rosemary sauce to accompany it – I've prepared this dish a hundred times and it never goes wrong.

Blinis with sour cream, whitefish roe and shallots for starters – that's a Nordic classic, and I want to give him something I don't think he's ever tasted before.

Mind you, at first I tried to stop him. Obviously, fitting him into my Swedish existence, overlapping his Exmoor and my Sweden in this way without any precautionary measures seemed both unmotivated and risky. But then he explained that he only wanted to meet me as usual. An evening, a night and a morning. Just as in Heathercombe Cottage. When I still protested he told me he had already booked flights – from Heathrow on Saturday afternoon and back again from Arlanda on Sunday afternoon. He didn't want to go on a guided tour of Stockholm and Sweden. He didn't want to meet my friends. Didn't want to visit the famous archipelago or see the Town Hall. He simply wanted to be together with me for half a day, as usual.

I gave way. He gave me no time to think it over: he rang on Thursday and today is Saturday. I asked if he wanted me to meet him at Arlanda, but he said I should stay at home and prepare a meal. He was very keen to become acquainted with my cooking skills.

He laughed. I laughed.

'And I suppose you'll then take another taxi to the airport on Sunday afternoon, will you?'

'Exactly,' said Mark Britton. 'You won't even need to step outside.'

'What about Jeremy?' I asked.

'My sister's coming here,' he said. 'She couldn't be away from home any longer than this, otherwise I'd have stayed for a few days. To tell you the truth.'

'I understand,' I said. 'Okay, you're welcome.'

'How long does it take from the airport to where you live?'

'About an hour and a half. The quickest way is to take the Arlanda Express into central Stockholm first.'

'I'll fix that. So I'll be at your place around seven. I'll ring if there are any delays. But you can count on my being there. Even if I have to swim over.'

'Give me a call when you've landed.'

'Of course.'

When we had hung up I passed by the hall mirror and saw my face in it. I smiled.

I shall drive Mark back to Arlanda. Of course I shall. I have to be out of the house tomorrow afternoon anyway, as there will be people coming to look it over then. The official viewing time isn't until next weekend, but the estate agent said he had a few very promising prospective buyers, and so it would be silly not to give them an advance viewing.

Everybody says I'm being too precipitate, but I let them think so. They reckon I should continue living here for at least six months, and see how it feels. But you don't know the whole story, I think to myself as I listen to their arguments. You don't understand. You shouldn't make important decisions when you're in a state of crisis, they say: you should at least finish mourning first.

I'm not in a state of crisis, I think. I'm not mourning.

Christa is the only one I've told that I can't bear the thought of carrying on living in this house. Not another week, barely another day. I think she understands me. Or at least, understands the fiction I present her with.

Gunvald and Synn have been here, then left again. We were together all last weekend, and as far as I was concerned it was a flawed and stiff theatrical performance. I know that they are both deeply affected by Martin's death, but we're simply not on the same wavelength. We are three individual instruments, all out of tune, trying to pretend that we are a trio – despite the fact that we have never been one, and have little prospect

of ever becoming one. But it seemed to me that despite everything, I might – eventually – be able to establish a better
relationship with Synn. I had that feeling, in brief moments
when our eyes met; but the presence of Gunvald and the situation we found ourselves in closed all doors for the time being.

Gunvald returned to Copenhagen last Monday. Synn flew
back to New York the following day. We are not yet thinking in terms of a funeral, but we agreed to have a sort of
memorial service at Easter. I've spoken to a clergyman, and
he said it was usual to make such arrangements, given the
circumstances.

Unless something new happens before then, that is. Assuming they don't fish up a dead body down at Fehmarn. A
police officer I spoke to explained that the sea currents in
that area are completely unpredictable. Some flow up towards
Denmark, others flow out into the Baltic – it's more or less
impossible to predict where things that have fallen overboard
will end up.

The day after I got home I composed a short e-mail that I sent
to everybody involved: Bergman, Soblewski, Christa, Martin's
closest colleagues in his university department, my closest colleagues at the Monkeyhouse, and a few others. My brother, of
course. People got in touch the first couple of days, but then
everything was remarkably silent. I think most of them linked
Martin's suicide with what happened in that hotel in Gothenburg almost a year ago. It would be rather odd if they didn't.

Bergman has been in touch several times, in fact. He rang

yesterday and said he had read Martin's play. Strong stuff, he said. It has every prospect of becoming a classic. I hope that can be of some consolation to you, if . . . well, if that was the last thing he ever wrote.

I replied and said I would try to see it in that light.

Did I have anything against his contacting a few theatre people already?

I said he was free to do whatever he found appropriate.

I start cutting up the shallots, and think it will be good to leave Sweden. I really didn't think I would ever make that decision, but after spending just one day in the house I was quite sure. I'm also clear about the fact that it's not only due to Mark: it's all the other things as well. Opening the door to a village pub you've never been to before, after a long walk. The gorse that is constantly in flower and permits you to make love all the year round. Dunster Beach. Simonsbath. The Barrett witches?

When I weighed all this up against ten years in the Monkey-house, I had no doubts whatsoever, and contacted the estate agent a mere three days after my return.

I long to be back on the moor, it's as simple as that. It's an almost physical perception, and I dream about it at night: the wind, the rain and the mists. I don't understand how this has come about – but then, it's not something you need to understand.

I look at the clock. Mark should be ringing from Arlanda at any moment now, to say that he's landed. I switch on the oven, and think it will be time to put the meat in as soon as I hear from him. I check that the bottle of white wine is in the fridge, and open the bottle of red.

There is a ring at the door.

What's all this? I wonder.

But then the penny drops. He has fooled me. He's taken an earlier flight and wants to surprise me. I can feel a hot flush like a teenager, and as I pass the hall mirror I see that I'm smiling again.

I look good and I smile. Perhaps you can only look like that when you're in love. The thought embarrasses me – it's not a thought that should occur to a woman of my age. I hurry to open the door.

Who's ringing the doorbell?

I'm writing this postscript a bit later – not all that much later, but not immediately afterwards. Time is something I have plenty of. Strictly speaking, that's all I have. My room is fifteen square metres, and from my window I have a view of the edge of a forest and the sky. I can see quite a lot of stars at night, and I often lie awake doing just that: looking at the stars. They say that the light we can see from them down here on earth is light they transmitted thousands of years ago, and it could well be that they have gone out now. That they are dead. I think that is interesting – it's reminiscent of life. It has already taken place, everything important has already happened ages ago. Always assuming it really was all that important, but we have now acquired an awareness that enables us to imagine all kinds of things. I agree with that professor of literature who said the brain needs all its many convolutions in order to make us feel unhappy. That seems absolutely right – but the very fact that we can imagine things at all is significant. Things that have never existed, or that did exist but have now disappeared. It was. It will never be again. Remember – how about that for an evocative summary of life in just eight words?

Moreover I am sure that we have been given our brains so that we can handle the passage of time. An awful lot of profound things have been written about the nature of time: most often the men who devoted themselves to studying the nature of time are desperate characters who are trying hard to somehow avoid being subjected to it. It can come and go as it likes. Seconds can expand and years can shrink, that's the way they are, after all. I think that is how our minds ought to deal with the matter. There are brief, beautiful seconds and minutes that really are so much more significant than masses of wasted rubbish years, and then – perhaps this is what I am aiming for, this conclusion I want to reach as I sit here looking at the extinguished or possibly not extinguished stars – then there are those pregnant moments that are so incredibly significant that they can barely contain the burden they are carrying. For my own part, since I landed up here, I think first and foremost about those seconds – there can't have been very many of them – when I go to open the door that evening in February. The brief moments in between my seeing my image in the mirror and discovering that I'm smiling and look rather beautiful, until the moment when I take hold of the handle and open the door. It can't have been more than three seconds. Four at most – it's not far from the mirror to the front door. But time has set itself free, it does whatever it likes, it creates its own freedom, or perhaps reclaims it: it has nothing to do with any intention or effort on my part, nor with what is happening inside my head: the thoughts that normally harass me – I can't think of a better word than 'normally', but no doubt I shall do so if I revise these notes tomorrow

– the thoughts that normally harass me wouldn't fit into those brief moments.

It begins of course with my excited expectations at the thought of seeing Mark Britton standing outside the door – I'm convinced he will be carrying a bunch of roses or perhaps a bottle of champagne, maybe even both. But then a cloud descends over that expectation: it stumbles off the straight and narrow path, gets completely lost and falls down into an abyss. The whole thing reminds me of a little girl who has got lost in the woods. I can see her quite clearly in my mind's eye: innocence, flaxen hair and lots of other details – I don't need to go into who she is.

It won't be Mark Britton standing out there, the left side of my brain tells me – the half that doesn't devote itself to sagas and that sort of thing: my happiness and lust for life have been a total waste of time. They are as false and unreliable as eyes: it will be somebody else standing there.

Is it somebody else? What does that question mean? Well, even an idiot can explain what it means – but is there more than one answer? Is there more than one person who could take on the role of 'some-body else' in this situation? How have I . . . How have I managed to scrape together all this fabulous belief in the future and this fruitless optimism in just a few weeks – an optimism that is now running off me like water off the back of the goose I clearly am.

'Don't open the door!' yells a voice inside me. It is almost bellow-ing: it really is strong, so strong that for a fraction of a second I have the impression that there is actually somebody else shouting at me. Yet another somebody else who is evidently standing behind me, somewhere inside the house, and is trying to warn me – to prevent me, to save me, I don't know what, but in a quick flash of inspiration

I conjure up the presence of a redeeming angel. Yes, now afterwards I am certain that it must have been an angel. A bellowing angel – is there such a thing? Whatever, there is not much point in warning or bellowing, not at this late stage in my life, not in the fifty-ninth second of the sixtieth minute of the twelfth hour.

But before I submit to this destructive avalanche taking place so suddenly and so unexpectedly inside me, I am raised up out of the darkness. I regain control of myself, terror loosens its grip, everything is repeated and retreats in the opposite direction, I am transported from the fear of death to a state of happiness and trust by the fastest lift in the world – or perhaps it's that angel after all – and when I turn the door handle that I have finally succeeded in coming to, the whole of my being is possessed by a sense of almost childish curiosity: who is it standing outside the door?

The fact is that until you have investigated, until you have lifted the lid, you can't possibly know anything about what is inside. Until we reach that very last second, everything is still possible.

Expectation, there is no sweeter sweetness in this life.

Who's ringing the doorbell?

58

There is a man in his sixties standing there. Slightly hunched, slightly overweight.

'Yes? . . .'

'Fru Holinek?'

'Yes . . . Yes, of course. What's it all about?'

He produces something from his inside pocket and holds it up. I don't understand what it is.

'Chief Inspector Simonsson. May I come in?'

I see that there is a dark blue car parked outside the gate. The engine is running, and another man behind the wheel is talking into a mobile phone.

'Yes, of course. This way . . . Forgive me, but I'm busy making dinner.'

He steps into the hall and sniffs the air. 'Yes, I can smell that.'

He hangs up his jacket. 'Is there somewhere where we can sit and talk? I have a few questions.'

'Is it about . . . ?'

'Yes, it's about your husband, fru Holinek.'

I show him into the living room and we each sit down in an armchair.

'Would you like anything?'

'No thank you.'

He takes out a small notebook and leafs through it for a moment.

'So your husband, Martin Holinek, disappeared from the ferry between Puttgarden and Rødby on the evening of the thirtieth of January, is that correct?'

'Yes . . . Yes, that's true. Why are you asking about that? I've already spoken several times to both the Danish and the Swedish police—'

He holds up his hand and I break off.

'The fact is that we might have found his body, fru Holinek.'

'You might have . . . ?'

For a brief moment my brain blows a fuse. I stare at him and try to remember what he said his name was.

'It's a possibility at least,' he adds. 'There are quite a lot of bewildering circumstances.'

'I'm sorry, what did you say your name was?'

'Simonsson. Chief Inspector Simonsson.'

'Thank you. I don't really understand . . . Bewildering circumstances?'

He clears his throat and looks at his notebook.

'I can't think of a better way of putting it. But maybe you can put us on the right track. Your husband is supposed to have jumped overboard from the ferry more or less half-way between Puttgarden and Rødby about . . . well, just over two weeks ago. And now a body has been found that might possibly be his.'

'What do you mean by "possibly"?'

He nods a few times and looks around the room before saying anything more. As if he were looking for an answer in the bookcase or up near the ceiling.

'In the first place we are wondering about the spot where he was found. It's quite a long way from where he is supposed to have jumped overboard.'

'I . . . I've been told that there are strong sea currents down there. That's what the Danish police said, at least.'

He nodded. 'That's true. But this body was found rather a long way to the east of Fehmarn . . . In Poland, in fact.'

'Poland?'

'Yes. That's one of the circumstances. The other one is the time aspect. The human body they've found has evidently been dead for several months . . . It's been very badly mauled, and to complicate matters further was discovered inside a bunker.'

'A bunker?'

'Yes. An old abandoned remnant from the last war . . .'

'But then it can't possibly be my husband. How . . . how on earth could he have ended up inside a bunker?'

I don't know where I got my neutral, almost slightly irritated tone of voice from.

Chief Inspector Simonsson sits up a little straighter in the armchair and leans towards me. 'That's a question we are also asking ourselves, fru Holinek. This body has been with the Polish police for quite some time, but they haven't managed to identify it because it is so badly mauled. As far as they can see the man must have died inside that bunker, but before he did so he might possibly have written something on the wall.'

'Written something . . . Now you said "possibly" again.'

'Yes. There are quite a lot of scribbles on those walls, it seems. Names and suchlike. But when the Polish police failed to get anywhere with identifying the body they sent out a list to police forces in other countries. That was about a month ago . . . Eleven names in all, and one of them might have been scratched in by this man before he died – that's what they are suggesting in any case.'

'Really? I don't think I . . .'

'Anyway, one of the names is Holinek. One of my younger colleagues happened to notice it and recognized it from that Rødby report. He's the one sitting out there in the car, incidentally. Stensson – a promising young detective officer.'

I swallow and try to think of something to say, but I can't find any words. Instead I look at the police officer with a calm and tolerant television smile.

'It's a pretty long shot, of course,' he says, closing his notebook. 'But we need to turn over every stone – that's the way we work . . .'

'I still don't understand. Of course it's not him. How could it possibly be?'

He raises his hand again. 'I agree that it sounds out of the question. But we thought we ought to look into it even so. After all, there are not many people around called Holinek. So we thought we'd investigate so that we could exclude the possibility – can I assume that's all right with you?'

'Of course. Naturally there's nothing I'd like more than Martin's body being found, so that . . . well, so that we know for certain. Are you intending . . . ?'

'Intending what?'

'Are you intending to test DNA and that kind of thing?'

He puts his notebook back in his jacket pocket and nods. 'That would be one method, of course. But maybe there's a shortcut in this case.'

'A shortcut?'

He stands up. Looks thoughtfully around the room again. 'Apparently there's not much left of that corpse in the bunker. Neither the body itself nor the clothes he was wearing. But there's one little thing that has survived intact. I had it delivered to my desk a couple of hours ago.'

'What's that?'

'A car key. He had a car key with him, and it seems the rats didn't find it edible. Forgive me . . . That's probably what he used to scratch things on the wall with. I take it that's your Audi parked out there on the drive?'

He has walked over to the window and I can see that he is giving some sort of signal to his colleague. Stensson.

'Come here, let's see what happens.'

I walk to the window and stand beside him. I watch as Stensson – a tall, well-built young man of about thirty – has got out of the car he's been sitting in while Chief Inspector Simonsson and I have been talking.

It strikes me . . . Yes, it suddenly strikes me that I am standing exactly where I stood that winter evening so long ago. Just as cold or even colder than this one: I'm standing here beside Martin and watching as his sister comes walking up to the house with her secret lover. Our children are small and we have all our lives ahead of us: there are so many wonderful opportunities open to us, so many days, but we don't think about that; we just stand here, in exactly the same place as Chief Inspector Simonsson and I are standing twenty-seven years later, Martin and I, trying to imagine who that man in the ordinary shoes and with his jumper pulled up over his head might be – and it occurs to me that life passes so quickly that one can remain standing there in the same spot and not notice that it's already too late. You can sail without any wind for years, and believe all the time that you are on the way to somewhere.

And then I come back down to earth and watch the young police officer open the front door of my car – as usual I haven't locked it – and see how he settles down behind the steering wheel and waves to us – possibly slightly embarrassed, it seems to me – before leaning forward and inserting the key in the ignition.

The ponies, I think. The pheasants. *The Protection* . . .

The headlights come on, and it starts at the first attempt.

'How about that?' says Chief Inspector Simonsson. 'It started. How do you explain that?'

I don't answer.

'Ah well, I think I must ask you to come with us, fru Holinek, so that we can continue our conversation in another place.'

I say nothing. Stand still and watch my car with its engine still running out there in the cold. Castor comes and sits down next to me. My mobile phone rings, I know who it is and don't need to check.

'I must just switch off the oven first,' I say.

NOTE

This novel is an imaginative creation of the author. This applies to Swedish professors and slim government ministers, it applies to English and American authors and it applies to people living in and around the village of Winsford in the county of Somerset, England. However, the Exmoor environment has been meticulously described in accordance with reality.